The Love Verb

Jane Green Warburg is a former journalist who gave up her job on the *Daily Express* to write a real woman's account of being single in the city. That account became Jane's first novel, *Straight Talking*. A huge success, *Straight Talking* was followed by nine more bestselling novels: *Jemima J*, *Mr Maybe*, *Bookends*, *Babyville*, *Spellbound*, *The Other Woman*, *Life Swap*, *Second Chance* and *The Beach House*. Jane lives in Connecticut with her husband, Ian Warburg, and their blended family of six children.

For more information, visit www.janegreen.com

The Love Verb

JANE GREEN

MICHAEL JOSEPH
an imprint of
PENGUIN BOOKS

MICHAEL JOSEPH

Published by the Penguin Group
Penguin Books Ltd, 80 Strand, London WC2R ORL, England
Penguin Group (USA) Inc., 375 Hudson Street, New York, New York 10014, USA
Penguin Group (Canada), 90 Eglinton Avenue East, Suite 700, Toronto, Ontario, Canada M4P 2Y3
(a division of Pearson Penguin Canada Inc.)
Penguin Ireland, 25 St Stephen's Green, Dublin 2, Ireland (a division of Penguin Books Ltd)
Penguin Group (Australia), 250 Camberwell Road, Camberwell, Victoria 3124, Australia
(a division of Pearson Australia Group Pty Ltd)
Penguin Books India Pvt Ltd, 11 Community Centre, Panchsheel Park, New Delhi – 110 017, India
Penguin Group (NZ), 67 Apollo Drive, Rosedale, North Shore 0632, New Zealand
(a division of Pearson New Zealand Ltd)
Penguin Books (South Africa) (Pty) Ltd, 24 Sturdee Avenue, Rosebank, Johannesburg 2196, South Africa

Penguin Books Ltd, Registered Offices: 80 Strand, London WC2R ORL, England

www.penguin.com

Published in 2010
1

Copyright © Jane Green, 2010

The moral right of the author has been asserted

Set in 13.5/16 Garamond MT Std
Typeset by TexTech International
Printed in Great Britain by Clays Ltd, St Ives plc

A CIP catalogue record for this book is available from the British Library

HARDBACK ISBN: 978–0–718–154530
TRADE PAPERBACK ISBN: 978–0–718–154547

www.greenpenguin.co.uk

Penguin Books is committed to a sustainable future
for our business, our readers and our planet.
The book in your hands is made from paper
certified by the Forest Stewardship Council.

In memory of Heidi Armitage
1965–2009

And dedicated to all the remarkable women on the
discussion boards of www.breastcancer.org

Chapter One

Steffi elbows her hair out of her eyes before grabbing a frying pan, splashing olive oil liberally into it and scraping the finely chopped onion onto the oil. Ignoring the sweat running into her eyes, she spins around, hurrying over to the counter opposite, where Jorge is slicing spring onions.

'More of the green,' she says, peering over his shoulder then leaning forward to show him. 'Take it all the way up to there.' She runs back to the frying pan and shakes it hard, turning down the heat for the onion to soften, before pacing quickly to another chopping board and thinly slicing a giant portobello mushroom.

The rest of the world might be falling apart, but you'd never know it to look through the window at Joni's on 12th Street, the tiny vegetarian restaurant downtown that is becoming almost impossible to get into.

The crowds come for the cosy atmosphere, the friendly staff and, mostly, the food, which garnered a rave review in *New York* magazine the other week, and is solely because of their scatty but brilliant chef, Steffi Tollemache.

In the past year, Steffi has been astonished to see how busy the restaurant has become. It is her first proper job as a chef, and she knew, within days, that she had finally found her calling.

It wasn't just the excitement of being given free rein to reinvent the menu that made it so perfect, but it was also the people. For the first time, Steffi felt part of a community, with most of the customers living in the neighbourhood and almost all becoming regulars.

The lunchtime rush is over when Steffi looks through the hatch and sees Mason at a table by the window, immersed, as usual, in a manuscript, and sipping from a mug of coffee.

She owes him a thank you – last week a box arrived containing advance copies of two new cookbooks that Mason had told her about, knowing she would be interested.

Wiping her hands on a towel and pushing the damp strands of hair off her face, she nudges the kitchen door open with her foot and walks over to the table with a smile.

The restaurant is almost empty. Just a table of four who are lingering over their mint teas and Middle Eastern orange cake.

'Are you the chef?' One of the table of four stops her as she passes, and Steffi nods.

'This. Cake. Is. Awesome.'

'It's incredible,' the rest of the table chorus. 'This is the most amazing cake I've ever had.'

One of the girls leans forward eagerly. 'I'm a serious cook, and I would love to have the recipe.'

'Thank you for all your great compliments,' Steffi says and grins, catching Mason's eye as he listens and looks up. 'And yes, of course you can have the recipe. I'll only have to charge you two hundred and fifty dollars for it.'

'What?' Their mouths fall open in shock.

'I'm kidding!' Steffi laughs. 'Didn't you ever hear the Neiman Marcus chocolate-chip-cookie story? I'm pretty sure it's apocryphal, but I couldn't resist.'

'Oh my God!' one of the group exclaims. 'I've baked those cookies! I love them.'

'I know,' Steffi says. 'Me too. I'll have to write down the recipe for the cake. Do you want to give me your email address? That's probably easiest.'

'That would be great,' the girl says. 'Thanks!'

'I think I under-ordered. I clearly need some of that orange cake.'

'*Everyone* needs some of the orange cake!' Steffi smiles, turning to call to Skye, the waitress who's hovering by the bar at the end. 'Skye? Can you bring Mason an orange cake?'

'Do you have time to sit?' Mason gestures to the chair and Steffi sinks down into it, relieved to be finally off her feet.

Skye comes to the table bringing the cake for Mason, two spoons and a cup of Lemon Zinger tea (her favourite) for Steffi, who smiles gratefully and squeezes her hand after she sets them down, then shakes her head as Mason tries to foist the second spoon on her.

'Oh come on, you have to. I can't eat all this by myself.'

'So eat half and take the rest home for Olivia.'

He splutters with laughter. 'Olivia won't eat this! She's allergic to carbs, wheat and sugar. Oh, and dairy.'

'She is? Properly allergic?'

'Of course not, but that's what she says now because it's easier than having to explain how she looks that fantastic after two kids. Mmmm. God. I have to say, she's seriously missing out on the fun stuff.'

Is she ever! thinks Steffi, who would never dare say anything.

Mason and Olivia live with their perfect children, Sienna and Gray, in a perfect apartment on Park Avenue in the East Sixties. And not just any building on Park Avenue in the East Sixties, but a building that is considered to be one of the top three buildings in Manhattan.

She only knows the apartment is perfect because a few weeks ago, waiting to see the doctor after a particularly nasty cold that had left her with a wicked sinus infection (dizzy spells and loss of balance were not great while working in a busy kitchen), she picked up a copy of *Elle Decor*.

There, on page sixty-five, was a giant glossy picture of Mason and Olivia, with Sienna and Gray looking adorably cute, in their stunning apartment. They were described as a serious power couple, he the highly respected publisher who formed his own imprint five years ago, and, thanks to three huge successes, is now regarded as a serious player in the publishing world.

His wife, Olivia, is a Bedale. Yes, from *those* Bedales. The super-wealthy Southern oil family. Steffi asked a friend who worked in publishing about them, and the money, it seems, the riches that funded their extraordinary apartment, is her *family* money. While he is now a player, that wouldn't earn him anything like the sort of income that bought this apartment, and the art contained within it.

They are not the sort of people that Steffi would usually know, but Mason works around the corner and comes in for lunch a couple of times a week.

Olivia met him there for lunch one day and Steffi was stunned. Though Olivia was charming to her, Steffi had never imagined Mason to be married to someone so . . . perfect.

Mason is always a bit of a mess. His hair is never brushed,

he often has at least a day's worth of stubble and his suits never seem to quite fit him, hanging off his lanky frame. There are times when Steffi wants to force-feed him, and although she knew, long before seeing the magazine article, that he was married, never did she expect him to be married to someone who looked like Olivia.

Olivia looks incredibly high-maintenance. The day she walked in, on her own, waiting for Mason, Steffi happened to be at the hatch and she was tempted to run out and tell this woman she was clearly in the wrong place, then redirect her to somewhere like Café Boulud or the Four Seasons.

What was she *doing* at Joni's?

A tiny symphony of blonde and white cashmere, her diamonds cast pinpricks of light on the ceiling, a veritable disco ball, as she turned to see if Mason was there.

Who *was* she?

'Excuse me?' Her voice was light and lilting, clearly Southern, and she laid a hand on the waitress's arm with a beaming smile. 'I am so sorry to bother you when you are this busy, but I think we have a reservation?'

'We don't take reservations.' Skye said. 'But you're welcome to wait in line for a table.'

Her face fell. 'Oh. I'm certain my husband would . . .' She trailed off as the door opened and Mason walked in. 'There he is!' she said delightedly, as Skye raised an eyebrow at Steffi, still peering through the hatch, and winked at Mason to indicate she would seat him as quickly as possible.

They may not have taken reservations, but they still tried to look after their most regular and valued customers, and Mason was definitely one of them.

As with all their regular customers, particularly the ones

who, like Mason, arrive after the lunchtime rush, she has got to know them, has even grown to consider some of them friends.

'I totally meant to thank you.' Steffi picks up her tea and sips. 'I can't believe you remembered to send me the cookbooks.'

'Of course. What did you think of them? This, by the way,' he gestures to the cake, 'is sublime.'

'Thank you. And I did look at the books. You were right about the slow-cooking one – there's a lot of meat in it so I had to look at it more carefully, but I loved the recipes, and I see how you could take the meat out and adapt them.'

'That was the point of me sending it to you,' he says. 'I knew you'd like the vegetables.'

'I have to say, the chilli is incredible. I made it the other day.' She sighs, barely perceptibly.

'You did? But doesn't it have turkey in it?'

Steffi laughs. 'Yes, but I made it for my sister's birthday. We're having a surprise party for her on Friday, so I made two batches, one with turkey for the party, and then I adapted it slightly for a vegan batch. Also, I added some allspice and cinnamon, which was gorgeous – made it ever so slightly sweet. And now,' she sighs again, heavily, 'I have to make it all over again tonight.'

'It was that good?'

'No. Rob invited a ton of people over last night while I was at work and, several pounds of grass later, they all attacked the chilli. Which would normally be fine, but I'd made it for my sister's birthday party this weekend, and Rob knew that,' Steffi says in disgust. 'Sometimes I think I'm living with a child.'

Mason laughs heartily. 'I think all rock stars are a bit like that.'

'I thought it was all *men*?'

'That too.'

'Christ.' Steffi shakes her head. 'And according to my dad *I'm* still a child. How is it I've ended up with someone even more irresponsible than me?'

'I take it he isn't the love of your life?'

'I can't even talk about it,' Steffi says sadly, for she recognizes this feeling, and knows it is now just a matter of time. Talking about it, even with someone as sympathetic as Mason, would just make it real; giving voice to her inner feelings would mean she would then have to make a change, and how can she run when she doesn't know where she's running to?

'So tell me more about the cinnamon with the chilli,' Mason says. 'I love that idea. It's very Moroccan, to mix the sweet and the sour. Interesting to do that with chilli. It worked, I take it?'

'Apparently so. At least according to the stoners lounging round the apartment last night. You should try it,' she says and grins. 'Or maybe I'll add it to the menu.'

'Do that and you'll have to pay me royalties.'

'Please tell me you're joking.'

Mason throws up his hands. 'Okay, I'm joking. So when are you going to write a cookbook for me?'

'When I can think of an angle that will sell it.'

'I asked you ages ago to start thinking.'

'Are you sure we really need an angle?'

'Yes. But when you're ready come and see me and we'll talk.'

Steffi sighs again. 'I must be the only chef in the country

who is being offered a publishing deal and is too busy to take it.'

Mason laughs. 'I haven't actually offered you a deal . . . yet. I just said come and talk to me when you have a good story to tell.'

'Isn't being a rock chick and vegan chef enough?'

'Sadly, no,' Mason says. 'Hey, there was something I've been meaning to ask you.'

'Ask away, but quickly.' Steffi checks her watch, and notes that Skye is getting itchy feet, clearly wanting to leave.

'So we're moving to London . . .'

'What?'

'We just bought a publishing house in the UK and we're merging the two businesses, so I have to spend some time over there to get this company going.'

'I can't believe we've been sitting here talking about chilli when you have this huge news. That's great! It's great, right?'

'It is great, and we're all really excited. Olivia's there now, working with the decorator to get the apartment ready. But here's the thing: we can't take Fingal.'

'Fingal?' Who is Fingal, Steffi wonders. Butler? Driver?

'Our dog. Fingal.'

'Oh!' She laughs. 'I thought it was a butler.'

'Don't be ridiculous!' Mason shakes his head and winks. 'The butler's coming with us.'

'Tell me that you're joking now.'

He shrugs. 'I know. It's really ridiculous. That we have a butler.'

'It's insane! What are you even doing here? You're much too posh for this restaurant.'

'It's not me!' He suddenly sounds like a little boy. Plaintive. 'It's Olivia. This is how she grew up, I guess.'

'Wow. So let me ask you a question.' There is a twinkle in her eye as Steffi leans forward. 'If you have a butler, how come your suits are always so horribly pressed? I think you should fire him.'

Mason sinks his head into his hands with a shrug. 'I can't help it. When I put them on they're perfect, but everything I wear looks like I've slept in it within an hour. It drives Olivia nuts. She makes me change my clothes every couple of hours when I'm at home.'

'She does?' Steffi is surprised.

'I know. But anyway . . . Fingal. He can't come with us – no dogs allowed in the apartment in London – so we need to find him a home. Do you by any chance know anyone?'

Steffi's eyes glaze over for a moment as she realizes what a dangerous conversation this is for her to be having. She loves dogs. She has always wanted a dog. She is known in certain circles as the dog rescuer, and has never been known to leave an animal rescue centre without a dog in tow.

The problem, she has repeatedly discovered, is that her life is simply too busy for a dog; and by the time she finishes work, the whole schlepping up the stairs to the apartment, getting the dog, going back down for walks, and all the rest of it, is just too much. Every dog has ended up being rehomed, usually with friends of her mother.

There was McScruff, the West Highland terrier, who now lives with Florence, her mother's hairdresser, in Maine. There was Poggle, the Maltese, who was the product of a divorce, and no one mentioned to Steffi that he wasn't house-trained. He now lives with Arthur, her mother's lawyer. And last year there was Maxwell, the eight-month-old golden retriever she fell in love with at the rescue centre.

She brought him home, only to discover that the reason a beautiful pure-bred golden retriever was in the animal rescue centre in the first place was because he was *crazy*. He was the most high-energy dog she'd ever known, manic, in fact, and within a week every single pair of her shoes had been converted to chews, and not the expensive Jimmy kind.

Maxwell had been shipped out to cousins on a forty-acre farm in Milbrook, where he has apparently decided that the sheep and donkeys are his playmates. They are, understandably, not terribly impressed, but Maxwell is beloved by his new family, and so Steffi considers herself something of a good Samaritan.

But a dog! She has always wanted a dog. Something small and cuddly who would love her to pieces. Or large and scary, like a Dobermann, who would actually be a pussycat and her best friend. A companion. Man's Best Friend – isn't that what they say?

And wouldn't this perhaps be a perfect solution? It wasn't permanent, but would break her in gently.

'How long for?' Steffi finds herself asking.

'A year.'

'Wow. That's a long time.'

There is Rob to consider. Rob hates dogs. Never trust a man who doesn't like children or animals. But what does it matter, given that they have neither? But she loves dogs. She wants a dog. She wants this dog. Even though she doesn't know what it is.

'What kind of dog is Fingal?'

She is thinking: small, terrier-type. Big brown eyes. Loyal. Loving.

'Scottish deerhound. But he's terrifically low-maintenance. Do you want to see a picture?'

'Sure.'

Scottish deerhound? What the hell *is* that? Steffi hasn't even heard of a Scottish deerhound.

Mason flicks through the photos on his iPhone and hands it over.

'Jesus Christ!' Steffi yelps. 'That isn't a *dog*. That's a *horse!*'

'He is quite big, but he looks much bigger in that picture because he's with the kids.'

'He's not with the kids. They're riding him.'

'That was just a joke. They don't really ride him.'

'I couldn't take care of a dog that size. He'd eat me for breakfast.'

'Actually he's very lazy. He could eat you for breakfast if he could be bothered, but trust me, he couldn't be bothered. Mostly he just lies around on sofas all day.'

'Always good to have a dog that's trained to stay off the furniture.' She peers at Mason. 'How does Olivia feel about having a dog lying around on the sofas all day?'

'Not happy. He's only allowed on two sofas, and she's covered them with special throws so his fur never actually touches the Fortuny fabric, heaven forbid.'

'Heaven forbid, indeed. God, Mason. I . . . I mean, I was going to say I'd take the dog, but he wouldn't even fit in our apartment. And he looks like you'd need to walk him eight miles five times a day.'

'He doesn't.' Mason shakes his head excitedly. 'He just

needs to be run. He's basically the same type of dog as a greyhound, so he needs a couple of short bursts of really intense exercise. And you wouldn't even notice him in the apartment. He's incredibly quiet and mellow.'

'Really?' Steffi looks at the picture dubiously.

'Really. And you would absolutely love him. He's the coolest dog in the world.'

'I guess he'd be something of a man magnet,' Steffi muses, handing the phone back to Mason.

'Why would you care? You have a boyfriend.'

'I won't have if I come home with Fingal. He hates dogs.'

'Oh. Never trust a —'

'Yes, yes. I know.' Steffi sighs. 'So here's the deal. I'll meet him. Which doesn't mean yes, it just means I'll meet him.'

'That would be fantastic!' Mason says. 'You'll love him and, honestly, I would feel so much better about him being with someone I know. You could feed him chilli spiced with cinnamon! He'd be in dog heaven!'

'What were you going to do if you didn't find someone?'

Mason's face falls. 'Olivia thinks we're going to adopt him out. Permanently.'

'Would you?'

He frowns. 'I wouldn't want to. I love Fingal. He's my dog.'

'Hey, given that I probably won't have a boyfriend to come home to if I decide to look after Fingal, you wouldn't happen to have a spare apartment I could live in as well?' Steffi is joking.

Half.

Mason looks at her curiously. 'I don't have an apartment —

we've already signed a year's lease with a couple from Belgium who are moving to New York, but . . . are you serious?'

'It depends. What are you thinking?'

Mason sighs, looks away, then back at her. 'You know what? Nothing. It's silly. You live and work in New York. Forget it.'

'What? Tell me. Now I have to know.'

'I do have a house. Not an apartment, but a wonderful old farmhouse in Sleepy Hollow.'

'Cooooool.' The word stretches out as images of roaring fires and long leafy walks flutter through Steffi's head.

'I've had it for years,' Mason continues. 'It's very old, but beautiful, and with twenty acres. Olivia hates it, so I just keep it rented out. However, the last tenants scooted out early and it's empty. I was waiting to rent it out after Christmas, but . . .'

'Would I like it?'

'I have no idea – I hardly know you.' Mason smiles. 'But I love it.'

'Sleepy Hollow's right by my sister, Callie. She's in Bedford,' Steffi muses out loud. 'It would be amazing, to be near her. One more question . . .' Steffi looks around and lowers her voice. 'Do you happen to know if there are any vegetarian restaurants in the area that might be looking for a vegan chef?'

Almost Flourless Orange Cake with Marmalade

1 orange
3 eggs
1 cup caster sugar
¼ cup plain flour, sifted
1 teaspoon baking powder
1 cup ground almonds
½ cup marmalade
icing sugar for dusting
Optional: small carton whipping cream, rind of 1 orange

Preheat the oven to 350°F. Grease an 8" springform cake tin and line it with greaseproof paper.

Put the orange in a pan, cover with water and simmer for an hour (or nuke in microwave for around 25 minutes) until soft. Cut the orange in half, remove pips and purée in a food processor.

Beat the eggs and sugar until pale and thick. Fold in the flour, baking powder, almonds and orange purée. Pour into the tin and bake for an hour.

Melt the marmalade in a small pan then pour through a fine sieve, pressing to get all the juice out. Spread the rind-free juice over the cake.

When cool, sift icing sugar over the cake. Mix whipped cream with the orange rind and serve alongside.

Chapter Two

The phone startles Steffi. She reaches for it blindly, then stumbles out of the room so as not to wake Rob.

'Shit.' She trips over her flip-flops outside the bedroom and kicks them viciously out of the way, collapsing on the sofa and rubbing her ankle.

"Lo?'

'Steff? Did I wake you?'

'Oh hey, Callie. Yes, you woke me. What are you doing calling so early?'

'Early? It's ten-thirty.'

'TEN-THIRTY?' Steffi shouts. 'Oh *shit*.'

'What?'

'Oh God. I overslept again. I was meant to go to the farmers' market this morning to get lettuce and peas for the menu tonight.'

'So . . . can't you go to Gristedes instead?'

'That's what I keep doing, and then I end up paying for it out of my own pocket. Dammit. I can't believe I over-slept again. And I'm supposed to be at work in half an hour. I'm never gonna make it.'

'Do you want me to call you back later?'

Steffi sighs. 'No. I'm going to be late whatever. A few minutes talking to you won't make any difference. How are you, sis? What's up?'

'Steff, I'm worried about you. You can't afford to lose another job. You have to be careful.'

'I know, I know. But they love me. I've totally changed the menu, and we're getting amazing crowds. I may drive them nuts with my lateness, but they would never fire me.'

'That's what you said the last time.'

'Right. But I was getting really bored there. It was time to move on.'

'So how do you feel about Joni's?'

Steffi hesitates. 'Bored.' She breaks out in a peal of laughter.

'You are a disaster,' Callie says, laughing. 'What's the record for holding down a job? Six months? Seven?'

'Nooo. That's not fair.' Despite being on the phone Steffi pouts, just as she has always done when teased by her big sister. 'Almost a year at the Grain Market.'

'A year? Are you sure?'

'Okay. So it was nine and a half months, but you always round up for your résumé. And actually, I was kidding about being bored. I'm not bored, I love it. But if a new challenge presented itself, I'd be willing to look at it.'

'Right now you're going to have to start praying for a new challenge,' Callie says sternly. 'And what about Rob? How're things going with him?'

Steffi drops her voice to a whisper. 'Would you be surprised if I said it wasn't going particularly well?'

'No.' Callie tuts. 'It's what I would expect. Oh Steff. When are you going to settle down?'

'Callie!' Steffi reprimands. 'Now you sound just like Dad. You've always been my supporter. Don't start giving me a hard time now! Anyway, this isn't my fault. I'm just getting fed up with the whole rock-chick lifestyle, and frankly, if I were to settle down, it wouldn't be with someone like

Rob. Plus, I'm only thirty-three so I've got plenty of time. Just because you were married at this age doesn't mean that's the right path for me.'

'You're right. I just . . . I guess I just want to see you happy.'

'I am happy,' Steffi says. 'It's just not the same kind of happiness as you, with a perfect husband, two perfect children and a perfect house.'

'If it makes you feel better, the husband is never home, those children ain't so perfect – the daughter, for example, is soon to turn nine and is developing a serious attitude that is making my hair stand on end – and the neighbours' septic tank has just exploded all over our yard.'

Steffi cracks up. 'I totally shouldn't say this, but yes, that does make me feel better. So I guess things aren't any different with Reece?'

'Different, as in does he get home before nine at night and does he ever stop travelling? Nope. Things are no different.'

'But you love it, right? The independence?'

'Yeah. I do. I guess I'm more like Mom than I realized.' Callie drifts into silence as she thinks about her solitary evenings, when Reece is still at work and the kids are in bed.

It is a time she loves. The house is entirely peaceful, and she can drift in and out of her office, Photoshopping pictures if she chooses, making herself tea, curling up on the sofa to watch some TV. It has become her favourite time of day – the hours when the phone doesn't ring, other than Reece to say what time he'll be home, and no one is demanding anything of her.

'How about your kids? Are they like you, or Reece?'

Steffi smiles, thinking of the niece and nephew she adores.

'Eliza's just as strong-willed and stubborn as I am, and moody as hell. God, Steff, I don't remember ever being this rude to Mom when I was young. Sometimes it just takes my breath away.'

'My perfect niece is rude? Seriously?'

'Not for the past couple of days, thank God. She's liking me this week because I just donated a family photographic session to the school auction, and apparently she overheard one of the ten-year-olds saying her mom was desperate to have me take their pictures. So this week I'm cool again. Jack, on the other hand, bless his soul, still adores me unreservedly. God,' she sighs, 'I love that boy.'

'Favouritism!' Steffi points out. 'And by the way, despite what Eliza may think this week, you're not cool,' she says. 'You're a total Stepford Wife.'

'Steff, if you weren't my sister, I'd kill you.'

'But it's true. How many times do I have to tell you there are wardrobe choices other than Gap shorts and Fit-Flops?'

Callie laughs. 'How do you know I have FitFlops?'

'I don't, but I took the train out to stay with Lila a couple of weekends ago, and every single woman I passed on Main Street was wearing those damned things. It's obviously some weird suburban Stepford thing.'

'Bedford isn't the suburbs, it's the country.'

'That's just what you tell yourself to make yourself feel better. Hey, by the way, this guy who comes into the restaurant may let me use his farmhouse in Sleepy Hollow. Wouldn't that be awesome?'

Callie lights up. 'Sleepy Hollow? That's so close! That

would be amazing. What would it be, a weekend place for you or something?'

'Something. Not sure yet. I haven't seen it but I'll keep you posted.'

'Hey, how is Lila, anyway? And how come you went out there? That's just sad. She's *my* best friend and you get to see her more often than I do.'

'I totally don't, but this boyfriend of hers, Ed, had his son staying, and the boy's a fan of Rob's so we came out to meet him.'

'That's adorable! She never told me!'

Steffi sniffs. 'Some kind of best friend . . .'

'No, it's my fault,' Callie says guiltily. 'I've been so busy with life, I've barely had a chance to speak to her, and she's terrible at email. So did you meet Ed? What did you think?'

'Yes. He seems like a great guy.'

'I think he is. In fact, for all the times Lila has said that this time she's met the one, this is the first time she hasn't actually said that. It seems more real than the others. Very measured and balanced. I think she may actually have found the guy.'

'She seems happy. They do seem right together, and she was calm around him.'

'That's exactly it,' Callie says excitedly. 'He calms her down, and that's what was always missing. Lila always got so completely amped up about her boyfriends that you knew it couldn't last.'

'Also, he does have that amazing English accent.'

'I know!' Callie giggles. 'If I close my eyes I can think of Hugh Grant.'

'So,' Steffi says, 'although, darling sis, I would love to

talk to you all day, they might very well kill me if I'm more than about twenty minutes late, so did you just call to chat or is there a reason?'

'Both. I called to chat, and to say that I'm kind of worried about Dad.'

'You are? Why? Is he sick?'

'God, no! Nothing like that. It's just that he's started calling me every day, which, as you know, isn't like him at all, and I just worry that he's really lonely.'

'That's because he's a bad-tempered old bastard and the minute all those lady friends realize it, they're off.'

'I don't think he has any lady friends right now. I think that's the problem. He's never been great at friendships, has he? And now he's sixty-nine and on his own, and I'm just worried about him.'

'So what should we do? Go up and see him?'

'That would be a start. Or maybe you could invite him to stay in New York with you. He loves the theatre and the opera and he probably wouldn't even be at the apartment much.'

'Callie? Have you *been* to this apartment? Dad would hate it here. And he totally wouldn't understand Rob's hours. It would drive him nuts that Rob stays up all night and sleeps all day. He'd probably shove him out of bed at six a.m. and force him to go for a run or something. Why don't you have him stay with you?'

'In Bedford? What's he going to do *here*? He'd have a much better time in the city.'

'So suggest he comes in and stays in a hotel. I'd take him out. I just don't think I can have him at the apartment. But anyway, it doesn't solve the larger problem. If he's lonely, what can we do?'

'I suggested online dating services but he freaked out,

which I guess is still the aftermath of Hiromi. Then he just said he's not the slightest bit interested in dating anyone. I even joked that he didn't have to date them, he could just sleep with them.'

'Ew. Gross. Do you have to bring that up?'

'Sorry. I was kidding.' Callie laughs.

'You know what I wish?' Steffi says. 'I wish that he and Mom would somehow find a way to be friends.'

'No you don't,' Callie counters. 'You wish that he and Mom would get back together.'

'Not really. I mean, there's a part of me that always wanted that when we were growing up, but now I just think they're both on their own, neither of them is exactly a spring chicken, and it would be so nice if they became, I don't know, friends. Wouldn't it be great?'

'Except you're forgetting that Dad's a starched right-wing, rigid, grumpy bastard who likes everything done his way, and Mom's a laid-back, left-wing, scatty free spirit who floats through life like a fairy.'

'She's on Planet Mom.' Steffi laughs.

'Yup. Still.' Callie sighs. 'All these years later and she still lives on Planet Mom. Or Planet Honor, as Dad calls it. She still loves her Chinese medicine and natural supplements. She'd drive him nuts. It's never going to happen.'

'Does he still hate her as much as ever?'

'Put it like this: when he talks about her, he still refers to her as "your mother", with a sneer in his voice.'

'God, you'd think that two marriages and one long-time relationship later he'd get over it.' Steffi shakes her head.

'I know. I think he still loves her.'

'And if by love you mean hates her passionately – absolutely.'

'I'm still amazed they didn't screw us up more.'

'Speak for yourself. I'm the younger one and, according to Dad, I'm a total mess.'

'He doesn't think you're a total mess. He just thinks you're completely irresponsible and still a child.'

'Thanks for the support.'

'I didn't say that's what I think,' Callie protests. 'That's what Dad thinks.'

'So what do you think?'

There's a pause. 'Pretty much the same,' Callie says, and they both burst out laughing.

'So maybe Reece and I will treat Dad to a stay in a hotel in New York for his birthday, then,' Callie continues. 'You're right about the apartment. Dad would think Rob was a disaster and it would put him in a permanent bad mood. Let me talk to Reece and see if he could get some time off work so we could all go out and do stuff together.'

'Time off work? Your husband?'

'I know, I know, but a girl can dream.'

'I've got to go,' Steffi says. 'Love you, Callie.'

'Love you too, baby.'

They put down their respective phones, each with a smile on her face.

Callie sits at her desk in her home office and grabs a pad and pencil. There is so much to do every day that the only way she can breathe is to make lists and systematically tick off each item as she gets it done.

1. Walk Elizabeth. Elizabeth is their devoted black
   lab, who is now the size of two black labs
   because, despite Jack pleading for a puppy and

swearing that he would walk her every single day, no one walks Elizabeth any more, and flinging a tennis ball from a plastic orange ball flinger in the garden twice a day doesn't seem to be making much of a difference. The vet now says Elizabeth has reached critical size and must be walked at least twice a day in the dog park, where she can jump and play with other dogs.

2. Register Jack for baseball; and sign Eliza up for drama classes, in a bid to channel the drama into something constructive, rather than the weeping and wailing when, say, Callie cancels a sleepover as a consequence for Eliza's backtalk.

3. Return the phone calls from all the sleep-away camps that have been leaving forced-cheerful messages on the answering machine for weeks. Oh how she wishes she'd never asked them for information in the first place. She had no idea quite how much they would want her . . .

4. Grocery shop. There is nothing in the fridge except drawers full of melting vegetables, which is what happens when you try to be clever by buying tons of food in the desperate hope that you won't have to hit the grocery store again for at least another week, and your husband doesn't get back until 9 p.m. every night and has usually grabbed a pizza on his way home.

5. Cook. Callie is hosting Book Club tonight, and has completely forgotten about it until this very second. She can't just serve ready-bought food.

No. She can't. The girls would never let her hear the end of it. She'll make Steffi's tomato tarts with puff pastry – easy and impressive. That'll keep the girls quiet.

6. Aaaargh. Run to the liquor store and get bottles of wine, and then to the gourmet food market for snacks. Having Book Club at her house tonight is also a problem because whoever hosts it has to introduce the book and give their opinion and some constructive thoughts as an opener, and Callie hasn't had time to even open the book. She does like the cover though, although she's not sure that's enough.

7. Get to the gym. She's been feeling extraordinarily tired lately, and she's convinced it's because she's let her exercise routine slide. There's no question that when she's working-out every day she is filled with an energy she doesn't otherwise have.

8. Check for paper plates in the pantry. One of those emails had gone out last week asking for volunteers to bring things in for Eliza's class performance of their Colonial Williamsburg project, and by the time Callie had got round to responding all the good stuff – cupcakes, biscuits, lemonade – was gone, and the only thing still left on the list were paper plates. She's pretty sure they've run out because no one's used them since the summer and she doesn't recall seeing any, so she will have to remember to add them to the shopping list.

9. Organize Eliza's birthday party. It may not be until next year, but Eliza's planning it already,

and Callie figures it's better to get it organized this far in advance. She has decided she wants a karaoke party, having heard about someone's big sister's bat-mitzvah extravaganza in New York City at an actual karaoke club, but given there are no karaoke bars in Bedford, Callie is having to use her imagination. Eliza has point-blank refused to have a party at home, and so Callie has found a Japanese restaurant with a private tatami room, available on the night of Eliza's birthday, and she has the number of Kevin the Karaoke King, who will apparently turn up with the machine, the video and the books. At what point, Callie wonders, did her daughter discover sushi and karaoke? What happened to mac 'n' cheese and disco dance parties in her bedroom?

10. Register Jack for football and basketball. She was meant to have done this weeks ago, but couldn't face all the additional driving. No one ever told her that motherhood meant you would spend three-quarters of your day as a chauffeur. She made a decision not to over-schedule the children, and now feels guilty because every boy in Jack's class is doing football, basketball, tae kwon do, baseball clinic and music. She draws the line at music because she just doesn't have the energy.

11. Copy-edit the ad that's going in the local paper next week, and ring back the journalist who's writing an editorial feature on her – an amazing coup that is likely to bring in a lot of

new business, plus ring back the three people
who have called this week to make an appointment for photography consultations.

Photography has always been something that Callie has
loved. As a little girl, she would grab her mother's camera
and snap away at people. It was clear, even then, that she
had an eye.

Without any sort of training, she instinctively knew how
to frame a shot, and one Fine Art degree plus several
photographic courses later, she had learned about shutter
speeds, apertures, lighting, developing.

For a while, after Eliza was born, she devoted herself
to being a full-time mother. They were living in the city at
the time, on the Upper East Side, having left the apartment
in Chelsea, and she would push Eliza in a buggy back
and forth to Central Park, weaving through the nannies in
a desperate attempt to find another mother, to find a
friend.

They moved to Bedford for more space, and Callie
jumped straight into playgroups and pre-school volunteer-
ing, figuring that was what you were supposed to do when
you were a full-time mother, that this was now her job, and
one she would take seriously.

But she could never put down the camera. It was always
in her bag, and she captured every change in Eliza and
Jack's life. When the kids were in school, or on play dates,
or there were other children around, she captured them
too, and people quickly started to ask her for shots, then
offered to pay her for formal shoots.

The thing was, Callie didn't like formal shoots. She didn't
like anything posed, preferring to get to know her subjects,

even if only a little, and to hover in the background and snap discreetly. She liked catching the true essence of a child, and, as time went by, of their families too.

Soon the wealthiest people in Bedford had huge, grainy, black and white Callie Perry prints of their families hanging on either side of the imposing stone fireplace in the drawing room.

'Who did those?' guests would inquire enviously. 'They're stunning.'

And Callie's business took off.

It is, she often thinks, the perfect job. She is at home for the kids whenever they are home, and yet has something that is wholly hers. She loves the excitement of downloading the pictures onto her computer, of scrolling through to pick the perfect shots, and of changing the shadows, the saturation, the exposure to make it even more perfect than it already is.

There was always something so meditative for her about exposing photographs the old-fashioned way, in a darkroom. About holding the sheet of paper between the tweezers and moving it gently through the chemicals, watching the image slowly appear, holding your breath with anticipation and excitement because you were never sure how it was going to come out.

And yet, although it isn't the same, she is surprised at how much she loves Photoshop, how much she loves the extent to which you can change a picture, improve it, correct mistakes with just the click of a mouse.

If only it were this easy with husbands. She picks up the phone to call Reece, but remembers suddenly that he is travelling, and she puts it down with a sigh. She thinks back to when they first met; his job was smaller then, and, although he was already travelling, when he wasn't away on business he would come home early from the office, would have dinner with her. But then the opportunity to shoot the car ads in South Africa came up and it was a huge career jump, far too good to turn down, bringing with it more travel, and later nights.

Tomato Tarts with Puff Pastry

1 pack puff pastry
2 red onions, finely sliced
olive oil
balsamic vinegar
1 tablespoon sugar
4–6 tomatoes, finely sliced
packet feta cheese
basil leaves, finely sliced

Preheat the oven to 350°F.

Roll out the puff pastry and cut out circles, roughly the size of a saucer. Score a circle (lightly track it with a knife) around 1 inch in from the edge.

Sauté the onions in olive oil until soft and caramelized (should take around 30 minutes on a low heat). Add a generous splash of balsamic vinegar and the sugar after about 15 minutes.

Heap the onions in the middle of each circle, with sliced tomatoes in a circle on top.

Place in the oven for 15 minutes.

Crumble feta cheese onto the tarts, drizzle finely with olive oil, sprinkle with basil leaves and serve.

Chapter Three

On nights like these, when Steffi has been working all day, and the restaurant has been packed, and she's barely had a chance to take a break, the last thing she wants to do is skid down the slippery stairs to a dank basement nightclub to watch Rob play a gig, but sometimes a girlfriend has to do what a girlfriend has to do.

Ordinarily she'd go out with the rest of the gang from the restaurant. Maybe to one of the neighbouring bars, or to someone else's restaurant where they'd close for the night and there'd be just staff and their friends sitting around, blowing off steam, wandering outside for the odd toke on a joint.

Or back to the apartment she now shared with Rob. Moving in with him was less of an indication of the seriousness of their relationship, and more because it was cheap and convenient; neither of them was under any illusion that this would be a leg up to the next level of their relationship.

But when Rob's band has a gig she knows she has to go for support, because he expects it, and also, frankly, to make sure the young girls who follow the band around from club to club know that Rob is very definitely not available.

She checks her watch. Ten-fifteen. They were supposed to go on at nine, but experience tells her they'll stall until ten-thirty, to give the audience time to build up a frenzy of anticipation. Steffi locks up the restaurant, inhaling sharply at the biting cold, then clutches her down jacket tighter and prays there is a cab nearby.

Usually she'd walk, but October in New York City can be vicious, and this is one of those nights when the wind chill takes the temperature down to a level that makes it clear that although winter is not yet here officially, it is definitely on its way. No one is outside unless they have to be. On the Upper East Side, the soignée women who are usually insulated in fur throughout the winter are already covering their faces with fleece balaclavas and giant ear muffs, trying not to expose an inch of flesh during their walk from their limousine to the waiting doorman.

Leaning back against the headrest as the cab jerks and lurches through every pothole on the Lower East Side, Steffi closes her eyes with a small smile and thinks about how lucky she is.

She may be sweaty, and tired, and dirty, and she may be off to watch a band she secretly doesn't think is all that good, but the one thing she's certain of is that she loves her life.

Her twenties were wild – all the partying, the craziness, the constant whirlwind of not knowing what was next – but there was always a feeling that she hadn't found her place in the world, didn't know who she was supposed to be, and she never felt settled back then.

Perhaps you are not supposed to, in your twenties, but Steffi always suspected that something would shift for her when she turned thirty. Callie, her older sister, had hated turning thirty all those years ago. She had phoned Steffi in tears, sobbing that she had no boyfriend, not a hope of marriage, nor of children, and thirty was the beginning of the end.

Nine years younger, Steffi had no idea what to say. Although she wasn't the slightest bit surprised that Callie met Reece just a few weeks later, and by the time she was thirty-one Callie was married, and a couple of years after that she had Eliza, her beloved baby daughter.

Steffi celebrated her thirtieth birthday on the ski slopes of Jackson Hole, Wyoming, giggling with her then-boyfriend, Bob, as they got drunk at the top of Corbet's Couloir, and somehow managed to make their way down.

Bob looked like a snow bum, which he was, but he also owned hundreds of acres of land in South America, where he grew roses for export to America, earning vast amounts of money in the process, hence his ability to stay in Jackson Hole for weeks at a time.

He looked and talked like a Californian surfer dude, and had adopted yoga and veganism several years earlier. Shortly after they met he urged Steffi to try vegan food, horrified at her penchant for meat, and spare ribs in particular. She wasn't convinced, but agreed she would do it for a couple of weeks, just to see what it was like.

She loved it. Instantly. She loved feeling clean and light. She used to say it felt as if her body didn't have to try in order to digest, and the benefits were huge. She honestly didn't think it would be something she would stick to, but after the two weeks she knew that her meat-eating days were over.

Always a keen cook, she started cooking foods with which she had only had a passing acquaintance before turning vegan: tofu, tempeh, quinoa, wheat berry. She would sit for hours and devise menus, making sure they had the right balance of leafy greens, protein, Omega-3s.

Her skin looked great, her body – always tending to the chubby side – seemed to find its natural weight without her even trying, and she became passionate about vegan cooking.

Bob looked at her one night after finishing a spinach and chickpea curry.

'You're really good at this,' he said. 'You ought to do it for a living.'

Steffi laughed. 'You mean, give up my wonderful job as receptionist extraordinaire?'

'You're only doing that because you haven't found your path,' Bob said. 'That's just killing time. And yes, I do mean give that up. If you follow your passion you'll be happy, and I can see that this is it.'

'What? Food?'

'Yes, but you're talented. You're always creating these amazing dishes, and I know you're not just following recipes. Half the time you're not using a recipe, you're just making it up. I've seen you scribbling notes when you get an idea. You should be a chef.'

It was one of those light-bulb moments, Steffi realized afterwards. As soon as he said the words, she knew that it was exactly what she wanted to do, indeed, what she had been destined to do.

She came back from Jackson Hole and Bob paid for her to enrol in a course at the Culinary Institute of America. It was the greatest thing he ever did for her, and in many ways more than made up for the fact that he left her for a nineteen-year-old Brazilian beauty shortly thereafter.

And now she works at Joni's, a hole-in-the-wall vegetarian

restaurant tucked between a laundromat and a pawn shop on 12th Street. It isn't exactly salubrious, but their reputation is such that it has become a destination, and every night there is a long line of people patiently waiting with bottles of wine in hand.

Even Walter, Steffi's dad, liked it, grudgingly admitting that perhaps he had been wrong about his daughter's 'latest crazy decision' to become a chef.

She couldn't really blame him; after all, he had been witness to every incarnation throughout her twenties, rolling his eyes each time and asking her when she was going to get a proper job.

'You don't understand,' she'd say. 'It isn't about pensions and security any more. No one wants that, Dad. And even if they did, companies aren't offering it. Life isn't the way it used to be.'

'Well some things haven't changed,' her dad would say. 'I notice you still come to me every time you need money.'

'Fine,' she would huff. 'I didn't realize it was a problem. I won't come to you any more.' And she wouldn't. For a while.

Her mother was more understanding. An artist herself, she had always encouraged Steffi to follow a creative path. When Steffi dropped out of Emory – she was far too busy partying and having fun to bother with work – her mother, while not quite actively encouraging it, said that she had never thought Steffi would thrive in an academic environment.

Her father, on the other hand, had almost had heart failure. There were only two things Steffi could do that would make him happy: work at a bank or insurance company, with a steady salary and a medical plan, or find a wealthy husband to take care of her. Given that she had been fired from every desk job she had ever attempted, and given her penchant for actors, musicians and writers, it was looking increasingly unlikely she would be able to make her father happy.

'When are you going to grow up?' he shouted a couple of times.

'You will find out what you are here for,' her mother said, and gently smiled. 'It just may take you a little longer to find out, but that's okay. It took me a little longer too.'

Steffi still cannot believe her mother and father had once been married. She doesn't remember a time when they were ever together. She was three when they split up, but spent her entire childhood dreaming of them remarrying, even though, for years, they quite clearly hated each other.

Now of course, as an adult, she has asked her mother.

'Tell me again why you married him?'

'I was young, he was handsome. I thought it would make my mother happy.'

'Did it?'

'Of course. To marry a Tollemache? My mother was over the moon.' Honor's eyes clouded over as she remembered.

'And they didn't care about what you wanted?'

'Things were different in those days.' Her mother smiled. 'You married for a variety of reasons, and true love was rarely one of them.'

'So you didn't love him?'

'Oh I did,' Honor said carefully. 'Your father is a good man. I absolutely loved him, but we were such different people. Truly, we should never have married each other.'

Her father still refuses to talk about her mother, unless it's a sarcastic dig. You would think, considering he has married twice more since then, not to mention having had a long-term live-in lover too, that he would have moved on, but he has never seemed able to let go of the anger. Callie has theorized that it is because their mother humiliated him by leaving him so unexpectedly.

And yet, when Honor's second husband, the man she described as the love of her life, died eight years ago, Walter wrote her a long letter, expressing his sorrow, and his regret that he hadn't been able to find the sort of happiness she had had.

Callie had been stunned at the generosity and genuine kindness contained within the letter. She suggested that their parents meet up again, try to become friends, but her father quickly reverted to the dismissiveness of old, and said he wanted nothing to do with their mother. It was bad enough he had to see her at weddings and christenings, he said. The last thing he wanted was her as a movie date.

Callie remains convinced it is because Walter is still in love with her. Throughout their marriage – fourteen years – he had been happy, had thought he had the perfect life. Walter hadn't realized that their mother was, much like Steffi, a free spirit, but one who was trying to be a good daughter, a good wife, a good mother. A woman who was trying so hard to be someone she was not in order to please other people that the weight of the pretence almost suffocated her.

Since her father's last divorce, some five years ago,

he has been on his own, and both Callie and Steffi are worried about him. Steffi has promised to go and stay with him up in Maine before Christmas, but she is dreading it. Her dad has invited Rob, but Steffi knows that he will hate him.

A long-haired, left-wing, laid-back musician, who doesn't have a clue what the word 'responsible' means, isn't exactly who her father has in mind for her.

To be honest, he isn't entirely who she has in mind for herself, but then he'll smile that devastating smile at her and everything will melt, and she will think that things can carry on as they are. For today.

'I like your bandanna,' a girl pipes up as Steffi inches past her, making her way through the crowd to their friends just in front of the stage.

'Thanks.' Steffi smiles, recognizing the girl as one of the groupies trying to befriend Steffi because in her teenage world there is cachet attached to knowing the girlfriend of a member of the band. 'Rachel, right?'

The girl's face lights up. 'Yeah. You're Steffi, Rob's girlfriend.'

Steffi nods. 'I'll see you later.' No point in pretending they have things in common, and having been working non-stop all day Steffi hasn't got the time for small talk, nor to explain that the only reason her dark-blonde hair is in plaits and bandanna is because she hasn't had a moment to wash it. It's not exactly glamorous.

'Hey, love!' Susie reaches over and gives her a hug. 'Cute plaits.'

'Thanks. What's going on?'

'They'll be on in about five minutes. How was work?'

Steffi reaches into her bag. 'You just reminded me – your favourite was on the menu today. I brought it for you.'

'Carrot cake?'

'Nope.'

'Lemon bars?'

'Nope.'

'Basil pesto quinoa?'

'Honey?' Steffi frowns. 'How many favourites do you actually have?'

Susie breaks out in a peal of laughter. 'Everything, sweetie. I love all your cooking. So, seriously, did you bring me my absolute favourite of all? A mushroom and pecan burger?'

'I did! And I brought you some sweet tomato pesto to go with it.'

'I love you, Steffi.' Susie reaches over to give her another hug, then takes the recycled cardboard box and puts it in the bag down at her feet.

'I love you too,' Steffi says, meaning it. It is perhaps the thing she cherishes most about this relationship: the wives and girlfriends of the other members of the band. They are the only other women who truly understand the nature of their rock-band life: that the fans at the concerts are constantly in competition with you, that you spend vast amounts of time on your own while your men are on tour, or recording, or doing press.

Steffi loves the sisterhood. Loves that on a Sunday, while Rob is at practice, Susie will drop in with baby Woody on her hip and drag Steffi out for a long walk and gossipy chats over steaming vats of green tea.

It is this she cannot give up, she realizes, for, eighteen months into their relationship, Steffi is beginning to wonder if she really wants to be a rock widow; she is beginning to question what she and Rob really have in common.

Not that she doesn't adore him, but Rob's world revolves very much around Rob, and Steffi is aware that she is growing ever so slightly tired of hearing the same stories again and again. If he were interested in other things, in . . . well . . . her, for instance, it might be okay, but Rob has to have the spotlight shine on him, and it's not that she minds that exactly, but she often feels they are two people living completely independent lives, coming together late at night for sex, a pretence at intimacy, before separating in the morning with a quick kiss and going out to live their respective lives. Alone.

Coming to gigs reminds her of all that is exciting about him. She knows it's superficial, but standing in a room and seeing how many women are screaming for him fills her with a sense of pride, because she is the one he loves.

Although lately she has been questioning even that. 'Love ya, babe', said frequently and in passing, isn't quite the same as a heartfelt 'I love you'. The word love seems to be used so loosely among their friends that she sometimes isn't sure of its meaning.

The band is great tonight. Steffi has learned that you can tell, as soon as you walk into the room, how the performance will be. It's not about the practice, or the moods the band members are in; it's about the energy in the room. When it is good, the show will be amazing; when it is flat, and no matter what the band tries to do, the performance will be off.

They finish their second song, and Rob spots Steffi in the front. Whatever happens between us, Steffi thinks, I will always look at you and find you devastatingly handsome, will always be sideswiped by that long dark hair and that smooth, tanned skin.

He grins at her and does his funny little strutting dance, which she always enjoys watching, raising an eyebrow and winking at her after his spin. She cracks up laughing and shakes her head. Even though she knows it's not going to be for ever, he has the ability to make her laugh, and for now, as she continues to try to convince herself, that *seems* like enough.

Spinach and Chickpea Coconut Curry

1 can chickpeas, drained and rinsed, or 2 cups home-cooked
    chickpeas
1 can organic diced tomatoes
2 medium potatoes, diced into 1-inch cubes, parboiled.
3 cups torn spinach leaves
5 cloves
1½ teaspoons turmeric
1½ teaspoons curry powder
3 garlic cloves, minced
1 can coconut milk

Combine all the ingredients in a pan. Bring to the boil, turn down the heat, cover and simmer for 30 minutes. Serve with rice or pitta bread.

Chapter Four

'Hi, I'm Emily Samek.' The pretty girl on the doorstep gives Callie a big smile and shakes her hand.

'I'm so glad you're here!' Callie steps aside and pulls her in. 'Especially since Jenn couldn't make it. Thank God she suggested you, or I don't know what I would have done. The kids can't wait to see this movie. Are you sure it's okay?'

'Of course!' Emily says. 'And you want me to keep them out for dinner?'

'I do. It's Book Club tonight,' she says with a shrug, by way of explanation. 'I've got all the girls coming round and I still haven't made the tomato tarts.'

'I'm happy to help, if there's time.' Emily follows her into the kitchen. 'I love cooking!'

'Really?' Callie hesitates. 'Oh God. Cooking or kids. Nope. I have to get the kids out of the way. Maybe if you're able to babysit for us again you could do some cooking with them?'

Emily beams. 'That would be great!'

'Kids!' Callie roars up the stairs. 'Emily the babysitter's here. Get your shoes on and get downstairs.'

'I don't wanna go,' Jack whines, his small face appearing at the top of the stairs. 'I wanna stay home.'

'Not tonight, baby,' Callie says. 'But you're going to see *Up*!'

'Really?' His face lights up. 'On a school night?'

'I know! You are so lucky!'

'Yay!' He disappears off to his room to find his shoes, cheering. 'Liza? We're going to see *Up!*'

Callie shakes her head in resignation. 'You can get them ice cream too . . . I know, I know, I'm a terrible mother.'

When the kids clatter downstairs she gives them giant hugs and closes the door gently behind them.

Callie was one of the founder members of Book Club. She'd never actually thought of herself as a typical Book Club woman – she didn't always enjoy large groups of women – but because it was only three of them in the beginning, and the other two – Betsy and Laura – were women she knew well, it felt like hers, and three years on she loves it.

As with so many book clubs, it is less about the book and almost entirely about camaraderie. It is about women remembering who they were before they had children. Women who can collapse into a sofa with a glass of wine and not have someone pulling at their T-shirt, or running in demanding Mommy punishes a sibling for hitting them.

It is about laughter. And friendship. And bonding. It has become a bright spot in all of their lives, and tonight, as with every other Book Club night, the women will dress up, put on make-up, sparkle just a little bit more. Not for their husbands, but for the other women.

When it's warm enough, Book Club has always been outside, or at least starts outside, with drinks in sun-filled gardens, around serene swimming pools, on fieldstone terraces overlooking hills, before moving inside or onto screened porches, while the drink continues to flow and the women get more comfortable.

During the summer, the women all wear dresses. Brightly coloured silk or chiffon sundresses with strappy sandals, their skin glowing as they sip their pomegranate martinis and throw their heads back with laughter, knowing how beautiful they all look.

But now, in the autumn, Book Club means fires, glasses of red wine, cosy sweaters and curling up on squishy sofas. It is the time of year that Callie adores, and she is looking forward to everyone arriving.

She flicks the light on in her dressing room and idly pulls out a couple of dresses. She isn't really a dress girl, has never felt entirely *herself* in dresses, although for special occasions she'll put one on. But tonight she thinks she'll wear jeans. She's always more comfortable in jeans, and she'll pair her favourite dark skinny ones with high boots and a pale pink chiffon blouse. A long delicate gold chain with a chunky crystal at the end, and she'll be perfect.

There is a uniform out here, and it is quite different to the uniform Callie wore when she lived in the city. In the suburbs, the women wear smarter clothes, more dresses, more colour.

In the city, Callie and all her friends wore jeans everywhere. Jeans with cute ankle boots and sweaters, or jeans with heels and gauzy tops in the evening. She's still fighting the suburban pull, although she did confess to Lila that she has succumbed, and – shh, don't tell anyone – actually has a couple of Lilly Pulitzer shifts at the very back of her wardrobe.

The coffee table is strewn with various copies of Anita Shreve's *Testimony*, half-empty glasses of wine, plates covered with crumbs. In the centre of the table is an almost-finished pumpkin gingerbread trifle, with a dozen spoons sticking out.

This has become their secret tradition. Every month a different member is assigned dessert. Everyone brings something – cookies, lemon bars, brownies – but they are always picked up at the grocery store, and only one has to cook a decadent dessert from scratch.

And it must be huge.

There are no plates for the dessert; only spoons are handed out. They all stand crowded round the dessert and on the count of three they plunge in, scooping dessert by the spoonful, figures, calories and men be damned.

Tonight Betsy made the trifle, and nobody spoke for a few seconds, just moaned with joy as they gorged.

'If no one pounces,' Callie says as she walks in from the kitchen, eyeing the trifle, 'I'm going to finish that up.'

'You can afford to,' says Laura. 'You're tiny. You could eat an entire trifle every day and it probably wouldn't show.'

'You know what's really weird?' Callie scrapes the last of the trifle and licks the spoon. 'I was way bigger before I had babies.'

'That *is* weird,' Laura says. 'And unfair.'

'I know. I wasn't huge, but always had, like, ten, fifteen pounds I needed to get rid of, and I always knew that once I had kids I'd get rid of it.'

'Instantly?' one of the other women asks.

'No. Until recently I still wanted to lose a few pounds, but strangely it seems to have simply dropped off. I guess I've been so busy I just haven't eaten that much. I'm making up for it now, though.' She grins, putting the spoon down and taking the empty dish into the kitchen.

So many things have changed, she thinks, as she quickly washes up the dish so she doesn't have to deal with it later. Her fortieth birthday was terrifying, but now, at forty-two, she realizes she is, indeed, in the prime of her life.

Her skin is glowing, her hair shines and she is completely comfortable in her skin. She wakes up every morning, loving her life. She has a husband she adores, children who light up her life (except when they're fighting and driving her nuts), and work that fulfils her.

She loves her family, her friends, her home. And tonight, as happens so often, she is amazed that she seems to be in the minority.

For so many of the women seem to be unhappy. Not on the exterior. If you didn't know, you would never know. You would think they had wonderful husbands, glorious children, beautiful homes and privileged lives.

It has been a shock, these past three years, for Callie to discover how few of the women are happy with where they are. Oh yes, their houses are beautiful, but they'd really like one with room for a swimming pool . . . *then* they'd be happy.

Or they adore their kids, but the live-in nanny/housekeeper just walked out – yes, she is the seventh in a row – and they can't possibly cope. Does anyone know anyone? Filipina, perhaps? Or Brazilian – they've had good luck with *those*.

And often, it is merely bitterness about their husbands that takes her breath away, couched in humour of course. Always couched in humour.

Callie puts the bowl on the draining board and goes outside to where the secret smokers are huddled on the bare teak furniture – the cushions having been put in the garage at the beginning of autumn.

'Hey, guys.' She sits down and reaches forward to borrow someone's glass of wine and take a sip. 'Aren't you cold?'

'Freezing.' Sue shivers. 'I have to stop smoking. I can't stand this.'

'Really?' Callie looks at her. 'But I thought you only smoke when you drink.'

'Right. And I only drink every day. At the witching hour. I keep telling the kids I'm just running to the postbox, and Sophie nearly caught me the other day.'

'Doesn't everyone drink every day?' asks Lisa. 'Seriously? How are you supposed to get through the evening without some help? My husband's not home until eight, I've spent the day running around like a crazy person, I've done homework with the kids, got through bath time and fed them, and I'm about to explode. It's just one glass of wine, though. Isn't that . . . normal?'

'Exactly!' Sue says. 'Callie? Don't you?'

'Of course!' Callie smiles, although it's not strictly true. If she's with another mother she'll always break open a bottle of wine, but it wouldn't really occur to her to have a glass of wine by herself.

'God knows I need the wine to get me in the mood,' Sue says. 'When Keith gets home from one of his bar-stops at the station, it's a disaster. Then I'm likely to drink the whole bottle.'

Lisa groans with laughter. 'What's happened to us?' she says, looking at Sue, then at Callie. 'I never used to be able to keep my hands off my husband. What happened? Honestly? I'd be happy if I never had sex again.'

'You said it, girl!' shrieks Sue, high-fiving her, while Callie smiles and stands up, excusing herself to go and get a frozen margarita.

Am I so unusual? she asks herself. Is there something wrong with me? For she does still love making love with her husband. After all these years they have grown closer, not further apart, and she never feels more connected to him than when they are in bed and he is moving gently inside her.

She cannot relate to what is going on for these other women. Doesn't judge them, but dares not reveal her truth, because she would then be the outcast, the one who was judged, or misunderstood.

How is it, she wonders, that they have managed to avoid what so many of these women are going through? Is it luck? Is it work? Not work, she thinks, since her relationship with Reece never feels like work. Luck? Partly. And communication. Taking, *making*, time for each other. Considering each other. Listening to each other. Avoiding those times when they are with other couples and could attempt humour, but it would come at their partner's expense – a biting comment that would elicit a smile or laughter from their friends, and an uncomfortable squirming from Reece.

She won't do it. She loves her husband and she knows she cannot take him for granted. She knows because of evenings like this.

It isn't as if Callie had a model for marriage, at least she didn't during the formative years, which is when, they say, it counts. She can barely remember her parents being together, and what little she does remember centres around two people who seemed to be entirely different, who lived separate lives.

48

Perhaps it was her mother's relationship with George that taught her the most. Her mother always said the joy of her marriage to George was that it was second time around. She didn't marry because she had to. Or because it was a way to leave her mother's house. Or because of any pressure she felt.

She married, despite thinking that she would never marry again, because a man came along with whom she fell completely in love. A gentle, kind man, who made her laugh, and who, she used to say, she thought was the best-looking man she had ever seen.

The fact that George always seemed, to Callie at least, very old and very craggy and not handsome in the slightest, didn't matter. Honor was smitten from the moment she met him, and remained smitten until the day he died.

'My handsome man' Honor would call him, leaning down while George was attempting to eat his breakfast, taking his face gently in her hands and kissing him.

'Look at that man,' she'd say happily, to anyone who would listen. 'Isn't he just the most glorious man you've ever seen?'

Everyone would agree. Not that George was the most glorious man they had ever seen, but that this was the most glorious relationship they had ever known. Being around Honor and George elevated everyone's spirits, it made them feel good. On a subconscious level, Callie must have taken notes, for she knew that it was possible to have something like that, and anything less would be settling for second best.

Reece grew on her slowly. She liked him enormously, and liked how she felt around him from the moment they met. But thirty was a dangerous age, she knew. She had watched as too many of her friends who were approaching thirty jumped into marriage with the first man who offered. They weren't relationships based on love or compatibility, but on the increasingly loud ticking of a biological clock.

She had been the bridesmaid at Samantha's wedding. Samantha was a friend from school, a bright, bubbly and gorgeous girl, who had a personality that was infinitely larger than life. She had spent her twenties on an emotional roller coaster, falling in and out of passionate love.

Samantha's husband, Alex, was, without doubt, the most boring man Callie had ever known. He was arrogant, dismissive and rude. He had the sort of good looks that weren't really good, but with the right clothes, the right haircut, a lot of working-out, could create the illusion.

Callie, who loved everyone, disliked him instantly. She could see immediately that he was entirely wrong for Samantha. She knew that Samantha was marrying him because he asked, and because she was terrified that no one else would; and he was marrying her because he couldn't believe his luck that someone as gorgeous as Samantha would even look at him, let alone marry him.

Callie sat through countless evenings listening to Alex pontificating about things he thought were important, always claiming to know just a little more than anyone else in the room.

She walked up the aisle in front of Samantha, praying for some kind of intervention, knowing that there was nothing she could do.

Their first baby came within the year. Their second twenty months afterwards. Their third two years later, and their fourth two and a half years after that.

'I guess I was wrong,' Callie said to Reece, who had refused to go out with them as a couple any more, Alex being so unbearable. 'I guess they're happy.'

When Samantha left Alex for her personal trainer, no one was surprised. Callie hadn't seen Samantha properly in years by that time, but they met for lunch one day in Greenwich and Samantha revealed all.

'I think I hated him before I even married him.' She shook her head in disbelief. 'I just . . . I guess I was convinced I could make it work. I thought he loved me enough for both of us, and I thought I'd learn to love him.'

'And you wanted babies,' Callie remembered.

'So much.' Samantha sighed. 'It clouded everything else.'

By this time Callie was married. Happily. Blissfully. She knew then just how lucky she was to have found the type of relationship her mother had found with George.

Even today, all these years on, if she arrives early at a party and sees Reece walk in the door, her heart still flips. He's with me! she thinks. See that gorgeous man over there? He's mine!

Callie stops just inside the kitchen, and looks at the photographs on the wall. She looks at ones of Reece and feels her heart swell. I love my husband, she thinks, feeling a shiver of excitement at the prospect of him coming home.

I am just so damned lucky.

Pumpkin Gingerbread Trifle

3 cups single cream

6 large eggs

½ cup granulated sugar

½ cup soft brown sugar

⅓ cup molasses

1½ teaspoons ground cinnamon

1 teaspoon ground ginger

1 teaspoon ground nutmeg

⅛ teaspoon ground cloves

¼ teaspoon salt

3 cups puréed pumpkin, or about 1½ cans

1 packet store-bought gingerbread mix

1 quart double cream

½ teaspoon vanilla extract

¼ cup crystallized ginger

½ cup gingersnap crumbs

Preheat the oven to 325°F.

Scald the single cream in a heavy saucepan (which means take it to the edge of boiling, then remove it from the heat).

Beat the eggs, sugar, molasses, cinnamon, ginger, nutmeg, cloves and salt. Mix in the pumpkin and single cream. When it is smooth, put in a buttered baking dish which you then put into a bain-marie: place the dish into a larger baking dish, and fill the larger dish with hot water to about 1 inch below the rim of the custard dish. Bake this for 50 minutes, then start to check it. You want a set, firm custard, and a knife inserted into the centre should come out clean.

Cool and refrigerate overnight.

Cook, cool and slice the gingerbread.

To assemble your trifle: get out your trifle bowl, or any deep glass or crystal bowl.

Whip the double cream with the vanilla extract, then fold in the crystallized ginger. Set aside.

Spoon half of the pumpkin custard into the bowl and layer half of the gingerbread over that, then half of the whipped cream. Repeat. Top the final layer of whipped cream with gingersnaps, or gingersnap crumbs, and, if you like, drizzle with Calvados.

Only about three million calories a serving, but worth it, and who counts when it's Book Club . . . ?

Chapter Five

Reece Perry settles down in the first-class seat and goes through his routine. He pulls out his DVD player, tucks it into the seat next to him, kicks off his shoes and pulls on the socks he always brings. His magazines are stuffed into the pocket in front, and his Kindle behind them – for when they are safely up in the air and it is safe to turn on all electronic devices.

His iPhone is on his lap and he picks it up, checking his email once more. Across the aisle from him is a man, similar age, holding his iPhone and playing some racing-car game. Reece grins. He downloaded a shocking amount of applications when he first got the phone, then found he was regressing to the age of about sixteen and was wasting vast amounts of time playing the games, so he got rid of all of them.

He checks his watch. Ten-forty p.m. in Cape Town, which means three-forty p.m. in Bedford. He picks up his mobile again to call Callie, thinking about how much he wants to see her, hoping she hasn't left to meet the kids from school.

'Hi, Loki,' he says, using his pet name for her, the same as her pet name for him. It started as a joke, when they saw the name on a sweatshirt and Callie decided it would make the perfect silly lovers' name, but then, somehow, it stuck.

'Lovebug!' The excitement is evident in Callie's delighted greeting. 'Are you on the plane?'

'I am. I can't wait to see you. I've missed you guys.'

'You always miss us guys,' Callie says. 'And we miss you too. Eliza made a chart and she's been crossing off the days until you come home. And this morning Jack was practically hopping with excitement, but I told him you'd probably be home after they're in bed. They both say you have to swear you'll wake them up.'

Reece smiles. 'Have you ever known me *not* to wake them up?'

'Right, and usually neither of them even remembers in the morning. But I'm glad you're coming home. When's your next trip?'

'Cal, don't ask when my next one is before this one is even done.'

Callie laughs. 'You're right. I'd just like to know I'm going to see you for a bit before you take off.'

'You'll see me a lot.' He smiles again, adding, 'You can see all of me if you want.'

'Promises, promises.' Callie laughs. 'I'd quite like to see all of you tonight.'

'You'll be up, right?'

'You can count on it. I have a ton of photographs I need to go through. Oh God, I didn't tell you, I did that shoot for those people at the end of East Magnolia Drive.'

'Which people?'

'The people who bought that huge house. The Kavanaghs. Remember, we met them at that cocktail party in New Canaan, at the Philip Johnson house?'

'Yeah, I remember. How's the house?'

'Really beautiful. I mean, it's huge — another big, new house — but she decorated it herself and I think she did an incredible job. Everyone around town is whispering about them being gauche, but I thought they were just lovely.'

'You think *everyone's* just lovely.'

There's a pause as Callie considers it. 'You're right!' Her laugh echoes down the phone line. 'I do. But she really was, and she served the most amazing chocolate cake — you would have died. Anyway, they're coming for dinner in a couple of weeks so you'd better be around.'

'Give me the date when I get home and I'll make sure I am.'

'Oh my gosh, look at the time. I have to go and meet the bus. Have a safe flight, baby. I love you.'

'I love you too.' And he puts down the phone feeling his heart soar.

He loves that she isn't needy. So unlike girlfriends before her. There were one or two he thought might have made the grade, but then they'd do things like pick up his phone and scroll through texts when he was out of the room, or give him a hard time because he had to go away again on yet another work trip, and no, they couldn't come with him because he'd be working round the clock and it wouldn't be any fun for them.

The stewardess walks past, flashing him a flirtatious look. 'Champagne? Orange juice? Sparkling water?'

'Champagne, please.' What a shame it is, he thinks, that such a pretty woman has ruined herself, for she has clearly done a significant amount of work to her face in a bid to retain her youthful looks, and now her lips are too full, her skin too tanned, her eyebrows too arched, and when she smiles the folds from her nose to her mouth look decidedly . . . odd.

'I'm Sally,' she says. 'Let me know if you need anything.

Anything at all.' It is not flirting, exactly, but there is a flirtatious lilt, although Reece is used to this, doing as much travelling as he does.

It is almost amusing, he thinks, how some stewardesses will respond delightedly to men travelling alone, their hopeful looks swiftly disappearing, replaced with a bored look of resignation, as they offer the same drinks to the woman sitting behind.

He would never admit this out loud to Callie, although she secretly knows it, but he loves travelling. It was the one thing that scared him when he met Callie and knew, very quickly, that she was the woman he would be spending the rest of his life with: what if she made him change?

He loves his career, climbing the ranks in his small advertising agency to Creative Director, and then switching over to directing for a large agency. The Creative Advertising Awards he has won for this agency line the glass shelves in his office.

He loves that he has worked his way up to a sleek, modern office the size of a small basketball court, with all the toys and accoutrements that creative people are supposed to have. There is, in fact, a basketball hoop. A pool table. A black leather and chrome Mies van der Rohe sofa, and a corner bar for those late-night brainstorming sessions.

He loves that, as his career progresses, he gets to go to more and more exotic locales to film the commercials, meets interesting people, eats unusual food, stays up late with the crew in assorted bars and nightclubs.

Before Callie, travelling also meant women. Lots of

them. From models and actresses appearing in the ads to, occasionally, women he met in bars. He is a tall, sporty American, with a winning grin and a wicked charm.

It isn't that Reece is the best-looking in the room, but he has a way of focusing his full attention on you, male or female, that always makes you feel you are the most interesting person he has ever met.

Almost everyone who has a conversation of longer than five minutes with Reece falls a little bit in love with him. It helps that he is six foot one, with tousled dirty-blond hair, and looks great in a pair of old jeans.

That is one of the things that first attracted Callie. That he looks equally good in a Brooks Brothers suit as in a polo shirt and jeans, with trainers and a faded baseball cap.

He always shied away from marriage, in fact from commitment of any kind, thinking that commitment meant change. But when he met Callie, it wasn't so much that she didn't want him to change – which she didn't – but that he wanted to.

Reece found he was no longer interested in the leggy model-types who starred in his shoots, wasn't swayed by a plunging neckline or a sultry look in the way he had been in the past.

In the early days, he hated being away from Callie; a couple of times he even cut his trips short to run back home. Then, when Eliza was born, he fell madly in love, but he started to welcome the nights away, the luxury hotels, the nights of unbroken sleep. And then came Jack, and with it a chaos that he still isn't entirely sure he is used to.

Now, Callie, Eliza and Jack manage perfectly well

without him, and while he misses them, he is also grateful that he not only gets to have some peace and quiet, but he gets to have a semblance of the freedom of a single man again.

Not that he's taking advantage of the women – never that – but he gets to stay up until late, drinking with the boys. He gets to have some downtime, lie by swimming pools with the papers and some great music playing through his earplugs – with no small people tugging on his arm, demanding he play a game, or throw a ball, or just give them some attention, any kind of attention, *please*.

Of late, though, he has found that while he still looks forward to the trips he's getting a little too old for the late nights and the drinking. The past couple of trips he has been the first to leave dinner, sometimes before dessert, yawning and excusing himself to go up to his hotel room and crash in front of the TV.

The will to party may still be there, or at least the idea of it, but the reality is something else entirely.

It's a bit like the year he stopped running, doing any kind of working-out. He'd lie in bed every night and decide that in the morning he would go for a run. There would be no decision-making involved: he would set the alarm forty-five minutes earlier then get up, pull on shorts and trainers and be out through the door before even the kids woke up.

Every morning, without fail, the alarm would go off, he'd groan, reach out a hand to bang it off and fall back to sleep.

The *idea* of running was so much more appealing than the *actual* running, which is exactly how the work trips are beginning to feel. God, is he happy to be coming home.

Reece sips his champagne and leans his head back, closing his eyes as the last stray passengers file down the aisle.

'I'm sorry.' His arm is bumped and he opens his eyes to see a woman standing over him, her bag resting on his arm while she steps back and attempts to lift what is obviously a very heavy carry-on case into the overhead locker.

'Let me help.' Reece's good manners take over and he jumps up and pushes the case in for her.

'Wow! Thank you.' She smiles and, naturally, sits beside him. 'I'm Alison.'

'Reece,' he says, thinking: Oh God. Please, no. Not a Chatty Cathy. It's a night flight, and the last thing he wants is someone who's going to yammer away all night long, even if she is, well, rather attractive.

On his flight over there were two businessmen sitting in front of him who got drunk and didn't shut up all night. Reece was furious. Tonight he just wants to sleep.

Please don't ask me what I've been doing in South Africa, he thinks, smiling tightly and wondering how to convey that he really doesn't want to talk, without being rude.

'Do you mind if I . . .' She gestures to her own iPod.

He smiles again, and this time it is with genuine gratitude. 'I'm planning on doing the same,' he says, and they both laugh.

Reece wakes up, sweating. He had turned his seat into a bed, wrapped himself up in a blanket and slept most of the way.

He pushes the blanket off and eases the bed up, seeing that the cabin is still dark, an eerie glow coming from one or two seats as people watch a movie.

He pulls out the toothbrush and gingerly climbs over the sleeping form of – what was her name? Alison? – and makes his way to the bathroom where he brushes his teeth and swirls the mouthwash around until he starts to feel vaguely human.

'Could I get some coffee, please?' he asks the stewardess when he walks out, and she smiles as he makes his way back to the seat.

Slowly people are starting to wake up, others moving blearily towards the washroom, beds turning back into seats, people stretching and yawning blankly in that slightly childlike, discombobulated way.

Alison stirs, pushes the mask off her face and sits bolt upright. She looks around, disoriented, then sinks back down, pressing the button until her bed is half elevated.

She catches Reece's eye. 'Did you sleep?'

'The whole time. I just woke up.'

'So you didn't hear me snore?' She grins. She is just as pretty, even now, with sleepy eyes and tousled hair.

'I did not, but I'm sure mine would have been louder.'

'So are you on your way home?'

Reece nods.

'You?' He doesn't really want to know, but it's only polite.

'Yup. I was in Cape Town for a vacation. Old boy-friend.'

'Sounds like fun.' Reece doesn't quite know what to say.

'Not so much. Turns out there was a reason it didn't work out the first time.' She sighs, and Reece knows she is trying to let him know she is single. Oh the signs that are so obvious, and so wrong.

'Navigating those relationship minefields is tough,' he offers with a smile, pulling out a magazine, hoping to put her off.

'Tell me about it.' She sighs again. 'How about you? You have a girlfriend?'

At this, Reece laughs. 'No,' he says, quickly adding, 'A wife. And two kids. This is the only chance I get to have a bit of peace and quiet.'

'Lucky you,' Alison says, picking up her headphones and plugging herself in.

*

Callie feels silly that she should still be this excited to see her husband after over ten years of marriage, but she is still this excited, and when he phones to say he is turning off the highway she feels her heart lift in anticipation.

Pouring herself a glass of wine, she perches at the kitchen counter so she can have a bird's eye view of Reece's headlights when he turns in the driveway, and as soon as she sees them she runs out of the house and over to the car to open his door.

'Loki!' she murmurs into his shoulder, burying her nose in his jacket, smelling his familiar smell. He nuzzles her hair and wonders how it is that he never quite realizes how much he misses her until she is in his arms again.

'Hey.' He pulls back and smiles down at her, lit up for a moment in the full beams of the hired limo as it crunches a lazy swing to make its way back to the city. 'Did you miss me?'

'So much.' She winds an arm around his waist as they head into the house.

'Daddy!' Eliza, fast asleep, wakes up and gives him a sleepy smile, throwing her arms around his neck as he bends down to hold her.

'Hi, baby,' he whispers. 'Mommy said I needed to wake you up. I'm home now. I love you.'

'I love you, Daddy,' she says, her eyes already closing as she turns on her side and clutches her rabbit close to her chest.

Reece tiptoes next door, to Jack's room. He is upside down on his bed, one leg flung over the side, pyjamas pushed up past his knees, blanket on the floor. Reece stands in the doorway for a moment, gazing at his son, filled with love as he walks over, picks Jack up under the shoulders and lays him back down with his head on the pillow.

He is hoping Jack will wake up, just a love-filled smile, perhaps an 'I love you' too, but Jack is dead to the world, and after tucking him in Reece leans forward and kisses him on the forehead, pausing for a moment outside their bedroom doors to watch their little sleeping bodies rise and fall.

I love them, he thinks. All of them. His children. His wife. His life. He loves this house, this antique farmhouse that they both fell in love with the minute they pulled into the driveway. He loves the dry-stone stacked walls that enclose the clipped boxwood balls in the front, and the heavy oak-panelled walls that make him feel safe.

He loves the wide corridor he is walking down, nursing his drink, wheeling his bag behind him – the corridor, lined with original built-ins and window seats covered in a pale grey chintz, that leads from the children's rooms to the master suite, a corridor they decided to carpet two years ago, to try to muffle the noise of the children stampeding like a herd of small elephants along the wooden floor.

He loves their bedroom, the soft blues and whites, the antique Swedish bureau and Gustavian side tables in rough painted greys, the canopy above the bed, a four-poster, the pretty fleur-de-lys curtains hanging down at all four corners, behind which he can just make out the curve of a naked leg.

Reece grins, leaves the case by the door, slides the glass onto his bedside table, and climbs on the bed, advancing towards Callie, who is lying there with her best come-hither smile, clad in her Lands' End cotton nightie.

'Grrrr,' he says and laughs. 'Someone really is happy to see me.' And he kisses her softly, then she yelps as he collapses on top of her.

'Can't. Breathe,' she gasps, but he doesn't believe her and she is laughing when he eventually lifts himself off, resting on the palms of his hands as he lowers his head and kisses her again.

'I love you, wife,' he says.

'I love you, husband,' she says, and soon they don't say anything at all.

In the middle of the night, Callie wakes up, soaking. Damn night sweats, she curses, getting up and going to the wardrobe, pulling off her nightie and sliding her head through one of Reece's oversized T-shirts.

She climbs back into bed, smiling as she snuggles against Reece's shoulder. She knows so many couples who just don't seem that happy. People who have children together and would never think of leaving each other, but don't seem to make their partner happy.

I am so lucky, she thinks, turning her head to plant a gentle kiss on Reece's neck. Reece isn't the man I married. He is so very much more. He is a greater husband, father and friend than I could ever have imagined. He is strong, and supportive, and loving.

As the years have gone by he has become more attractive, sexier, softer.

I am the luckiest girl in the world, she thinks, turning over and closing her eyes as sleep comes to take her away.

Chocolate Chestnut Truffle Cake

1 cup dark chocolate, in chunks
1 cup unsalted butter, cubed
1 cup peeled, cooked chestnuts
1 cup whole milk
4 eggs, separated
½ cup sugar
Optional: chocolate shavings to garnish

Preheat the oven to 350°F and grease and line a 9" spring-form cake tin.

Melt the chocolate and butter together in a pan over a very gentle heat. In another pan, heat the chestnuts with the milk until just boiling, then purée.

Mix the egg yolks and sugar together until pale and fluffy. Add the chocolate and chestnuts, and blend until smooth.

Whisk the egg whites until stiff, and fold them into the batter. Transfer the mix to the tin and bake for 30 minutes. Serve warm (when the cake will be more like a mousse) or place in the fridge to firm. Garnish with chocolate shavings, if you would like.

Chapter Six

'How are you doing, Louis?' Mason pauses in the foyer to greet the doorman.

'Good, good, Mr Gregory. How are you?'

'I'm great,' Mason lies enthusiastically. 'Isn't it your daughter's birthday coming up? How old will Sophia be? Four?'

The doorman's face lights up. 'Yes. She is four, and so cute!'

'Does she like Barney?'

'No. She wants to be like her older brother. She likes Spongebob.'

Mason makes a mental note – he will get hold of some Spongebob books for her – and he waves goodbye as he steps onto Fifth Avenue.

It is a beautiful autumn day. The sky is blue, the air is sharp and clear, despite the biting cold. As always, as soon as he steps outside his building, looks across the street at the trees lining the park, he feels his heart lift.

And more than that, he feels a weight lift off his chest.

He strides down Fifth Avenue – it is twelve blocks to the office – and pauses only to lift up his BlackBerry when it buzzes. Olivia. It can wait. She can leave a message. She will not be calling with messages of love or endearment, she will be calling to remind him to do something, or be somewhere, or look after the children because the nanny has cancelled and she is going out.

He is beginning to realize that he may be living, but this really is no kind of life. His happiest hours are those spent in the office, when he is surrounded by dynamic, clever people who respect him and listen to him.

He lunches with authors, agents, editors. He is funny and perceptive and, most of all, light. He dreads having to leave, his footsteps infinitely heavier as he walks home up Fifth Avenue, focusing on the children, hoping that Olivia will not be home.

He has become an observer. A bystander on the sidelines, watching his life from a distance. He doesn't want it to be this way, but he and Olivia have nothing in common, and he wonders, now, what on earth he was thinking when he asked her to marry him.

What on earth she must have been thinking when she said yes.

Olivia hated her mother. She hated her mother's snobbery, her mother's constant demands that she marry 'someone of our class'. Mason was no slouch. A graduate of Harvard Business School, he was already, when they met, a bright star in publishing, but his beginnings were humble, and Olivia's mother never thought he was good enough.

Of course Olivia wanted to marry him. It was the ultimate snub to her family.

And Mason? Surely he should have known better? He did, but he was intoxicated by Olivia's world; it was so very different from anything he had ever known and he was swept away by the romance and the possibility of it.

And that Olivia, this golden beauty who was so tiny and delicate, and had such sweetness, should be interested in him was extraordinary. The fact that, even in the early days of dating, they seemed to have different interests was charming back then. He found her social nature adorable. It was a perfect foil for his more introverted personality, forced him to go out more, which seemed a good thing at the time.

Her extensive involvement in charity was impressive. He thought she was a genuinely good person, sitting on all these boards, raising so much money for so many good causes. He remembers being truly shocked when he asked her about one of her charities and she had no idea what they actually did. It wasn't about raising money, he quickly discovered, it was about remaining at the top of the social ladder.

She is obsessed with appearing in the *New York Times* diary, is on air-kissing terms with all the photographers, friends with all the fashion designers, who make dresses for her, gratis, in return for publicity.

Mason is an accessory, a shadowy figure in black tie who stands awkwardly with the other shadowy figures in black tie, being pulled out by their wives for the occasional photo opportunity.

He has thought, often, about leaving, but if the thought itself is exhausting, the actual physical process of doing so would be utterly overwhelming. It isn't that he hates his wife, or even dislikes her. He just has no idea what they are doing together. They barely speak, and if they do have a meal together – like Olivia coming to Joni's the other day – it is because they have something concrete to discuss, in this case the logistics of their move to London.

Then there are the children to consider. He has to stay, because if he weren't there their lives would be filled with a series of nannies. Olivia loves her children, of that he has no doubt, but she loves them more when they are beautifully behaved, when they are dressed impeccably, when there are other people to see her perfect family.

When the children are tired, or whiny, or acting up, as all children do, Olivia will step out of the elevator yelling, 'Christy?' or 'Elena?' or 'Dominica?' to whichever nanny or housekeeper is around that afternoon.

It is not Olivia's fault, he thinks sadly. Her own mother stayed in hospital for ten days after she gave birth to Olivia, sending Olivia home with a baby nurse and nanny.

She would see Olivia in the morning, when Olivia was sent downstairs for breakfast, dressed and washed, and for a short while again in the afternoon, before Olivia was taken to the nursery for tea. Her mother was English and, despite living in Texas, followed the English upper-class traditions exactly.

When Olivia was excited, or upset, or had cut her knee, or had a fight with her best friend, or got into trouble in school, or didn't like her music class, or fell off her pony, the person to whom she ran was Nanny.

Her mother was busy lunching and socializing, and had little time for Olivia unless it was on her rigid terms.

Now the pattern is being repeated with Olivia's own children. Except instead of one long-term nanny to love them and raise them, there is a series of young girls, none of whom has ever lasted beyond a year.

When their knees are scraped, or they are happy, or sad, it is Mason to whom they come running.

This is why he will never leave.

He is in the office by six o'clock every morning, and home by six every night. He thanks the nanny, tells her she

70

can leave, then gets down to the serious business of what to make the children for dinner.

If Olivia is there, she insists on taking over, but it's never for long. One cry, one raised voice, one meltdown, and she immediately hands them over to Mason, and they are his for the rest of the evening, or until they go out.

'Jim? It's Mason.'

'Hey! I haven't heard from you in ages. Where've you been?'

'Busy as ever. I was wondering if you wanted to grab a beer tonight.'

'Great. Usual place?'

'Sounds good. Six?'

'See you then.'

O'Hanrahan's is dark, crowded and loud. Mason pushes through the crowds to the bar, raising a hand and waving at the barman, who reaches over to shake his hand.

'Haven't seen you in an age,' he says. 'How are ya?'

'Busy, Declan,' Mason says. 'Have you seen Jim?'

'Down the other end. Pint of the usual?'

Mason nods and shuffles through Manhattan's chattering workforce, everyone delighting in letting off steam at the end of the day.

Olivia has just returned from London, and tonight she is taking the kids to some charity tea party, hence his ability to meet Jim. They were college room-mates, but don't see each other much any more. Once a month they try to meet up for a drink. It used to be several times a week, but Mason is busy with work and family, and Jim is busy chasing women.

'Buddy!' Jim's face lights up. He reaches over and they grip each other in the universal man hug.

'You look good!' Mason steps back. 'Have you been working-out?'

'No. You won't believe it, but I think I'm finally in love.'

'What? You? You're quite right. I don't believe it.'

'I know. The eternal bachelor may be about to retire. Cheers!'

'Cheers. So who's the lucky girl?'

'Françoise. She's French. Came here as an au pair years ago, and stayed.'

'Uh-oh. Years ago? She's eighteen, isn't she?'

'I wish.' Jim grins. 'She's thirty-five.'

'No! You're kidding. A grown-up!'

'I know. Who would have thought it?'

'I thought your cut-off was twenty-five.'

'It was, until I met Françoise.'

'So what's the secret?'

Jim sips his beer and shrugs. 'She gets me. And I get her. She's independent, clever, hard working. She wasn't looking for a man and doesn't want to get married. She loves me, but not in a needy way. She's just . . . cool.'

'That sounds great, Jim,' Mason says. 'It's about time the beast was tamed. But not marriage? She doesn't want to get married?'

'That's the thing. She doesn't want to and I do. For the first time in my life, I want to get married.'

'There's no rush,' Mason cautions. 'Are you living together?'

'She's agreed to move in. That's the first step.'

'Marriage is a big commitment. You don't want to make

a mistake. Trust me. Get to know each other really well before you even think about marriage.'

'Speaking of which, how are things with you?'

'Two ships passing in the night,' Mason replies. 'Same as always. Kids are great, though. You should see them.'

'Maybe we should all get together,' Jim says. 'Françoise and me, and you, the kids . . .' His voice trails off. 'And Olivia, of course.'

'That sounds great,' Mason says, knowing that it will never happen, at least not with Olivia there, for she has never approved of Jim, doesn't approve, in fact, of any of his friends. 'But, with London looming, I don't know if we're going to be able to do it.'

'Christ.' Jim hits his head. 'I totally forgot. London. That's huge.'

'I know,' Mason says and sighs. 'But I really don't know if this is a good thing or not.'

Mason gets home just after seven, stepping out of the elevator to find the apartment quiet. He drops his briefcase in the hall and walks into the kitchen, where the children are sitting at the kitchen counter, tucking into a bowl of berries, while a housekeeper cleans up the room.

'Daddy!' Sienna leaps off the stool and throws herself into Mason's arms.

'Hi, baby!' He squeezes her tightly, opening his arms to encircle Gray, who appears seconds later. 'How was the tea party?'

'Boring,' Sienna says. 'Charlotte was mean to me again.'

'I'm sorry, sweetie. Were you sad?'

Sienna nods.

'They had giant cupcakes with M&Ms on them,' Gray says, his eyes lighting up. 'It was awesome!'

'It sounds awesome,' Mason says with a laugh, looking over at the kitchen counter. 'No wonder you're not eating any dinner. Where's Mommy?' Sienna shrugs, then climbs back on her stool.

'Mrs Gregory is in her room.' Elvira, the housekeeper, turns from Windexing the microwave door. 'She is getting ready to go out.'

'Again?' Mason frowns. 'I thought it was just the tea party tonight?'

'Dinner for the Central Park flower thing.' Elvira shrugs.

'Oh God.' Mason has clearly forgotten something important. He grimaces as he walks down the corridor to Olivia's bedroom and knocks on the door.

'Come in.' Her voice is faint; she is clearly in the dressing room.

'Olivia? It's me.' He pushes open the door into what used to be their shared master bedroom until Olivia complained that his snoring kept her awake, and he was relegated to a different room at the other end of the corridor.

'In the dressing room,' she calls. He walks in to find Olivia sitting at her dressing table, with Megumi expertly applying her make-up. On the table, Megumi's curling iron heats up, with an assortment of hair products standing at the ready.

'Hi, honey,' she says smoothly, opening her eyes for just a second to glance at him. 'We're almost done with the make-up. Megumi, as usual, is doing a spectacular job.'

'Olivia, I feel horrible. I totally forgot about tonight. It must have just slipped my mind, but I don't think I can make it,' he says. 'I have a ton of work that has to be done by the morning . . .'

Olivia opens her eyes and raises a hand, Megumi obediently stepping aside so she can talk to Mason.

'It's okay, honey,' she says, for she always uses an endearment when there are other people around. 'I know how you hate these things. Kent is taking me.'

'Oh.' Mason inwardly breathes a sigh of relief. 'So I didn't forget?'

'No. I didn't tell you about it.' She turns to Megumi and beckons her back, raising her face for Megumi to finish brushing the blush on. 'I hope that's okay,' she adds quickly, as an afterthought.

'Of course.' Mason starts to leave. 'Kent has always been much better at these things than I have.'

'He'll be here soon. Would you mind giving him a Scotch when he gets here? Tell him I'll be ready in just a minute.'

'Sure.'

Great, he thinks, walking back towards the kitchen. Kent Beckinsale, formerly gay walker to the stars, and now, it seems, to his wife. Kent with his good looks, effusive charm and funny stories. Kent, whom he doesn't trust for a second.

Kent lives in an apartment left to him by Rose Thorndike in a surprise last-minute change to her will. A surprise because she was so addled by Alzheimer's she didn't know who anyone was, and why she should suddenly change her will, leaving all the important items to Kent rather than her beloved charities, was something of a mystery.

Nor was it the first time wealthy dowagers had left surprising gifts to Kent. A part of Mason thinks there is an element of quid pro quo: he looks after them, which he does beautifully, so then it is only fair they should look after him.

He doesn't like the fact that Kent has become Olivia's companion du jour. Not that he can say anything to Olivia. If he were to say anything, the rebel in Olivia would probably have her seeing him even more.

The phone rings – the doorman announcing Mr Beckinsale is here – and Mason walks quickly into the kitchen and grabs the kids.

'Elvira?' he says. 'I'm taking the kids to give them a bath. When Mr Beckinsale gets in can you pour him a Scotch and sit him in the living room? Tell him Mrs Bedale Gregory will be in shortly, and apologize that I am not there, but explain I am with the children.'

A lucky escape, he thinks, hurrying the kids down the corridor and quickly hustling them into the gleaming marble bathroom.

Whipped Honey Ricotta

2 cups whole-milk ricotta cheese
4 oz. cream cheese, room temperature
4 tablespoons sugar
3 tablespoons honey
¾ teaspoon vanilla extract

Whip all the ingredients together in a food processor or with a hand-held blender until entirely smooth. Delicious served with summer berries.

Chapter Seven

Lila smiles as she hears Callie's familiar voice on her answering machine.

'You witch!' Callie barks, but Lila can hear her smile. 'You never told me my sister came out to see you. I can't believe she sees you more than I do. Where are you, anyway, and why don't I ever hear from you? And don't use that old excuse of being in love because I'm your oldest, bestest friend, and I'm not buying it. And I know you've forgotten my upcoming birthday, and when can the four of us have dinn –' Beeeeeeeeeeeep.

Lila calls back and leaves her own message. 'Phone tag. You're it.' And she puts down the phone and starts to get dinner ready.

It is a little late, Lila realizes, to become a domestic goddess at the ripe old age of forty-two, and yet, as her mother always says, better late than never. She had grown up presuming she would be doing this – cooking for a husband, children – decades ago, but the right man had never come along.

Elderly relatives had accused her of putting her career before a man, but they hadn't realized it hadn't been her choice: she had focused on her career only because she didn't have a man. In her twenties she had been desperate to be married, had viewed every date through the lenses of husband-potential, had, for many years, secret scrapbooks filled with vision-board-style pictures of her dream wedding.

Her dress would be Vera Wang, floaty chiffon with a huge skirt. Her hair would be swept up and back, with a delicate pearl and Swarovski crystal tiara, the flowers would be hand-tied white hydrangeas and peonies.

She would be transformed from a five-foot-one, frizzy-haired, big-bottomed Jewish girl, into Audrey Hepburn. She was never sure exactly how this would happen, but she was certain it would.

And her husband, in turn, would be like Harrison Ford. Only Jewish. Or a Jon Stewart-type, she thought. A neurotic, funny, cute New Yorker with a wicked sense of humour, who looked great in a polo shirt and chino shorts.

The problem was, she discovered, much to her chagrin, that Jewish Harrison Fords and Jon Stewart look-alikes didn't have much of a penchant for short, round, frizzy-haired girls who looked like Lila. She may have been brilliantly clever, with a sharp wit and a heart the size of the Amazon Basin, but the men she was drawn to were only ever interested in her as a friend.

Time after time she developed searing secret crushes on men who became her best friend, and she hoped they would wake up one morning and realize that she, Lila Grossman, their confidante and chief adviser, was in fact the love of their life.

And time and again she would seize up in pain as she attended yet another of their weddings. Always to the same girl. Petite, skinny, with naturally curly hair expertly blown out on a regular basis to a long, sleek sheath of silk; a girl who looked great in Seven jeans, a personalized Goyard bag slung casually over her shoulder.

Lila spent years trying to be that girl. She has been on

every diet known to man, but nothing has reduced the size of her bottom and, frankly, she loves food too damn much to worry about fitting into a size four pair of jeans. Or even a size ten. There is a cupboard in her bathroom spilling over with hair products and appliances that promised to give her silky smooth hair, but nothing has been able to tame her frizz.

She even bought a Goyard bag, except it was from a street vendor in Chinatown and if you look closely you will see it says Coyerd. She didn't think anyone would notice, but when she passed the identikit princesses she saw their eyes flick disdainfully over the bag, and she knew they knew. She sometimes thought she should care more, instead of finding it funny, and she only found it funny because it was easier to laugh than to admit how painful it was that she lost countless men to women she didn't understand.

She almost married once. She was thirty, and dating Steve, whom she didn't particularly like. He was arrogant and charmless, but he was clever, a lawyer, and Jewish.

He treated Lila like his servant from the first time she made him dinner, something she had been trained to do as she was growing up, by watching her mother prepare for her father's home-coming every night.

'Always set the table even if dinner isn't ready,' her mother would tell her, laying out place mats and napkins. 'That way they'll always feel looked after.'

Her mother had her father's drink ready as soon as he walked in the door – a small tray with a vodka martini and a bowl of nuts. No one was allowed to talk to her father until he had 'decompressed' in his study, emerging to sit down at the dining-room table and be served dinner by

Lila's mother, while Lila and her brother and sister were ushered upstairs to 'leave your father in peace'.

Like her mother, Lila is a nurturer. She shows her love for people by cooking for them. Not, as her mother did, with chopped liver, roast chicken dripping with schmaltz, brisket simmered for hours until it was so tender it was falling apart, but with recipes culled from *The Barefoot Contessa*, Martha Stewart, Mario Batali.

Steve was the perfect recipient of her nurturing. He loved her cooking and she, in turn, loved to feed. The fact that they didn't have much conversation mattered less than knowing he was exactly the type of man her father would want her to marry.

Steve encouraged her to cook Friday Night Dinners and invite her entire family. She played hostess instead of her mother, serving up her father's favourite food, feeling a glow of contentment as her father slurped up her chicken soup, sighed dreamily and complimented her on the *kneidlach*: 'As light as a feather.'

'He's a mensch,' he'd say about Steve, who would give her father the honour of saying the prayers over the bread and the wine. 'And he's a lawyer. You could do worse.'

'*Nu*?' her elderly relatives would ask at first-night *Seder* at her parents' house. 'When's the wedding?'

When Steve asked, on bended knee in the New York Botanical Garden, proffering a box containing a large, sparkling, emerald-cut diamond that had belonged to his grandmother, she didn't know what to say other than yes.

She chose to ignore the feeling she had never quite been able to shake off since she started dating him: Is this all there is?

Not that Steve was a bad person; he just wasn't ever

what she had envisaged for herself. She was this marketing guru who loved her career, who had spent her twenties waiting for her knight in shining armour to come and sweep her off her feet.

And instead this sweet, schlubby mensch had shuffled along, and was already treating her as if they had been married thirty years. There was no excitement, no passion, no thrill. Just the routine of stepping into the role of her mother: housewife, cook and at-some-point-in-the-very-near-future-if-Steve-had-anything-to-do-with-it mother.

But it should have been enough. Isn't this what everyone wanted? A decent guy who treated her reasonably well, who had a great job. And he wanted to marry her! Not like all those tall, handsome men she had spent years falling in love with who had broken her heart, over and over again. Here was someone who actually loved her. He wasn't going to break her heart. They would have a life just like her parents; he was already talking about moving out to New Rochelle once they were married. And he definitely wasn't going to cause her any more pain.

She didn't love him.

It took months for her to realize this. She tried being the good girl, doing everything she was supposed to do to make everyone else happy. She waited patiently in line at the Vera Wang bridal gown sample sale, with her mother and future mother-in-law chattering excitedly about the bargains to be had inside, then she ran in, joining the stampede, furiously trying on dresses her mother and Carol threw at her, and wondered why Vera Wang hadn't considered five-foot-one size twelves when putting together her samples.

She went to the Roosevelt Hotel and met with the

banqueting manager, the catering manager, and sat blankly sampling the wedding menus, all the while feeling as if she were having an out-of-body experience.

Just get through this, she told herself. This is pre-wedding jitters. Everyone has them. She'd look at Steve, sprawled on the sofa after dinner, watching television, which had become their nightly routine, and will herself to feel something. And when she didn't, she put it down to stress. Or nerves.

Callie took her out one night to plan the hen-night party. They had a quiet dinner at Atlantic Grill, and Callie, watching carefully as Lila mechanically worked her way through the sushi on the table in front of them, suddenly asked the question Lila had been trying to avoid.

'I know you're getting married in four weeks,' Callie leaned forward and lowered her voice, 'and I know this sounds like a ridiculous question, but do you love him?'

'Of course,' Lila responded, for the words came easily. Steve called her several times a day. To ask what they were having for dinner, to put in a date for dinner with friends of his, to tell her about some movie he thought they ought to see, and at the end of every conversation he said, 'Love you,' to which she replied, equally flatly, 'Love you too.'

'That's not what I mean. I mean, are you absolutely crazily in love with him?'

Lila laughed awkwardly. 'You mean, do I feel about him the way you feel about Reece?'

'Exactly!' Callie's whole face lit up at the mention of Reece's name. She had only recently started dating him, but she was giddy with excitement.

'Callie, not everyone has the same relationship. Steve is

a great guy. He's incredibly good to me, and he has a great job, and he'll make a wonderful husband and father.'

'Jesus, Lila. Who's that speaking? Is that your father? Because it sure as hell isn't you.'

And Lila realized that indeed it was her father. That he was the very reason she was sitting at this table, with the final alterations being done to her wedding gown (they were letting it out, rather than taking it in – Lila had to be the only bride in history who, rather than losing tons of weight before her wedding day, was putting it on since she was eating and eating, to try to push down the feelings she didn't want to admit were there).

'Oh Callie.' Lila's mask started to slip. 'Help me?'

'Of course. Whatever you're doing, you need to stop it now.'

'But how?' Lila's voice dropped to a whisper. 'How do I let so many people down? How do I tell Steve? It will ruin his life. And my father! And all the people who are coming. I don't know if I can do it.'

'Would you rather walk down the aisle knowing you're making the wrong decision? Have to go through a painful divorce?'

'I'm standing under a chuppah,' Lila said, attempting humour.

'Whatever. You know what I mean.'

'What if we make it work?' Lila grimaced. 'Because not everyone has what you have with Reece. If I thought a Reece was waiting for me in the wings it would be easy, but that doesn't exist for me. I've only ever known pain from falling in love, and there's no pain with Steve. I'm making a pragmatic choice, choosing with my head rather than with my heart.'

'Oh Lila.' Callie's eyes welled up. 'You are a beautiful, strong, brilliant woman who deserves to fall in love, and to be loved in return. What makes you think that you have to settle? What makes you think that you have to marry Steve just because he asked?'

'What if no one else does?' Lila's voice was laced with panic as she voiced a fear she had never admitted to anyone.

'So what? So you'll buy a fabulous apartment, sleep with lots of toy boys, and have sixteen cats. So the fuck what?'

And Lila started to laugh. 'You're right. So the fuck what?'

'Thank you. You do not have to be your mother in order to have a fulfilling life, and you do not have to please your father in order to be okay. This isn't the sixties any more, and you absolutely do not have to marry someone just because he asked, or just to make your father happy.'

Lila, crying and laughing at the same time, overcome with relief, happiness and sadness, reached over and clutched Callie's hand. 'Will you help me?'

'I will. And I'll even help you return that God-awful vase from your Great-Aunt Sadie. What were you even thinking, putting that on your wedding list?'

'I didn't.' Lila started blubbering with laughter. 'Steve insisted on putting it on the list. His mother has the same vase.'

'Jesus. Does it look as ugly in her house?'

'Yes! God, I hate her house. Oh God, I can't believe I'm going to admit this, but I can't stand them! Any of them. I can't stand his family. And I can't stand his friends. Oh God, Callie. What the hell have I been doing?'

Callie leaned back in her chair and threw her hands

to the ceiling. 'Praise the Lord!' she shouted, giggling as diners around them turned to stare.

As Lila progressed through her thirties, she often wondered if she'd made the right decision, but she knew she was indeed better off alone than married to a man she didn't love.

(For the record, Steve got married six months later to a girl he had known for ever, the daughter of his parents' best friends. She gave up her job immediately and they moved to Englewood, New Jersey, where she is President of the local Hadassah chapter and mother to their three adorable children. Lila still feels lucky to have escaped.)

Two years ago Lila's company moved to Norwalk, Connecticut, and although she tried the reverse commute for a while, she found herself sitting on the train and fantasizing about a little house, a garden of her own, sitting on a porch and sunning herself with a glass of wine and a cat curled up on her lap.

She was tired of New York, she realized. She had heard it said that once you were tired of New York, you were tired of life, but she knew that wasn't true. She just wanted a different kind of life, a move away from the rat race, from the dating scene that had got so much harder as she got older.

Jdate, or match.com, it didn't much matter, it was always awful. Nobody ever looked like their picture, and actual romances were few and far between. It was time for a fresh start, somewhere she could be happy, just Lila and her cat.

She found a little Victorian cottage in Rowayton, almost on the water, in need of serious renovation, and while it took a good year to feel settled, to find her feet, to find her friends – a hard task when surrounded by married couples and children – she also found a peace that had been missing from her life in the city.

And then, last year, she met Ed. She heard him first, on his mobile phone in the Starbucks at the bottom of Greenwich Avenue, and it irritated her beyond belief, because she was firmly of the opinion that you need to take your phone calls outside so as not to disturb other people.

She tried to ignore it, but he was having an argument with his wife – although as the conversation escalated it became clear she was an ex – and she was accusing him of not returning her son's clothes, and he was attempting to tell her he had bought the child's clothes himself and always made a point of returning hers.

It could have been interesting, if it hadn't become quite so loud.

'Excuse me?' She turned around, frowning, now hugely irritated. 'As interesting as it is to hear about the three Ralph Lauren polo shirts you swear aren't at your house, and the Merrell sandals, I'd much rather read my *New York Times* in peace. Would you mind taking the conversation outside?'

To be honest, Lila was gearing up for a fight. She quite wanted him to be rude back because she needed to let off some steam and found a satisfying fight was sometimes all it took to put her in a really good mood.

The man's face fell. 'I'm so sorry,' he said, looking distraught and immediately standing up and heading outside. 'I'm just . . . mortified. I'm so sorry to disturb you.'

'It's okay.' Now it was her turn to be embarrassed. 'Don't worry about it. Just keep it down.'

She buried herself in her paper, and looked up ten minutes later to find the same man standing in front of her, clearing his throat.

'Again, I apologize,' he said, the apology sounding far more sincere given that it was delivered in a crisp English accent. 'May I buy you a coffee, something to eat, perhaps?'

'Sure.' Lila grinned, folding her paper and putting it down. 'Apology accepted, and I'd love a grande skim latte and a slice of low-fat cherry berry cake. So where'd'you get that accent? Brooklyn?'

And now, at forty-two, Lila knows what it means to fall in love. She understands that it isn't fantasizing about men who are unavailable or unattainable, who will only ever look at her as a friend. It isn't about playing games – not returning his call, pretending to be busy when you are not – in a bid to try to keep him interested, or perhaps get him interested in the first place.

It is about peace. And joy. And happiness. It is about the way her heart starts to smile when she hears Ed's car pull up in the driveway. It is about feeling safe; sure that there are no games, that he will call when he says he will; knowing that when he gazes at her as they sit on the porch, he does not see her as she sees herself: a five-foot-one, dumpy, frizzy-haired Jewish girl with a long nose and double chin. He sees Audrey Hepburn.

And when she looks at him, this six-foot-three, sandy-haired, slightly shy, impeccably mannered, self-deprecating English journalist, she feels her heart quite literally burst open with love.

It may have taken forty-two years, but it was worth the wait.

Fish Balls

1½ lb. haddock fillet, skinned
1½ lb. cod fillet, skinned
1½ medium onions
3 eggs
3 teaspoons salt
pinch white pepper
3 teaspoons sugar (I actually ended up adding much more – am guessing it was around 5–6, but you want it to taste slightly sweet and salty)
1 tablespoon oil
½ to ¾ cup breadcrumbs or matzo meal

Wash the fish and leave it to drain.

Peel and chop the onion into 1-inch chunks. Put into a food processor with the eggs, seasoning, sugar and oil. Process until the mixture is a smooth paste.

Pour into a large bowl, add the breadcrumbs, stir and leave to swell.

Cut the fish into 1-inch chunks and put them into the food processor, half at a time. Process for 5 seconds until the fish is finely chopped.

Add to the onion purée and blend by hand.

The mixture should be firm enough to shape into balls about the size of a large meatball. If it is not firm enough, add a little more of the breadcrumbs; if it is too firm, add a little water.

Add enough oil (about 1 inch deep) to a frying pan and heat. Carefully lower the fish balls into the oil and fry, turning often over a moderate heat until they are an even brown. Remove when cooked and drain on kitchen roll.

They can be served hot or left to cool.

Chapter Eight

Callie exhales a long slow breath and smiles to herself as the masseuse deftly rubs out the tension in her shoulders.

And she thought Reece had forgotten her birthday!

This morning, there was nothing from Reece. He had gone by the time she woke up, and Callie assumed he had forgotten, sighing sadly as she hit the snooze button on the alarm clock.

But then Eliza ran in, closely followed by Jack, carrying a tray on which were some scrambled eggs, some leftover chicken from last night's dinner, two pieces of burned toast, and a cup of coffee which was a rather suspicious shade of grey.

'Is that for me?' Callie asked in delight.

'We made you breakfast in bed,' Jack announced proudly, climbing into bed next to her and snuggling up. 'Happy birthday, Mom.'

They wriggled with excitement as she ate her breakfast – good Lord, did she really have to eat that black toast? – before handing over their 'surprise', which was wrapped loosely in activity paper Callie recognized from the craft cupboard downstairs.

Callie welled up as she opened it to find a photograph of herself and Jack when Jack was a baby, in a large brown-paper frame that had clearly been made by Eliza. There were tiny delicate shells stuck all over it in swirling patterns, and Callie immediately pictured Eliza, shut in her room, head bent low as she concentrated on sticking the shells just right.

'I love this picture!' She threw her arms around both her children in a group hug. 'It's always been my favourite of the two of us, Jack. And this frame is gorgeous! Where did you find something so beautiful?'

'I made it!' Eliza said proudly. 'All by myself! That's why I couldn't let you into my bedroom last week.'

'And I wondered what you were doing in there so long! Oh Liza, it's just beautiful.'

'Do you like the circles?'

'I do!' Callie nodded enthusiastically. 'Those are my favourite parts. And I particularly love this bit here – it kind of reminds me of a wave.'

'That's what I wanted!' Eliza beamed, before jumping off the bed and running downstairs to the TV room to watch *Camp Rock*. Again.

'Love you, Mom!' Jack shouted, running out of the room after Eliza, the temptation of television, as always, being too strong to resist.

Callie allowed herself a minute to feel sorry for herself. Last night she had reminded Reece, just before going to sleep, that it was her birthday the next day and that the very best present he could give her would be to take the day off work today and spend it with her. Even as she said it, she predicted his answer.

He laughed and kissed her, and said he had another surprise up his sleeve, and not to worry.

'No, but seriously,' she said, 'I don't want a present. I know it's a Friday but I want you at home.'

'You know I have to be in early,' he said. 'But I'm going to try to come home by six, okay?'

She still hoped that she might wake up in the morning and find him there.

He had surprised her, though. At two p.m. a huge bouquet of flowers was delivered with a note attached, telling her she would be picked up at three p.m., and a babysitter had already been organized for the kids.

She tried to call Reece to find out if she needed anything, but he was in meetings all day and couldn't speak, so she changed out of the ubiquitous FitFlops and into ballet flats and white pants, with a pretty tunic – the sort of outfit that would easily take her through dinner at a decent restaurant, if that was what he had in mind – and waited for the car.

Something was clearly afoot, because the kids jumped off the school bus just before three, and while Jack disappeared inside to flick on the TV, Eliza could barely contain her excitement.

'You don't need anything, right, Mom?'

'Apparently not.'

'But you don't know where you're going?'

'No, but I have a feeling that you do.' Callie leaned forward conspiratorially. 'Can you tell me? Pinky swear I won't tell anyone.'

'Mom!' Eliza said in disgust. 'I'm too old to pinky swear.'

'Cross my heart and hope to die?'

'No! I'm not allowed to tell you. You're gonna be happy, though.' And she skipped up the stairs to phone her friend.

*

At three p.m. precisely a limo cruised down the driveway, crunching the gravel as it pulled to a gracious halt outside the door of their antique farmhouse.

The door opened and out jumped their babysitter with a huge grin on her face.

'Jenn? Is there any reason why you're turning up to our house in a huge limo?' Callie asked, trying not to laugh. Oh the lengths Reece has gone to.

'Isn't it awesome? It picked me up and I made sure all the kids on the street saw me! Now it's your turn. I'm going to look after the kids and you have a great time. There's champagne in there and everything!'

'I hope you didn't drink any?' Callie teased her. 'You may be in college but you're still underage.'

'No! Of course not!'

With a hug for Jack and Eliza, and a wave for Jenn, Callie climbed in the car.

And it was only when the car finally pulled out of the driveway that Jenn took out her mobile phone and hit redial.

'It's Jenn, the babysitter,' she said. 'She just left. Coast is all clear.'

The limo dropped Callie off at a luxury hotel and spa, one she had been longing to see, and she was led to a light bright suite, where there were more flowers and a box of her favourite chocolates.

Hanging in the wardrobe was a dress she had bought last year but never actually worn, because she'd caught the flu and they hadn't gone to the party. She was still waiting for an occasion to wear the dress, but nobody seemed to have parties any more and it had been hanging, miserably, in her wardrobe ever since.

Her strappy sandals were there, and her make-up bag. Even her hairdryer and brushes. Bless her husband. He had truly thought of everything.

First a facial, and then the most blissful massage she has ever had.

She wraps herself up in her robe and staggers back to the bedroom, fumbling with the key card until the door opens and Reece is standing there, a huge grin on his face.

'Baby!' Callie squeals, flinging her arms around him.

'Happy birthday, baby!' He squeezes her, nuzzling her neck, then draws back to drop a small box in her hands.

Callie grins. 'I love surprises. But it'd better be jewellery.'

'I know, I know,' Reece mutters. 'All girls should get jewellery on their birthdays.'

Like a little girl, Callie rips off the paper and opens the box, gasping when she sees the earrings. Huge delicate gold hoops, speckled with tiny sparkling diamonds.

'You spoke to Lila!' she says, her eyes wide with delight.

'Of course! You think I wouldn't seek expert advice?'

She and Lila had been shopping in the city when they passed a jewellery store.

'Let's just go in and have a look,' Lila said. 'Maybe I can try on engagement rings.'

'Engagement rings? Really?' Callie's face lit up. 'Is there something you need to tell me?'

'Not yet,' Lila said happily. 'But I'm pretty sure this is it.'

Once in the shop, while Lila was happily lining up enormous diamonds on the third finger on her left hand, Callie stopped short when she saw these earrings; she had fallen in love.

'Maybe Reece would get them for you for your birthday?' Lila barely looked up from the enormous pear sparkling away.

'He'd never spend this sort of money,' Callie grumbled, reluctantly handing them back.

'Couldn't you have bought them for yourself?' Lila asked after they had left and Callie was continuing to talk about them. 'I thought you were doing really well with the photography.'

'I am,' Callie said sadly. 'But that's college money for the kids. Not my frivolous jewellery money.'

'There was nothing frivolous about those earrings,' Lila said.

'How would you know? You barely took your eyes off the engagement rings to notice.'

'You're right, you're right. I'm sorry. But I did see them, and now we both have something to aspire to.'

'I love you.' Callie's eyes fill with tears as she puts the earrings on, admires them in the mirror – they are just as beautiful as they were the first time she saw them – and walks over to the bed, where Reece is now lying. She leans over to kiss him.

'I love you,' he says, drawing back to look her in the eyes, to make sure she knows just how much, and he kisses her again, pulling her on top of him and slipping the robe gently, but firmly, off her shoulders.

Callie finishes her make-up with a dash of clear gloss, smacks her lips together, then twists her hair up behind her head, securing it with a large, glittery clip.

'You look beautiful.' Reece comes up behind her and kisses her neck, and she smiles at him in the mirror.

Eleven years, and she loves him as much today as the day she married him. No, not as much. More. Her love for him has deepened and strengthened, and there has never been a moment when she has doubted him, or their relationship, or thought that the grass may be greener somewhere else.

Their relationship is, in many ways, an anomaly. None of her friends fully understand it. With him away so much, there must be problems, they figure. She must be so lonely. Poor Callie, having to do so much on her own.

But the distance is precisely what makes it work. The fact that they are two independent, self-sufficient people who love each other, but do not spend their lives thinking they desperately *need* each other, is what makes their partnership stronger.

Callie is the love of Reece's life, and he of hers. When he is travelling she is thrilled. She gets to organize Girls' Nights Out with her closest friends, or crawl into bed at eight p.m. with Eliza – shh, don't tell anyone – and watch silly movies and eat popcorn and chocolate for dinner.

And when he comes home she is thrilled to see him, marvelling at how handsome she still finds him. She looks at him across a room and feels her heart flutter, filled with a sweet smugness that he is hers.

She loves his smell, his touch, his taste. Often, during the night, when he is fast asleep and she is restless, tossing and turning, she will lean over and kiss his shoulder or his arm. He will not wake up, but even in his sleep he will reach for her and stroke her hand, before falling deeper into sleep.

They have never been the couple to sleep spooned together. Callie can't sleep spooned together. But she likes knowing he's there, watching him when he is sprawled, like a little boy, legs splayed across the blankets.

*

Lila peers out of the window, waiting for Steffi to arrive.

'Christ,' she mutters out loud. 'I love her like she's my own sister, but why is she always so damned late?'

'She'll be here.' Ed calls from the hallway, where he's setting up the bar. 'Do you want me to slice the lemons and limes for the drinks?'

'You're the best,' Lila says and smiles at him. 'My big lovely Waspy man.' She walks over to him and puts her arms around his waist.

'Will you stop calling me Waspy?' He looks down at Lila. 'I'm English. It's different. We don't have Wasps there.'

'But you still are,' she says. 'That's why you're in charge of the alcohol.'

'What?' He pulls back, confused. 'What's that got to do with anything?'

'Wasps drink, Jews eat. Okay, so not Wasps – Christians, whatever. Non-Jews, okay? Jews don't do alcohol. Not well. Have you ever been to a Jewish wedding?'

Ed shakes his head. Lila never fails to make him smile with her stories and her forthrightness.

'I'm telling you, it's all about the food, never about the alcohol. You're lucky if you get a glass of kosher wine. At my cousin's son's bris the table almost collapsed there was so much food, and when someone suggested proposing a toast, my cousin suddenly realized she'd forgotten to order anything to drink.'

'So what did you do?'

'Milk and water. That was all she had.'

'Well at least we'll be okay with the food tonight,' Ed says.

'If Steffi ever gets here. Even if she doesn't I've made enough hors d'oeuvres to feed a small advancing army of hungry teenage boys. I can't help it,' she adds with a shrug. 'It's hard-wired into my genes.'

'You make me laugh,' Ed says affectionately, reaching down and kissing her. 'I think you are the most extraordinary woman I have ever met.'

'But do you *fancy* me?' Lila uses the English expression that she always finds so amusing.

'I fancy you rotten.' He raises an eyebrow and gestures upstairs.

'Ew!' Lila pushes him away. 'You can't seriously be suggesting we run upstairs for a quickie in my best friend's house while we're getting ready for her surprise party and her eight-year-old and six-year-old are downstairs watching TV?'

'That's exactly what I'm suggesting.' He laughs.

'Well the answer is no. But if you behave well you may get lucky later tonight . . .' She reaches up and pulls him down for a kiss, just as they hear the sound of a car.

Lila looks out of the window. 'Yay, she's finally here. But Jesus Christ, what the hell is *that*?'

'This is Fingal,' Steffi pants, pointing to the huge, skinny but shaggy, horse-like animal standing next to her. 'I have him for the weekend.'

'You haven't rescued another creature that will be sent off to one of your mom's poor friends again, have you?' Lila looks suspiciously at her after releasing her from a giant bear hug. 'Because I think your mom may not do it again.'

'No, I haven't. He's really not mine. He belongs to a customer. I'm thinking of maybe dogsitting him while his owner goes to London, so I'm just taking him for this weekend to see if we like each other.'

'What is he?' Lila asks. 'He's enormous.'

'If I'm not mistaken, that's a Scottish deerhound.' Ed walks over and bends down to give Steffi a kiss, then scratches Fingal behind the ears. A delighted Fingal leans into Ed for more attention. 'They're wonderful dogs. Very aristocratic.'

'That's not a dog, that's a pony,' Lila says cautiously.

'He's very mellow.' Steffi leads him in. 'He's actually very easy.'

Lila peers out towards the car. 'Where's Rob?'

'Not here.'

'Uh-oh. Everything okay?'

'Not really.' Steffi walks over to the sofa at one end of the kitchen and points to it. 'Load up,' she says to Fingal, who leaps up and curls into a surprisingly compact ball, then rests his head elegantly on his paws to survey the room.

'That's impressive,' Lila says.

'I know!'

'So . . . Rob.'

'Men,' Steffi mutters, quickly shooting an apologetic glance at Ed. 'Sorry. Not all men, obviously.'

'Men named Rob?' Ed offers.

'Exactly. So I'm mad with him because he brought all his stoner friends back the other night and when the munchies hit they ate all the chilli I'd made for tonight, and then he never even apologized but just said if I wanted to save food for something I should keep it in the fridge at work.'

Lila shakes her head in disgust.

'I told him about the chilli and he said he didn't remember, so I said that was because he was so stoned all the time the weed had fried the few brain cells he had left, because, God knows, guitarists weren't exactly known for their intellectual prowess.'

'You said that?' Lila is horrified.

'Well, yeah. I was mad.'

'Is that true?' Ed muses. 'I always thought it was drummers who weren't known for their intellectual prowess. A lot of the famous guitarists are actually quite brilliant. Look at Queen. And Coldplay. They're all university educated and very bright.'

Steffi is looking at Ed as if he is nuts, while Lila gazes at him adoringly. 'Isn't he wonderful?' she says to Steffi, who nods quickly.

'Well I don't know. I don't know any drummers. Or any other guitarists. It was just one of those stupid things I said because I was mad.'

'And that was how the fight started?'

'Uh-huh. And then . . .' She looks sheepish for a moment. 'Then I brought Fingal home.'

'Let me guess. You hadn't told him.'

'Only because I knew he'd say no!' Steffi says plaintively.

Ed starts to laugh. 'Oh! So that makes it all right then!'

'And, um, whose apartment is it exactly?'

'Ours,' Steffi says petulantly.

'How long have you lived there?' Lila pushes.

'Four months.'

'And how long has Rob lived there?'

'Twelve years,' Steffi mumbles.

'I'm sorry,' Lila cups her hand around her ear, 'I can't hear you.'

'TWELVE YEARS. Okay, okay, I get it. It's his apartment and I didn't ask and I know he hates dogs.'

'He what?' Lila stares at her in disbelief. 'Did you just say he hates dogs?'

'Well . . . yeah.'

'Does he like small ponies, by any chance?'

'Not really. He doesn't like any animals.'

Ed shrugs. 'You know what they say, never tr –'

'Yes! I know! So that's the point. I brought Fingal home knowing it would make him even madder, and now we're on a break.'

'Oh sweetie. Are you okay?'

'Yes, I'm okay. I'm better than okay. Frankly I'm relieved. I'm fed up with not being able to sleep because he's sitting around the apartment with all his friends practising riffs until six in the morning.'

'When does he sleep?' Ed is intrigued.

'Daylight hours. It's like being married to a goddamned vampire.'

'Doesn't sound like a whole lot of fun, I have to say,' Ed concurs.

'It's not.'

'So . . . have you found yourself another apartment yet?'

'No. I'm going to stay with a friend for a few days, but there's another thing.'

'Uh-oh. Why does my heart feel like sinking again?'

'No, it's nothing bad. It's just that the guy who owns Fingal also has this cottage in Sleepy Hollow, and it's empty, and he said I could stay there. I'm kind of thinking that I'm a bit done with the city, so I was wondering about going out there for the winter.'

'Steffi?' Lila says sternly. 'Without wishing to sound like your father, when the hell are you ever going to settle down?'

Chilli

1 green pepper
½ large white onion
2 cups baby carrots
3 garlic cloves
3 tablespoons olive oil
1 teaspoon chilli powder
2 teaspoons ground cumin
1 teaspoon ground coriander
½ teaspoon Jamaican allspice (or any other kind – I just happened
to have that)
½ teaspoon cinnamon
1 teaspoon paprika
½ teaspoon turmeric
1 lb. minced chicken/turkey (for meat eaters)
2 small cans kidney beans
1 small can black beans
1 large can chopped tomatoes
dash of Worcestershire sauce

Chop the pepper, onion, carrots and garlic in a blender, then gently sauté in olive oil until soft and flavourful (about 5 minutes). Add all the spices; stir well.

For vegetarian chilli, omit the meat step and carry on. If adding meat, add it now and keep stirring and turning until the meat changes colour.

Add all the beans, making sure you rinse them well in a colander beforehand. Then add the tomatoes and a dash of Worcestershire sauce.

Bring to a boil then turn down the heat and cover, leaving to simmer for around 30 minutes. The longer you simmer it the better the flavour will be. Also, it's best to make it a couple of days in advance and leave in the fridge for all the flavours to fully absorb.

Serve with sour cream, fresh coriander, guacamole and shredded cheese.

Chapter Nine

'I can't believe you.' Callie, now dressed, fully made-up, feeling beautiful, tries to fight the tears in her eyes. 'It's my birthday, and we're about to go in for dinner. Why do you need your goddamned BlackBerry?'

'I'm sorry, Callie,' Reece looks contrite. 'I just need to send one quick email and then I'm done, I swear. I can't believe I didn't bring my BlackBerry.'

'Can't you send it from your iPhone?'

'No, sweetie. All the back-up emails that reference this campaign are on the BlackBerry, and I need to be able to type properly.'

'Can't you access your email account from the hotel? I'm sure they have a computer you can use.'

'Callie, Loki.' Reece puts his arms around her and pulls her close. 'I can't. I already checked. I know it's your birthday, and I know how you hate me having to work on nights, but I swear this will be quick. We'll just run home and pick up the BlackBerry, and come straight back. If you drive, I can get the email out while you're driving, and then I am all yours for the rest of the night, I swear. It will take twenty-five minutes, tops. Come on, baby. Don't let this ruin your birthday. Please?'

Callie sighs dramatically and turns her head, eventually shrugging her acquiescence as she grabs her evening bag and shawl. 'I'm still not happy, Reece,' she says, using his name instead of the more familiar term of endearment, which she only does when she's angry with him. 'But okay. Let's go.'

*

In the TV room of 1024 Valley Road, Honor Wharton gives her grandchildren a kiss each, and reluctantly pulls herself away to go back to the kitchen to help out.

'Hey, I like your skirt,' Eliza calls nonchalantly as Honor is walking out of the room. Honor walks back in and twirls, the sequins and tiny mirrors sewn all over the bottom of the floor-length skirt catching the light as she turns, and she blows her granddaughter a kiss of thanks as she leaves.

She is constantly amazed by the love she feels for these grandchildren, quite different from the love she has for her daughters, and, more, by the love they have for her. If she could, she would live next door, but Maine has been her home for forty years and she cannot see herself ever leaving.

Three times a year she plans her big trips to Bedford, with day trips to New York to spend time with Steffi; and now, this year, there is a fourth visit to celebrate Callie's birthday.

And despite seeing their grandmother less than a handful of times each year, Eliza and Jack beam with love every time they see her; they hurl themselves into Honor's open arms, cover her with kisses, crawl onto her lap as they did when they were babies. Eliza always asks whether Googie – their name for Honor – can sleep in her room tonight.

Which Googie invariably does. She forgoes the guest room downstairs, with its en-suite bathroom and beautiful canopied bed, for the twin bed in Eliza's room, because there is nothing more magical for her than being woken up at six a.m. by a small nose, inches from her own, a hand on her arm, and a plea for Googie to wake up and play horses with her.

Which Honor does willingly and joyfully, drinking up everything about her granddaughter and marvelling at the bond they have, despite the distance and the scarcity of time together.

'Googie! We were looking for you!' Lila looks up from where she is pulling the Boursin triangles out of the oven. 'Do you know where the name tags are?'

'I do.' Honor opens a drawer beside her. 'I put them in here for safe keeping. Do you have the table plan?'

'I'll get it for you in a moment. Have you met Kim and Mark? Callie and Reece's friends?'

'Of course I've met Mark.' Honor reaches up and kisses him hello with a warm smile. 'But I don't believe I've had the pleasure –' She turns to Kim, ignoring her outstretched hand and giving her a warm hug instead. 'I'm Honor.'

'So nice to meet you!' Kim says. 'I've heard so much about you! Did you say your name was Honor? I thought I just heard Lila call you something else?'

'Googie.' Honor smiles. 'It's what Eliza has always called me and it seems to have caught on. Now I'm Googie to the whole family.'

'So should we call you Honor? Or Googie?'

'Whichever you prefer. I'll answer to pretty much anything these days.'

'I'll let Dad know.' Steffi, busy refilling her wine glass, looks up with a grin. She checks her watch. 'Mom, I'll come with you to do the place mats. I know the table plan. They should be here soon and we have to get everything ready. Lila? Is all the food done?'

'I think so. I'll just plate these and put them in the living room.'

Steffi and Honor walk into the dining room, and Honor admires the table. 'Is this you, darling? Did you set the table?'

Steffi nods.

'You're so creative, darling. I love those flowers, and in paper bags! Adorable!'

Steffi bought armfuls of green hydrangeas and has put them in glasses and jam jars, then covered the jars with white lunch bags, tying them up with raffia and placing them all the way down the centre of the table.

The name tags are brown-paper luggage tags, tied around tiny little terracotta pots stuffed with lavender.

'I thought it was very spring-like.' Steffi shrugs, unable to hide her pleasure. 'And it smells good too.'

'It smells better than good, it's divine.' Honor buries her nose in the lavender, just as a blood-curdling shriek is suddenly heard from the living room.

They look at each other in alarm and turn to race in and find out what has happened.

'FUCK!' Lila yells. 'Oh CHRIST,' then, spying Honor, 'Oh God. I'm sorry. My language. BUT STEFFI! That GODDAMNED DOG has eaten all the pâté.'

'It wasn't Fingal,' Steffi says defensively. 'He's in the TV room with Eliza and Jack, and I told them to keep the door shut.'

'So who's that under the table?' Lila gestures to a large snout poking out from under the table at the other end of the room. 'My imaginary friend?'

'Oh shit,' mutters Steffi, before turning to shout, 'Eliza! Jack!'

'It's not their fault,' Honor says. 'They're children.'

'Yeah?' Eliza wanders into the living room, balancing a hot cheese triangle on her fingers and blowing on it. 'These are really good.'

'Where's Fingal?' Steffi puts her hands on her hips.

'He's . . . Uh-oh. I kept the door closed. I swear. It wasn't me. It was Jack.'

'I don't care who it was,' Lila says. 'But he ate all the pâté. Good thing I came in when I did, or he would have eaten everything.'

Eliza's face falls. 'I'm really sorry.'

'It's okay.' Lila feels the anger seep out of her just as quickly as it arrived. 'Don't worry. It's not like we don't have enough food. It was good pâté, though.'

'Thanks,' Steffi said. 'Mushroom pecan. You can also form it into burgers and grill it.'

'Will you give me the recipe?'

'Sure.'

'And more importantly, will you get the damned dog out of the way?'

'I will. Here, Fingal. Good boy. Come on, let's go back to the TV room.'

'Darling —' Honor stops Steffi as Fingal lopes next to her, both of them heading out of the living room — 'don't you think a dog this size is a little much for you? I'm not sure you should agree to dogsit him again. He is lovely, but he's enormous. I think next time you need to say no.'

Honor looks closely at Steffi's face. She knows this look. Very well.

'Oh no. This isn't just a weekend thing, is it?'

Steffi shrugs and looks away. 'It is just this weekend . . .'

'So what aren't you telling me?'

'I kind of said I'd look after him for a while.'

'Oh Steffi. Why do you do these things? How long is a while? A week? Two?'

'No, a bit longer.'

'How long?' Honor pushes, but she already knows the answer. 'It's permanent, isn't it? This is your new dog. Oh Steffi. Really. Is this wise?'

'No, Mom. He's not my new dog. I'm just looking after him for a year, that's all. I'm taking him back to his owner on Sunday, I think, but then I get him in a couple of weeks. He's really easy, even though he's big – and guess what? In exchange for me looking after Fingal, I get a farmhouse in Sleepy Hollow!'

'Sleepy Hollow? You mean, right by here?'

'Yes. I'm so excited!'

'But . . . it's a bit more of a commute from here to the city for Joni's. And you'll be hitting rush-hour traffic.'

'I know,' Steffi says happily. 'I've thought about all of that. I was going to just use it at weekends, but . . . Honestly? I think it's time for me to leave the city. I need a quieter life, and this is exactly what I've always dreamed of: an old farmhouse and a big hairy dog.'

'But Steffi, what about your job? Your boyfriend?'

'Oh Mom. I love my job, but that's the great thing about doing what I do: I can do it anywhere. And Rob and I are on a break.'

'A year-long break?'

'Okay, so that's my way of dealing with our break-up, but Mom, you have to be happy for me. You know how much I've always loved the country. Look at how much I love being up at home in Maine. Haven't I always said I loved living in the open air? Didn't you always say that I was just like you? That I would be happy living up in Maine too? Well, maybe eventually I will come home to Maine, but right now I have this amazing opportunity to live rent-free in the country – and he has animals too. I just feel, in every bone in my body, that this is the right thing for me to do.'

Honor shakes her head, but she can't help a small smile. 'I know I should tell you no, but you're so like me, sometimes it's terrifying.'

'Really?'

'Yes, but with more courage. You're doing all the things I always wanted to do, but instead I tried to please my parents by marrying your father. You remind me so much of me, and you're right: I shouldn't judge. I think it's wonderful. I just wish Fingal were a bit more manageable.'

'He's great. Don't worry about us. We'll be fine. OH SHIT! What time is it? They'll be here any second. Lila? Hit the lights!'

*

'Loki? Honey?' Reece calls over to the car, where Callie is sitting, still in a bad mood, refusing to talk to Reece for ruining her birthday, furious that even on this night work has to come first.

She presses the switch to move the window down.

'What?'

'Eliza just wants to give you a birthday kiss.'

'Tell her to come out to the car.'

'She doesn't have shoes on. She says can you come in.'

'Oh for God's sake,' Callie mutters, swinging the door open and marching into the house.

'Eli . . . ?'

'SURPRISE!'

The lights flick on and there are the people she loves most in the world, standing in the entrance hall with smiles of delight on their faces and champagne glasses in their hands, and Callie stands there in shock for two seconds, then bursts into tears.

Five minutes later she is beaming, wiping the tears away.

'I'm sorry, baby,' she says as she cuddles up to Reece. 'I was so mean.'

'I know!' He grins, looking down at her. 'And all the time we'd worked so hard to give you this wonderful surprise and you were just in the worst mood ever.'

'Oh my God, don't! I'm so embarrassed! I had no idea. And Mom's here! This is just the best. Did you . . . is . . . any chance you might surprise me with Dad?'

'I tried, Cal. I'm sorry. I think he was really conflicted. He badly wanted to be here, but he just couldn't deal with being around your mom.'

Steffi walks up and overhears. 'Good Lord. It's about time he got over it.'

'That's the problem with men who are divorced and angry,' Callie says. 'They never get over it because they never talk to anyone about it.'

'Are you suggesting Dad has therapy?' Steffi says, and both Callie and Steffi then burst out laughing.

'Can you imagine?' Callie asks. 'Dad having to reveal his childhood? Someone saying, "So, Walter. Tell me how that made you *feel* . . ."'

'Oh God!' Steffi holds her stomach. 'Don't make me laugh, it hurts!'

'You two,' Honor says as she joins them. 'You're still giggling just like you did when you were girls. What are you laughing about now?'

'We were just imagining Dad going into therapy,' Steffi says.

'And how does that make you feel?' Callie says again, in a smooth low voice, and even Honor starts to laugh.

'Do you mean that's something he's considering?' She is stunned.

'Not before hell freezes over,' Reece says. 'They're just being silly.'

'It's a shame.' There is sadness in Honor's eyes as she waits for the girls to stop cracking up. 'I'm sad for him that he can't be here for his own daughter's birthday party. We've been divorced almost thirty years and he still can't be in the same room as me. I'm sorry for him. I just . . . it just seems that he's missing out on such a lot by being so rigid.'

'But that's Dad,' Steffi says. 'He's as stiff as a poker.'

'Really? Still?'

'Well . . .' Callie cuts in. 'You have to admit that Eleanor loosened him up a bit.'

'Was that the last wife?'

'One before last.'

'You both liked her, didn't you? You thought she was great for him.'

'She was. But all the spiritual stuff and meditating got a bit much for him. She was really laid-back though, and every time he'd have a shit fit about something she'd just tease him. I was really surprised when they split up,' Steffi says.

'Surprised? Eleanor was devastated. She didn't see it coming at all.'

114

'So why did they split up?'

'I think Dad just got increasingly irritated with her way of life. In the beginning it was new and exciting, but after a while? Not so much. He said if he never ate another veggie burger again for the rest of his life, it would be too soon.'

'Veggie burger? Your father?' Now Honor starts laughing again. 'You mean, she made him give up rare steak?'

The girls nod.

'Well no *wonder* it didn't last.'

'And she said he had to stop drinking too. One time I was there she found a bottle of Scotch he'd hidden in the office and she poured it down the sink in front of him. I thought he was going to burst a blood vessel.'

'Oh my goodness.' Honor shakes her head. 'She's a braver woman than I am. That Hiromi was a drinker, though, wasn't she?'

The girls catch each other's eye and shudder with horror at the memory of Hiromi.

'Let's just try to forget about Hiromi,' Steffi says.

'You wouldn't mind if Walter were here?' Reece asks.

'Goodness, no. Not at all. I haven't seen him since Eliza was born, but it's all water under the bridge. And look, between the two of us we produced these two beautiful girls. What would be the point of hating him now?'

'Ladies and gentlemen!' Reece taps his glass with a spoon until the clinking brings a quiet to the room.

'I know we're all going to go into dinner in a moment, but I have a few words to say before we go in. First, I want to say thank you to all of you for coming and sharing this special night with us.

'Lila and Steffi, you have created a feast of feasts, and despite our unexpected guest, Fingal, stealing the pâté –' he shoots Eliza a grin – 'a little bird told me about that . . . everything is delicious and, best of all – thank you, ladies – healthy! And Lila, thank you for introducing Ed to our lives – he seems like an excellent fellow and we look forward to celebrating many more happy occasions with him.

'Honor, we couldn't be happier that you have driven all this way to be with us – our celebrations are never the same without your warmth and love.

'Kim and Mark, thank you for sharing this night with us. I love that our daughters are such good friends, but mostly, Mark, I thank you for changing our life.

'And last, but by no means least, the woman we are celebrating today. My beautiful, talented, gorgeous, grumpy wife.' Reece looks down at Callie with love, as she nudges him and rolls her eyes.

'But seriously, these past eleven years have been the happiest of my life. I never dreamed that I would find someone as wonderful as Callie, and I wake up every day feeling blessed that I have a relationship that is still so filled with love, and wonder, and joy, that I truly do feel like the luckiest man in the world.

'And the other reason we are celebrating today is not just that it is Callie's birthday, that she has reached the ripe old age of forty-three yet doesn't look a day over thirty-five, but that we have almost reached four years.'

Reece's voice turns serious, and his eyes take on a watery sheen as he stops and swallows.

'I know we are not supposed to be celebrating until the four-year mark, but I know we're going to make it. Almost five years ago, as you know, Callie was diagnosed with breast cancer. It was a hard battle, and the scariest thing we have ever been through, but with the help of amazing doctors – Mark –' he and Mark exchange a tearful nod – 'and the entire oncology team at Poundford Hospital, we got through it. Callie was declared cancer-free, and next month will mark the four-year all-clear.

'I never thought that cancer could bring good things with it, but I can tell you this: I never thought that our marriage could be better than it was during the first few years, but I have learned that it can always be better. Cancer taught me what love is. It taught me how to appreciate. It taught me never to take a damn day for granted, that every day that we wake up together, strong and healthy and filled with love, is a day to be cherished.

'I want to thank my wife, Callie, for being the best wife, the best mother, the best daughter, the best sister, the best friend and the best patient any of us could ever ask for. She is the love of my life, and I wouldn't be the man I am without Callie standing by my side. Callie? I love you.'

And everyone in the room gratefully pulls a tissue from the pack Honor happened to have in her bag.

Mushroom and Pecan Pâté

2 onions, finely chopped
3 garlic cloves, minced
2 cups dried assorted mushrooms, soaked
1 cup sliced fresh mushrooms (garden variety is fine)
2 tablespoons olive oil
½ cup fresh parsley
1½–2 cups breadcrumbs, or cooked quinoa
3 tablespoons tahini
2 tablespoons hoisin sauce
¾ cup toasted pecans or walnuts, chopped
3 tablespoons tamari soy sauce
1 teaspoon dried oregano
½ teaspoon dried sage
salt and ground pepper, to taste

Sauté the onions, garlic and mushrooms in olive oil over a medium heat for around 6 or 7 minutes. Set aside to cool, then purée in a food processor, with the parsley.

Transfer the onion-mushroom mix to a bowl, and add the rest of the ingredients. Place in the fridge for at least an hour to cool.

Either serve with vegetables and crackers as a pâté; or preheat the oven to 350°F, form mixture into patties with cool, wet hands, brush with olive oil and cook for 20 minutes, or until crisp.

Chapter Ten

'Morning!' Lila sings as Reece stumbles into the kitchen.

'Hey.' Reece has never been particularly good in the mornings, not helped by the amount of alcohol he consumed the night before. 'Where is everyone?'

'Your mom took Eliza out to the diner for breakfast – she said it was a weekend tradition, Ed's in bed reading the papers, Steffi took Fingal out for a walk, and I'm making breakfast.'

'You're the best,' a sleepy Reece says, bending down to give Lila a kiss on the cheek, then reaching up to the medicine cupboard.

'Hangover?' Lila grins.

'Only minor. Callie's got the big one.'

'Shall I make her some coffee?'

'That'd be great. I'll take these up to her and I'm sure she'll be down in a minute.'

'Let me take it up. It's not like I've never seen your wife in pyjamas before.'

Callie and Lila should not, by rights, have been friends. Callie was skinny, pretty, one of the popular girls, and Lila was not.

But the great thing about Manitoba Summer Camp was that who you were at your high school didn't matter; the minute the buses or, if you were geeky, your parents, drove you past the giant totem poles at the entrance, camp became the great equalizer.

Girls who were used to being queen bees at their high schools were suddenly out of their depth in this camp where no hairdryers were allowed, no weekly mani-pedis, no make-up (although they all sneaked eyeliner, lipgloss and blush into their trunks).

And the girls who were ignored the rest of the year had a chance to come into their own – and would beat the princesses at kayaking, field hockey and soccer.

Lila was last to arrive. As usual, her parents had insisted on driving her themselves, her mother alternately turning her head and telling Lila how lucky she was to be going to camp, and how much she'd love it, and perhaps she'd do some sport and lose a little weight, and wiping tears from her eyes and wailing about how much she'd miss her.

Lila sat in the back, catching her dad's eye from time to time in the rear-view mirror, and they would exchange an eye roll and a small smile.

She got to her dorm to find every bed taken, her bunk-mates already touring round the camp, and only one bottom bunk left. Her face collapsed in disappointment. This was her first year at camp – her mother had refused to release her in previous years when all her friends were off to camp, although with hindsight she knew her parents struggled to afford luxuries such as these – and she had romanticized visions of how it would be.

Part of her vision involved seeing herself as queen of the bunk. She would have the prime spot – top bunk, command central, from which point she would amuse, entertain and, in general, feel the love.

Bottom bunk in the corner of the room did not have quite the same feel.

The door burst open as Lila and her parents stood there, Lila reluctant to even put her stuff on her bed, as the others had done. In the doorway stood a tall, skinny girl with a huge smile.

'Hey!' she said, as if Lila were an old friend.

'Hi,' Lila offered cautiously.

'I'm Callie. You're the new girl, right? Lila? Everyone took all the best beds but I was hoping you might swap with me. I love being cosy and in the corner, and I love bottom bunks. Can we swap?'

'Where are you?'

Callie pointed to the best bunk in the room. The top bunk, slap bang in the middle. The bunk, in fact, of Lila's romantic imaginings.

For that entire summer Callie swore that she did love the bottom bunk, but months later, when they were pen pals, she admitted that she felt horrible that Lila, as the new girl, should have the worst bed in the place, and that she hated the bottom bunk, but she didn't regret it because otherwise they would never have become best friends.

It was perhaps an unlikely friendship. The suburban Jewish girl from Long Island and the native New England Yankee who lived a few miles down the road.

'I'm supposed to be a day camper,' Callie had grinned, 'but I begged and begged and begged, and eventually my dad gave in.'

'Even though you live five minutes down the road?'

'Yeah. And I have this baby sister who is adorable, but I just needed a break from the whole babysitting stuff.'

'You babysit?'

'Sure. All the time. But I just kind of needed to be a kid, you know?'

'I know,' lied Lila, who had felt like she was thirty-five years old since the day she was born.

They wrote to each other every winter, were inseparable every summer. When they graduated high school they went to different universities – Callie to Brown, Lila to SUNY Binghamton – and after university they roomed together in New York in a great loft downtown, where, although they had separate bedrooms, nine times out of ten they would end up falling asleep on Callie's great big king-sized bed – a gift from her father.

Everything seemed to revolve around Callie's bed when they were in New York. Friends would come over and everyone would crawl onto the bed, swiftly renamed the Magic Carpet, with bottles of wine, food, magazines.

People would come and go; some would fall asleep and wake up there the next morning. When Lila thinks back to those days in New York, as she is doing now, she can only picture one room: Callie's bedroom.

Marriage and children always change friendships. For a while, after Eliza was born, Lila was terrified she had been replaced with the burst of new friends from Callie's Mommy and Me group.

One weekend she came up to Bedford to stay – Eliza must have been two – and Callie took her to a playground where the rest of the group were meeting.

She introduced Lila as her best friend, but Lila saw that these women knew Callie better than she expected; they were part of her daily life and there was an easy intimacy between them of which Lila, suddenly and shockingly, felt jealous.

They knew more about Callie's life, her present life, than Lila did. They talked about pre-schools, and babysitters, and other mothers – things that Lila couldn't possibly understand. She grudgingly confessed her jealousy later that night, and Callie burst out laughing.

'You will always be my best friend,' she said. 'No matter who else comes and goes.'

The thing with Callie was that everyone wanted to be her best friend, and because she was so easy, and open, and loving, and warm, everyone thought they were. And in some respects it was true – Callie had always had the unique ability to light up every room into which she walked.

After a while, as Eliza grew up and Jack was born, Lila stopped minding all these other people. When she was diagnosed with breast cancer, Callie was always surrounded by these girlfriends and Lila stopped being jealous, because there was just no room for it; she saw how much they loved Callie, what wonderful friends they were.

Meals were dropped off at the house every day, children picked up and taken to school, gifts and flowers left on the doorstep.

Friends organized a schedule of who would pick Callie up, bring her to chemo, who would visit, who would take her home.

More than once Lila would find herself sitting with Callie's friends in the car park, after a session, sharing hugs and a bucketful of tears.

This is why Lila insists on taking the coffee up to Callie as she's lying in bed wishing the damned headache would disappear.

As Lila opens the door quietly and edges in the room, Callie winces with pain.

'I cannot believe you are forty-three years old and

drinking enough to give yourself this kind of a hangover,' Lila says with a laugh, taking one look at her. 'What are you, like sixteen or something?'

'I swear I didn't think I had that much to drink.' Callie slowly eases herself out of bed and Lila slides a mug of fresh coffee in front of her.

'That's probably because you were too drunk to realize it.' Lila grins.

'Was I that drunk? Because I didn't feel it.'

'Nah. You didn't seem to be. I think it's just the problem with getting older. We can't handle our alcohol any more.'

'You must be right.' Callie carefully lifts the mug to her lips, wilfully not moving her head. 'I can't handle it at all any more. One glass of wine at night and I'm waking up with a killer headache.'

'It could be menopause as well,' Lila offers, sitting on the bed.

'What? Are you kidding? I'm forty-three, not fifty.'

'I meant peri-menopause. I've started having signs.'

'You're kidding! What signs?'

'Total night sweats. It's disgusting. I wake up in the middle of the night freezing cold and completely drenched. Most nights I have to change PJs, and then I have to scooch over to Ed's side of the bed where it's nice and dry.' Lila laughs. 'He thinks I've suddenly become super-affectionate, but I am not climbing back into wet sheets.'

'I've had that a few times recently too. What else?'

'Itching like crazy. I had no idea that was even a symptom until I Googled to find out. I keep a hairbrush next to my bed and sometimes my skin itches and crawls so bad I literally scratch with a brush until it bleeds.'

'Ew. That's attractive. I bet that's a total turn-on for Ed.'

'Luckily he loves me, so he loves my bleeding legs too.'

'Nice. But no itching for me. What else?'

'Headaches are a total symptom, as is depression, irritability, mood swings. Oh, and loss of sexual desire, but I'm not there yet. Hey, are you okay?'

Callie, white as a sheet, shakes her head then bolts for the bathroom. There is the unmistakable sound of vomiting, then she re-emerges, as Lila is pouring her a glass of water.

'You really are hungover. Did that help a bit?'

'Yes. It always helps a bit.'

'Really? Your headaches make you throw up a lot?'

'Not always. Sometimes. Go on then, Dr Grossman. What's your diagnosis?'

'I think it might be a migraine. It sounds exactly like one of my migraines. I always used to throw up. I have Imitrex on me; maybe you should try it, because if it is a migraine this should blow it out of the water. Why don't you call Mark and ask him if it would be okay to take it?'

'Just hand it over. I'm not taking any other medication, and my body's been through so much with drugs it can definitely handle it.' And Lila runs downstairs to where her bag is, presses the pill out of the packet she always keeps with her and goes back up to Callie, who swallows it quickly then waves Lila away in a bid to try to sleep the headache away.

An hour later Callie rejoins the group, now all sitting around the kitchen table tucking into scrambled eggs, bagels, smoked salmon and bacon.

'It's the Waspy Jewish breakfast,' Lila explains. 'I can't live without my weekend-morning breakfast of bagels and salmon, and Ed can't live without his scrambled eggs and bacon.'

'Actually,' Ed interrupts, 'that's not strictly true.' He looks at the others. 'I told her that what I truly can't live without on a weekend morning is a fry-up, but she can't stand how it makes the house smell, so this is our compromise.'

'It's true,' Lila says. 'You can't even imagine what he makes for a fry-up. Fried eggs, fried sausages, fatty soft-fried bacon, fried tomatoes and, get this, fried bread! Can you stand it? Talk about a heart attack waiting to happen.'

'You forgot the baked beans.' Ed looks at her affectionately.

'Oh gross.' Steffi, spreading tofu cream cheese on a bagel, makes a face. 'How can you eat that crap first thing in the morning?'

'I'm telling you, it's the best cure for a hangover. Speaking of which, Callie, I heard you had a bit of a rough morning. You look fine now.'

Callie smiles as she pulls out a chair. 'Lila, that pill was amazing. I feel great. I think you might be right about the migraines. As always, you have saved my life. I'm going to have to get some.'

'That's my job,' Lila says. 'Getting you out of trouble.'

Reece narrows his eyes. 'I thought it was Callie's job getting *you* out of trouble, not the other way round.'

'It's Callie's job getting everyone out of trouble.' Steffi laughs. 'Isn't that right, Mom?'

Honor smiles. 'I have to say, out of the two of you, Callie has always been the sensible one. And yes, I do seem to remember a time when you, Lila, held a party when your parents were away and Callie was the one who spent the night cleaning so you wouldn't get into trouble.'

'Oh my God!' Lila's eyes are wide. 'How do you even remember that?'

'Wow, Mom!' Callie laughs. 'That's impressive. I bet you never knew that Lila and I once borrowed your fur coat when you were in Palm Beach. And it was her idea.'

'You big fat liar,' Lila splutters. 'It was your idea.'

'Was *not*.'

'Was *too*.'

'Children, children!' Laughing, Reece puts up his hands to stop them. 'Enough fighting or you'll have to leave the table.'

'Anyway, I did know,' Honor says and winks. 'I found some ghastly, cheap, roll-on chocolate-flavoured lipgloss in the pocket. I just decided there was no harm done so no point in saying anything.'

'God. Fur,' Lila says. 'Isn't it weird how everyone's mom back in those days wore fur?'

'Don't even talk about it,' spits Steffi. 'Mom would still have hers if I hadn't forced her to get rid of it.'

'I loved that mink coat.' Honor sighs. 'But I take your point. It is unfathomably cruel. What *is* that buzzing noise? I keep hearing this infernal buzzing that's driving me nuts.'

'Oh God, sorry,' Ed, red-faced, apologizes as he draws his BlackBerry out of his pocket and hits a button. 'I keep it on vibrate and I'm so used to it that it doesn't bother me.'

'What's the buzzing? The usual?' Lila, suddenly stern-faced, looks at him.

Callie peers at both of them. 'The usual? What's the usual?'

'It's my ex.' Ed shrugs unhappily. 'She's trying to get hold of me.'

'Shouldn't you answer?' Callie is confused. 'It might be important.'

'Trust me,' Lila says with a sniff. 'It's never important. It drives her insane when Ed doesn't pick up the phone, so she just keeps ringing, every two or three minutes. Honey, why don't you just put the phone on silent?'

Ed nods, and presses more buttons.

'Oh go on,' Lila bursts out. 'I know it's mean, but humour us. How many times has she phoned you this morning?'

Ed looks at his screen and scrolls down. 'Twenty-seven.'

'What?' Callie bursts out. Even Reece looks shocked, and they start to laugh.

'Oh that's nothing,' Lila says lightly. 'The other day it was forty-something.'

'But . . .' Honor is concerned. 'How do you know it's not an emergency? It sounds like it could be something very serious.'

'It's not.' Ed sighs resignedly. 'She's texting me too, and leaving messages. She's shrieking about me picking up Clay to buy him new baseball cleats this afternoon. She wants me to keep him for the night.'

'Again?' Lila asks. 'But this is her weekend.'

Ed now looks perturbed. 'Lila, you know how I feel. It's my son. If he wants to be with me I'm not going to say no to him. Let me call them. Sorry, chaps. I'll be back in a minute.'

They all sit and quietly watch as Ed takes the phone out to the back yard, then Callie turns to Lila.

'I guess that's his fatal flaw?'

'What?'

'Having a crazy ex.'

Lila sighs and buries her head in her hands. 'I know. I can't stand it. Finally I meet the man I've waited to meet my whole life, and not only is he not Jewish, he has a crazy ex-wife.'

'Has she always been crazy?' Reece asks.

'I think so, but it's been markedly worse since I came on the scene. I guess she knows it's serious and she's not handling it well. Ed has basically been her lapdog since they split up, because he's terrified of her rages.'

'She rages?' Steffi looks up.

'Totally. She can be perfectly fine one minute and then all of a sudden she's like a screaming, crazy nut job and, seriously, she will literally just scream. It's like watching a five-year-old have a tantrum.'

'Sounds terrifying.'

'It is pretty shocking.'

'So you're the Wicked Witch of the West?' Callie asks.

'And how. I'm like the controlling, demonic, selfish bitch from hell as far as she's concerned – which, frankly, is all total transference as far as I'm concerned.'

Callie looks round the table with a grin. 'Let me tell you, if Dr Grossman says it's transference, transference it is.'

'But don't you have a great relationship with her son?' Steffi asks. 'Surely she'd be grateful to you for being so nice to her kid, no?'

'That's what a sensible person would think. I don't know. There I was thinking he was perfect and had no baggage, and I discover this.'

'There's no such thing as no baggage in your forties,' Reece says.

'Yes, there is,' Lila says. 'Me. I have no baggage. Well, not much.'

'That's what I love about you,' Callie says. 'You're practically perfect in every way.'

'Have you met the ex-wife?' Honor asks. 'Perhaps you could sit down, woman to woman, and chat about what's best for all of you? Maybe you could help her see reason?'

'She hates me,' Lila says. 'She's always making little digs about me, and some of them are so mean. A couple of weeks ago she told Ed that I was really too overweight to wear the skirt I was wearing, and a client had some leftover Nutrisystem meals which she thought I might like.'

'Oh I get it.' Reece nods with a smile. 'Passive-aggressive.'

'Completely. Then . . .' she pauses for dramatic effect, 'she emailed me a coupon for some new treatment for eye bags.'

'Seriously?' Callie gasps.

'I know! Can you believe that? They're not that bad, are they?' She turns to Callie, head down, and Callie laughs.

'What eye bags?'

'Exactly. Nasty, right?'

'Breathtaking.' Callie shakes her head. 'I wish you'd told me.'

'I find it somehow makes it worse when I talk about it. I'm trying to just take the high road, and always be kind and gracious, no matter what, and I guess it could be so much worse.'

'But what about Ed?' Callie asks. 'Can't he say something? Stand up to her?'

Lila says, 'It's precisely what I love about him that makes it so difficult. He's the most gentle man I have ever known, and kind beyond belief. He's trying so hard to keep everyone happy, he just feels caught in the middle.'

'Wow,' Steffi says. 'I was just thinking exactly that. He needs to –'

'Shh,' Lila interrupts. 'He's coming back.' She turns brightly to Ed and her voice changes. 'Hi, sweetie. Everything okay?'

'Fine.' He sits back down and picks up a piece of bacon. 'We have to collect Clay at four.'

'She can't drop him off?'

'There's a problem with her car.'

Lila looks at Callie and suppresses a sigh, while Callie shrugs.

'I knew he was too good to be true.'

*

Walking through the streets of New York, hand resting on Fingal's large head, Steffi is enjoying the attention she's getting.

'Whoa? Is that a horse?' and similar comments are happening every few feet, it seems, and Steffi is more than happy to stop and chat with the people who are genuinely interested in Fingal.

'You really are a conversation starter,' she murmurs to him as they stand on a street corner, waiting for the lights to change. She bends down to rub his side then he leans into her and looks up into her eyes, and she smiles.

'I think I might be falling in love with you,' she says, and Fingal, in return, gives her hand a big lick.

The doorman sends her up to Mason's apartment, and

this time there is no one there to greet her. The elevator opens directly into the apartment, into a large round hall-way that has a walnut table with a huge arrangement of peonies, and vast canvases on every wall.

'Hello?' she says tentatively, dropping the leash as Fingal lopes off around a corner. Steffi has never been into an apartment like this one and only a select few, the crème de la crème, can afford to live here. Steffi is curious, *fascinated*, as to how these people live, for it is a world that is so different to hers.

Steffi comes from old money, money so old, she likes to joke, it has now disappeared. She comes from a world where it was considered déclassé to display your wealth, where rules dictated that you live quietly, and graciously.

It was a world that died when her grandparents died. Even towards the end of their life the money had mostly gone. They no longer lived on the family estate, but in a tiny house on the other side of the village.

Walter's inheritance was negligible – corruption on the part of the financial advisers and lawyers, combined with a lack of willingness on his father's part to admit he didn't understand finances or to let other people take control. Callie and Steffi were brought up with the name, but without money.

Nothing like this.

Her Vans make no sound on the marble floor, and she peers through vast arches into glossy mushroom-coloured rooms, the walls and ceilings lacquered to a high-gloss fin-ish, reflecting antique lamps, acres of windows, sculptures and artwork everywhere she looks.

And, in a corner, she suddenly spies a dog bed, with a small curled-up dachshund, fast asleep.

Fingal has disappeared, and she is still waiting, uncomfortably now, for someone to appear, so she walks over and crouches down by the dog.

'I had no idea Fingal has a brother,' she says softly, reaching out a hand to pet the dog. Wow, she thinks. This must be a really old dog, because the fur is slightly matted and coarse to the touch.

'Are you sleeping, baby?' she croons, scratching the ears, waiting for the dog to open its eyes and look at her, and then she freezes.

'Fuck,' she whispers, swiftly standing up just as Mason appears in the doorway.

'It's stuffed,' he says with a grin. 'Actually I'm not supposed to say that. I'm supposed to say it's an Installation.'

'You mean, it's art?' Steffi is praying that her cheeks stop burning very shortly.

'Yup. If I told you how much it cost you might have a heart attack and die on the spot. But please don't do that, because it would be very inconvenient.'

'Okay, can I just say that I am so mortified right now I would be very happy if your marble floor would, in fact, open up and let me fall through.'

'Don't worry about it. Everyone does it. Unless of course they read the art papers and know the artist and that Olivia paid a record price for it, and so on and so on. Then they're all impressed and ooh and aah over it.'

'So how much was it?'

'Too much.'

'Do you actually . . . this might be a rude question . . . but . . .' Steffi frowns.

'Do I like it? A manky stuffed dachshund that looks as if

it's about a hundred and fifty years old?' He snorts with laughter. 'What do you think?'

'Okay. Good. For a while I was questioning your taste. Don't you and Olivia talk about stuff like this?'

'Not art. I'm not the slightest bit interested. I let her do what she wants when it comes to art, and she keeps saying it's a great investment.'

'Really? Even though the world is collapsing all around us?'

'Give it ten years and hopefully we'll see some return.' He shrugs. 'Who knows?'

Steffi looks around her happily. 'Wow. This is some place. This is, like, seriously impressive.'

'I know. Who would have thought it, looking at me in my creased suits?'

'Actually, you look better in jeans.' Steffi looks him up and down appraisingly. 'Much better, in fact. You should go to work like this. You look like you're way more comfortable.'

'Thanks.' There is delight in Mason's face. 'Not often I get compliments these days. It was a compliment, right?'

'Definitely.'

'Come on into the kitchen. Do you want some lemonade? And . . . you won't believe this . . . but we made the Neiman Marcus chocolate chip cookies.'

'You did? You're kidding! Who's we? You and Olivia?'

'Olivia cook? Don't be ridiculous! No, me and the kids, and I have to thank you because they are the greatest cookies I've ever had.'

'You don't have to thank me. I had nothing to do with it. Where did you get the recipe?'

'Online. But I wouldn't have known about them if it

weren't for you. I think you may have changed my life.' He grins, placing the cookies on the counter. 'Try one.'

'Oh. My. God.' Steffi sighs, crumbs spraying out of her mouth. 'These are good.'

'Told you. Oh shit!' The smile leaves his face. 'Oh Steffi. They're not vegan. I'm so sorry.'

'Don't be.' She adds, 'I break the rule for chocolate. And I have been known to fall off the wagon for my mom's roast chicken.'

Steffi perches on a stool. Fingal is already curled up in a custom-built dog bed tucked underneath the kitchen counter.

'So how did you and Fingal get on? Did you fall in love?'

She nods. 'I really did. He's amazing. He was a bit naughty at my sister's house – my niece let him out of the TV room and he proceeded to eat the mushroom pâté, but other than that he's just so easy. And I love the way he leans into you.'

'He only does that if he likes you.'

'Aw, you're just saying that to persuade me to have him for a year.'

'Is it working?'

'It already worked. I'm persuaded. I love him. So when can you let me see Sleepy Hollow?'

The sound of the elevator is followed by a clatter of high heels and a small blonde woman appears, sweeping in then stopping abruptly when she notices Steffi.

'Oh . . .' She looks at Steffi, with raised eyebrow. 'Hello?' She is no longer the friendly woman who showed up at Joni's; she is now imperious, and wondering who this blonde girl is, sitting at her kitchen counter.

'Hi!' Steffi jumps up with outstretched hand and a big smile. 'We met at Joni's? The vegetarian restaurant? I'm the chef?' She can't help it; every word she utters becomes a question, aiming to please Olivia.

'Steffi is the girl who's going to look after Fingal,' explains Mason. 'Remember? I told you she was taking him for the weekend to see how they got on.'

'I love him!' Steffi babbles. 'What an adorable dog he is. I can't wait to look after him!'

'Oh!' Olivia smiles coolly. It doesn't reach her eyes. 'I had no idea who you were! Of course! The chef!' And quick as a flash she excuses herself and disappears.

And even though she was smiling, and even though she was friendly, something about her words − 'The chef!' − makes Steffi know, instantly, she has been dismissed.

Neiman Marcus Chocolate Chip Cookies

5 cups blended oatmeal

2 cups butter

2 cups sugar

2 cups brown sugar

4 eggs

2 teaspoons vanilla essence

4 cups flour

1 teaspoon salt

2 teaspoons baking powder

2 teaspoons bicarbonate of soda

1½ lb. chocolate chips

8 oz. good-quality dark chocolate (grated)

3 cups chopped nuts (your choice)

Preheat the oven to 375°F.

Grind the oatmeal in a food processor until it is a fine powder.

Cream the butter and both sugars. Add the eggs and vanilla essence. Stir the flour, oatmeal, salt, baking powder and bicarbonate of soda into the mixture. Add the chocolate chips, grated chocolate and nuts.

Roll into balls and place two inches apart on a cookie sheet, or drop by teaspoonful onto the cookie sheet.

Bake for 8 to 10 minutes – or 10 to 12 minutes for a crispier cookie.

Chapter Eleven

Lila's last high school reunion was five years ago, but she didn't really need to have been there to be able to tell you what had happened to the vast majority of her class.

Even before going, Lila knew that the girls would all be pencil thin, with long, dark, straightened hair hanging from a centre parting in a glossy sweep. They would be wearing tight boot-cut jeans and high-heeled boots. They would have diamond studs in their ears, of varying sizes depending on how well their husbands had done, and would be carrying the latest designer handbag. Their husbands would stand in a corner of the room and talk about sports and trading and where they had gone on their most recent holidays. No one would come out and say it, but there would be an undercurrent of who was worth the most.

Even before going, Lila knew that Alissa Goldbaum, now Alissa Goldbaum Stern, would still be queen bee. She would live in the biggest house on the best street in Great Neck, would drive a very large and impressive car, and would be swathed in the latest, trendy, designer gear.

Even before going, Lila knew that the women would all look a thousand times better than the men. Even the girls who had big thighs, or bad teeth, or large noses when they were all in high school together would have *Pilated* their thighs down to nothing, spent hours in the dentist's chair having Lumineers expertly stuck to their teeth, fixed their noses . . . and added cheekbones, smoothed frown lines and removed double chins, thanks to liposuction, Botox, Restylane.

The men would be much the same, only chubbier, their success apparent in their jackets that didn't quite fit. Their teeth would be as before, their hair thinning, their chins slack. But none of them would see that when they looked in the mirror. They had made fortunes. When they looked in the mirror, all they would see was that they were kings of the world.

Even before going, Lila knew that she would still not be one of them. She would still be regarded as someone who was an oddity, who didn't fit in.

Years ago, in eighth grade perhaps, or ninth, Alissa had turned to her at someone's party. 'You could be really pretty,' she said, 'if you just lost a bit of weight and had your hair straightened.'

Lila hadn't been particularly offended. Even at that age she was secure enough in herself to find it funny, and she knew Alissa had thought she was being kind, was offering advice that she thought would help Lila be a better person.

Lila isn't thin, doesn't have straight hair, and didn't spend her twenties living on the Upper East Side and prowling the singles scene before finding a husband, having a baby then moving back to Long Island or Westchester County, within a five-mile radius of the house in which she grew up, getting involved with the local Hadassah, becoming a mover and shaker on the board of the new Conservative Synagogue.

And more to the point, Lila hasn't been married. She hasn't married a nice Jewish boy and gone on to have two point four children. She doesn't live in a big colonial and put said children in the pre-school of new Conservative Synagogue.

Lila has never wanted children in the way her peers did. She hasn't wanted the life she was destined to have, the life that all her school friends have. She has never thought of herself as particularly maternal, and in fact always jokes that she is slightly allergic to small children.

She doesn't mind older children, very much enjoys their company, actually, but she finds today's children increasingly hard to stomach. What has happened to rules, she wonders. To boundaries? When did it become acceptable for small children to butt in on an adults' conversation whenever they have something to say, without so much as an 'excuse me'? And worse, when did the parents stop speaking in mid-conversation and turn with beatific smiles to respond to their children's question, leaving their conversation partner stopped and shocked in mid-stream?

When, she wonders, did parents stop teaching their children to say 'please' and 'thank you'? Sitting in cafés these days, she most often hears children say, 'I want', with not a hint of a 'thank you' when the food arrives.

They climb on the seats in the booths, their muddy shoes all over the banquettes, and grin playfully at the people sitting in the booth behind them, while the mothers ignore them, presumably thinking that everyone in the restaurant will find their children's behaviour as adorably cute as they do.

They get down and run around, swerving round waitresses carrying hot food aloft, shrieking and bumping into people, while the mothers don't see, or choose not to look.

Lila walks into shops and small children come tearing

out under her arms as she pushes the door open – not a hope of any of them standing aside to let the adult through.

Oh GOD, she sometimes thinks. I am turning into my grandmother. I am becoming a curmudgeon, and surely forty-two is too young to be turning into this. But she doesn't understand what is happening to today's parents.

And of course she cannot understand, for she is not a parent herself. She cannot possibly know what it is like to be exhausted, overwhelmed, to know that your children are behaving appallingly but you have already had words with them a million times today and frankly you just do not have the energy any more.

Lila cannot know that you spent years trying to get your children to say please and thank you, but you are only human and you cannot do it all the time, and sometimes you are just too damned tired.

Sometimes it is easier to just tune out, because no one can be one hundred per cent vigilant all of the time.

But Lila doesn't know this. She only knows that once upon a time she presumed she would find a nice husband, probably sometime in her late twenties or thirties, and they would have a couple of children, and she would live in a small colonial somewhere. She thought this not because it was something she wanted, but because it was what her parents expected of her. What her world expected of her.

And now, at forty-two, her life is not at all what she expected. She is no longer employed by a large company, but struggling to find work as a marketing 'consultant', grateful only that her prior company paid her such a large severance.

She is not married, and doesn't want children. She is

very happy in her cottage with her big Waspy English boy-friend, and every other weekend with his lovely nine-year-old son, Clay, who is surprisingly well-behaved and chatty.

So when Ed asks the following question, she is nothing if not a little surprised. They are flopped on the sofa on Sunday night, watching a pay-per-view movie while wait-ing for *Entourage* to start. Lila is alternately flicking through the pages of *Martha Stewart Living* and watching the movie, which has a little too much action, blood and guts to really capture her attention, and Ed is stroking her legs, which are flung over his lap.

'I've been thinking . . .' Ed says, gazing at Lila.

'Yes?' she says, looking up at him, wondering what he's going to say.

'How do you feel about children?'

'I think they're perfectly fine as long as they belong to other people. Although I adore Clay. He's not really a child, though. He's a twenty-year-old trapped in a nine-year-old's body. Why?' She peers at him. 'Is that what you're asking or are you asking something far more specific?'

Ed laughs. 'A little more specific. I was just wondering whether you had thought of having your own.'

'Thought about it, yes. A long time ago. A very long time ago. I thought about it and concluded the answer was no.' Lila squints at Ed, thinking. 'Is this some convoluted way of trying to tell me you want me to bear your chil-dren?'

And Ed, much to her surprise, blushes.

'Oh God!' she blusters, kicking her legs off his lap and sitting up. 'I was kidding. Oh Ed. What is this? What are you asking?' Her voice is now gentle as she takes his hand and looks him in the eye.

'I don't even know,' he says. 'It's just … I suppose I always thought I would have a big family. I grew up as an only child, and I hated it. I determined that when I grew up I would have three or four children, and probably raise them on a wonderful old farm in the country, and have this idyllic family that was filled with love and laughter.'

'Because your own childhood wasn't?' Lila asks softly.

'It was, to a point,' Ed says. 'But it was very … ordered. Orderly. My parents treated me as something precious. They took me to concerts, and art galleries, and the theatre. I learned how to discuss the merits of Picasso, the merits of the Bach symphonies, but all I really wanted was to live with the Campbells.'

'The Campbells?'

'They lived at the end of our road. Four children, three boys and a girl, and their house backed onto a big playing field. All the neighbourhood kids would be at their house all the time, or in the fields behind, but Mrs Campbell always made a huge cake for tea, and enough food to serve an army, and I just remember how much I wanted the chaos. Everyone was always welcome there, and because there were so many kids I think she just got used to other children joining the group.'

'I bet they never went to art galleries and museums, though.' Lila smiles.

'I don't think they did, but their house was always fun. Lots of noise, delicious smells, animals everywhere.'

'Animals?'

'They had two red setters, a couple of cats, and there were usually small rodent-like creatures around the rest of the house. Anna had a rabbit called Timmy who thought he was a cat, and the boys had hamsters and guinea pigs. Oh, apart from Roger, who had an iguana.'

Ed smiles at the memory before continuing.

'But it felt like the family I should have had. I used to walk past every day praying that someone would see me, or that the kids would be outside, because I was always too self-conscious to just knock on the door. And that's what I always thought I would have. A house filled with children, and animals. I thought I'd have it with Mindy, until . . . well . . . until I realized she was a complete nutcase. And then I just spent years miserably trying to leave.'

'I still don't understand. Why didn't you leave sooner?'

'I tried so many times. But every time there'd be another crisis, another drama. She'd be desperately sick, or something would happen with her family, or she'd just make me feel guilty. And it worked. How could I leave my wife and small child? It was unthinkable.'

'Of course it was. Because you're a knight in shining armour and you thought your job was to rescue everyone.'

'God, you're so American.' He grins.

'It's true though.'

Ed shrugs. 'Maybe. The point is, I thought I'd have tons of children. And now I have Clay, who I love more than anything in the whole world, and I was honestly resigned to having just one perfect child. There was no way I was having another child with Mindy, and I had accepted that this was clearly my fate; it just hadn't turned out the way I had always thought.'

'And . . . now?'

'Well . . . that's the thing. Whenever I thought about having another child when I was married to Mindy, the thought filled me with abject horror. But now, with you, I realize that for the first time in years I can see me having another child. I can see us having a child.'

Lila looks away for a second, unable to bear the softness in Ed's eyes, and when she looks back her own eyes have filled up.

'Oh Ed. I wish I had met you years ago. I wish I had met you when I was thirty-two, not forty-two. I'm not going to pretend I haven't thought about it, thought about how miraculous it would be to have a baby with the man I love, to create a person out of this extraordinary love we have for each other, but . . . I'm forty-two, Ed. First, I think it's unlikely that I would even get pregnant. And secondly, I don't want children, Ed. Not now.'

Ed cannot hide the sadness in his eyes as Lila talks.

'I love my life. I love you. I love living here. I'm too old, and too selfish, and too set in my ways to have children. And I see how hard it is. At thirty-two I might have been under some illusion that raising children was easy, that they would be these gloriously adorable appendages who I could dress in cute clothes from Gap, who would accessorize me perfectly. But I haven't got the energy. Nor the inclination. Which doesn't mean I love you any the less. It just means I think my time has passed.'

Ed nods, considering all that she has said. 'I'm not trying to change your mind,' he says finally, 'but can we at least continue the conversation about it?'

'Yes, my darling.' She smiles, drawing him close for a kiss. 'This is why I love you. Because you leave no bridge burned, no stone unturned. Yes, we can continue the conversation about it, but I must warn you I will not be changing my mind.'

'As long as you're willing to keep talking about it, that's all I ask.'

'Have I ever told you how much I love you?' Lila places a hand on each of his cheeks and looks him in the eye, her nose inches from his.

'Not half as much,' he says very seriously, 'as I love you.'

*

'Are you *sure* you're not having an affair with him? Oh shit, hang on.' Callie drops the phone into her lap as she drives past the policeman, shooting him a big smile. 'Hang on,' she shouts, 'police alert.' She picks up the phone again after she rounds the corner. 'Sorry, I'm in the car.'

'I figured. Where's your Bluetooth thing?'

'I lost it again.'

'Another one?' Steffi laughs. 'Callie, you're as bad as me. How many have you lost in the past year?'

'Only four. Don't try to change the subject. So this guy, Mason. Rich wife. Sounds like a bitch. Interested in you.'

'No. Not clearly interested in me at all. Why do you always have to be so suspicious?'

'Because it's just weird. I understand him wanting you to dogsit, particularly because he can clearly see your bleeding heart, but then offering you his house in Sleepy Hollow? For free? He must get a fortune renting that. I just don't understand why he would give you his house unless you were secretly having sex with him and not telling me because I'm your older wiser sister and I would disapprove massively.'

Steffi splutters indignantly. 'First of all, I would not have an affair with a married man. Ever. And secondly, have I ever kept secrets from you?'

'Yes.'

'I have not! When?'

'When you last had an affair with a married man.'

'What? What are you talking about?'

'That artist you had a thing with. Paul something. Remember? You definitely weren't honest with me, and you never told me he was married until afterwards. So, wrong on both counts. You have had an affair with a married man, and you kept it a secret from me.'

'Jesus, Callie. It doesn't count if you didn't know. I had no idea he was married until we'd been dating for six weeks.'

'How do you not know someone's married?'

'Because he kept his wife out in Woodstock and told her he was in New York painting at his studio all week, and he told me he was painting in his studio in Woodstock on the weekends and he had no phone because he couldn't be disturbed, it would ruin his creativity.'

'And you really believed that?'

'Yes! It sounded totally credible at the time. I swear, if I'd had the slightest idea that he was married I would have had nothing to do with him. And that was the only time, and it doesn't count because I really didn't know.'

'So what about Mason, then? Do you find him attractive? Come on, be honest. Because I think there's something you're not telling me.'

'I really don't. No, that's not true. I think he's a great guy, and there's something about him that is attractive, but I swear to you, Cal, on my life, I am not physically attracted to him, and I am not, nor ever will be, having an affair with him. Honestly, we just like each other. As friends. His wife seems to be a bit of a bitch, and I think he comes into the restaurant because he feels comfortable with me. He can talk to me.'

'So how come he's giving you the house?'

'He's not giving it to me. It's . . . payment, I guess, in return for looking after Fingal. And Callie, these people do not need the money. Whatever they get for renting the house, they can live without. This apartment was like nothing I've ever seen. She's a Bedale, and worth gazillions. Money isn't an issue.'

'So when are you going to see the house?'

'I think this weekend.'

'Tell me you're not driving down together, because then I'd get suspicious again.'

'We're not driving down together, okay? Actually, we're really not. He said he's going down this week to make sure it's all cleaned up, and I'm going to hop on the bus on Saturday.'

'So, if you like it, when do you move in?'

'I'm sleeping in Susie's spare room right now, so I'm kind of hoping I can just stay from Saturday.'

'Did you tell Mason that?'

'Nah, but I think he'll be cool with it. I've got hardly any stuff so I'll take a big bag, and I can always come back up and get the rest of my things once I've settled in.'

Callie laughs. 'I can't believe you're doing this. Again.'

'What? Changing my life?'

'Yes. In a way I'm kind of jealous. You're such an adventurer.'

'You're kidding, right? You? Jealous of me? Callie Perry! You have an enviable life! Not only are you beautiful and brilliant, your husband is creative, talented and gorgeous, you have the perfect kids, you live in an amazing house, and you are loved by everyone who knows you. You have an incredible career as a photographer, and I would swap lives with you in a heartbeat.'

'Are you trying to tell me you would sleep with my husband?' Callie asks suspiciously.

'Wha –? Yes! Yes, I would! Okay? Happy now?'

'No . . . Oh Christ!' Callie yelps, looking at the clock on the dashboard. 'Speaking of photography, I'm supposed to be shooting someone now.'

'Now?'

'Fifteen minutes ago. Oh my God, I can't believe I forgot. I love you, Steff,' she shouts as she clicks off the phone.

'Love you too,' Steffi says, to nobody at all.

Warm Chocolate and Banana Cake

1 cup plain chocolate
1 cup unsalted butter, softened
1 cup sugar
3 eggs, beaten
1 cup plus 2 tablespoons flour
1 teaspoon baking powder
2 tablespoons cocoa powder
3 ripe bananas

Preheat the oven to 350°F. Grease and line a 9-inch cake tin.

Melt the chocolate over a bain-marie (or my lazy way of VERY, VERY slowly melting it in a microwave).

Cream together the butter and sugar until pale. Add the eggs gradually, while beating. Stir the dry ingredients together and fold into the wet mixture. Add the mashed bananas and melted chocolate. Mix well.

Bake for 45 minutes.

Chapter Twelve

'Wha –?' Steffi, head thumping, attempts to open one eye as Susie stands over her proffering a mobile phone.

'Honey? Your phone kept ringing so eventually I answered it. It's your mom.'

Reaching out a reluctant arm, Steffi brings the phone to her ear. One eye is half open, the other very definitely closed.

'Mom?'

'Darling?' Honor's voice is loud and clear, too loud for Steffi, who winces. 'You sound terrible. What on earth's the matter? Are you sick?'

'Just a late night,' Steffi says, thinking it best not to mention the copious amounts of drink that accompanied the late night. Oh God. And the man. What was his name? Luke. What on earth happened to him? She turns over and checks the other side of the bed. No sign of him. She could have sworn he slept over.

'So what time should we pick you up?'

'What are you talking about?'

'Darling, I spoke to you last night, remember? Callie's photo shoot is cancelled so we're going to come into the city to pick you up and bring you back here.'

'Oh GOD!' Steffi sits bolt upright in bed. 'I'd forgotten entirely. Jesus. What time is it?'

'Eight-thirty.'

'Eight-thirty? Mom! I thought it was eleven. I'm going

back to sleep. We're not meeting Mason at the house until three so we can leave here at two. I'll see you later . . .'

'Steffi Tollemache! We will not come at two. We will be there to pick you up at eleven, and we will find somewhere lovely to have lunch. It's not often I get to spend the day with my two daughters, and I do intend to make this the whole day. No discussion. See you soon. I love you.'

Steffi groans as the phone clicks, then throws the mobile to the other side of the room.

'Suse?' she yells. 'Suse?' No sign of her, so Steffi throws back the covers and goes into the living room – hair tousled, eyes still half-closed, wearing a man's pair of boxer shorts and oversized T-shirt that she somehow must have got from somewhere at some point during the night.

'Can you wake me up at . . . Oh!' She colours instantly as Susie gestures to two steaming mugs of coffee on the table.

'Shit,' Steffi whispers in a panic, her hands flying up to her hair. 'Is he still here?'

'No.' Susie laughs. 'He just left. Cute!'

'Was he? I don't even remember what he looked like.'

'Yes, you do. Sandy-coloured hair, messy, great smile. Preppy.'

'Preppy?' Steffi looks horrified. 'Are you sure? That's not my type. I would never have had a fling with someone . . . preppy.'

'Well, you did. He was preppy, and very cute. He left his number with me and made me promise to give it to you.'

Steffi grabs the card Susie is holding and bursts out laughing. 'He's an architect! No way!'

'You mean he's not a struggling musician?' Susie, married to a struggling musician, raises an eyebrow.

'Right! Or a wannabe actor, or a novelist who's written the greatest American novel since Tom Wolfe and is waiting tables until he's discovered . . .'

'Or a drug addict, of course. You've always said those have had particular appeal for you,' Susie adds.

'Exactly. An architect! Now that's funny.'

'So are you going to call him?'

'A preppy architect?' Steffi peers at Susie closely. 'Are you out of your fucking mind? Of course I'm not going to call him.' And with that she rips up his card and walks over to put it in the trash can. 'Much too normal, plus I don't even remember him.'

'Let me remind you.' And she does, shaking her head in dismay. Then she says, 'I can't believe you're not going to call him. He was a good guy.'

'How many times have I told you?' Steffi laughs. 'I don't do good guys. Well okay, let me rephrase that, I might do them for a night, but I know myself. I get bored. I need a bit more excitement. And a tattoo.'

'What?'

'A tattoo. I've never dated anyone who hasn't had at least one tattoo.'

'Really?'

'Really. And nor do I intend for that to change.'

'So you now remember that architect-boy didn't have a tattoo?'

'I now remember. Great body, no tattoos.'

Susie sighs. 'It just seems a shame. So what did you want to ask me?'

'I was going to ask you to wake me up before my mom gets here, but now . . . Jesus, look at the time. No point going back to sleep. Maybe I'll sleep in the back of my sister's car.'

And picking up the cup of now-cold coffee on the table, she drains it before heading into the bathroom to take a shower.

*

'Wake up, sleepyhead.' Honor turns around from the front seat. 'We're almost there.'

'Wow!' Steffi sits up and stretches as she emits a loud groan. 'That was awesome. I slept the whole way.'

'We know.' Callie tuts. 'You snored too.'

'Sorry.' Steffi shrugs lightly and gazes at the landscape shooting past, the trees which clear every so often for a gorgeous old house or horses grazing behind a white split-rail fence.

'This is pretty. Are we here?'

'We decided to go to New Canaan for lunch,' says Honor. 'We're going to grab something to eat and do some shopping. Oh my!' She looks out of the window at the storefronts. 'Isn't this pretty!'

'This is gorgeous,' Callie says. 'I can't believe I don't come here more often, but – Oh. My. God! Steffi!'

Steffi turns her head, and at exactly the same time they both excitedly shout, 'Ralph Lauren!'

'What?' Honor frowns.

'My favourite store!' Callie exclaims, now jiggling up and down in the car seat with excitement. 'And I never get to go!'

'It is her favourite store,' Steffi reaffirms. 'Much too preppy for me, even if I could afford it.'

'It's not preppy,' Callie says, and sighs. 'It's classic. Let's find a parking spot. I have to get in there.'

'Jeez, Callie.' Steffi starts to laugh. 'Calm down. You're like an addict needing a fix. Relax.'

'No, seriously, I can't relax. Did you see that patchwork coat in the window? I want it.'

Honor looks at her daughter in amusement. 'Callie! I never knew you were such a shopper.'

'I'm not,' Callie says. 'But this is Ralph Lauren, Mom! This is a whole other world.'

Once inside, Callie becomes businesslike. A salesgirl stands just behind her, her arms piled high with clothes that Callie hands back.

'Do you have this in a medium?' she says, or 'Does this come in any other colours?'

Honor walks over to Steffi, who is wistfully fingering a silk tunic. 'Darling? Aren't you even going to try anything on?'

Steffi shakes her head. 'There's nothing in here for me, and anyway it's too expensive. The only thing I quite like is that scarf, but I wouldn't spend the money.'

'I'll buy it for you,' Honor says, and Steffi's face lights up. 'I'm your mother,' she adds with a smile. 'It's my job.'

Eventually the three women leave the store laden down with bags. Callie has indeed bought piles of clothes, Steffi has a bag of her own, and even Honor found a long, cream, cashmere wrap she fell in love with.

'I'm starving,' Steffi says. 'All that shopping worked up an appetite. Can we go and get something to eat?'

'Maybe we can find somewhere for you to work?' Callie says. 'A little vegan restaurant around the corner?'

'Doesn't have to be vegan.' Steffi shrugs. 'That would be perfection, but I've cooked everything before and I can certainly do it again.'

'So you'd be happy to shove your hand up the inside of a chicken and pull out the gizzards and the liver and feel it all slimy on your hands?' Callie teases.

'Ew!' Steffi makes a face. 'God, Callie. Do you have to be so gross?'

'Just checking to see how willing you are.'

'You do what you have to do,' Honor interjects. 'And Steffi would be fine. How about over there?' She gestures to a pretty sidewalk café with a small fenced garden and tables outside.

'You go in. I'm just going to stand outside for a minute,' Callie says.

'Is everything okay?' Steffi asks.

'Just a bit of a headache coming on, and the cool air helps.'

'Another one?' Her mother looks concerned, so Callie goes on to explain Lila's theory about the menopause.

'You need to go to the doctor.'

'I will, I will. I had an appointment the other day but then a client called and I had to run over there. I'll go next week. Definitely. So what do you guys feel like eating?'

Some time later, the salads have been eaten, the sparkling mineral water drunk, and the bill has been called for – Honor's treat – when Steffi's phone rings.

'Oh hey, Mason! We're just finishing lunch in New Canaan . . . You are? . . . Sure, we can come now . . . Don't worry, I'm with my mom and my sister and she has GPS in the car so we can just plug it in. Okay . . . Great.' She finishes the call and looks at Honor and Callie. 'Mason's already there,' she says. 'And he says we can come over now if we're ready. Callie? Do you want me to drive? You look terrible.'

'I'll be okay.' Callie squints; the pain is now significant. 'I think this is turning into a migraine. Can we stop at that drugstore we passed at the top of the street and get some painkillers? This is pretty bad.'

'Let me drive,' Steffi says.

'No, no.' Callie shakes her head, wincing as she does so, then stands up slowly and gingerly. 'Honestly I'm fine, and I'd rather drive.'

Steffi and her mother exchange a look, but Honor shrugs. There is no arguing with Callie when she makes up her mind, but the sooner they get some painkillers into her, the better.

Callie drives with her eyes now half-closed against the pain, concentrating furiously on getting to the pharmacy. The pain is like a vice in her head, and she is feeling increasingly nauseous. This is like the others, but stronger.

Just get to the pharmacy, she tells herself, the voice in her head drowning out concerned mumbles from her mother and sister. And then everything goes black. She isn't even aware of slowly driving across the road and into a street lamp. As Honor screams and tries to grab the wheel, Steffi covers her head in horror.

Spiced Black Bean Fritters
(I have made this recipe with black beans, chickpeas, haricot beans, and even the dreaded lima beans, and they are all equally delicious – it's the perfect pantry meal when you're stuck.)

2 tablespoons olive oil
1 small onion, finely minced
1 large green pepper, finely chopped
dried red chilli (to taste), minced
2 teaspoons ground coriander
2 teaspoons ground cumin
1½ teaspoons turmeric
1 can black beans
2 handfuls fresh coriander
½ teaspoon grated lemon rind
juice of 1 lemon
3–4 tablespoons soy yoghurt
salt and pepper
½ cup wholewheat or chickpea flour
2 tablespoons sesame oil
2–3 garlic cloves

Heat the oil, add the onion, pepper, and chilli to taste: a slight sprinkling for those who don't like heat. (If you add too much, you can cut it with lemon juice.)

Cook for about 5 minutes until soft, then add the coriander, cumin and turmeric, and stir-fry for another 30 seconds. Remove from the heat and set aside.

Transfer the beans and fresh coriander to a blender and process until evenly chopped. In a medium bowl combine the beans, cooked onion mixture, lemon zest and juice, and soy yoghurt. Season to taste.

Form into 8 patties, roughly half an inch deep, and coat them with the flour. Heat the sesame oil over a high heat in a frying pan. When hot, fry the patties a few at a time, roughly a minute per side. Drain on kitchen roll for a few minutes and serve with mango chutney, or tofutti sour cream with chopped garlic and coriander added.

Chapter Thirteen

Walter Tollemache sits down at his computer and sighs wearily as he opens his inbox and sees yet another email from Hiromi.

And his morning had been going so well.

He misses being married, certainly misses having someone to look after him, and yet . . . and yet there is something so nice about being in the house by himself, not having anyone chatting away to him first thing in the morning, being able to enjoy his cup of tea as he sits on the bench outside and pets the cat – the only good thing to have come out of his brief marriage to Hiromi.

In the early days, when they were courting, when she was still pretending to be sweet and docile, she brought him a kitten that she had 'rescued' from the pet store. Walter had never been a cat person, but Hiromi adored the kitten and so he tried very hard to like it too, and it quickly became clear to him that this was a very unusual cat, much more dog, in fact, than cat, and so he and Brutus became firm friends.

They stayed firm friends, he and Brutus, through the marriage.

Hiromi insisted on Brutus being at the wedding itself, dressed in a miniature tuxedo, which Walter found completely mad, not to mention rather cruel, as Brutus seemed terrified by the very loud drinking and singing, and ended up miaowing rather pitifully in his crate in another room.

Walter was rather terrified too. He had thought this was going to be a tiny, private wedding. So tiny and private that Hiromi said it would be just the two of them. It would be more romantic, she said. He told Callie and Steffi hours before the wedding, attempting to brush over it nonchalantly in the hope they wouldn't be upset.

They were less upset at not being invited to the wedding than they were by the very fact that he was marrying Hiromi.

'She's very nice,' he kept repeating. 'And she looks after me.'

'I don't trust her,' Callie said. 'And I think she's a gold-digger.'

'Ha!' Walter barked with laughter. 'She'll be disappointed there, then. This stream of gold doesn't run particularly deep at all. The glory days of the Tollemaches are long gone.'

'I don't think Hiromi knows that,' Callie said. 'How did you meet her again?'

'Through friends,' he said. As he always did.

Which wasn't actually true. He had in fact met her through a website specifically designed to introduce Japanese ladies to American men. The website was clear that the purpose of these introductions was to help the men appreciate the glories of a subservient, docile, sweet and charming Asian wife.

There were pictures of older gentlemen who were thrilled with their gorgeous younger – much, much younger – wives, and testimonies by the men, saying they had never been happier, nor better looked after, in their lives.

It was about time, Walter thought, that he had some looking after. Honor had looked after him for a while, until she decided their fourteen years together and two daughters had been a terrible mistake, and she couldn't possibly stay in such an unhappy and dreadful situation.

And then came Sally, who was forever having crisis after crisis, and looked to Walter to sort them out. He was enormously flattered for a while – he hadn't played the knight in shining armour role, and he found it suited him. But ten years of drama was exhausting, and when her drama ended up being an affair with a work colleague, he almost clapped with relief.

Sally begged for forgiveness, and Walter honestly had to use all the acting skills he had to pretend to be furious.

Luckily, they had never actually formalized their arrangement, hence – thank you, God! – no alimony with Sally. Then came Eleanor, who was delightful, but a little too space age for his tastes; and suddenly a younger, malleable wife seemed . . . appealing.

When Hiromi started corresponding with him, enclosing pictures of her sweet, shy smile, he was captivated. She was forty-six, which he decided was a perfect age. Not so young that it would be inappropriate, but mature. A woman, rather than a girl. She had been married once, when she was young, but, she said, it had been more of an arranged marriage, one to please her parents.

She had joined the Dreamy Asian Wife site a few weeks ago, she said. Had received emails from several men, but hadn't found any of them very interesting. Walter, however, she found intriguing.

'So handsome!' she wrote. 'And clever!'

She was big on exclamation marks.

And Walter allowed himself to be charmed.

He paid for her ticket and drove to the airport to pick

her up, gruff with nerves and second thoughts, but as soon as she walked through, a beaming smile on her sweet face, he was thrilled.

'So much more handsome than in your picture!' she said, as they walked to the car, then she giggled, adorably, behind her hands, embarrassed.

'And you are so much prettier,' he said, instantly flushing at how clichéd that sounded.

It didn't feel clichéd, though. It felt . . . wonderful.

She waited on him hand and foot. She cooked him the most delicious Asian steamed sea bass he had ever had. She gazed at him as he spoke, as if he were the most interesting, intelligent, amazing specimen she had ever seen, and truth be told, Walter found it all rather addictive.

When she returned to Japan after six weeks – he had extended her ticket – he missed her. Plus, he was fairly certain he had fallen in love. Their relationship had not become physical, but he knew that it would, that she felt the same about him but was shy, demure, wanted to be married first.

'Dad?' Steffi said, when he mentioned he was quietly 'dating' a lovely Japanese woman. 'You'd better not have gone to one of those websites.'

'What are you talking about?' he said quickly. 'What websites?'

'Mail-order bride? Because that's all about getting a green card, and it's a total scam.'

'I didn't meet her through a website.' He forced a laugh. 'But how can it be a scam? Even the young people are dating through websites now,' he said. 'Maybe you should try it.'

'No thank you. My friend Erin's dad married some Thai woman he met through a website, and he thought she was the love of his life. Okay, so she was about thirty years younger than him, but as soon as they were married she turned into the witch from hell, and left him for the plumber, taking half his life savings with her.'

'Ah.' Walter made a mental note to call his lawyer immediately, but swiftly forgot the warning from his younger daughter. This wasn't a scam; it couldn't be. This was true love.

Hiromi moved in, and after a while she moved into his bedroom. Then Brutus moved in, and then, because it seemed like the right thing to do at the time, he proposed.

Hiromi squealed with excitement, jumped up from the table and flung her arms around him. Her joy and happiness was so delirious that Walter went to kiss her, but she leaped off and immediately rushed to the phone. Walter sat, smiling at her affectionately as she phoned her family back in Japan. Then her friends, then everyone she had ever met, talking so fast, her fingers moving prettily as she spoke. After two hours Walter whispered he was going to bed, and Hiromi laughed happily and nodded, reaching up for a quick kiss before going back to her call.

Walter got undressed, put on his pyjamas, brushed his teeth and climbed into bed, waiting for her to come up. She obviously hadn't heard, so he went back to the bathroom and flushed the toilet, knowing she would hear that because the plumbing was terrible in the house.

She still didn't come. He put his reading glasses on, picked up the biography he was reading and thought he'd give it ten minutes, and then he'd tell her to come up. He wanted to celebrate, after all. With his . . . fiancée!

'I'm coming, I'm coming!' She giggled up at him, looking so adorably cute when she was excited. 'I just have to tell my great-aunt.'

'I thought you already told your great-aunt?'

'On my father's side. And my cousins. You go upstairs, I will be quick.'

An hour later, while Walter was gently snoring, his book having dropped onto the floor, Hiromi continued giggling away downstairs.

All was forgotten by the morning. Later that day he went to see his lawyer, his old room-mate from Yale, to arrange a pre-nup. He felt strangely guilty doing so. Surely legal arrangements to protect yourself were not the way to start a marriage, but he couldn't quite put Steffi's story about her friend out of his mind, and it was always good to be on the safe side.

Just in case.

He started to think he might have made a mistake on the night of the wedding. A dozen Japanese people showed up outside the town hall, showering them with confetti.

'Cousins,' Hiromi turned to him and explained delightedly. 'Surprise!'

It certainly was a surprise. He had booked a romantic dinner for two at a special occasion restaurant, but instead found himself, after first taking Brutus back home, in a very seedy bar with lots of happy Japanese people who didn't really speak any English, but did do a very good job of running up the drinks bill.

They drank and drank. And then a couple of men walked in with equipment, and the Japanese people cheered.

Karaoke night was, it seemed, a regular here, and as the vodka flowed they all started singing.

And his demure Hiromi? What had happened to her? She was drunk. And shameless. She kept grabbing the microphone from whoever was singing, and gyrating on the stage, while her friends cheered her on.

Walter was horrified.

He carried her to his car, for she was in no state to walk, and spent the rest of the night Googling how to annul a marriage.

Happily, in the morning she was deeply apologetic. She said she was taking antibiotics for a 'woman's issue', hence not telling him, and it had reacted horribly with the small amount of alcohol she had ingested.

He was quite certain he had watched her drink vast amounts of alcohol, but after consummating the marriage she was just as wonderful as she had been before their wedding night. So it was clearly a blip.

Until the next time. And the next.

Each time an entourage of smiling, charming, bobbing friends of hers showed up, none of them speaking English, and he began to dread going out at all.

Suddenly she started shouting at him, telling him he was a 'stupid old man', and when she was unhappy she refused to lift a finger in the house. Shortly thereafter being unhappy seemed to be a pretty permanent state of affairs with her, and he moved out of the master bedroom and into the spare room downstairs, just to get some peace and quiet.

He'd been had.

And he was ashamed.

Too ashamed to tell anyone.

'How's married life?' his friends would ask, busting his chops about having such a gorgeous young wife, and he would force a smile and nod. 'Fine, fine. You know. It's . . . married life,' he'd say, then try to change the subject as quickly as possible.

He would lie in bed, Brutus on his chest – for Brutus didn't seem too terribly impressed with Hiromi either, although he did pretend when he was hungry – and feel hollow inside. And he would think about Honor, and Eleanor, and even, sometimes, Sally. Women who may not have been perfect, but he understood them.

He had no idea what to make of Hiromi. Sometimes she would just laugh when he said something, and he would be flooded with relief; other times he might say exactly the same thing and she would fly off the handle in a rage.

It was terrifying.

He served her divorce papers after a year. It felt like the longest year of his life. He did it when she was at work – she had recently got a job as a hostess in a restaurant – and changed the locks on his house, packaging up all of her stuff in neat boxes and leaving them outside the front door.

He knew that if she got back into the house, she might never leave. As it was, she stood outside screaming and rattling on the door for a good hour, during which time Walter breathed a sigh of relief that he didn't have any close neighbours.

And then she left, and the emails started.

They have been divorced for five years, and still the emails come.

She is convinced he has stolen something from her. A

pair of purple and black panties and matching bra that were from Victoria's Secret and her favourite set. She accuses him of being a dirty old man, but he hasn't the faintest idea what she is talking about, and is pretty sure that he wouldn't have forgotten a purple and black pantie and bra set from Victoria's Secret. No siree.

Asian Steamed Sea Bass

2 lb. sea bass (preferably one fish if you can get it)
½ teaspoon salt
½ teaspoon sugar
1 inch fresh ginger root, peeled and julienned into very thin slices
8 spring onions, finely julienned in 2-inch lengths, green and white
    parts separated
6 tablespoons groundnut or corn oil
4 tablespoons soy sauce

Rinse the fish and pat dry. Make 2–3 diagonal slashes on both sides of the fish.

Steam in a fish poacher or steamer over a high heat for about 8 minutes, or until the fish is cooked and flakes easily.

Carefully place the fish on a serving platter and sprinkle with the salt and sugar.

Spread the ginger over the fish, then the green part of the spring onions, followed by the white part.

Heat the oil in a small pan over a high heat until smoking. Pour it little by little over the spring onions and ginger, which will sizzle and cook as the oil hits them.

Finish by drizzling soy sauce over the entire fish.

Chapter Fourteen

'I'm fine,' Callie keeps insisting. 'I just want to get out of here.'

'But you had a blackout.' Honor winces from the bruise of her seat belt, but nothing else, thank God, thank Volvo. 'You can't go home until they find out what caused it.'

'They said we're all fine. There's nothing wrong with us now, just shock and a few bruises, and I don't want them to do tests here, okay? I swear I'll go and see my doctor when I get home, but I don't want to stay here in the hospital.'

Honor and Steffi look at one another. They understand. Of course they understand. Ever since her cancer Callie has hated hospitals, has hated the memories that come flooding back every time she steps through the doors, for all hospitals look the same, smell the same, feel the same.

'But, darling,' Honor attempts again, 'didn't that doctor say he wanted you to have an MRI to try to establish the cause of the headache?'

'Yes, but I'm not going to do it here. I'll have the MRI, but Mom, if I'm going to do it, it needs to be at Poundford Hospital. I need to be with people I know, all right? It's just too traumatic for me to be in a strange hospital, okay?'

Honor and Steffi back down immediately. The last thing anyone wants is for Callie to be traumatized.

'Okay. But you have to see someone very soon. I'm going to tell Reece.'

'Fine. Can we just get out of here?'

'Guys?' Steffi is driving. 'Mom? Would it be okay, do you think, if you drove instead?'

'I *can* drive.' Honor is cautious, shooting worried glances at Callie, who is lying down on the back seat. 'Why?'

'It's just that I told Mason what has happened and he offered to come and get us. I told him we were fine. He's staying the night here now, and I said I'd try to come over later, but I know you need to get back.'

'You're leaving us?' Honor is horrified.

'But you're fine, Mom. You heard Callie – she's fine too.' They both look over their shoulders at Callie, who doesn't look very fine at all.

'Cal? You okay?'

'Just a headache,' Callie says.

'Oh goodness. I think we should turn back. What if it's brain swelling? We have to go back.' Honor starts to tremble.

'No!' Callie's voice is surprisingly forceful. 'I didn't even hit my head, okay? It's not brain swelling. It's the same headache I always get. Migraine. I think it's stress.' She opens her eyes and manages an evil glare at her mother and sister. 'Just get me home. Please.'

'Steffi, I need you to stay with us,' Honor mutters, her teeth clenched in anger.

'But I need to see this house, Mom. I'd planned it, and everyone's fine. You'll be fine to drive home.'

'I am not fine to drive home. I am shaking. There is absolutely no way I can drive us home. I know it's not far to Bedford from New Canaan, but the answer is still no. I'm not giving you a choice. I refuse to drive, and you, young lady, need to grow up.' With that, Honor crosses her arms and stares resolutely at the road in front of her, while Steffi sets her lips in a tense scowl.

God, she thinks. Sometimes I really can't stand my mom. Then she instantly feels ashamed at regressing to around twelve years old.

*

Lila sits on the floor of her dressing room with her head in her hands. What on earth is she going to wear? Who, more importantly, does she want to be tonight?

It is Clay's recital this evening. He is playing the cello, and while school orchestra performances are not her preferred method of spending the evening, she recognizes it is a big deal, not only that Clay wants her there, but that Ed does too.

For Mindy will be there. It will be Lila's first introduction to the school as Ed's girlfriend, and one serious enough to bring to recitals. She will meet Clay's teachers, his friends and the parents of his friends.

Ed has often talked about the school, about how much he likes it, how it feels like a family, and yet he sometimes feels disenfranchised because, as a divorced dad, he is not included in the way the other couples are. There are none of those 'we must get together' comments at the end of Back to School night or parent–teacher evenings, when all the parents bump into one another milling around the school corridors.

And Ed has confessed to Lila that he misses that, he feels distanced from the other parents as a single father, and because Mindy is the one who has befriended them.

'Really?' Lila laughed. 'They all like her?'

Ed nodded. 'On a superficial level, yes, of course. She can be . . . charming.'

'So I've heard,' Lila said. 'Not that I've seen much evidence.'

'She'll be on her best behaviour tonight,' he assured her earlier on the phone. 'I guarantee it.'

Lila is so different with people. Where Mindy is all about artifice, Lila is real. Where Mindy is cold and judgemental, Lila is warm and accepting. She may not look like Mindy, who is coiffed, designer-labelled, golden-highlighted and cashmere-clad, but people warm to Lila in a way they never have to Mindy, and Ed cannot wait to introduce Lila to his world at school.

So what will Lila wear? She doesn't usually care, but tonight feels different.

'It doesn't matter what you wear,' Ed said. 'I love you just the way you are.'

'That's not helpful, honey,' Lila said. 'What do the other mothers wear at these things? Are they dressed up? Trendy? Classic? Do they do make-up?'

Ed laughed and shrugged. 'It's a mix. A little bit of everything. But don't worry about them; they'll love you whatever you wear.'

Ed continued along these lines, firmly stating, as all men do, that it didn't matter what she wore. But it matters. Tonight, it really, really matters.

Black, maybe. Slimming. Oh God. Why did she have to have that chicken and pasta dish for lunch? Her stomach is now blown up like a balloon. As a consequence perhaps her favourite and most flattering black trousers and a black cashmere poncho-style top. It hides her greatest flaws – certainly hides her post-pasta stomach – and makes her feel surprisingly elegant, particularly teamed with high-heeled boots.

Amber earrings . . . and Lila looks at herself approvingly in the mirror. But there's still something missing. Something that isn't quite right. Sighing as she leaves the bathroom, passing the range of Ouidad products lined up on the shelves, she walks to the corner of her bedroom and dials her hairdresser.

'This is Lila Grossman. Is there any chance Toni can squeeze me in for a blow-out in about fifteen minutes? Please? I'm desperate . . . Yes? I love you! See you then.' And she scampers out of the door.

'I'm nervous,' Lila says, as they pull into the parking lot behind the school.

'Don't be nervous, darling,' Ed says. 'Everyone's incredibly nice and I'm sure Mindy will be on her best behaviour.'

'Not about tonight,' Lila says. 'About Callie.'

'What did her mom say again?'

'That she'd blacked out. She almost *killed* them, Ed. She almost killed herself. Do you have any idea how lucky they were that no one got hurt? And she's still getting these headaches, but she hasn't been to see anyone. The fact that her mom had to even call me scares me.'

'But she's going to see the doctor?'

'Apparently this time she really is going. And Reece has banned her from driving until they've got to the bottom of it. But, Ed? I'm scared.'

'I know,' he says, parking and turning to her, taking her hand. 'I know how much you love her, and I know she was sick before. This could be nothing, and they'll run the tests they need to run and find out what's wrong with her, and then they'll treat it. There's no point worrying about something that hasn't happened.'

'But what if it's . . .' She can't say the C word.

'You'll cross that bridge when you come to it.'

'I just . . . I just have this feeling that it's not good.'

'That's just a feeling, and feelings aren't facts.'

'You're right. But I hate walking around having this cloud of anxiety hanging over me.'

'It won't be for long. The doctor will figure it out. It's probably just some vitamin deficiency. There was a woman at the paper I used to work on in England who used to black out, and it turned out that she wasn't getting enough Vitamin B1. She'd developed some syndrome that caused the blackouts, but they treated it and she was fine. I'm sure it's something like that with Callie.'

Lila takes his hand. 'You always make me feel better.'

He smiles. 'Good.' Then leans in to kiss her. 'Can I just say something about your hair?'

Lila grins. 'I know! Isn't it gorgeous? Don't tell me you want me to wear it like this all the time, though, because it took about two hours to straighten and I can only go through that for special occasions. I could get it professionally straightened, I guess, but I think I'd look kind of ridiculous with poker-straight hair, I need some bo –'

'Lila? Shut up!' Ed says, not unkindly, and with a smile. 'I think it looks lovely, but I have to tell you that I prefer it curly.'

'You do?' She is shocked.

'I do. Because it's natural. And it's you.'

'Thank you, sweetie.' She opens the door.

Ed doesn't need to know that she didn't have her hair straightened for him; she had it done for Mindy.

Lila is not a competitive woman and she thought she had learned not to feel inadequate among other women, particularly if they were taller, thinner and prettier than her, but Mindy is something different and, given the constant digs Mindy has made, Lila needs to prove herself, needs to prove she is as good as Mindy, even though, as Ed has pointed out, she is a million times better.

Lila spots Mindy as soon as they walk into the school foyer. Squeezed into a pair of jeans that might fit one of Lila's ankles, she is teetering in skyscraper heels, with a fur-lined cream bomber jacket. She is standing with two identikit women and she gives Lila a cool smile and a wave before leaning in to the women and saying something, causing them both to look over at Lila.

'Oh please,' Lila hisses under her breath. 'I feel like I'm back in high school.'

'What?' Ed looks down, oblivious.

'Your ex. She just . . . she gets to me.'

'She's here?'

'Yup. Her broomstick's propped up by the door. It's the one with the big Chanel logo on top of the bristles.'

Ed grins. 'You may be nasty, but you're pretty funny.'

'Well I'm serious. How else do you think she got here since her personal chauffeur went out of business?'

'You mean me?'

Lila puts her hands on her hips and gives him a slow stare. 'Who else? Do I need to remind you?'

'Let it go,' Ed soothes her, rubbing her back then

bending down and giving her a long kiss. 'She's in the past. She's the mother of my child, which is the only reason I have to have anything to do with her. What matters is now. You're my present. And my future.'

And once again Lila looks at this man and knows what it is to truly feel loved.

Mindy disengages from the other girls and approaches them with a smile that reaches nowhere near her eyes.

'Hi, Lila!' Mindy says, smirking slightly as, to Lila's surprise, she leans forward to give her a kiss.

'Mindy!' Lila beams. 'You look beautiful.'

Mindy, unexpectedly, flushes with pleasure. 'Oh . . . thanks. You look . . . nice too. Ed? Can I talk to you, please?'

Lila turns to look at Ed, wondering, not for the first time, what in the hell these two people were ever doing together, let alone married for as long as they were.

'Of course,' Ed says. 'What's the matter?'

Mindy gives Lila a sideways glance, as if to say 'in private', although she doesn't want to say it out loud in case she offends Lila.

'It's fine to talk in front of Lila,' Ed says wearily.

Mindy huffs. She wasn't expecting this. 'Fine,' she says suddenly. 'It's about child support. I need to talk to you about increasing child support.'

Lila resists the urge to laugh. Try getting a job, she thinks.

Ed's jaw clenches. 'I hardly think the school orchestra performance is the time to talk about this,' he says.

'Well, you never respond to my emails any more, so how else am I supposed to get in touch with you?'

Lila stands there, uncomfortable. She wants to excuse

herself to go and get a drink, or use the restroom, or hang her coat – something. Anything. But she doesn't want to leave Ed alone with Mindy.

'We can talk about it on Monday,' Ed says.

'I don't want to talk about it on Monday,' Mindy whines. 'I want to talk about it now.'

'*Can everyone please make their way into the auditorium? The performance is about to start.*' The voice echoes loudly from the speakers in each corner of the room.

'Oops,' Ed says. 'Let's talk about it after the show.'

'Did you mean that about discussing increased child support after the show?' Lila looks at him in disbelief as they sit in the auditorium, far away from Mindy.

'No. I plan on running over to give Clay a hug, then running out as quickly as possible.'

'Tell me again why you married her?'

'It was an out-of-body experience.' He shakes his head. 'Honestly? No idea. I think I must have been abducted by aliens.'

'Aliens who found volatile crazies attractive?'

'Clearly!' He smiles and leans towards Lila for a kiss just as the children file in with their instruments and take their seats.

Clay is towards the end, and once he is seated he scans the auditorium, his eyes finally alighting on Ed and Lila, who is waving furiously. Clay flashes a megawatt smile before leaning forward and adjusting the stand.

Venetian Chicken and Pasta with Rosemary

3½ lb. roasting chicken
2 tablespoons extra-virgin olive oil
salt and freshly ground black pepper
½ cup pine nuts
rosemary needles, finely chopped
⅓ cup sultanas, soaked in warm water for 30 minutes
1 lb. tagliatelle or fettucini
2–3 tablespoons chopped fresh parsley

Preheat the oven to 350°F.

Rub the chicken with the oil and sprinkle with the salt and pepper, then place it breast-down in a roasting pan and roast for about 1½ hours or until well browned, turning it over towards the end to brown the breast.

Take the chicken out of the oven, let it cool for about an hour, then pull the meat and skin off the bones. Discard the carcass and any fatty bits of skin, but keep all the lovely crispy pieces.

Heat the pine nuts in a small frying pan, browning them slightly.

For the sauce, pour all the juices from the roasting pan into a saucepan. Add the rosemary, the drained sultanas and the pine nuts. Begin to simmer the sauce when you're ready to cook the pasta.

Prepare the pasta, salting it when it boils (a bit of olive oil helps too). Drain, then toss it with the sauce, chicken pieces and parsley in a large warmed bowl.

Chapter Fifteen

'Mom?' An insistent voice whispers loudly, inches from her face, and Callie opens her eyes to see Jack hopping from one foot to the other.

'Jack? Do you need the bathroom?'

'No. Yes. But, Mom? Eliza's being mean to me.'

Callie sighs as she pushes the covers back. 'Okay. I'll go and speak to her. Now YOU go to the BATHROOM,' she demands, smiling as he weaves through her bedroom and into the bathroom.

God, he is just so damned cute.

When Eliza was born, she never thought she could love anyone as much, ever again. Not even Reece. Her world revolved around this tiny little dark-haired creature, this little girl who won her heart the minute she was placed in her arms.

Callie loved everything about Eliza. She was conceived on a cold spring night, in their little apartment in an old Brownstone in Chelsea. That was their first apartment together, before they moved to the bigger one on the Upper East Side, a move which Callie always regretted.

And Callie swears she knew, even while making love, that she and Reece were making a baby. She remembers going into the bathroom and looking at herself in the mirror and seeing that something had changed, and she smiled a small, secret smile, and rubbed her stomach.

'Hey, baby girl,' she whispered.

'You are completely nuts,' Reece said, when she ran back into the bedroom and pounced on him, telling him the news.

'That may be true, but it doesn't change anything. We just made a baby! And it's a girl, and we're going to call her Eliza.'

'Fine.' Reece shook his head with a grin before bending down and talking to Callie's stomach. 'Hello, Eliza. Daddy here. Everything all right in there?' And they both laughed.

Reece would come home and find Callie scouring baby sites, reading everything there was to read about pregnancy.

And this was only the first three weeks.

She started buying pregnancy tests, but it wasn't until two days before her period was due that a faint blue line showed. The line became stronger and stronger with each one of the countless tests Callie performed over the next two days, and a visit to the doctor confirmed what she had known from the first second.

She was pregnant.

That it was a girl called Eliza took a little while longer to confirm.

She loved every second of being pregnant. Her body bloomed: lush and ripe and gorgeous. She talked to her baby every day, and as soon as Eliza smiled her first smile, giggled her first giggle, Callie knew that if, God forbid, anything happened to her child, she would not be able to live.

Jack was unplanned. Callie wasn't even sure she wanted another child, so scared was she that she wouldn't have enough love in her for two, but Reece wanted a boy. Her father wanted a boy, and there was still a part of her trying to please her daddy. She knew that at some point the likelihood was that she would have another baby, and she couldn't help but think that if it were to happen, it would make everyone happier if it were a boy.

Still, this time she didn't know. She felt very tired and only realized her period hadn't arrived after seven weeks. The pregnancy wasn't as easy and she felt enormous. She put on sixty pounds, hauling her body around, resenting it all the while.

When he finally arrived, Jack was colicky. In the mornings he would be fine, but by mid-afternoon he would be screaming, for no reason whatsoever.

Callie was trying to look after Eliza, only two herself, while trying to rock Jack – the only thing that seemed to quieten him down was being rocked, or pushed in a buggy, for hours, and hours, and hours.

She tried everything. Gave up dairy in case he was lactose-intolerant and unable to handle any dairy he was ingesting through her breast milk. Then gave him formula. Soy formula. Goat's milk formula. Pre-digested formula. Nothing stopped the screaming.

Days would go by when Callie spent hours walking around like a zombie, wondering what the hell she was thinking in having another baby, and wishing she could turn the clock back to what was before – just the three of them.

The guilt was enormous. Looking at Jack she felt nothing like the overwhelming and all-consuming love she had had for Eliza from the first second. Looking at Jack, she felt . . . hate would have been too strong a word for it, but *dislike*, certainly. Which she couldn't admit to anyone.

At three and a half months, everything changed. Honor showed up, unexpectedly, with a great big suitcase and a truckload of patience. She scooped up Jack and shooed Callie out of the room.

She decided to start Jack on solids, which Callie's paediatrician had said not to do until he was six months old, telling her that babies' digestive systems aren't properly formed and they can't handle the solids before then.

'Well that's just not true,' Honor sang, rocking Jack in her arms. 'You and your sister both started on baby rice at three months. Everyone did. And you both slept right through the night after that. We're going to try it.'

Callie was too tired to argue with her.

Honor spooned a little baby rice mixed with formula into Jack's eager mouth that evening and he slept until two a.m., in the little cot next to Honor's bed in the spare room. ('I won't hear of it,' Honor protested, when Callie weakly said that Jack ought to be in with her. 'You need to sleep, and I need to spend time with my grandson.' Callie had the first proper night's sleep in three months. In the morning, for the first time, she started to think that perhaps there was a light at the end of the tunnel after all.)

Honor gave him a bottle when he woke that night, and within a week he was off the two a.m. feed and sleeping through the night. He also, miraculously, turned into a happy little boy, and one day, as he looked at Callie and smiled with delight, her heart opened up, and from that moment on she loved him just as much as she loved Eliza.

And he adored her. Oh how he adored her. Even now, at six years old, he is so different from how Eliza was at this age. She was independent, strong-willed, stubborn.

Refused to be kissed or cuddled by Callie unless she was in the mood, but Jack?

Jack snuggles with her all the time. He flings his arms around her legs and squeezes tightly, looking up at her adoringly.

At night, when she goes to kiss them goodnight, Eliza gives her a perfunctory peck, occasionally requesting a proper snuggle, but Jack shifts over in his little twin bed to make room for her, and when she lies next to him he reaches an arm around her neck, pulling her close and stroking her cheek, unmitigated adoration and bliss in his eyes.

'Eliza?' Callie calls, pulling on a robe and stuffing her feet into slippers, wincing at the headache that seems to be constantly present these days. 'What's going on with your brother?'

'Nothing,' Eliza yells from her bedroom, appearing briefly in the doorway in skin-tight leggings, a T-shirt with a peace sign and a long, ratty pink scarf wrapped around her neck. 'It wasn't me, it was him.'

'Eliza, you're older, okay? It's up to you to set the example. Just be nice. Please.'

And as Eliza huffs and puffs, Callie goes downstairs to make breakfast.

'Why can't Daddy ever stay and have breakfast with us?' Eliza asks when Callie places a plate of scrambled eggs in front of her.

'He's working,' Jack says, in irritation.

'He's always working.' Eliza is grumpy, and Callie turns her back so Eliza doesn't see her expression, because she agrees with Eliza: sometimes it would be really nice if he left for work a little later, or came home a little earlier. Just spent a bit more time with the children.

'He's always here at the weekends,' she says brightly, 'and he spends lots of time with you then.' Which is true.

'But I want him here on school days,' Eliza whines, 'and I want Googie too. Why can't we wake her up in the mornings?'

'Because Googie won't be a very happy Googie if she doesn't get enough sleep,' Callie warns, to which Eliza has no response, so silence ensues as she quickly finishes her eggs then pushes her chair back to go and sit at the computer in the kitchen and play Club Penguin.

Jack comes up behind her, rapt, as a cartoon penguin surfs the screen, and Callie stacks the dishwasher and wipes down the table.

'Come on, guys,' she says, checking her watch. 'Five minutes till the bus. Brush teeth. Eliza? Brush hair. Shoes and coats on. Let's roll.'

When she gets home, Callie takes an Imitrex then goes back upstairs to try to sleep off the headache. It is true that often the headache gets better as the day progresses, but right now she needs to lie down.

Honor sits down gently on the bed, sliding a cup of hot camomile tea onto Callie's bedside table.

'How are you feeling, honey?' she says when Callie opens her eyes.

'I'm okay,' Callie lies.

'You're going to the doctor today?'

'Yes.'

'Your regular doctor?'

There is a pause. 'No. Mark.' Her oncologist.

The blood drains out of Honor's face as she places a hand on her heart to still it.

'What? It's . . .' She can hardly speak, a wave of nausea coming over her.

'No, it's not.' Callie attempts a smile. 'Reece insisted on calling Mark yesterday because my scan is due next month, and Mark said he'd rather see me himself. I don't think it's anything to worry about, Mom, and I'm more comfortable with Mark anyway. I barely even know my internist, and I know Mark will refer me to the best neurologists, or whoever I need to see.'

'Okay.' Honor exhales loudly. 'I just . . . I just got scared.'

'Don't worry, Mom. I'm not. Even Mark said it could be any number of things.'

'Like migraine? Or peri-menopause?'

Callie smiles. 'Yes. Exactly.'

But that isn't really how Callie feels.

Just as she knew the minute she was pregnant with Eliza, she has a knot in her stomach, a feeling of dread, a certainty that something is very wrong, and she has been trying to bury her head in the sand, hoping that tomorrow morning she will wake up and everything will be fine.

Tomorrow morning keeps coming, and each morning she wakes up and it is not fine, and she is so scared she can't even think about it; every time she does think about it she finds herself unable to breathe.

She doesn't even know why she is so scared. When she was diagnosed with breast cancer she never had a flutter of fear. She knew she would be fine. This is not the same thing. Not that there were any symptoms with breast

186

cancer the first time round, and she has no idea what this is, whether it is cancer, or whether it is something else, but whatever it is, she is pretty certain it is serious.

Which is why she has refused to go to the doctor. She doesn't want to know. She refuses to accept that there may be anything wrong with her, because, as she has said before, bad things do not happen to Callie Perry, and if, perchance, they do, they will still end well.

Look at the cancer. It brought her and Reece closer than she could have ever imagined possible. For four years she had been immersed in her children, had not forgotten about her husband, but he had no longer been her priority in the way he was pre-children. The diagnosis made her open her eyes and pull her husband close again.

Reece didn't change his travel schedule, but he came home from the office a little earlier, left the house a little later, was at most, not all, of the appointments with the oncology team at Poundford Hospital.

They took the time to be together again, just the two of them. Reece even surprised her with a 'second honeymoon' after she was declared cancer-free, or, at least, showing no evidence of the disease.

They went to Paris. Of course. They stayed in a little hotel behind Sacre-Coeur, where they lay in bed all morning eating buttery croissants and drinking huge bowls of café au lait, and spent the afternoons touring the museums, the Tuileries, a trip out to the Chateau de Vaux le Vicomte. And late-night dinners in candlelit bistros, falling in love with each other all over again over a sparkling Burgundy and a pear tarte tatin that was heaven-sent.

Life, despite having been so complicated that past year,

suddenly seemed so simple again. Reece loved Callie. Callie loved Reece. They both loved their children. And life was good. Better than good. Wonderful.

Thinking back to those days almost feels like a distant dream, and Callie can't even imagine, or remember, what it is to feel that good, that optimistic. She just wants the pain to go away.

Honor leaves her daughter and goes down to the kitchen. She will drive Callie to the hospital, for Callie is no longer allowed to drive until they can get rid of this headache and find out what is wrong with her, and she leans her hands on the kitchen counter and drops her head.

She is scared in a way she too has not been before. But she cannot be scared. She has to be strong for her daughter. But is she the only one who has noticed how Callie's appetite has dropped? How Callie is pretending to eat, but only takes one or two bites before announcing she had a huge snack just an hour ago and she's practically full to the brim.

Is she the only one to have noticed the worrying shadows under Callie's eyes, her pallor, her skin?

Please God, she closes her eyes and prays. Please let it be nothing. Please let Callie be fine. She knows this probably isn't quite right. That it might be better to pray for the strength or the fortitude to get through whatever it is that He decides is going on, but she can't quite bring herself to do that.

Praying is something she is not wont to do that often, for while she believes in the Universal Spirit, in a guiding force, in protective angels that watch over us, she has spent many years questioning the God of her Catholic upbringing, and found the only other time she turned to him for help was almost five years ago.

When Callie was first diagnosed.

*

Reece checks his watch and swears under his breath.

'Shit, I have to go. Al? Can you take over?' His creative partner nods, and Reece grabs his jacket and waves a group goodbye as he leaves the meeting room.

'I'll be back later,' he shouts to his assistant. 'Doctor's appointment.'

His assistant stands up. 'You have a four p.m. with –'

'I know, I know.' He pauses by the door. 'Don't worry. I'll be back by then. But now I'm late.'

He is always late, which he tries very hard not to be, but life is so busy, and he gets so distracted, and there is always somewhere he needs to be.

Today, he thinks he doesn't necessarily need to be with Callie for this doctor's appointment. He is sure that this will just end up being a consultation, and that Callie will be sent home with a list of other specialists she will have to see, but Callie has clearly not been feeling well, and when she turned to him last night and said, 'I need you to come with me,' he heard.

He runs up 52nd Street and speed walks across Lexington to the car park, waiting only a few minutes for the guys to pull his Audi out, gleaming black, brand new.

He folds his body inside and guns the engine, loving this car just as much today as when he had the casual thought that he might like an Audi S5, and spent the next few hours in his office with the door closed, salivating over pictures on the Internet.

The traffic in midtown is terrible, but there is nothing he can do now. He should have left twenty minutes earlier, and it can't be helped. He rings home to tell Callie he'll meet her at the hospital and that he may be ten minutes late.

Honor picks up the phone.

'Honor? It's me. The traffic's horrific, so it's going to take me longer than I thought. Can you drive Callie? I'll meet you at Mark's as soon as I can.'

'Of course,' Honor says. She knew this would happen, as it so often does. It has become a standing joke that they have to bring two cars to every social occasion, for Reece will always show up half an hour late.

She feels a surge of irritation, because this isn't a social occasion but something important, and then she suppresses it. She loves her son-in-law. Loved him the minute she met him and saw how he looked at her daughter; more importantly, she has learned to accept him, with all his foibles and idiosyncrasies.

'We'll see you there. Have you eaten?'

'No,' he says and smiles, as he heads onto the West Side Highway.

'Want me to bring you something?' she asks.

'I'd love you to bring me something!' He is enthusiastic. 'What are my choices?'

'Leave it to me. I'll surprise you,' she says, walking over to the fridge.

It is no surprise to Honor that Steffi became a chef, because Honor was always cooking. Both Callie and Steffi, when young, would perch on stools and help her, and she remembers Steffi cooking herself elaborate meals when she was only, what, five? Or six?

Today's child would never be allowed anywhere near a hot stove, or boiling water, but Honor has a clear memory of Steffi making scrambled eggs first of all, when she was around four, then the obligatory cookies and muffins, and then devising entire menus for the whole family.

She would sit at the kitchen table with Honor's cookbooks all around and choose something. She used a lot of pork, because George, Honor's second husband, adored pork, and Steffi adored George.

For a very long time, Honor stands at the counter and thinks. She has had a perfect life. Good God, it was hard when George died. So hard, for so long. But she continued with her life, started a book group, attended classes; all things she would not have had time for in her marriage.

And she found that life could be good again. Better than good. Wonderful. Surrounded by family and friends, she tries very hard not to dwell on loneliness.

Or fear.

She wishes she didn't feel quite so fearful now.

Roasted Tenderloin of Pork with Fig, Prosciutto and Sage Stuffing

1 loin of pork, around 1½ lb.
½ stick butter
6 dried figs
4 slices prosciutto
1 garlic clove
8 fresh sage leaves, or about 1 teaspoon if using dried (it is far
   more pungent)
seasoning
1 tablespoon Dijon mustard
2 tablespoons honey
olive oil

Preheat the oven to 350°F.

Cut a pocket along the length of the pork, almost going through to the other side, but being careful not to. (Think of the *Muppets*, and you will get the idea.)

In a food processor, pulse the butter, figs, prosciutto, garlic, sage and seasoning, until a paste forms. Fill the loin with the paste, and tie it with string to keep it together.

Mix mustard and honey to a paste and cover the meat with it.

Drizzle with oil, then cook for an hour.

Chapter Sixteen

Now that it's about to become reality, Steffi is really not sure about this whole moving to Sleepy Hollow business. Had it been San Francisco, for example, or even Portland, Oregon, she would have jumped at the chance, but Sleepy Hollow, New York? What is there for a single girl to even *do* there?

Aren't places like Sleepy Hollow for married people like Callie and Reece? For married couples with small children who are looking for a proper house and space in which their children can play?

Granted, it will be free accommodation, and there is a part of her that has already started romanticizing about her life in the country: big roaring fires; long walks with Fingal loping by her side; cosying up on the sofa next to some long-haired rock star who, miraculously, lives at the end of the dirt road and has been looking for a gorgeous woman just like – well, who would believe it! – just like Steffi.

Then she thinks about what it will actually mean: getting up at the crack of dawn to feed the chickens and the goats, never being able to find a plumber who can come within less than a week, so having to live without essentials, like toilets, for example. On top of which the sheer loneliness may be enough to drive her crazy.

Where will she work? Who will she talk to? Will she be accepted? Mason assured her it would be fine, that there are tons of interesting people around and it isn't exactly deepest darkest countryside. But what would have felt like a fantastic adventure in her twenties, now, at thirty-three, just seems like it might be a big, bad mistake.

Steffi steers the rental car off the highway and peers out of the window at the sky. It has rained all morning, but the sun is now struggling to break through, and she thanks God, again, for GPS, which was surely the only way she was ever going to make it here without a minor heart attack.

She may spend time close by in Bedford, and she may have been in New Canaan just the other day, but she has never actually been to this town before, and a sense of direction has never been her strong point.

It looks much like suburbia, she thinks, following the GPS, but as she keeps driving and the sun comes out at last she passes through a pretty town with old-fashioned stores and a true country village centre, and smiles at the charm.

She follows on down the road, past white clapboard antique houses, falling-down iron picket fences, past a few barns that have clearly been there for well over a hundred years.

The next left, Matilda tells her – Matilda being the calm and assertive voice of the GPS – and she turns left, then right, then right again, onto exactly what Mason had described: an old dirt road that looks as if it will lead to nowhere.

As she makes the turn, Fingal, who has been fast asleep on the back seat, suddenly lifts his head and stands up, his tongue hanging out as he starts panting and whining in pleasure.

'You know you're home, boy, don't you?' she says, and Fingal's tail whacks her on the shoulder.

She bumps down the track, glimpsing the roof of the house as she rounds the corner, and then over the cobbled apron, along the gravelled driveway and up to a pretty, Italianate farmhouse, with strategically placed rocking chairs on the wide, wrap-around porch.

'Wow!' Steffi whistles to herself, getting out of the car and standing for a moment, while Fingal whirls around in delirious circles with, Steffi would swear, a genuine smile on his face.

She watches him for a few seconds before doing a slow turn to take in the view. Next to the house is a large wooden barn and behind it she can see the corner of a cage – must be the chicken coop.

'I'm so sorry I can't make it down again to show you myself,' Mason apologized the other day, as he handed her a key. 'But you'll be fine. There's no one living there now, but there's a guy down the road who's helping me out with caretaking stuff. I'll try to get hold of him to explain who you are.'

She walks down past the side of the house, and grins when she sees the chickens, squatting down on her haunches to get a closer look and clucking gently at them, surprised and delighted when they strut over to see if she has anything for them.

'Sorry, girls,' she says. 'Not this time. But maybe next.'

Standing up, she holds her breath for a moment, for Mason had said nothing about the stunning views from the back porch, stretching out over the hills for miles.

'It's beautiful,' she whispers, before nosing round the corner to where the miniature goats are grazing. They too are friendly, and she scratches their heads in delight as she croons softly to them.

After a wide stretch, she steps up to the back porch, calls Fingal to her side, and walks around to the front door.

Mason has told her he never bothers locking it when he is there, but the house has been empty for a while, hence the need to give her a key. It turns easily and the door pushes open to reveal a large hallway with a curving staircase on one side and a marble fireplace on the facing wall.

A small sofa is on one side of the fireplace, a wing chair on the other, and Steffi sinks down on the sofa. There is no fire in the grate, but it is easy to imagine one, and what could be nicer than walking into an entrance hall that feels like a living room with a roaring fire and squishy sofa?

She gets up, almost reverentially, and peeks through the archway into a gracious living room with original floor-to-ceiling French doors on one side. The wide-planked floorboards are stained a dark ebony, with worn Tabriz rugs, and every wall is lined with bookshelves, thousands of books everywhere she looks.

The sofas are a dark grey, with large, soft, grey and cream striped cushions; there are faded ticking curtains. The aura is one of shabby elegance, much like, Steffi thinks, walking around and examining the small porcelain boxes grouped on an end table, Mason himself.

Lithographs are propped up here and there, framed, resting on the bookshelves, leaning on the books themselves. She has no idea if they are valuable, if they are original lithographs, numbered or prints, but she recognizes some: a couple of Picassos, a Matisse, a Leger.

Back through the hallway Steffi finds his study, and she smiles at the thought of Mason sitting here, for his personality is imprinted on every surface. From the large old mahogany desk with the antique reading lamp to the many more prints and pictures covering every spare inch, to the haphazard piles of books on the floor, all around the edge of the room, each of them threatening to topple over.

Big rattan baskets hold dozens of magazines. *Architectural Digest, Publishers Weekly, Time, The New Yorker.*

A cracked-leather wing chair sits next to the fireplace, with a high footstool, a mohair blanket thrown over the arm. Steffi sits down and puts her feet up, leaning back and smiling as she surveys the room.

This is indeed a room in which she could be happy.

Onwards and upwards, she thinks, standing up to move through the corridor under the stairs, and into the kitchen.

'There you are!' she says, kneeling down to pet Fingal, who is already curled up in a huge dog basket in the corner, gnawing on what looks like a well-loved rubber toy.

Large and bright, the room is airy, the table a large scrubbed farmhouse, the cabinets a pale grey. It isn't perfect – the marble countertops are marked and stained, scratches from many decades dug deep into its patina – but this is what Steffi would call a true cook's kitchen.

She turns to see a professional La Cornue oven in the corner, complete with raised hotplate. Well, of course. As if she would expect anything less from Mason.

Copper pots hang from a large baker's rack above the island, and as Steffi moves around she keeps one hand on the marble, stroking it gently as she walks, feeling the love the stone has absorbed over the years.

Yes, she thinks, breathing in deeply. This feels right. I *belong* here.

The words come to her without her even thinking about it. But there is no longer any doubt. This house has been waiting for someone to come and breathe some life into it.

This house has been waiting for her.

Upstairs she finds the master bedroom at the back of the house, with those incredible views. A canopied bed piled with pillows; a Victorian claw-footed tub in the en-suite bathroom that is bigger than the bedroom she grew up in; a fireplace – another one! – at the foot of the bed. Steffi kicks off her clogs and falls back on the bed, grinning.

She shifts her bottom up into the air and digs her phone out of her back pocket. Forgetting about the time differ-ence in London she types a text message.

It's perfect. I LOVE it . . . may never leave.

Minutes go by, then her phone beeps.

I knew you'd love it! When are you moving in?

Now? ☹

Is Fingal happy to be home?

He's thrilled. He's downstairs chewing on a
ratty-looking rubber monkey.

That's no rubber monkey. That's Parsley! His
best friend.

Oh sorry! (I thought you were his best friend?)

I compete with Parsley on a regular basis.

Srsly, I wasn't planning on moving in properly until next w'end, but I don't think I can ever leave now. r u ok if I stay?

Of course. That's the whole point! ;-)

How's London?

Wet. Grey. Fun. Amazing food.

Oh ha ha.

I'm not kidding. You should visit.

I will. Soon as I find myself a rich boyfriend.

No replacements for the rock star?

Nope. Free as a bird and happy to stay that way.

Sure it won't be long before you're snapped up.

Not this time. Need a break from men. Will get it here! So beautiful!

Don't! * groaning * makes me miss it ☹

Come visit me!

Not sure wife would approve.

Bring her!

Told you – she hates the country. Unless it's in
a Four Seasons.

Fingal wants to go out. Thanks, Mason. So
much. Not enough words . . .

My PLEASURE. Thrilled. Xx

xx

*

Mason drops the BlackBerry on his desk, stands up and
stretches, a smile on his face. His heart is warm, he realizes. His beloved house is no longer sitting cold and empty,
or rented to an unknown tenant, his most treasured pos-
sessions having to be boxed up and locked away in the
attic.

His beloved house now has Steffi inside. The thought
spreads, warm and comforting, feeling very, very right.

Vegan Spinach Quiche with Herb and Quinoa Crust

For the crust
1 cup cooked quinoa
2 tablespoons quinoa/spelt/rice/wholewheat flour to bind
2 tablespoons flax seeds
small bunch basil and thyme, finely chopped
salt and pepper

For the filling
1 packet firm tofu, drained
juice of 1 lemon
10 oz. fresh spinach
1 garlic clove, minced
½ teaspoon turmeric (for colour)
½ teaspoon sea salt
½ teaspoon nutmeg
¼ cup nutritional yeast
1 tablespoon Dijon mustard
¼ cup roasted pine nuts

Preheat the oven to 350°F.

Mix quinoa, flour, flax seeds and herbs together, add seasoning. Grease a flan tin with a removable base. Press the quinoa evenly over the base and up the sides.

Purée the tofu with the lemon juice in a blender. Add the spinach leaves and pulse until blended, then add all the other ingredients except the pine nuts, mixing until combined. Pour into the base, sprinkle the pine nuts over the top and bake for 30–40 minutes.

Serve warm or cold.

Chapter Seventeen

Callie sinks back on her hospital bed and watches blankly as the nurse inserts the IV. Once upon a time she was frightened of needles, of nurses, of medical procedures such as this. Once upon a time the thought of having an IV – something alien permanently in her body – would have made her feel ill.

But the months of chemo five years ago have made her immune, and now she is just grateful that Mark is keeping her in to try to find out what is wrong.

The good news: the scans do not show cancer. Nothing in her breast, and no metastases that are detectable. Lymph nodes, bone, brain: all clear.

The bad news: they do not know what it is, but it clearly is something. An infection of some kind, perhaps? Meningitis? A Staph infection? Bacteraemia? They do not know, but they are putting her on antibiotics, steroids and a narcotic pain reliever to be on the safe side.

Reece sits in the corner, his face as serious as Callie has ever seen it. She looks up at him beseechingly as the small plastic tube is taped to her arm, and he stands up and quickly comes to her side, sitting on the bed and taking her other hand, stroking it gently.

'How are you doing, Loki?' he whispers.

'Okay,' she says, attempting a smile.

'You're going to feel a whole lot better soon,' the nurse

says cheerfully as she adjusts the bag. 'The Dilaudid will kick in and the pain will go away, and there are all kinds of other good things in here to make you better. You'll start to feel sleepy, but the sleep is good; that's how your body heals itself.'

Callie, in too much pain to move her head, rolls her eyes up to look at her, suddenly seeming so like Eliza that it makes Reece's heart want to break.

'Really?' she says. 'What's going in?'

'The Dilaudid, the Decadron, which are the steroids, and then some regular old antibiotics in case it's an infection.'

'And Mark – Dr Ferber – said that both the steroids and antibiotics are precautionary, right?'

'That's right.' The nurse nods. 'Better to be safe than sorry. He'll be in soon. I'm going to call him now and have him check in on you.'

'Thank you.' Reece looks at her gratefully as she goes out of the room.

'Don't look so worried.' Callie smiles. 'I'm going to be okay. And honestly? I'm happy they admitted me. I'm just . . . relieved they can make the pain go away.'

'I didn't realize it was that bad,' Reece says. For Callie has been insisting she's been okay during each of these headaches, but earlier, when they asked her to number the pain on a scale of one to ten, she gave it a seven, which for Callie, who does not complain, is about as bad as it gets.

Callie says nothing.

'I hate this,' Reece says suddenly.

'What?'

'This. That you're here. I just can't believe we're back in this fucking hospital, and in the cancer ward too.'

'Shh.' Callie reaches up her arms and draws Reece down for a hug. 'Mark said we ought to be on the cancer ward only because he's here all the time and can keep a proper eye on me. It doesn't mean anything. And I know you're scared, but I'm not going anywhere, I promise. They'll do some more tests, they'll find out what it is, and they'll treat it and I'll come home, okay?' She pushes Reece back so she can look him in the eye.

'I'm not ready to go anywhere, you hear? I have you, Eliza and Jack, and you all need me. This is just a temporary blip.'

Reece smiles though his eyes are watery. 'A bump in the road?'

'Exactly,' Callie says. 'Just like before. Another fucking bump in the road.'

The door opens and they both look over, expecting to see Mark, but it is Lila standing there, laden down with bags.

'Jesus!' Lila marches in. 'Could you have picked a room that was any further from the elevator?' She dumps the bags and walks over to the bed. Reece gets up and moves back to the chair, making room for Lila to sit in his place. She sits, takes Callie's hand and leans over, kissing her gently.

'How are you, sweetie?' Her voice is low as she strokes Callie's cheek softly.

'I've been better,' Callie says. 'What are you doing here? Shouldn't you be working?'

'When my best friend is in hospital with some mysterious ailment? Not on your life. It's not exactly as if they're breaking down the door to use me. Great timing. I leave my job, albeit with a massive payout, and the world decides to collapse. Typical goddamned Lila.'

Callie smiles as Lila talks.

'Anyway, I've brought a few things,' she says, glancing around the room, 'to make this room look a little better. Nothing worse than a hospital room.'

Reaching down, she starts pulling things out of her bag. First a series of framed photographs – Callie and Reece, Callie and the kids, Elizabeth the dog, Callie, Steffi and Lila on vacation in Mexico, many moons ago.

Callie, starting to feel sleepy, closes her eyes briefly as Lila places them on the windowsill, resting against the slatted blinds.

'What else?' she whispers.

'Supersoft blanket.' Lila shakes out a pale pink blanket, as soft as feathers, and lays it on top of the hospital-issue blanket. Callie sighs with delight.

'Peanut M&Ms for when the cravings strike.'

'My favourite!'

'I know! A stack of magazines in case you feel up to reading, and an iPod loaded with audiobooks in case you don't.'

'You brought me an iPod?' Callie's eyes are starting to close. 'Oh God. I feel stoned. I feel like I'm drifting away.'

Reece grins. 'You're supposed to. That's what the nurse said would happen. How's the pain?'

'Better,' Callie murmurs.

'On a scale of one to ten?' He is already adopting the hospital lingo.

'Four,' she mutters. Her eyes close, her mouth falls slightly open and she is fast asleep.

Lila doesn't move. She sits, watching her friend, still holding her hand, stroking it back and forth with her thumb. After a while she lets go, folding Callie's hand gently on the blanket.

When she turns to Reece she is dripping tears, and when he stands to comfort her Lila dissolves into quiet, hiccuping sobs in his arms.

Driving home, her mind full of Callie, Lila wonders whether to tell Callie's friends, the ones who see her every day: Betsy, Laura, Sue, Lisa.

She picks up her BlackBerry at a red light and hits the address book, about to call, but then she thinks: no. Not until Callie has said it's okay. For while Callie is open, has no secrets from her friends, she has not told anyone quite how bad these headaches are, and perhaps she doesn't want everyone to know.

Not yet.

Back home in Rowayton, she expects to see Ed's Volvo in the driveway, but he is not there, which is no bad thing. She wants to talk to him, be comforted by him, tell him how scared she is, but first she wants to regroup: pour a glass of wine, light candles, take some deep breaths and try to centre herself.

Her phone rings as she walks in the house.

'Hi, darling.' Ed's warm voice instantly makes her feel better, and suddenly, more than wanting to regroup, drink wine, gather her thoughts, she wants Ed's arms around her, wants to bury her head in his shoulder and not think about anything at all.

'Hey.' Her voice is sad.

'How is she?'

'She's . . . I don't know. It's scary. They don't know what's wrong, but the good news is, it's not cancer.'

'That's not just good, that's great, isn't it?'

'Yes. I mean, of course. It's just that she looks so frail. She looks ill.'

'But she's in the best possible place, with a doctor who knows her well. Do you want me to make some calls?'

Oh bless him, thinks Lila. As a journalist he has contacts in every walk of life, and as a thoroughly good, likeable man his contacts often become friends, and when anyone needs help, Ed always knows the right person to ask.

'No, sweetie. Let's figure out what it is first, then you can pull in some favours.'

'How are the kids?'

'Eliza and Jack? They're fine. Why would they be anything otherwise? They don't even really know, other than Mommy's not well. Honor's there, and Reece left the hospital and went straight home. I think they're fine.'

'And Reece?'

'Reece is scared too. He would never say it, but I can tell. Hey, how come you're calling me anyway? You're supposed to be home by now.'

'Well –'

Before he says anything, Lila feels herself tense. These conversations always start in the same way. Ed has to let her down because Mindy is demanding he do something with Clay. She forces Ed to make the choice, more and more often it seems, now that he and Lila are so serious: Lila or Clay? And she knows that his guilt over the divorce, over not being a father who can be present one hundred per cent of the time, will always have him choose Clay.

'Good Lord, what does she want *now*?' Lila interjects, wishing she could keep the irritation out of her voice.

'It's not her,' Ed warns. 'It's Clay. He has a sore throat and he said he wants to be with me. I can't say no when he's sick.'

Lila takes some deep breaths. Don't explode, she thinks to herself. Don't explode.

'But . . . we were going to have a quiet night tonight, just us. You and me,' she says. 'Did you even speak to Clay?'

There is a pause. 'No, but that's not the point.'

'Of course it's the point. Mindy always does this when she has a date. She comes up with some reason why you need to take Clay and you always say yes.'

'Lila, relax!' Ed soothes. 'It isn't nearly as menacing as you think. You always assume the worst . . .'

'I'm not assuming the worst.' Lila feels the tears rise. 'I just sometimes need to have some alone time with you, and tonight, of all nights, was one of those times. If Clay wants to come out here that's fine, but you can't leave me to go and stay in the city with him, that's just not acceptable.'

'Lila, I –'

'No, wait.' Her voice is now calm. 'My best friend has been admitted to hospital today and they don't know what's wrong with her, and I'm scared, okay? I'm terrified. And I need you tonight. I need you here with me. Not on the phone, but here. With me. I was going to make dinner, and I just needed us to sit quietly and process this. That's all I'm trying to say.'

'Okay,' Ed says quietly. 'I hadn't called Mindy back. I'll

tell her it's impossible. I'm sorry. I do completely understand what you're saying. Maybe she will let him come out here and stay with us tonight, even though it's a school night. I'm sorry, baby. It's just hard for me to say no to my son.'

'It's not your son you're saying no to.' Lila sighs. 'It's your ex-wife.'

Salmon Parcels with Watercress, Rocket, Spinach and Cream Cheese

1 bag watercress
1 bag rocket
1 bag spinach
8 oz. cream cheese
zest of 1 lemon
seasoning
1 pack puff pastry
4 salmon fillets
1 egg
1 tablespoon milk

Preheat the oven to 350°F.

Blend the watercress, rocket and spinach in a food processor until finely chopped. Add the cream cheese, lemon zest and seasoning, and pulse until blended. Put half to one side to serve alongside the salmon parcels.

Roll out the pastry and cut into four squares. For each parcel place one salmon fillet in the middle of a square, season, spread a quarter of the cream cheese mixture over the top. Pull the corners of the parcel over the fish and seal at the top. Beat the egg with the milk and use this to brush the parcels. Cook for around 25 minutes, or until the pastry is golden.

Serve with the rest of the cream cheese and a green salad.

Chapter Eighteen

Honor places the phone back in its cradle and checks her watch. She left Callie at the hospital in order to come home and babysit the children. She knows she has just told Reece she would look after the kids, but how can she look after them when her daughter is in hospital and all she can think about is whether her daughter will be okay?

How can she be present for these children, explain why Mommy didn't meet the school bus as she does every day after school, when her daughter is sleeping, knocked out by one of the heaviest narcotics available, and the doctors don't know what is wrong with her?

She desperately wishes that it was possible for Lila to come tonight so that she could go back to the hospital. It is a waiting game, and she knows she cannot do anything more at the hospital, but today, the first day Callie is there, Honor needs to be with her. This, after all, is what mothers do.

She goes into the bathroom and stares at herself in the mirror. All of a sudden, she thinks, she looks old. Grey skin, deep hollow shadows under her eyes. Her entire face seems to have fallen overnight.

She turns on the tap, waits for the water to become icy cold, then splashes her face with it in an attempt to wake herself up, tighten her skin, make herself look better.

And when she has finished she looks at herself in the

mirror again, and sighs, because she still looks like a woman twenty years her senior.

Honor had been a great beauty when she met Walter Tollemache, the life and soul of the party, a butterfly who flitted around the town of Bar Harbor, Maine, waiting to spread her wings and fly to somewhere, something, far bigger and better.

Until she met Walter. So impeccably behaved, so well-mannered, so solicitous and kind, he took care of her from the very first date in a way she had never been taken care of before.

Of course we all marry for different reasons, and Honor, who had lost her father at a young age, and had been raised by a devoted mother, had not had the unconditional love and adoration that every little girl needs from her father.

She came into her own in the sixties, went to parties and dances and social gatherings where men crowded around her, just as they would later do to her daughter Callie, and didn't realize how long she had spent looking for someone to take care of her.

When Walter appeared, looking down his aquiline, elegant nose, introducing himself then whisking her off to supper, taking her home to her door afterwards and telling her that he would be taking care of her from now on, she turned into the little girl she had never been able to be, sinking into the arms of her daddy.

For a while, they were happy. As a wedding gift his parents gave them the carriage house on their estate, and Walter's mother, Mrs Tollemache, taught Honor how to entertain.

Honor didn't particularly want to learn how to entertain, although she loved cooking, but Mrs Tollemache told her she should not cook meals herself: that was what the staff were for. Her job was to be a gracious and perfect hostess, and Mrs Tollemache took her under her wing, introduced her to all of Boston society, had her dressmaker sent up from the city to measure Honor for a full wardrobe of clothes she would need for the season, and treated her much like the daughter she had never had.

She taught her to wear bouclé suits and pearls, or large colourful clips in her ears. She brought Honor up to the main house every Friday for the hairdresser to set her hair in much the same way as Mrs Tollemache's.

Jewellery was bestowed upon Honor, the likes of which she had never imagined wearing: diamond and enamel earrings, large citrine bracelets, Jean Schlumberger rings.

Honor tried so hard to be the woman they all seemed to want her to be: a younger, prettier, carbon copy of Mrs Tollemache.

For a few years, she managed it. She threw summer cocktail parties and dinner parties, planning menus like a pro – loving cooking herself, rather than, as her mother-in-law tried to insist, delegating to the staff, and her boeuf en croute was legendary. She sat on the boards of various museums and ballet organizations. She was a Tollemache, after all, and, as her mother-in-law kept reminding her, being a Tollemache entailed great responsibility; noblesse oblige meant having to give back.

From time to time she would accompany Mrs Tollemache on a tour to see how the *disadvantaged* lived, smiling and shaking gloved hands with those less fortunate, who seemed utterly shell-shocked at the arrival of these perfumed, bejewelled visitors, bewildered by these strangers who had just co-chaired a gala that had raised enough money to put their children through school.

For a while, it was fun. It was like stepping into one of the black and white movies that she had loved so much when she was growing up. She was Grace Kelly. And Walter? Well, Walter had to be Cary Grant.

Honor had always rather liked acting, had, as a child, hoped that she would grow up to be a movie star, and although this wasn't quite the acting she had in mind, she loved the glamour and excitement of it all.

For a while.

Then Callie was born – Caroline Millicent – and that changed everything. Mrs Tollemache expected Honor to do exactly what she had done: hand the baby over to the nurses and carry on as if nothing were different.

During Honor's pregnancy, Mrs Tollemache kept eyeing her growing bump with distaste.

'One mustn't let one's body go,' she would insist, horrified when Honor reached for another slice of cake. 'It is a discipline, my dear, and one must keep in shape for the menfolk.'

But Honor, for the first time, ignored her. She stopped wearing the patent pumps and tiny bouclé suits, even though Mrs Tollemache had suggested the dressmaker let them all out to accommodate the pregnancy. She replaced them with flowing kaftans that were just becoming fashionable – they were in *Vogue*, for heaven's sake! – and started growing her hair out.

From a perfect sprayed set, Honor let her hair go long and blonde, parted down the centre in a glossy silk sheath, and she saw no reason to change once Callie was born.

As for handing the baby over to a nurse, Honor couldn't

bear to be away from Callie for a minute. Callie was either cradled in a sling over her shoulder – it was so much easier to nurse her that way – or carried in Honor's arms. As she grew older Callie followed her mother around, holding on to the hem of her floor-length skirt.

It was when Callie was around eight that the discontent started to fully set in. Walter had not been keen on this new, relaxed version of his wife. Women should be lady-like, he thought, dressed at all times, not floating round the house in diaphanous gowns with no make-up and bare feet.

Honor still dressed the part when she had to. No more sitting for hours under a hot dryer with rollers in her hair, but she scraped her hair back in a long ponytail, and trussed herself up in the obligatory suit when she had to be wheeled out as the younger Mrs Tollemache.

She did indeed feel as if she were being wheeled out. Like an accessory. Which, she supposed, was exactly what she was. Walter loved her, of course. And what his parents loved was not *her*, but that she could be moulded into a Tollemache, someone to carry the name forward through the generations with pride.

Until she refused to be moulded any more. Until she stopped being quite so willing to fit into the Tollemache role. Then Walter and Honor started to drift apart.

Walter was bewildered. What had happened to the woman he married? Particularly after she met Sunny, a woman from California who had ended up in Maine and had turned her house into an impromptu market. Various friends had set up stalls in each of the rooms and people would come to shop and stay for hours, sitting around the kitchen table, or lounging on the velvet floor cushions in the living room, passing around beaded necklaces and glasses of wine, the scent of patchouli and the sounds of Neil Young filling the air.

When Honor first walked in, saw the posters of Jimi Hendrix and the Rolling Stones, heard the music, saw the people, she felt . . . assaulted. There was so much to take in. She was curious, repelled, excited.

She couldn't keep away.

At first she would drop in on the pretext of buying a beaded necklace, or another flowing top, or some flat leather sandals from India, but soon she was just dropping by for a glass of wine. When the joints started being passed around the table, it would have been rude not to try them.

Walter knew little about her other world, her new friends. He was so stiff, so strait-laced and starchy, she knew he would have hated them, would have insisted she didn't see them. So rather than have to actively disobey him, she just didn't tell him.

Callie did, though. She told him all about Mommy's other friends. But times were different then and Walter didn't realize that it wasn't just that Honor had friends of whom he'd disapprove, but that in finding these other people she was beginning to find herself.

One of Sunny's friends started offering art classes during the school day, and after Callie had gone to school Honor would throw a smock into the back of her station wagon and head over there.

As a small child, Honor had had a talent for art, but it had never been fully formed. Now, she had the confidence and willingness to pursue it, and she had an eye for the nude form that her teacher said was unparalleled.

Hours would go by, Honor lost in a meditation, brush in one hand, palette in the other, capturing the exact formations of the light on a woman's thigh, or the sweep of a shoulder and the curve of a chin.

It was, she slowly realized, the first time in years she had been truly happy. And she only knew this because of the contrast with how she felt every night when Walter walked through the door.

She would be in the kitchen, cooking – by now she was refusing to listen to Mrs Tollemache at all, and did all of the cooking herself – with Callie perched on a stool, helping and chattering away. Sometimes they would put an eight track in the player and dance around the kitchen, giggling.

Until she heard the crunch of gravel that told her that Walter was home, and she would quickly usher Callie upstairs to brush her hair and put her socks and shoes back on.

It was as if a black cloud appeared. Nothing terrible. Nothing earth-shattering. Nothing that would cause a woman to leave, but a black cloud of depression that muted her, overshadowed the developing Honor, who was only able to re-emerge the next morning when Walter leaned down, kissed her cheek and disappeared down the driveway again.

Art was her salvation. It kept her busy, kept her from dwelling on the fact that she knew, almost without a shadow of a doubt, that she had married the wrong man. She was not only a wife and mother, but she was married to a Tollemache. What woman would possibly leave a husband like Walter, and who, after all, would want her?

Steffi was a surprise. A huge one. Honor had told herself

that as soon as Callie was old enough, perhaps even boarding at school – the girls in the family all went to Putney – she would leave. Then her period didn't come. She didn't take much notice, and a few months later – yes, honestly, it took her that long – she realized that she wasn't just getting fat, she was pregnant. How could she possibly leave her husband now?

But although she tried hard for the sake of the girls, when Steffi was still practically a toddler, Honor knew she couldn't carry on. She had reached the point where she couldn't stand feeling every day that a little bit more of her was dying.

Mr and Mrs Tollemache sat at opposite ends of the formal mohair sofa in the drawing room and explained that it was perfectly all right to be unhappy in a marriage, but duty called and you just had to grit your teeth and get on with it. At least, that was what she thought they were saying. For much of the time she simply attempted to tune out.

Walter was devastated. That was the hardest part. He lost vast amounts of weight in what seemed like minutes, his suits all hanging off him, prompting people to whisper that he must be terribly ill.

He would come to pick up the girls – he had moved out of the carriage house and into the barn at the far end of the property, several acres away, in fact – and as soon as Honor opened the door, he would burst into tears.

Which was heartbreaking. Walter had never been a man who wore his emotions on his sleeve, and the fact that he was not able to contain himself made things so much harder.

Time and time again Honor would ask herself whether she was doing the right thing in leaving Walter, the Tollemache family, the lifestyle; but every time she thought of the elegantly panelled living room, the antique chinoiserie desks, the bronze busts and collections of enamelled pill-boxes on every surface, she felt herself suffocating.

She may not have known what she wanted, but she knew what she *didn't* want.

The Tollemaches eventually accepted that she was not going to bend to their will, and she ended up with enough money to buy herself a house on the outskirts of town. An antique farmhouse that had small, cosy rooms, huge fireplaces and creaky floorboards. She loved it.

Callie had a beautiful sun-filled room at the rear, and Steffi, barely out of toddler stage, a tiny bedroom next to the master, which was only the master by dint of being one foot larger than Callie's bedroom.

Friends came to visit every day. Fires roared in the grate, bottles of wine were always open, music was always playing. Walter, poor, stiff Walter, would arrive to pick up the girls, and he would stand awkwardly on the doorstep as people hustled and bustled about inside.

After a while his discomfort turned to hate, a tremendous source of sadness for Honor, who only ever wished for him the things she wished for herself: peace, happiness, joy, and perhaps love, for everyone deserves to be loved. She continued to feel guilty that she was never able to love him in the way he wanted, the way he deserved.

She always hoped they would be able to be friends, partly to assuage her guilt, and mostly for the girls, but as time progressed he seemed to find it harder – so often he could not even meet her eye – and before long he started sending emissaries to get the girls, so he wouldn't even have to see her.

And then, when she least expected it, and when she was truly happy, she met George, who was indeed the love of her life. He was everything she had hoped she might find, and so very much more.

He started talking to her in a bookstore, commented on a book she had chosen, and they ended up going for coffee, sitting and chatting for hours. Honor felt immediately as if she had known him for ever. He was funny, and clever, and humble, and kind. And above all he was entirely accepting. He loved Honor for who she was, not for who she could be, or for who he wanted her to be.

His death was brutal. Eight years ago and still it seems like yesterday; and yet she refuses to not *live*. George would have wanted anything but *that*. Some of the time she loves being on her own – cooking for herself, especially food that George never liked, pasta and lamb; or, as is so often the case, *not* cooking: eating whatever concoction she can throw together from what she finds in the fridge, food that others would never admit was palatable.

And bed is glorious. Her large, soft bed piled high with pillows; magazines, books, art journals, sketchbooks all stacked up on what used to be George's bedside table, spilling onto the bedcovers. And no one to complain, no one to click his tongue on the roof of his mouth when he opened the bedroom door and found, yet again, that 'fourteen bombs have exploded while we were out'. Although, to be fair, he always said it with a smile in his eyes.

She does not sleep much these days, or not, at least, at night. Not in the way she used to. She can go to bed at midnight and still be wide awake and raring to go at four. She has always loved peaceful mornings, and often gets up, makes herself some tea and reads on the sun porch, lying on the wicker chaise longue with a blanket flung over her, where she always manages to doze off. Other times, she crawls back into bed at five, drifting off to sleep until mid-morning, rarely feeling truly well-rested.

It is coupledom she misses. Sharing. Companionship. Someone with whom to dissect an evening, someone to share an interesting article with, someone to . . . talk to. She misses the ease of walking into a party as half of a whole, of being introduced to other couples and being able to refer to 'my husband'.

She misses fitting in.

Not that it matters much in her circle of friends, in the town in which she has lived for over forty years; but at those times when she ventures out of her comfort zone she finds herself wishing for a companion.

Those times she circles a play she wants to see, an opera she'd love to go to, a talk she'd find interesting. She'll call around the other unattached or widowed friends she has, and sometimes, even if they are all busy, she will still go, taking just her bag and her smile for company.

She always talks to people, but people aren't always so willing to talk to her, and she misses the car ride home, talking about why the play was so disturbing, or how much better this production was than last year's.

But she has been lucky. She has had three great loves, far more than most people ever get. George, Callie and Steffi.

Losing George was numbing. Losing Callie . . . it is unthinkable. And Honor has been through this before, five years ago, and she is still not entirely sure how she got through it.

You do not lose your children first. It should not, and cannot, happen.

'Not to me,' Honor whispers, looking at herself in the mirror before she goes out to start making the children's dinner. 'Not again.'

Lamb Shanks with Figs and Honey

4 tablespoons olive oil
10 lamb shanks
3–4 stalks thyme
2 lb. onions
2 garlic cloves
2 tablespoons rosemary needles
15 oz. can pumpkin purée
3 cups dried figs
1 teaspoon ground allspice
1 teaspoon cinnamon
⅓ cup honey
1 bottle red wine
2 cups water

Heat the oil in a very large casserole dish, brown the lamb shanks in small batches and transfer them to a plate.

Pull the leaves off the thyme stalks and discard the stalks. Finely chop the onions, garlic, rosemary and thyme (a food processor is easiest). Fry them in the oily pan until the onion is soft.

Add the pumpkin, figs, allspice, cinnamon, honey, wine and water. Stir well, bring to the boil, and put the lamb back in. Turn down the heat and simmer for 1½ hours.

When possible, make this dish the day before serving and place it in the fridge overnight. The next day the flavours will not only be enhanced but the fat will have risen to the top. Skim this off before reheating and serving.

Chapter Nineteen

'It's my baby sister!' Callie is sitting cross-legged on the bed in her favourite brushed-flannel pyjamas and a nurse is adjusting the bag on her IV stand, when Steffi walks in.

'Steffi, this is Rita,' she introduces her to the nurse. 'She is doing an amazing job of looking after me. I swear she's the only person around here who I want giving me shots.'

A knock on the open door and a young man walks in with equipment. Steffi gives Callie a questioning look as Callie holds out her arm.

'They come in every hour to take my vitals.'

'Doesn't that drive you mad?'

'A little.' Callie gives the male nurse a sly smile. 'That's why I requested they only send in men who are young and hot.'

Another knock and a woman walks in with a tray and places it on the table. 'Chicken soup and meatloaf, right?' she asks with a bright smile.

'Thanks, Rose,' Callie says, while Steffi takes the steel dome off the plate to inspect the food.

'Do you know everyone's name in here?'

'Only the people who come in this room.'

'You're amazing. And you look amazing. From what Mom said I thought you'd be on death's doorstep.'

Callie starts to laugh. 'If you weren't my sister you'd never get away with saying that.'

'If I weren't your sister I'd never have dared say it.' Steffi grins. 'You can't seriously eat this stuff, can you?' She gestures to the greying meat, cold cooked carrots and stodgy mashed potato.

'The chicken soup is pretty good.'

'I guess it's amazing that you want to eat, right? You haven't eaten anything for days.'

Callie smiles. 'I am feeling better, but now I realize it's the drugs. I asked them not to wake me up last night for the pills, just to let me sleep, and I felt horrible this morning.'

'Sick?'

'Nauseous, and in a tremendous amount of pain. They said it can take a while to figure out the pain management and get it right.'

'But you're good now?'

'Better.'

'So what is it? Do they have any idea yet?'

Callie shrugs. 'More tests today, waiting for the cultures to form on the tests they did the other day. Someone on the team suggested it might be migraine . . .'

'Lila *said* it was migraine!'

'I know, so now they're bringing in a neurologist.' She sighs, pulling the food closer to her.

'You can't eat that.' Steffi pushes the tray away and reaches into her bag, bringing out a Thermos flask and some Tupperware containers.

'You cooked for me?' Callie is delighted.

'Of course. I don't want you eating this crappy hospital food and, more to the point, I don't want you eating meat. We've spoken about this before, and now you're sick again, you cannot eat this stuff any more, okay?'

Five years ago, when Callie was first diagnosed, Steffi went rushing over with stacks of books and Internet research, all suggesting that animal products were the primary cause of common diseases in the West, especially heart disease and cancer.

She implored Callie to give up meat and dairy, would sit next to her chair in the chemo ward and read her horrible statistics, and Callie always said she would try.

But then Steffi would walk into her kitchen and find Callie eating a BLT for lunch, or scrambled eggs for dinner, and she knew she wasn't trying that hard.

It was the most frustrating thing in the world. Steffi was certain that cutting animal products out of her diet would make a difference. If Steffi were diagnosed with cancer, she knows she would do anything and everything that had been shown to help beat the disease, particularly if it were as easy as changing her diet.

Cancer loves sugar, she discovered. She highlighted passages in books, emailed reports, but Callie was never without her peanut M&Ms and her Butterfingers.

'I'm not giving up the sugar,' she would say with a sigh as Steffi moaned. 'I'm having chemo, for God's sake. You can't take away the one thing in life I look forward to.'

Steffi unscrews the lid of the Thermos flask and Callie dips her head forward and smells.

'Mushroom, lentil and barley soup.'

'Mmm. What else?'

'Spinach quiche.'

'No eggs or milk?'

'Of course not. But . . . I made this the other day and I figure a tiny bit of dairy won't kill you, so I brought one for you – orange almond cake.'

'Yum! How come this one is dairy?'

'I have a job. Kinda, sorta. Part-time cooking for a local store. The owner's not so interested in the vegan stuff, though, so I'm cooking just about everything for them.'

'Oh my God!' Callie shrieks. 'I am so selfish. I haven't even asked about you! The house! The giant pony dog! Your new life! Tell me everything.'

Steffi grins. 'Callie, I am so happy it's almost ridiculous.'

If you had told Steffi, just a few months ago, that she would be waking up before six every morning, and not only that but she would be happy about it, she would have laughed in your face.

But that was in New York, when she was out every night, drinking with the rest of the gang from Joni's, or with the band and their cronies, ending up at clubs, eventually crashing in the early hours.

She felt herself longing for a quieter life, but didn't im-agine she would fall in love with it quite as much as she has.

Susie instant-messaged her last night on her way out to a gig, to tell her that Rob has a new, twenty-two-year-old girlfriend. Steffi felt absolutely nothing, just happiness that he had moved on so quickly, and also relief that at the time Susie popped up on her computer screen, made-up, dressed up, great new high-heeled black boots she'd bought down-town, Steffi was curled up on the sofa with Fingal's head on her lap, in a long white nightdress and with the fire slowly burning itself out.

She'd never owned a nightdress in her life. Steffi was the kind of girl who always slept in her boyfriend's T-shirts and boxer shorts, but she went to check out the village on the first day, and she walked into one of the little mom-and-pop stores where they had a stack of old-fashioned Victorian nightdresses piled on a shelf.

'Those are the best things in the world,' the owner exclaimed. 'I haven't slept in anything else for years and they get softer and softer with every wash.'

'I'm not really a nightdress kind of girl.' Steffi smiled.

'You will be,' the woman said. 'Are you the gal who's living in Mason's place?'

Steffi's eyes widened. 'Yes! How on earth did you know?'

'I've lived here my entire life. There's very little that goes on around here I don't know about. I heard there was a pretty young thing who was a chef, and I took a chance. Tell you what. Why don't you take a nightdress home, sleep in it, and if you don't like it I'll give you your money back?'

'I couldn't do that.'

'I insist. I promise you, it will change your life. I'm Mary, by the way.'

'Steffi.'

'I know. How about I pour you a cup of coffee and you can tell me all about yourself?'

By the time Steffi left, with the nightdress, a bottle of Soft Scrub, a pack of two sponges and a bag of oranges, she also had a list.

Mary had written down the numbers for Stanley the handyman, Mrs Rothbottom who ran the church charity sale, Mick the caretaker, and the Van Peterson family, who lived in the big house on West Street and might be interested in having someone cook for them.

'You may as well ask,' Mary said. 'She's in here every day begging me to start selling healthy ready-made meals because the big supermarket doesn't have much in the way of organic prepared food, but I'm worried there isn't enough of a market for it. Anyway,' she sighed, 'I bet if you telephoned her and said you would be interested in cooking for her, she'd jump at the chance. Three young children, a huge house and a husband who's never there. Poor girl could use a friend as well. Amy is her name. You tell her I passed on her number.'

'That would be great,' Steffi said. 'And you know, I could always make some healthy food for you and we could see if it sells. Maybe we could start with some delicious home-made vegetable and barley soups . . . maybe some maple and pumpkin muffins?'

'What if they don't sell?'

'You wouldn't have to buy them. I'd make them and you would just have to make space for them. I could do plates of muffins that you could just put there, next to the coffee. And the soup could go in canisters on that table over there where you have the leaflets. You wouldn't have to pay for the food, maybe just take a percentage of what sells.'

'Oh I don't need a percentage. I tell you what. You take the nightdress and I'll take the soup and muffins, and we'll both see if it works out. How does that sound?'

'Perfect.' Callie grinned, and they shook hands.

'Oh, and by the way, watch out for Mick the caretaker. He's a bit of a ladies' man, that one.' Mary raised an eyebrow. 'Don't let him charm you, because he's broken a few hearts in his time.'

'Don't you worry,' Steffi said with a laugh. 'I'm taking a break from men for a very long time.'

That night, when Steffi pulled on the nightdress, she cracked up looking at herself in the mirror. Where was the hip downtown chick who went clubbing? She looked like she'd stepped out of the early nineteenth century, but she felt cosy, and feminine, and she immediately understood what Mary had been talking about.

Susie had gasped as Steffi walked the computer round the house, showing her each room on the video cam.

'It's amazing!' she breathed in envy. 'But don't you miss New York a little bit?'

'I really don't,' Steffi says again, to Callie this time, as Callie finishes every drop of the soup, then eagerly pulls the orange and almond cake towards her.

'Mom always said you were a country girl at heart,' Callie says. 'God, this is so good. Thank you, Steff.'

'You're welcome, and yes, I guess Mom was right. There's something about the peace there. About waking up in this blanket of darkness where you can't see anything at all, and it's so quiet and so unbelievably peaceful.'

'So what do you actually do all day?' Callie thinks of her busy life, getting up with Eliza and Jack, feeding them, getting them on the bus, answering emails, editing photographs, going through paperwork, running to a shoot, grocery shopping, picking up the kids, driving them to activities, making dinner, going through the bedtime routine.

Oh God. The kids. She has to force herself to stop thinking about them, because although they are coming in every night to visit her, bringing in their dinner and eating it with her, curling up next to her on the bed and watching a movie with her, she is missing them desperately.

She is missing her life. Her routine. Her husband. She knows she cannot think about it too much, because she is powerless over it, and thinking about it will make her upset, and there is no point because until they know what is wrong with her they cannot send her home.

This morning was a shock. She had been feeling so much better yesterday that she started to consider that she might be home by the end of the week. It became more than just a thought; it swiftly became a fantasy, and then Callie's reality. So much so that she informed the nurse, Rita, that she would be home by Friday; she missed Rita's sceptical glance.

It hadn't occurred to her at that stage that she wasn't actually getting better, that it was just the copious and constant amount of the strongest drugs available to man that was helping her feel better.

Until this morning, when the pain rushed upon her like a vice, making her throw up twice, causing her to look longingly at the window, high on the thirteenth floor, and seriously consider smashing it and leaping out. Anything, *anything*, would be better than this pain.

She actually moaned. Continuously. And then she cried, because she didn't know what else to do, and she kept crying, not making any noise, just tears running down her face, until the drugs started to take effect and the vice started to ease.

And now, hours later, she feels almost normal. The pain is still there, but it's a dull throb, bearable, almost as routine to her now as breathing.

'What do I *do* all day?' Steffi grins. 'Are you kidding? Well, first, I let Fingal out. Apparently you're totally not supposed to let deerhounds out without a leash, but Mason says squirrels have been known to lick his paws and he hasn't done anything.'

'Lick his paws? Really? Do squirrels lick?'

'I don't know, but you know what I mean. So I let him out and build a fire –'

'You build a fire? Yourself?'

'I do! I learned from a video on YouTube!' She chuckles in delight.

'Okay. I'm impressed. Then what?'

'Then I make breakfast – steel-cut oats and fruit for me, and I made some great bread the other day so I've been eating toast too – and then I feed Fingal; later, when it starts to get light, I go out and talk to the chickens.'

'You talk to the chickens? Oh God. Reece was right. You are going mad living in the country.'

Steffi giggles. 'I love them. I find them completely fascinating. I take my coffee out there and talk to them.'

'Do they, by any chance, say anything back?'

'Okay, now you're the one going mad. I'm living in the country, not turning into Sybil, for God's sake.'

'Kidding, okay?'

'Okay. So we sit for a while and I just watch them. They make me laugh. And then I have to feed the goats or they'll be jealous . . .'

'Didn't you say something about a caretaker? I thought there was a caretaker who feeds the animals.'

'There is, kind of, but I think he's part-time. Mick. I think that's part of the problem – Mick never seems to show up, which is why Mason wanted someone living there full-time to pick up the slack.'

'What's the matter with Mick?'

'I don't know. Mason said he tended to be unreliable.'

'Okay,' Callie says, nudging her. 'So you've covered about half an hour. What do you do for the rest of the day?'

'I start cooking. There's this great woman, Mary, who owns the general store, and she's letting me sell some food there, so I make up big batches of soup and muffins and I drop those off to her in the morning. Then I usually hang out with her for a bit. I'm getting to know the town and the people, and I'm discovering the best perch is at Mary's counter, so I spend a couple of hours there, reading the *New York Times*.'

'You actually read it?'

'Cover to cover. I know! Can you believe it? I don't think I've ever read the whole paper in my entire life, and now I read it every day. Of course the irony is I now know every-thing about the arts scene in New York, and who's doing what, and where, and I'm not there any more.'

'It's not exactly far. You could drive in and do stuff.'

Steffi pauses, for she has thought exactly the same thing. Susie keeps telling her to come in, since she is only an hour away . . . and yet it feels as if she is a lifetime away, and for the time being she needs to stay out of the city.

Steffi has spent her life running. She isn't sure what from, or perhaps what to, but she has spent her life going from one relationship to the next, from one job to the next, from one group of friends to the next. Everything has been a drama, a whirlwind, a flurry of activity, and suddenly, out here, she has found something she never realized she was looking for: peace.

And the thought of jumping on a train, of elbowing through Grand Central, of weaving through the streets of New York and pushing her way into a crowded bar, or club, or restaurant, fills her with anxiety.

'I'm not ready to go back, you know?' she says to Callie. 'Of course I'll start going in, but I feel like this is my new life and I want to just embrace it for now. I'm loving it so much, I want to immerse myself in it totally. Does that make any sense?'

Tears fill Callie's eyes. 'Okay,' she says. 'I know I shouldn't say this because you've only just moved in, and it's all so new, and knowing you, you could turn around in three weeks and say you hate the quiet and you miss the buzz of the city and you could move back there ri –'

'I'm not going to,' Steffi interrupts.

'That's my point. I know. I think you've finally found where you belong.'

'That's it!' Steffi says. 'You've put your finger on it. It feels, oh God, I can't believe I'm going to say something as clichéd as this, but it feels like I've come home.'

'Well it's hardly surprising,' Callie says, pushing the tray away and leaning back on the bed as the nurse comes in. 'You're a vegan chef with an inner earthy crunch goddess who's been held down by this rock chick you always thought you were supposed to be.'

'So I'm not really a rock chick? I'm an earthy crunch goddess?'

'Yeah. Just make sure I don't see you in any of Mom's floor-length mirrored skirts.'

'Don't worry.' Steffi grins. 'There's only so far I'm prepared to go.'

Cauliflower Soup with Parmigiano Reggiano and Truffle Oil

2½ slices chopped applewood-smoked bacon rashers
1 cup chopped onion
¾ cup chopped celery
2 garlic cloves, chopped
6 cups cauliflower florets
3½ cups chicken stock
3 tablespoons grated Parmesan cheese, plus more to garnish
½ cup whipping cream
white or black truffle oil for drizzling

Sauté the bacon in a heavy pan until golden brown. Add the onion, celery and garlic. Cover and cook until soft, stirring occasionally, for around 7 minutes. Add the cauliflower, stock and cheese. Bring to the boil, reduce the heat, cover and simmer until the cauliflower is tender – about 20 minutes.

Purée the soup and add the cream. Return to the heat and bring the soup to a simmer. Season. Garnish with the cheese shavings and drizzle with the truffle oil.

Chapter Twenty

'Mommy!' Eliza and Jack run in and crawl on the bed, both of them fighting to get to their mother first, while Honor gives her daughter a kiss then settles herself in the armchair in the corner of the hospital room.

'Babies!' Callie croons, stroking their heads and kissing them.

'I have lots to show you,' Eliza says, first to crawl off the bed and go to her backpack on the floor by the door. 'I did this project on kangaroos, and Mrs Brumberger said I could bring it home to show you even though no one else was allowed to bring theirs home, but because you're in the hospital and you can't come in to our presentation I brought it to you. I have to bring it back to school tomorrow so it can go up on the wall with everyone else's, okay?'

'Okay,' Callie says, as Jack cuddles into her, one arm flung across her chest, a beatific smile on his face as he raises his head from time to time to gaze at his mother with infinite love in his eyes.

He raises his hand and strokes her cheek then leans in and kisses her before resting his head again on her shoulder, happy to just lie there, close to his mother.

'He would crawl back inside, if he could,' had always been their joke, her and Reece, for never had they known a boy love his mother quite as much as Jack loves Callie.

This is the highlight of her day, when her children run

in, filled with energy, chattering away to the nurses, asking lots of questions. Yesterday they were sad, but today they are bubbling, climbing all over her, covering her with kisses and knocking into the IV stand every few seconds. She doesn't mind. She is tired, happy to just lie and be with them, her heart bursting with love.

An hour later they are squabbling, as they so often do during 'the witching hour'. Honor shoots a worried glance towards Callie, who suddenly looks ill and worn-out, and announces it is time to go.

And then the tears start.

'Mommy!' They both cling to Callie, refusing to be pulled off the bed, while Honor tries to explain that Mommy is sick and it's time to take her medicine.

'I don't want to leave,' Jack cries, his little body heaving as Honor tries to lift him.

'Where's Reece?' Callie implores her mother. 'I thought Reece was bringing the kids tonight.'

'He got stuck at work,' Honor says, feeling guilty that she even has to tell Callie that. 'He said he's coming straight to the hospital but he wouldn't be here until around eight.'

Callie says nothing, but her mouth is set in a straight line. She doesn't have the energy for this, but what choice does she have?

Callie has told the story of her marriage so many times, of how independent she is, how much she loves her space, how their time apart keeps the romance alive, gives her and Reece something to look forward to. And yet . . . when she is not around, like now, *someone* needs to be.

When Reece shows up at the hospital, at nine o'clock,

Callie wakes up slowly, kisses him and cuddles with him. She drifts up through the layers from her deep sleep, the time with the children having exhausted her, and after a few minutes, when she is fully awake and present, she looks at Reece.

'We need to talk.'

'I know, I know.' He runs his fingers through his hair as he sighs. 'I'm late. I'm sorry. The traffic was terr —'

'Enough.' She holds up a hand. Her voice isn't loud, but it is determined. 'I don't want to hear excuses. You said you would bring the children here at six o'clock, and you weren't here, and that isn't good enough.'

'I'm sorry, Callie, but when work gets —'

'Reece? I don't give a fuck what happens with work.' She is so angry, she spits the words. 'I care about what happens to my children, and what they are feeling, and how they are coping with their mother not being there *at all*. Do you understand? This isn't the same as when I had cancer and came in for chemotherapy while they were in school, and okay, was tired a lot of the time, and in bed a lot of the time, but I was *home*. Nothing in their lives changed. They didn't *need* you.

'Reece, they need you now. And I will not let you use work as an excuse. This is more important than work will ever be. And if I am not around, you will not bury yourself in work because it is easier to be at work than to deal with your children.'

Reece has turned white. 'What do you mean, if you're not around?' he says, after a long pause.

'If I die,' she says simply. With no emotion.

'Do you . . . have the results come back? Is there something you know?' He can barely speak; his voice is a strained whisper.

'No, there are no results back that tell us anything. And I have no idea what's going to happen, but I am scared. Actually, no. I am terrified. And what terrifies me the most is what will happen to the children if you continue living the life I have always allowed you to live, and you do not step up to the plate.

'Do you hear me, Reece? If I die, I cannot let the children fall through the cracks. I won't allow it. You are their father and you have to start *being* their father. That means if you say you'll be here at six o'clock, you will be here at six o'clock. Fuck work. Fuck the traffic. Right now, until they adjust, and until we know what is wrong with me, I don't want you going to work. You can work from home. And once we know what's wrong, and how long I'll be in for, you will still be home every night at six o'clock, and you will be there to give them breakfast in the morning.

'Not Jenn,' she continues, on a roll. 'Not a babysitter. Not my mom, or my sister, or anyone else. And you have to step up now, Reece. Right now. No more excuses, no more travelling. I am asking you to be their father, and to be present in their lives. I am asking you to put them on the school bus every morning, and sit at the table with them for dinner every night. It has to start now, Reece.' Callie is crying. Sobbing. Her words are barely decipherable through her sobs, but Reece hears, and he is frightened.

'Jesus, Callie. Stop. You're talking as if you're going to die. Will you just *stop*?'

'No, Reece. I hope I'm not going to die. God knows I'm nowhere near ready to die, but do I feel as if I'm going to die? Yes. A lot of the time I do. And I cannot leave my children if I don't think that you are going to be there for them, and I need to see it now.

'Hopefully I will be fine but, whatever happens, while I am not around, you need to be, and you need to promise me.' She puts her hands on either side of Reece's face and brings him inches from her own. 'Do you understand, Reece? I love you so much. I have never loved a man like I love you, and I know you are capable of it. I know you can do it, and you have to promise me.'

There are tears running down Reece's face now. She pulls him down, his head on her chest, and they cry together.

'It's going to be fine,' she whispers, after a while. 'I'm just looking at the worst-case scenario, okay? I'm playing devil's advocate, but right now, while I'm in hospital, you need to be there. My mom is there, which is great, but they need you.'

'Okay,' he says, into her chest. 'Okay.'

'Okay what?'

'Okay, I'll do it.' He lifts his head up, his eyes red and swollen.

'You have to promise.'

'Okay, I promise.'

'What do you promise? You have to actually say it.'

'What do you want me to say?'

'I promise to put the children on the bus every morning, and to be home for dinner at six o'clock every night.'

'I promise to put the children on the bus and to be home for dinner at six o'clock.'

'Every night.'

'What?'

'Say it again, on the bus *every day*, and home for dinner *every night*.'

And he does, his voice hoarse and cracking.

'You can do this, honey,' she whispers. 'I think I'll be home by the weekend at the latest, so it's just a few days, but even if it takes a bit longer, you can do this. You are the best dad in the world. You're fun, and loving, and kind, and patient. They love being with you more than anything. They just need you to be around a little more.'

'Callie?' he whispers back, after a long silence. 'Do you really think you're going to die?'

'Yes,' she says. 'But not right now. I'd like to think I have another fifty years or so.' She smiles and he raises his head and kisses her.

*

Reece pours himself some coffee and pokes his head round the door of the TV room. Eliza and Jack are both sitting quietly on the sofa, watching some Disney Channel show. They have eaten cereal and Dad's speciality: scrambled eggs, cheese and ketchup. The plates are in the dishwasher, Elizabeth has been fed and let out, and all is quiet.

What on earth is Callie complaining about, he wonders, thinking of all the times he phones at breakfast time and there is screaming in the background, the children are fighting and Callie snaps that she'll have to speak to him once they're on the bus.

This is easy.

He sits at the kitchen table and flicks idly through the local paper, then glances up at the microwave: 7.47.

Oh SHIT. Doesn't the bus come at seven-fifty?

'Eliza?' He runs into the TV room. 'What time does the bus come again?'

She shrugs, eyes glued to the screen.

'Seven-fifty,' Jack says, and Reece runs over and turns the TV off.

'Three minutes, guys.' His panic is becoming evident. 'Shoes and coats on.'

'But I haven't brushed my teeth,' Jack says.

'Why not? I thought you brushed your teeth when you woke up?'

'He never brushes his teeth,' Eliza says. 'He always tells Mom he has but he hasn't.'

'Quick!' Reece's anxiety is rising. 'Get your shoes on. Don't worry about your teeth. We'll do double-brushing later, okay?'

'No!' Jack says in horror. 'I *have* to brush my teeth.'

'Jack, please.' Reece is exasperated. 'We'll just do it later.'

'No!' Jack starts to wail.

'Oh God. Okay. Fine. Brush your teeth. But quickly.'

Please be late, he thinks. Please, bus driver, whoever you are, be held up.

He flings the coats on and opens the front door.

'Eliza? Where are you going?'

'To get my homework.'

'Where is it?'

'I don't know.'

'Okay. You look in the bedroom, I'll look in the kitchen.'

Ten seconds later he finds the homework in the kitchen. 'Eliza?' he yells up the stairs.

Nothing.

'Eliza? I have your homework. Let's go!'

Nothing.

Reece starts up the stairs. 'Eliza?' He is now yelling at full volume.

'Coming!' she shouts back.

They race out of the door, to see the bus disappearing down the street.

'Shit,' he mutters. Now he'll have to drive them, and it will take an extra twenty minutes, and he still has to make that conference call in twenty minutes. Oh God.

'In my car,' he orders, and they both cheer, for being driven in by a parent is their most favourite thing of all.

'Mommy always puts my homework in my backpack at night,' Eliza mutters.

'Well, good for Mommy.' Reece bites his tongue. 'But Mommy isn't here and I'm doing my best.'

'Daddy?' she says suddenly. 'If Mommy dies and you die, will we be orphans?'

Jack starts to cry.

'Oh Eliza!' Reece shakes his head, thinking: why ask that now? 'Don't worry, Jack, no one's going to die. And Eliza, first, Mommy isn't going to die, and I'm not going to die either, so there's no point even talking about it.' He pauses, unsure of whether he should be saying this, knowing that he should be more honest, but now, on the way to school, is not the time to have this conversation.

'But if you both did, then we'd be orphans?'

Reece sighs. 'Technically, but that's never going to happen, okay? It's just not going to happen.'

'It happened to the children in *Lemony Snicket*,' Eliza says knowingly, looking out of the window, while Jack's sobs continue to escalate.

'Jack, honey, there's nothing to cry about. Mommy is sick, and they're going to give her medicine and then she's going to get better. Remember when you had your tonsils out?'

In the back seat, Jack nods.

'And it really, really hurt for a lot of days, but you kept taking your medicine and then you got completely better?'

Jack nods again, the sobs subsiding.

'That's what it's like with Mommy. It's really hurting right now, but when she takes her medicine it stops hurting, and soon it's going to get better.'

'I thought it was cancer,' Eliza says suddenly.

'No, sweetie. It isn't cancer.'

'Julia says her mom told her that Mommy's cancer is back.'

'Julia is wrong.' Reece wonders if he ought to speak to the school. 'Mommy doesn't have cancer any more. This is something else.'

'What is it, then?'

'I'll find out from the doctor.' For now, he has run out of answers, and unlike when Callie is truly exasperated and cannot answer any more of their questions, he cannot simply direct them to 'ask your father'.

They pull up outside the school and as they unbuckle Eliza says, 'What's for snack, Daddy?'

'*Snack?*' Reece's heart sinks. 'What snack?'

'Snack! You have to pack us a snack every day. In a brown bag. With our name on it and a big heart, like Mommy does.'

Oh shit. Why couldn't someone have told him? Honor, who had clearly been up all night, judging from the empty mugs in the kitchen sink, has been snoring away in the damned guest room this morning and he's supposed to figure this all out by himself.

'I'll bring the snack back,' he says slowly. 'I'm sorry, honey. I didn't know.'

'Okay. So can I have the pink wafer cookies, please?'

'Sure. Are they in the pantry?'

'No. You have to buy them. And some marshmallows.'

Jack's face lights up. 'Yeah! Marshmallows.'

'Marshmallows for snack? Mommy gives you marshmallows for snack? Are you sure?'

'Every day,' Eliza says solemnly. 'All the kids get marshmallows for snack. Bring them back, okay?'

'Okay, sweetie.' Reece sighs.

'And Dad?' Jack kisses him goodbye. 'Did you put the note about my play date with Jasper in my folder?'

'What play date with Jasper?'

'I'm going to Jasper's house after school today and his mom is picking us up and you have to send in a note.'

'Can I just email?' Reece says, not really thinking Jack will know the answer, but this all suddenly seems very complicated.

'Yes,' says Jack confidently. 'You can email. I love you, Dad.'

'I love you too, buddy,' Reece says, and with an unexpected surge of relief, and love, he watches his children bundle into school.

Today has been surprisingly peaceful. The house is quiet, Reece was only a few minutes late for the conference call, and he has been able to successfully manage his work from home.

Honor has gone to the hospital to sit with Callie, but not before making him a grilled tuna melt for lunch. He could kind of get used to this.

At three-twenty he stands up and stretches, then grabs his coat to go and meet the bus.

'Reece!' April, their neighbour from up the street, presses the switch to open the window of her Porsche Cayenne. 'I didn't expect to see you here. How's Callie?'

'She's good,' he says, for what else do you say?

'Really? Honor seems to be very worried. Do they know what it is yet?'

Wow. How much do they know? He had forgotten how much women talk. 'Not yet,' he says. 'But the next round of results should be in tomorrow and I hope they'll tell us something.'

'It's so awful,' April says. 'Especially after the . . . well, a few years ago. But I hear it's not cancer, which must be a huge relief, right?'

'Huge,' Reece agrees.

'So, Jack has tae kwon do tomorrow with Will. Callie and I carpool but I'm really happy to take them.'

'Oh.' Reece has no idea what the children do after school. He makes a mental note to actually read the kids' schedule that is stuck to the front of the fridge. 'Thank you. That would be great.'

'He can stay for dinner too, if he wants. Nothing fancy. Pizza.' She shrugs in resignation.

'I . . . Thank you. Another time would be great, but I'm taking the kids to have dinner with their mom, in the hospital. It's kind of a nightly thing.'

'Of course. I totally understand. That's so nice. Listen, do you need anything? Anything at all? Maybe food? I cook every day for my family and it would be no problem to drop some food in . . .' She looks up at him expectantly.

Reece stands and looks at her, not sure what she is talking about, and then he remembers, from last time, that this is what people do when you are sick: they cook for you. But how do you say yes? Last time, when Callie was having chemo, she was still seeing everyone, she was dealing with everything. He never had to field offers of food, and he'd feel oddly helpless and vulnerable if he said yes, even though it might be really nice to have her cook for him.

Honor had been doing the cooking, but now she is tending to spend her days in the hospital with Callie and picking up food from the market to bring in for the kids, because she says she doesn't have the time.

Reece has been getting home so late, up until today, that he usually grabs a slice of pizza on the way home, or a bowl of soup at the diner next to his office. Often, if Lila has been to the house to watch the kids, she will have brought something delicious, but to have a neighbour he barely knows cook for him? That's just weird. Nice, but weird.

'That's so kind of you,' he says. 'But my mother-in-law is staying with us, so it's really not necessary.'

The next morning, when he leaves to take the children to the bus, he finds two aluminium trays, one lasagne, one chicken and spinach, on his doorstep, still warm. No note.

Grateful, he takes them inside, and puts them in the fridge.

Chicken and Spinach

2 packets frozen chopped spinach, defrosted and liquid
  squeezed out
8 chicken breasts, boneless and skinless
seasoning
1 medium jar mayonnaise
1 medium carton Greek yoghurt
1 small carton single cream
1 tablespoon curry powder
¾ cup breadcrumbs

Preheat the oven to 350°F.

Cover the base of a large rectangular dish with the spinach. Season. Place the chicken breasts on top of the spinach and add seasoning.

Mix together the mayonnaise, yoghurt and single cream; add more or less curry powder, according to taste. Spread the mixture liberally on top of the chicken breasts and spinach until all is covered.

Sprinkle the top with breadcrumbs and cook for 45 minutes.

Chapter Twenty-One

Mason thought he had seen enough British films, read enough books by British authors, knew enough about the culture to know what to expect, but he is finding it is almost entirely different to his expectations.

Not that he expected all Londoners to be charming chimney sweeps with bad cockney accents *à la* Dick Van Dyke, but he hadn't expected it to be quite the melting pot it is, nor had he expected people to be quite so brusque – good Lord, there were times when he felt as though he was still in New York.

There are things he is finding he *loves*. He is fascinated by the design, the architecture, the sophistication. He walks the streets, just as he does in New York, but in London he looks up every few feet, amazed at the sheer brilliance of the architecture.

And the food! What an unexpected pleasure to find that the food in London equals, and often, in fact, surpasses, that in New York. He wanders round the markets, delighting at the fresh produce; it is far smaller than anything he is used to seeing in New York, but the taste! The flavour! Never has he enjoyed biting into a juicy tomato as he has here.

He delights in the black cabs, quizzing chatty cab drivers as they weave through the streets in a way that made his heart almost stop the first week, but which he now trusts.

He had always thought that New York was the most

vibrant city in the world, and perhaps it is the energy of London that has so surprised him.

It is palpable on the streets, and in his business. The marketing departments are run by bright young things who love what they do; the editors are exciting and excited; the publishing house feels more alive than anything he is used to.

And yet he wakes up every morning, conflicted.

This morning he woke up at six, showered – and yes, it is entirely true what they say about English showers being hopeless – and dressed, then crept past Olivia's bedroom – her door was closed, meaning she was asleep, and doubtless would be for the next three or four hours – and past the vast arch into the living room towards the kitchen.

Sienna and Gray were both sitting on the sofa, mesmerized by a television show, not seeing Mason, nor hearing when he tried to say good morning.

He was about to ask if anyone wanted pancakes when a door opened and quick, heavy footsteps came down the corridor.

'Oh! Mr Gregory!' Nanny Bea stopped, startled. 'I am so sorry. I didn't realize the children were watching television. Come along, children, you know the rules. No television in the mornings. I do apologize,' she said, turning to him. 'It won't happen again.'

Mason laughed, awkwardly. 'Don't worry about it, Nanny Bea. And please, you can't call me Mr Gregory. It makes me feel so old. It's Mason. Please.' He'd quite like to call her Bea, or her full name, Beatrice, because it feels so silly, always prefacing her name with 'Nanny', but she made it clear from the outset that she should always be called Nanny Bea by the children, and by the adults.

'Of course, Mr Gregory. I mean . . . Mason.' And a slight blush rose on her cheeks.

'Don't worry so much,' Mason said gently. 'It's fine if the children watch some TV. God knows, they watch it all the time at home.'

'But Mrs Gregory made it quite clear.'

'Mrs Gregory makes a lot of things quite clear,' Mason said with a sigh. 'But if you won't tell, I won't tell.'

For a moment, fear left the nanny's eyes. 'Really?'

'Really, and it's not like she's going to know. She doesn't emerge from her crypt until at least nine, right?'

Nanny Bea's eyes widened in shock and she tried, and failed, to suppress a smile. 'You're a very good father,' she said. 'Relaxed. It's good for the children.'

'Thank you, Nanny Bea, and you'd feel even better if you relaxed a bit more around Olivia. I know, I know – it's hard. I'll talk to Olivia. How's that?'

'Please don't tell her I said anything . . .'

'Absolutely not. She just seems to have these ridiculous expectations since we moved here. I won't get you in trouble. Promise. Now, how about coming into the kitchen with me and I'll teach you how to make proper American pancakes?'

'Would you?' Nanny Bea's face lit up. 'Count me in.'

Mason thought about it all morning, how Olivia seemed to be taking more and more of a back seat with the children – if, my God, that were even possible – since they moved to London, but at the same time had become frighteningly controlling.

She finally had what she had been waiting for all these years: a proper English nanny. She had grown up with one, as she never tired of telling anyone, and when the children were still babies she had attempted to bring one over, but they had never worked out.

Now, with Nanny Bea, she had a uniformed, vocational English nanny, and seemed to think that her job as a mother was to instruct Nanny Bea on how to do all the things that Nanny Bea had clearly been doing for years, and to micro-manage her children's lives, even though she didn't seem to be around to witness the results.

All of a sudden, Olivia insisted the children should watch only twenty minutes of television a day, and only once they had been bathed. They were not allowed white flour, refined sugar or anything processed. However, this did not include the hot dogs that entirely filled the freezer as a safe fall-back for when the children failed to eat their gourmet dinner, which Olivia now called 'high tea', as they almost always did.

They were to spend at least half an hour a day practising their reading, and Nanny Bea was to take them out to the park, or a museum, for at least one hour a day.

The Xbox and Wii and PlayStations – all the tools that Olivia had relied upon as alternative babysitters until the actual babysitters showed up – were banished now that she had a full-time, live-in nanny, and they were only allowed to use the computer if it was for educational purposes.

Sienna and Gray had always been relatively ignored by Olivia, and this new obsession with what they were doing all the time seemed out of character. And where was she, anyway?

She seemed to have found a crowd of girls almost immediately. A handful of wealthy ex-pats from New York and some of the London society girls. They were lunching every day and, as she was jumping on committees for various charities, she had picked up exactly where she left off, but now there was theatre as well.

She was never home, and Mason's presence at her side seemed to be required even less than it had been in New York.

He was using the opportunity to get to know London. After he sat with the children during their evening meal, then read them a story, he waited until they were asleep and then he went out, leaving Nanny Bea in charge.

He would take the tube to different neighbourhoods and wander around, getting a feel for the place. When he found a restaurant he liked the look of, he would have dinner by himself, with a couple of glasses of wine, and listen to the conversations at the surrounding tables. The insight he was getting into the human condition was fascinating and he wondered why he had never thought of doing this before.

The only place he had ever been truly comfortable eating alone before now was Joni's. Ah, Joni's. How he missed it. For however fascinating the neighbourhoods here were, however much he was enjoying being an innocent abroad, he missed the feeling of walking in somewhere and feeling at home.

He missed catching sight of Steffi, who, he was somewhat startled to realize, he considered a friend long before there was talk of her living in his house; he missed seeing her long hair scraped back off her face as she dashed around the kitchen making sure everything was fine.

He missed the way she would look through the hatch to check on the tables and see him there, in the corner, a delighted smile flashing onto her face as she waved to him. And he missed how she always came and sat with him at the end of a busy lunchtime, when the restaurant was almost empty, and teased him, made him smile, made him forget about the weight that was his life, if only for a while.

He could do with a friend here, he realized. A big city can be a very lonely place for a man on his own, which was how he felt much of the time.

Which was why he walked the neighbourhoods – walking meant he didn't have to think about being lonely, he could, instead, soak up the atmosphere, learn things, make notes about the areas he loved. He fell in love with Bayswater, with Queensway, and how everything stayed open so late. He had the best chicken he had ever tasted, in a tiny Moroccan restaurant off the beaten track, and sat drinking Turkish coffee, feeling as if he were in Beirut, long into the night.

He adored Westbourne Grove for its chic boutiques and great cafés. He had cappuccino and croissant at Tom's Deli early one morning, before a meeting, and delighted in the people-watching.

He poked around Pimlico, and wished they were living in Barnes.

The only place he didn't love, the only place he felt no desire whatsoever to explore, was Belgravia. His doorstep. The vast stucco sweeps of houses with imposing front doors flanked by perfectly groomed topiary plants. The streams of maids and housekeepers going in and out through the basement. American accents everywhere he turned, for it seemed to be most popular among his countrymen, sent over here for work.

He didn't love it, didn't desire to know more, because it felt soulless.

It didn't occur to him that it wasn't the neighbourhood that was soulless, it was his marriage.

Mason sends his assistant out and closes the office door. Eleven-fifteen. Surely Olivia will be awake now? She will have had her morning delivery of Starbucks, will be ready to talk.

He dials home, listens to the answering machine pick up and puts the phone down, swiftly dialling her mobile, imagining her digging in her bag, then her face falling when she sees it is him.

Sure enough, she answers brusquely. 'Hello?'

'Hi. It's me. How's your day?'

'It's good.' She softens slightly. 'I'm getting ready for a lunch. Scott's in Mayfair. It should be fun.'

'Excellent food,' Mason says. 'You'll like it.'

'You've been?' She sounds irritated.

'For business lunches,' he assures her. 'Don't worry, you haven't missed anything.'

There is a pause. 'I'm kind of busy,' Olivia says eventually. 'Was there something you needed?'

'I just wanted to know how you thought Nanny Bea was doing.'

'I think she's great.' Olivia is on her guard. 'Why? Is there something I should know?'

'God, no! I think she's wonderful and the kids adore her. It's . . . well . . . I notice that she seems to be a little intimidated by all the rules and, frankly, by you. I thought it would be easier if she were a little more relaxed, but, obviously, that's hard with all the rules she has to enforce.'

Another pause. 'Has she said something to you?'

'No!' Insistent. 'Absolutely not. It's something I've become aware of, and I thought I should say something. You know, the kids managed perfectly well without all these rules. I think life would be more fun for everyone if things were a bit less structured.'

'We've had this discussion before,' Olivia snaps. 'You and I have very different ways of parenting. I think Nanny Bea is doing a fine job, and to say she's, what, frightened of me? Well that's just ridiculous.'

'You know what?' Mason feels his temper rising. 'It's not ridiculous. You bark orders at her like she's the staff.'

'Which she is,' Olivia interjects.

'No. She's not. I mean, technically, perhaps, because we employ her, but she isn't "staff", Olivia. We aren't living in a bygone age. She's part of our family and we should treat her as such.'

'How you can even think you know the first thing about how to treat staff is beyond me.' Olivia's voice is icy cold. 'Given you grew up on some fifties ranch with nothing, I find it extraordinary that you would even have this conversation. You have no idea.'

'Maybe not, Olivia. But here's what I do know. These children are growing up with a mother who's too selfish, and too self-absorbed, and too intent on social climbing even to have a conversation with them. You don't care about them, you barely see them, you hand them off to whoever's willing to take them, with thousands of pointless instructions that you think makes you look like a good mother.'

'Oh my God!' Olivia shrieks. 'And you think slapping some pancakes on a grill in the morning makes you a good father? Are you kidding me? How dare you!'

Mason's shoulders collapse. He cannot believe he just said what he said. He cannot believe he had the courage, and it is terrifying, because once the words are out there, words that perhaps should never have been said, how can they be taken back? Where is there to go?

'I'm sorry,' he says, not knowing what else to say. 'I didn't mean . . . I'm sorry.'

There is a long silence.

'I'll be home tonight,' Olivia says quietly. 'We need to talk properly. There's . . . we need to talk.'

Moroccan Chicken with Tomatoes and Saffron Honey Jam

8 pieces of jointed chicken
seasoning
olive oil
1 large onion, roughly chopped
3 crushed garlic cloves
2½ teaspoons ground cinnamon
1½ teaspoons ground ginger
1¾ lb. diced tomatoes (I used canned)
1 cup chicken stock
½ teaspoon saffron threads
5 tablespoons honey
1 teaspoon orange flower water (I order mine online, but you could substitute orange juice)
handful of toasted flaked almonds
small bunch of coriander, roughly chopped

Season the chicken pieces and quickly brown them in a casserole dish. Remove, and cook the onion in the same pan until soft and just colouring. Add the garlic, cinnamon and ginger, and stir for around a minute. Tip in the tomatoes, mix together well, turn the heat down and cook for another 5 minutes or so, stirring from time to time.

Boil the stock and dissolve the saffron in it. Pour over the onions and spices and bring to the boil. Set the chicken pieces on top, together with any juices from the chicken, and spoon the liquid over them. Turn down to a gentle simmer, cover and cook until the chicken is tender – around 30 minutes.

Remove the chicken pieces, set aside, cover and keep warm. Bring the juices to the boil and simmer until well reduced – there should be nothing sloppy about it. Add the honey and continue to cook until it is well-reduced and jam-like. Check the seasoning, add the orange flower water. Put the chicken pieces back and warm through in the sauce.

Serve scattered with the toasted almonds and chopped coriander, with couscous or flatbread on the side.

Chapter Twenty-Two

Steffi cups her hands around her Lemon Zinger tea and digs her feet deeper into her Uggs as the chickens peck around her, then reaches next to her for the cookbooks stacked on the bench.

This morning she is going to meet Amy Van Peterson, and she needs to impress. They had a great phone conversation yesterday, although Amy could hardly be heard with children shouting in the background, but she managed to convey that they liked simple, fresh food, and she was desperate to wean her children off the chicken nuggets and pizza they had been force-fed at their previous school before they moved here.

Steffi sat at the kitchen table last night preparing some sample menus. She wanted it to be delicious, without being too complicated. Good, fresh food. Guacamole, hummus and cut-up vegetables that the children could eat when they got home from school. Soy lime chicken, turkey and lemon meatballs, with wholewheat pasta and brown rice.

As a sweet treat she has made date and coconut balls and figgy oatmeal bars, packaging them up in white take-out boxes with green tissue paper.

She needs two more meals, one of which she will cook today for her mom, Reece and the kids, Lila, Ed and Clay, who are coming up for lunch.

She scours the books, finally slipping small pieces of paper between the pages with the curried parsnip and apple soup, and salmon, watercress and rocket parcels. The market got their fresh fish this morning, so that's perfect. She can substitute tofu for herself. She slips the books under an arm and stands up.

'See you later, girls,' she says, turning as she suddenly hears the gravel crunch.

Pulling into the driveway is an old red Ford truck. Damn. She had forgotten Mick the caretaker left a message saying he would be coming over to see if everything was okay.

'Of course he's coming,' Mary said, when Steffi dropped the food in yesterday and told her she'd had a message. 'He's probably heard there's a cute young lady living there now. I'm surprised it's taken him this long.'

And look at her. Not that flirting with a cute caretaker is something she's the slightest bit interested in, not with her sister in hospital and most of her day taken up with worrying about that, but still . . . She'd rather not be in a nightgown, fleece and Uggs, given the choice.

Steffi walks towards the van, putting on a smile, as a man climbs out with a huge grin.

'I'm Mick,' he says, and Steffi suppresses a giggle. Was Mary kidding? Mick is quite . . . *rotund*, with a long grey beard and twinkly blue eyes. He looks like a lovely man, but a ladies' man? Hardly.

'I'm Steffi,' she says, and Mick shakes her hand firmly.

'I heard there was a gorgeous lady up on the farm,' he says. 'I thought I'd have to come and meet her for myself. And you cook too – I had some cookies the other day that were delicious. Now here's a girl after my own heart, I thought.'

'Thanks,' Steffi says. 'Are you here to feed the animals? Because I just fed the chickens and the goats.'

'Oh I'm just here to have a look around and make sure everything's in working order. Ladies included.' And as he gives her a cheerful wink, Steffi's eyes widen in horrified amusement.

'O-kay.' She steps backwards. 'I'll just let you get on with it.'

'What's that you're drinking?' He leans over and sniffs her cup. 'Lemon Zinger, is it? I wouldn't mind a cup of that. It's a bit nippy out here now and I've been out in the fields for the past hour.'

Mick marches past Steffi and into the kitchen, while Steffi stands there helplessly. Oh God. How is she supposed to get rid of him now?

'I haven't got long,' she says as she places the tea in front of him. 'I have to run into the village and get some groceries. Family coming up for lunch.'

'Husband? Children?'

'No,' she says weakly. 'Mom, brother-in-law, few others.'

'Do you have a husband, then?'

'No.' She sighs. 'And before you ask, no boyfriend either. And –' she leans forward and looks him straight in the eye – 'I'm not in the market.'

'Oh I get it.' Mick nods his head knowingly. 'You've an eye for the ladies. I don't blame you. If I were a woman I'd definitely be a lesbian.'

'I'm not a lesbian,' she says. 'Not that there's anything wrong with that. I'm just single and happy about it.' And I certainly wouldn't be interested in a sixty-something man like you. What on earth was Mary talking about?

Mick sits back and puts up his hands. 'Okay, okay. I'm just teasing. I have a bit of a reputation around here and

I do my best to live up to it. You don't have to worry about me. I'm old enough to be your father.'

Steffi breathes a sigh of relief.

'Not that I wouldn't have chanced my arm were I a few years younger. Don't you get lonely up here on your own? I always think the same thing about Mr Mason, always here on his own. This is a house for a family.'

'Mason was here on his own? I thought he had it rented out before I moved in, and he wasn't ever here.'

'There was someone here this past year, but before that he came most weekends. Sometimes with his children, sweet little things, but that hoity-toity wife of his never came. Doesn't think this village is good enough for her.'

'Really?' Now Steffi's interested. 'I don't really know her at all . . .'

'I'm not one to gossip,' says Mick, who clearly loves to gossip. 'But let's just say she never tried to fit in here. I always felt a bit sorry for him; she seems so negative, and she wasn't exactly polite to the locals. You don't talk down to people if you have class. Now Mary, at the general store? She may not come from Texas oil money, but she has more class than anyone I've ever met.'

Aha, Steffi registers. There's obviously mutual admiration, hence Mary's flattering description of Mick. She smiles.

'Mary seems like a lovely lady.'

'Oh she is. Husband's a drinker, though. Such a shame. Woman like that ought to have a good man to take care of her.'

'Someone like you?' Steffi ventures.

Mick colours then suddenly becomes gruff. 'Well, thanks for the tea. Ought to be getting along.' And off he goes, pulling out of the driveway with a crunch and a squeal.

'So much for my cute-caretaker fantasies.' Steffi sits on the sofa next to Fingal, who sighs with pleasure and raises a lazy paw, placing it on her arm. 'Looks like I'll have to be a lonely old spinster here. You and me. We can grow old together.'

Fingal sighs, as if he understands, then closes his eyes.

'Yeah, okay. So I'm boring you. I'm going out to do some shopping then I'll be back. You watch the house.' She leans down and gives him a kiss, noting, with only a tiny amount of alarm, that she is now having conversations with a dog.

The front door of the Van Peterson house opens and there is no one there. Steffi looks down to see a very small, blond, curly haired person, with chocolate all around its mouth.

'Hello.' She crouches down. 'I'm Steffi. I think I'm here to see your mommy.'

The small person turns around and wanders off, leaving Steffi on the doorstep, not sure what to do.

'Um, hello?' she calls into the hallway, admiring the polished black-wood floor and sisal rugs, albeit with a couple of large dog pee stains in the corner. 'Hello-oo?'

No answer. She steps inside and pushes the door closed, then follows the direction the small child took, down a hallway lined with pictures of a perfect family, and into the type of kitchen that Steffi has always dreamed of having.

Huge, with two islands, sofas at one end and a big fireplace, French doors open along one entire wall onto a lovely stone terrace flanked by a grand old hedge of clipped yew.

'Hello?' she tries again. 'Anyone here?'

Hearing children's voices, she passes through a doorway

in the kitchen and finds two children in the pantry. One of them is on top of a stepladder, passing chocolate from the top shelf down to the little blond boy who answered the door.

'Ah,' says Steffi. 'Um. I'm not sure you should be doing that. I think that's perhaps a little dangerous, standing on the top of that ladder, and I'm quite sure you shouldn't be eating chocolate at ten o'clock in the morning. Is your mom around?'

The little girl at the top of the ladder looks at Steffi. 'I think she's upstairs in the laundry room. Would you like some chocolate? You can go upstairs.'

'Actually, I think I'd be a lot happier if you got down from that ladder. How old are you?'

'Six and a half.'

'And how about you?' She turns to the little person, who holds up two fingers.

'Two? That's very old.'

'Can you help me?' The girl holds out her arms and Steffi swings her down.

'I'm Amelia.' She extends a hand and formally shakes Steffi's. 'Nice to meet you.'

'Goodness, that's impressive,' Steffi says. 'It's nice to meet you too. And what's your name?'

'His name is Fred,' Amelia says. 'He doesn't talk much.'

'Oh. Okay. Do you want to come with me while we go and try to find your mom? I don't know where the laundry is.'

'Okay,' Amelia says. 'And I'll show you my room too.'

Steffi is sitting on Amelia's bed, with a silver plastic crown on her head and an American Girl doll on her lap, when a small blonde woman sails past the bedroom carrying a basket of laundry. She glances in, keeps moving, then swiftly doubles back just as Steffi stands up and starts to apologize.

'I'm so sorry. I didn't know where you were and Amelia –'

'Oh GOD! *I'm* so sorry. I totally forgot you were coming.' She gestures to her pyjamas. 'Who let you in?'

'Fred.'

The woman groans. 'I can't believe it. The children know they're not supposed to open the door to strangers. Amelia, you should be keeping an eye on Fred. Where's Tucker?'

'Playing Wii.'

'Oh God. I'm sorry, I'm sorry. You're Steffi.'

'Yes.' Steffi remembers the crown and whips it off her head. 'And you must be Amy.'

By the time they are sitting together at the kitchen counter, Steffi already knows that she and Amy are going to be friends. She has always trusted her instincts, and immediately, from the very first second Amy opened her mouth, she knew she'd be her kind of person.

'I'm a total disaster in the kitchen,' Amy is confessing as she tucks into one of Steffi's figgy oatmeal bars. 'Big Tucker – that's my husband, everyone calls him Big Tucker – well, Big Tucker despairs of me. He keeps buying me cookbooks –' she gestures over to a groaning bookshelf above the desk in the kitchen – 'but it's like reading double Dutch, to me.'

'So what do you eat?' Steffi is genuinely interested.

'Anything that can be heated up. I'm excellent at take-out food too, but the choice here isn't terribly good. That's the thing. We were in the city for so many years I never had to cook. When we first bought out here we thought it was going to be a weekend place; I never thought it would be permanent.'

'So how long have you been out here permanently?'

'Almost a year. I know, I know, why did we move?' She talks quickly, with a smile, and her hands flutter as she talks. She is very expressive, has large brown eyes, a quick mouth, a ready laugh. 'The kids. Three kids and the city – it was just too . . . oppressive. But this is really my husband's dream. I sort of feel I'd be happy anywhere as long as I have my family and a couple of friends.'

'Have you found the friends?'

Amy nods enthusiastically. 'Lots. Well, maybe not friends, to be honest. Lots and lots of other mothers from the school, but not really close friends. That's okay, though. I'm very self-sufficient.'

'Me too.' Steffi smiles. 'And you only need one or two.'

'Right! So tell me about you. How on earth have you ended up here? And are you loving the peace and quiet – I suspect you are – or are you dying of loneliness?'

'Right first time,' Steffi says, and goes on to tell her how she came to be living at Mason's farm. She is just telling her about Fingal when the back door slams shut and a man appears in the kitchen.

He must be Big Tucker, Steffi thinks, before remembering that she had walked down the hallway of family photos, and if Big Tucker looked like the man standing in the kitchen, she would definitely not have forgotten.

So who the hell *is* he? One thing's for certain: if she thought she'd left all the cute men behind in New York, she was sorely mistaken, for he is *exactly*, but *exactly*, her type. Dark skinned, large brown eyes, rumpled dark hair.

He stares at Steffi, whose heart skips ever so slightly, their gaze holding for a split second longer than it needs to, before she cracks first and looks away.

'Hey, Stan,' Amy says, entirely unaware of the effect he is having on Steffi. 'Are you done?'

'Yup. Bookshelves are up.'

'Do you know Steffi? She just moved into Mason's farm. Steffi, this is Stan.'

'I heard about you.'

Stan walks over and shakes hands with Steffi, who is turning information over in her mind. Stan, Stan, why is this familiar?

'I meant to come over and check up on you but haven't had the chance. I'm sorry.'

'That's okay. Oh, you're Stanley the handyman!' she yelps, suddenly realizing.

'Most people just call me Stan. Stanley makes me sound like a sixty-year-old.' He grins.

'That's what I thought.' She grins back, and then the awkward silence descends.

'I need to pay you!' Amy shrieks, breaking it, as she leaps up from the chair and grabs her bag. 'I'm so sorry. I always forget. Here.' She stuffs a pile of notes into his hand and Stan thanks her then turns to leave.

'Is he as hot as I think he is?' Steffi leans forward, whispering, when he has left.

'Who? Stan? Are you kidding? You think he's hot? He's a kid!'

'What? How old do you think he is?'

'I don't know. Twenty-nine? Thirty? How old are you?'

'Thirty-three. So I'm pretty much a kid too.'

'Nah. It's just that I'm forty so I'm older than everyone

now. Anyway, no idea if he's single or not. Want me to find out?'

'No. Absolutely not. The last thing I need right now is some sexy, heartbreaking handyman.'

'Sexy!' Amy spits out the tea she was drinking, with laughter. 'You and I sure as hell don't share the same taste in men.'

Two hours later, they are still sitting there, covering all the topics in each of their lives. Steffi, quite unexpectedly, has found herself telling Amy about Callie. She isn't even sure why, or how it came out, but Callie fills her thoughts almost all of the time, and she hasn't been able to talk about it with anyone.

Amy's eyes fill with tears as Steffi tells her how scared she is, and she reaches over and lays her hand on Steffi's. 'Any time you need to talk, you come and sit here with me,' she says, and Steffi nods, swallowing the lump in her throat.

'I mean it,' Amy says. 'My mom died of cancer. I've been through it. I know what it's like. And I also know what it's like to be going through this alone. I have this feeling you and I are going to be great friends anyway, so we may as well skip the whole getting to know you bit at the beginning and jump straight into crying on each other's shoulders, don't you think?'

Steffi nods again, then glances behind Amy at the clock on the microwave.

'Oh shit!' She leaps up. 'Sorry, sorry,' she apologizes, glancing around, looking for the children, but they have long since disappeared. 'My family are coming in an hour and I totally forgot to go shopping. I'm making lunch.'

'What are you making?'

Steffi tells her, then promises to make some extra to drop in later for Amy and Big Tucker.

'This will be the first meal of many.' Amy walks her to the door and reaches out, giving Steffi a huge bear hug, surprisingly firm for someone so tiny. 'Stay strong,' she whispers.

Steffi waves as she pulls out of the driveway, her heart singing at the knowledge that she will not be entirely on her own any more. She loves this life, loves the solitude, and knows it will be even better if she has friends.

She doesn't need many. Lord knows she doesn't have time for many, at least not now, not until Callie is better. She is going to the hospital again today, with the rest of the family, and she will go every day to accompany her sister on this journey.

So, just a friend or two, and perhaps a distracting affair with a dangerous-looking handyman who is *exactly*, but *exactly*, her type.

Figgy Oatmeal Bars

For the filling
8 oz. dried figs
4 oz. dates, pitted
2 tablespoons slivered or chopped almonds
1 tablespoon maple syrup
2 tablespoons water
1 tablespoon lemon juice
¼ teaspoon cinnamon

For the crust
1 cup regular or quick oats, ground in blender until fine
1 cup regular oatmeal
1 teaspoon baking powder
¼ teaspoon salt
3 tablespoons maple syrup
4 oz. unsweetened apple sauce
¼ cup water

Preheat the oven to 375°F.

Place the figs, dates and almonds in a food processor and grind to a coarse paste. Add the rest of the filling ingredients, pulse until mixed, then set aside.

Combine the dry ingredients thoroughly, then add the maple syrup, apple and water. Stir well. Press half the crust mixture into a greased rectangular pan. Cover with the fig filling, then smooth the remaining crust mixture on top. Bake for about 30 minutes, and cool completely before cutting into bars.

For optional icing: mix icing sugar with water, or milk, until thick. Add vanilla extract to taste, and drizzle over the top.

Chapter Twenty-Three

'Oh Steffi!' Honor's eyes fill with tears as she stands at the kitchen counter and pours out glasses of champagne. 'It is just beautiful here. I can see exactly why you love it.'

'It's the freakiest thing.' Steffi grins, accepting the champagne and calling Reece and the kids in. 'I've never been so happy in my life! Who woulda thought I was such a country girl?' She laughs.

'It's awesome,' Reece says, turning to the children. 'Guys? What do you want to drink?'

'Can I have a Coke?' Jack says hopefully.

'A *Coke*? Are you *kidding*?' Reece looks at his six-year-old in horror. 'Since when do you drink Coke?'

Jack shrugs. He tries again. 'Sprite?'

'Nope. No soda.'

'Honey,' Steffi says, crouching down. 'I don't have any soda anyway. I do have apple cider, though. I could warm it up for you. How does that sound?'

'Great!' he and Eliza say gleefully.

Steffi turns to Reece and silently mouths, 'Coke?' And he shrugs and grins. As far as they're all aware, Callie has a strict no-soda rule.

And a strict no-gum rule. And a strict no-TV-before-bed rule. And a strict no-food-outside-the-kitchen rule. None of which have been adhered to particularly since she has been in the hospital.

Reece is trying his best. He has Honor to help, but

Honor is flying out to be with Callie for most of the time. Reece is managing to work from home, so he is the one who is trying to sort out the play dates, and the classes, and the library books to be returned.

He is managing, but most of the time it's only just. If this hospital trip is extended for much longer, he's going to have to think seriously about bringing in some help. A babysitter, an au pair, something. He just can't do it all by himself.

On the weekends, it is easier. He has always taken over the weekends, and driving out to see Steffi's new place he can't wait to take the kids for a hike, to see their faces when they first see the animals. He just can't manage it every day. Frankly, he isn't entirely sure how Callie manages it either.

'This is like the perfect country house,' Reece says. 'What are you paying for rent?'

'I'm not!' Steffi says, setting out a platter of cheese with fig jam. 'The house is in exchange for looking after Fingal.'

'This guy must totally have the hots for you,' teases Reece. 'How much would it cost to pay someone to dog-sit? A hell of a lot less than the monthly rent on this place I would think.'

'Daddy!' Eliza tugs on his shirt. 'You said the H word.'

'I did? I'm sorry.'

'That's twenty-five cents in the curse jar when we get home.'

'Okay,' he says with a shrug, waiting until she leaves the room to add, 'Good job she doesn't follow me to work. She'd be a millionaire by now.' He peers out of the window as another car turns slowly into the driveway and pulls up to the house.

'Who do you know that drives a silver Volvo? Oh! It's Ed and Lila and a young boy. I didn't know they were coming.'

'The more the merrier. That's Clay, Ed's son.' Steffi goes to the front door, and soon the kitchen is filled with noise and movement as they all help Steffi with the finishing touches, gathering round the counter to eat the hors d'oeuvres and drink the champagne that Honor has brought.

Clay kicks around the edges of the room until Eliza corners him and questions him, then he starts to relax. Soon the three children are tearing round the house, making so much noise that Reece commands them all outside to play, and Steffi tells them to take Fingal with them.

'Just keep him away from the chicken coop!' Steffi shouts after them, and they raise hands to indicate they've heard, trooping off like a row of ducks, Eliza already having fallen in love with Clay, and Jack wanting to be wherever the big kids are.

They sit, eventually, in the dining room, which is beautifully set with Mason's white Wedgwood china and crystal wine glasses, but with a classic Steffi touch: there are three galvanized steel pots on the table containing growing lettuce, and bowls of crisp red radishes, a heaping mound of soft beansprouts and a dish of roasted pine nuts, so everyone can pick their own lettuce leaves straight from the pots and assemble their own salads.

It is, like so many family gatherings, easy and comfortable, with much laughter, and the great grey elephant in the room is not remarked upon. The children sit for a while, gobble up their food – they eschewed the tuna and took the turkey lemon meatballs as an alternative – and then go out to feed the chickens.

'How is she today?' Steffi is first to broach the subject. 'I went in again yesterday afternoon and she was amazing – she was chatty, and eating, and she honestly looked great. Is there any news?'

Everyone looks to Honor, who is devoting most of her time to being with her daughter and is a fairly constant presence at the hospital: a book in hand, a blanket, a cup of tea, for the many times when Callie is asleep and Honor still cannot leave her side but sits peacefully in the room until she wakes up.

'She wasn't so great this morning.' Honor sighs. 'She was in pain again.'

'She was?' Lila jumps in. 'But I thought they were managing it. I thought the pain that other time was just because she didn't let them give her the oral medication at night?'

'That's what we thought too, but she had it last night and still had breakthrough pain.'

'So what are they doing for that pain?' Lila asks. 'Other than the IV of Dilaudid?'

'When I left they were talking about Oxycodone.'

'On IV or orally?' Lila asks.

'Orally.'

'And is that okay with the Decadron and the Zofran? Are there any adverse interactions? Did anyone ask?'

They all look at Lila blankly.

'What is Deca-what? And Zofran?'

'They've been giving her Decadron, which are the steroids, and Zofran, which is an anti-emetic, it stops her throwing up.'

'How do you *remember* that?' Reece is amazed.

'I wrote it down, and then I looked it all up on the Internet.'

'Wow.' Reece looks at her. 'You're pretty impressive.'

'No, I just know that you have to be your own advocate these days. You have to know exactly what's going on and not be afraid to ask what you're getting, and ask for other things if it's not working.'

'Lila, we could do with you at the hospital,' Honor says thoughtfully. 'I get a bit overwhelmed by all the terms and the names, and I'm not very good with doctors and nurses. My generation still thinks they're all-powerful. I wouldn't dare ask about anything.'

'Really? But . . . don't you want to know?'

'I just trust that they're doing everything in their power.'

'That's just it. We always think that, but everyone's fallible. They're only human. Callie doesn't have the strength to fight for herself right now, so someone needs to do it for her.'

All eyes are on Lila.

'What?'

'Seriously, Lila,' Reece says. 'I'm there as much as I can be, but you're amazing. I can't be at the hospital during the day as much as I'd like to be so maybe . . .' He tails off, starting again: 'I guess what I'm trying to say is maybe you could be her advocate.'

'Yes.' She nods, after a long pause. 'Of course. It's not like I'm run off my feet with work.'

'It's not? I thought you were starting a new business, dear?' Honor asks.

'I was planning on it, but I hadn't planned on the worst recession since the thirties. Right now I'm a consultant, which basically means I have two clients, and can't see myself getting any more in the immediate future.'

'But you're okay financially, right?' Reece asks.

'Thank God they paid me a huge severance as part of the buy-out.' She looks at Ed and laughs. 'Sorry. I keep forgetting that Ed goes into heart failure every time we talk about money.'

He grins. 'It just that the English never talk about money. It's the one thing I'm still not used to about living here.'

'And his Long Island Jewish love,' Lila puts on a thick accent, 'talks about money all the time. I can't help it. I have no shame. But, thank *God*, financially I am fine, and heaven knows I have enough free time on my hands. Do you know,' she says suddenly, leaning forward, 'I had never seen the inside of a Starbucks at eleven o'clock in the morning before?'

'Is it . . . different?' Reece smiles.

'Yes! It's hell! Tons and tons of young mothers with small children who run around screaming and laying their sugar-coated fingers on you, while the mothers ignore the horrible behaviour and would be shocked to think anyone could possibly find their brats anything less than adorable.'

'She loves children.' Ed shrugs. 'What can I tell you?'

'But you do love children,' Reece says. 'At least, you love ours. And they love you.'

'Yes, well. That's different. First of all, they're the children of my best friend, and secondly, they are spectacularly well-behaved. I bet they've never run around Starbucks screaming. Even if they did Callie would have grabbed them and marched them out of there, putting their doughnuts in the trash can on the way out.'

'She's right.' Reece grins. 'My wife has always been the disciplinarian in our house.'

A fresh wave of silence and sadness as it hits them, yet again, that Callie is not there, and the reason why she is not there.

'So,' Steffi says, 'we know she was in pain, but do they have any more results?'

'We should be getting some later today,' Reece says. 'I'm going back to the hospital after I drop the kids home with Honor. I hope we'll have some news soon.'

Reece and Ed are taking the kids for a hike, Lila and Honor are inspecting the garden, and Steffi is clearing up in the kitchen when a small blue truck appears. She frowns, then gasps as Stanley the handyman climbs out.

'Oh shit,' she mutters, smoothing her hair back and dashing to the mirror to wipe down her shiny skin – there was no point in bothering with make-up for her family, but she wasn't expecting this guy to show up this afternoon.

She slides to the back door just as he is about to knock.

'Hey.' He nods, a half smile on his face. 'I just thought I'd been really rude in not coming over, so I wanted to see if there was anything you wanted.'

'Oh. Wow. That's really nice of you. No, I . . . Do you want to come in?'

'Sure.' He lopes in, and as he passes her she breathes him in, and yes, he smells just as delicious as she had hoped. And now he is in her kitchen Steffi feels as light-headed and giggly as a schoolgirl.

'Oh man, I didn't realize you had people.'

'It's okay. It's just my family.'

'Really? Where are they all?'

'Outside. Do you want some . . . champagne?' She feels stupid saying it, but he's looking at the half-empty champagne bottle on the counter, and it is what they have been drinking, after all.

'Nah. I'm not really a champagne guy.'

'Let me guess. Budweiser.'

He laughs. 'Right first time.'

Steffi smiles to herself. Oh I so know you, she thinks. I know you better than you know yourself. And she feels a shiver of lust go through her.

'I'm really sorry, I don't have any in. I'll stock up, though.' Shut up! That implies you want him to come back, she thinks to herself. That's not exactly playing it cool.

'Great,' he says. 'That'd be good.'

'So . . .' she says, feeling slightly awkward. 'How did you end up here?'

'In Sleepy Hollow? I've lived here my whole life. My parents run the gas station. I moved to Seattle for a bit when I was fresh out of school, trying to do the whole musician thing, but it didn't work out so I came back.'

I knew that already, Steffi thinks. I've met you a million times before. But, just to be on the safe side, she asks the obligatory question, already knowing his answer.

'Did you have a record deal?'

'Oh man!' He starts to laugh. 'You know which questions to ask. We came this close,' he moves his finger and thumb an inch apart, 'but the lead singer blew it. He just wouldn't take the deal and they walked away. Why are you smiling?'

'You just . . . remind me of someone I once knew.'

'A boyfriend?'

'Maybe.' She shrugs. She could have said, more accurately, 'Every single one of my boyfriends.'

'Listen, I'd better go. I just wanted to make sure you had all my numbers in case you need anything. And if you ever want to hit the Horseshoe for a Bud, give me a call. The nights can get pretty dull when you live up here on your own.'

'You're on your own?'

'Yeah.' Once again he holds her gaze for just a second longer than is altogether necessary, and her heart does a tiny flip.

Honor bends down to finger the hydrangeas, which are dried to a pale papery brown on the stem. Although she and Lila watch the blue truck pull up, neither of them makes a move to see the new visitor.

'I'm really worried,' Honor says slowly, straightening up to meet Lila's eye. 'I haven't said this to anyone, I haven't even wanted to say the words out loud, but I'm so scared.'

'I know,' Lila says, reaching out a hand and rubbing Honor's back. 'We're all scared.'

'I just . . . I just have this feeling that . . . Oh Lord. I shouldn't even say it.'

'Don't,' Lila says. 'I know what you're going to say and I feel it too, and we mustn't say it out loud. We mustn't even think it.'

'I just feel so helpless.' Honor starts to well up. 'This feels so different from before, with the cancer. The . . . unknowing makes it feel so serious and so frightening. This . . . waiting game. It's like being trapped in hell, and even though you don't know the outcome, you know it isn't . . .'

'It's okay.' Lila shushes her. 'We don't know the outcome but we're going to pray that it is going to be good. And I'm going to do everything I can, Honor. I will be there every day, and I will fight to make sure she gets the best possible treatment available. I won't let a single stone go unturned, I promise you that.'

'You're a good friend,' Honor says, with a small smile. 'You've always been a wonderful friend to Callie.'

'She's always been a wonderful friend to *me*,' Lila says, swallowing the lump that has just crept into her throat.

'So who was the hot guy in the blue pick-up truck?' Lila demands, passing Stanley on their way back into the kitchen.

'Oh *him*? That's just the handyman.'

'*Just?* You mean you just happen to move out to the boondocks and the handyman looks like a total rock god who is *exactly*, but *exactly*, your type?'

'I know!' Steffi grins. 'And he's single! I thought I'd be celibate for the next year, but Mr Handyman may be the answer to my prayers. Sorry, Mom.'

'Oh don't worry, darling. I came of age in the sixties. Nothing shocks me.'

'So what's his name?'

Steffi pauses. 'It's Stanley,' she says eventually, reluctantly.

'*Stanley!*' Both Honor and Lila whoop with laughter.

'He's not a Stanley,' Lila says. 'He looks like a Rip, or a Thorn, or, at the very least, a Jack.'

'Sexy Stanley,' Honor muses, and they all crack up.

'So? Nice guy? Or total loser like the rest of the rock gods you usually date? Oh I'm sorry, rock gods slash waiters slash handymen.'

'If you weren't practically family I'd think you were a total cow,' Steffi shoots back.

'Girls, girls,' Honor says, theatrically. 'Behave.'

'I forgive you,' Lila says. 'And anyway, if I were a total cow, which I am not, I'd be a total cow who loves this family as much as her own. Actually, make that a tiny bit more than her own.'

'You're not a total cow,' Steffi says. 'You're amazing. And to answer your question, I have no idea yet whether he's a loser or not. I don't know anything about him but he just invited me to the Horseshoe, which is the local bar, for a drink.'

'Really? He asked you on a date?' Honor asks.

'Well, not exactly. He said that if I ever wanted to grab a beer I should call him.'

'Shouldn't he be calling you?' Honor says.

'Oh Mom. You're so old-fashioned. It's totally fine to call guys now.'

Lila purses her lips. 'No, I agree with your mom. He should be calling you. And I bet that if he doesn't hear from you in the next few days, he will.'

'But I don't want to play games,' Steffi says.

'I agree. You shouldn't have to play games, but look at him! This is a guy who has played more games in the past year than I've probably played my entire life. Seriously. Doesn't he look like a game player to you?'

'I don't know,' Steffi says. 'Anyway, it's just a drink. I'm not going to marry the guy.'

'Don't call him,' Lila says. 'Please. Pretend to be an old-fashioned girl, just for me.'

'Hey! Speaking of old-fashioned, you have to see my nightgown!' Steffi runs upstairs and puts it on, over her clothes, swanning down the stairs to show it off.

'Oh my God!' Lila announces. 'I love it! Where did you get it? I want one!'

'Me too,' Honor says, admiring the lace. 'I haven't seen one of these in years.'

'They're at Mary's store,' Steffi says. 'Come on. Jump in the car and we'll go shopping!'

Tuna with Coriander Lime Sauce and Avocado

4 tuna steaks
2 handfuls chopped coriander
1 teaspoon grated ginger
1 garlic clove, minced
juice of 2 limes, zest of 1
2 tablespoons soy sauce
pinch of sugar
seasoning
2 tablespoons olive oil
1 avocado, pitted, thinly sliced

Season the tuna steaks. Mix together all the remaining ingredients, except the avocado. Add the tuna then marinate for at least 2 hours, and preferably overnight.

Remove the tuna from the marinade and grill for 3 to 5 minutes on each side.

Pour the marinade into a small pot and reduce on a high heat until thick.

When ready to serve, pour the sauce over the tuna and fan sliced avocado on the top.

Chapter Twenty-Four

There is nothing quite like setting three women free in a quaint country store to revive their spirits and take their minds off whatever in life is dragging them down.

Mary makes a huge fuss of Honor, pouring on compliments about what a wonderful daughter she has, while Lila swoons over the home-made chutneys, shopping baskets and coasters.

'God, I love shopping,' she says happily to Steffi as she sweeps through the store, putting more and more items in her trolley.

All three women have been consumed with fear for Callie. She has taken up space in each of their heads. They have woken up each morning with her the first thing on their mind, and have continued to think about little else for the remainder of the day.

Of course, life goes on, even with the weight that is now permanently on their shoulders, and they are adjusting to this new version of their lives.

Steffi has a new path to forge. She has Fingal and the farm animals to take care of, menus to plan for Amy Van Peterson and hours of cooking and baking for Mary's store. She is getting to know the locals, and becoming used to hours passing with no one around.

She never would have expected to enjoy this quiet, coming, as she did, from the hustle and bustle of the city, the craziness of being a chef in a popular restaurant. But it is precisely the quiet that she loves. It is as if it has centred her, calmed her down, and for the first time ever Steffi doesn't feel as if she has to constantly keep running.

Lila too is adjusting to the quiet, with less ease than Steffi. She is still not used to being self-employed, and particularly in a world that is no longer spending money, no longer bringing in marketing consultants in the way it once did.

Her quiet is accompanied by a constant low-grade anxiety. What if she doesn't get enough work . . . what if she has to find another job . . . could she, in fact, go back to working full-time . . . what if she can't pay the bills . . . From time to time she shares these fears with Ed, who has a magical ability to calm her down. He tells her they are in this for the long haul, and they are in this together. That everything will be fine. And for a while, when he says this, she believes him.

Of the three women, Honor is perhaps the one who is handling the weight of sadness the least well. She does not have a fresh start, a new home, a new job to occupy her. She does not have a supportive partner to whom she can turn when her anxieties threaten to overwhelm her.

Honor is not at home, surrounded by things that may be able to comfort her, but she lives each day dragged down with fear.

For Honor the fear is *constant*. Her only breaks are when she is at home with the children, when she can pretend that she is not sick with fear, but it *is* a pretence. There is no place to go, physically or mentally, to get away from her thoughts.

Today, now more than ever, these women need to be together. They need to be shopping, laughing, having fun.

They need to stop thinking about the missing link, even if only for a few minutes.

They drive back home, giggling with excitement about their new nightgowns, and walk into the house to find absolute quiet. Ed is on the computer doing something with the kids, and Reece is standing up by the counter, pale.

'Mark called,' he says quietly. 'He says we have some results.'

'What? What did he say?'

'He said I have to come in. He wants me to go to the hospital now.'

There is a dull silence before Steffi's hand flies up to her heart. 'Oh God,' she says. 'I think I'm going to throw up.'

The drive to the hospital seems to take a lifetime. The kids stay with Steffi and Ed, and Reece drives in with Honor and Lila.

'Are you sure you want me there?' Lila says, not for the first time.

'If you're going to be Callie's advocate, you need to hear it from the horse's mouth,' Reece says, but other than that, there is little conversation.

'I know it's not *nothing*,' Reece says finally, as he is turning into the driveway for the hospital. 'Or, not nothing, but . . . maybe they just know what it is, and now we'll work out a treatment plan.'

'What's the worst-case scenario?' Honor attempts. 'That it's cancer? She's beaten it before, she'll beat it again.'

'If it *is* cancer,' Reece says.

Lila doesn't say anything at all.

*

Words have failed them again by the time they reach the thirteenth floor. They file down the corridors, Honor looking in each room, all of them filled with the elderly, the infirm, people who you would not be surprised to see in a hospital.

How can my *daughter* be here, she wonders. How can my lovely, vibrant daughter be *here*?

Callie has just woken up, and is having her vitals taken when they walk in. Lila is shocked at how thin and drawn Callie appears. She does not look well. Mostly because there is no smile on her face and the light has gone out in her eyes. This is the biggest shock of all, and Lila swallows her lump, again, and walks over to kiss her friend hello.

'Hey, sweetie.' She leans over Callie, stroking her cheek, holding her hand. 'How are you doing?' Her voice is a soft whisper.

'Not so good today,' Callie says. Her eyes are suddenly too large for her face, and she looks so tiny in her hospital bed it feels, Lila realizes, as if she is a child again.

'I know, sweetie.'

'Mark said he wants to see me and Reece. Will you stay with me too?'

'Yes, baby. Of course. If you want me to.' Callie nods her agreement. 'I'm not going to let them give you anything but the best treatment,' Lila says.

'I'm scared, Lila.' Callie stares her straight in the eye, and Lila doesn't know what to say.

'I'm scared too,' she says eventually, for she cannot tell her it's all going to be okay. She just doesn't know.

Mark appears five minutes later. He steps into the room and shuts the door softly, then comes and kisses the women hello, shaking hands with Reece. But there is nothing in his manner that is light. He is as grave as Reece has ever seen him.

Callie, lying prostrate, follows him round the room with those huge eyes.

Mark clears his throat, clutches his clipboard, then perches on one of the chairs.

'As you know we did the lumbar puncture the other day, and the results were negative,' he says.

'That was good news, wasn't it?' Reece says.

Mark pauses. 'In forty to fifty per cent of lumbar punctures performed we see a false negative. What we did find were mildly elevated protein levels, but given the possibility of the false cytology, we performed another one.'

He pauses again and takes a deep breath.

'We confirmed the results today with an MRI. Callie has a disease called Leptomeningeal Carcinomatosis.'

There is a long silence, broken by Reece. 'What is that?'

Mark goes on to explain that leptomeninges are the innermost layers of the system of membranes that envelop the central nervous system, and their primary function, together with the cerebrospinal fluid, is to protect the nervous system.

'Leptomeningeal Carcinomatosis is, essentially, a tumour that has diffused within the leptomeninges. It means the tumour is in the cerebrospinal fluid and travelling around Callie's nervous system, hence the headaches and,' he sighs, 'a new symptom these last twenty-four hours of weakness and numbness on her left side.'

'When you say tumour,' Reece says and swallows hard, 'do you mean the cancer is back?'

Mark lifts heavy eyes. 'It does not present as a tumour in the way other cancers do, but five per cent of breast cancer sufferers will get this disease, and this is the same cancer as the primary breast cancer.'

'So what is the treatment?' Honor asks quietly.

Mark turns to her, looking between her and Callie as he speaks. 'We will start with whole-brain radiation therapy. I have called the radiologist to come up here to consult on the amount needed, but I would say three weeks of radiation.'

'And then?' Callie asks, and Mark turns to address her directly.

'Then, if it is successful, we can start intrathecal therapy, where an ommaya port is inserted directly into the brain to target the chemotherapy.'

'So what is the prognosis?' Callie is the only one who has the courage to ask. It is what everyone is thinking, but no one is daring to put it into words.

Mark hesitates. 'It's difficult to say. This is rare. We don't see it very often. But Callie, Reece, you know we will do everything we can. The treatment is palliative, but can be very effective in easing the sympto –'

'*Palliative?*' Lila jumps in, her professional voice belying her thumping heart. 'You mean it won't make her better, it will make her more comfortable?'

He nods.

'So she's not going to get better?' Reece looks white with shock.

Everyone in the room seems to have forgotten that Callie is there.

'I'm sorry.' Mark then looks at Callie, reaches over and takes her hand as a silence falls. 'I'm sorry.'

'You're my friend, Mark,' Callie whispers, the only person who seems able to speak. 'You know my family. You know my kids. You've been to my house. If I'm to get my house in order, how long have I got?'

Mark swallows. 'If the treatment is successful, maybe six months to a year.'

No one says anything.

'And if it's not successful?' Callie's voice is surprisingly strong.

'Four to six weeks.'

Mark leaves, and Callie turns her head to look at her husband, her mother, her best friend. No one can speak and, as Callie looks at them, tears start to trickle down her face.

Reece rushes over and puts his arms around her, and Honor and Lila stand up and leave the room.

They walk silently to the waiting room at the other end of the corridor, and as they walk in they look at each other, both bursting into tears, clutching each other for support, Honor heaving like a child as Lila sobs.

A nurse comes in, rubs their backs then places a fresh box of tissues on the table, and leaves them alone in their grief.

After they finally pull apart, they sink into chairs, numb, to stare at the wall with tears dripping down their faces until Reece comes to get them.

'She wants to see you,' he says to Honor, who nods and makes the weary trek down the hallway, while Reece sinks into the chair next to Lila, leans his head on her shoulder and starts to cry.

'You need to take care of my children,' Callie says, when Honor has stopped crying. 'Reece is an amazing dad, and he can't do it himself. He needs a shitload of help. You have to be there for them.'

'I will. Of course I will.' Honor feels ready to explode with tears, but she cannot do it here; she has to be as strong as she can be for Callie.

'Six months to a year means I can plan,' Callie says softly. 'We can make videos for Eliza and Jack, write them letters. I can organize things. Oh Jesus —' And she stops and looks away.

'What?'

'I just . . . I can't believe it. I'm not . . . ready. I'm not ready to die. There's too much I need to do.'

'I'll help you,' Honor says, not able to believe it either. 'I'll do whatever you need me to do.'

Lila is the last to go in. She cannot pull herself together enough to see Callie, and so she waits in the waiting room for an hour. Eventually, when Honor and Reece have gone downstairs to the cafeteria to grab some coffee – even though neither of them wants it, but they don't know what else to do – she takes a deep breath and walks up to Callie's room.

Perhaps Callie is sleeping, she thinks, tiptoeing round the bed to see Callie's head resting on her folded hands on the pillow, her eyes wide open and staring out of the window as tear after silent tear slowly slides down her cheeks, soaking the pillow beneath.

Lila wants to gather her up, fold her into her arms and make everything better, but there is nothing she can do. She sits on the bed and leans her head down on Callie's shoulder. She realizes, in all the years she has known her friend, she has never seen her cry.

For Callie is the girl who can do anything. She is the girl who is always happy. The girl who seizes life and wrings out every last drop.

How can this possibly be happening?

They stay there, for a long time. Eventually Callie turns her head and looks Lila deep in the eyes. 'I'm scared,' she whispers. 'I don't want to die.'

'I know.'

'Who's going to raise my children? Who's going to look after Reece?'

'I'll find someone for you,' Lila says. 'I'll speak to the agencies. I'll find them a nanny-governess person. I'll find someone amazing to raise your kids.'

Callie nods. 'And you? And Steffi, too. Both of you. You have to make sure they're okay. You have to help Reece. I love him to pieces but you know how hopeless he is.'

Lila smiles through her tears. 'You'd be surprised if you saw how amazing he has been.'

'I would.' Callie smiles back through tears of her own.

'I love you,' Lila says softly, leaning forward and kissing Callie on the cheek, then the other cheek, then her forehead. She would keep kissing her for hours if she could. As it is, it seems she cannot be in this room without physically touching her – sitting on Callie's bed and holding her hand, resting a hand on her back, leaning her head on Callie's shoulder and leaking tears. It is as comforting to Lila as it is to Callie.

'I love you,' Callie says, and they lie there, holding each other, until Reece comes back upstairs to take Lila's place.

'We have to call Dad,' Callie says, exhausted now, the emotions and the pain meds too much for her.

'I'll call him tonight,' Reece says.

'No,' Callie says. 'Tell Steffi. Then let her tell Dad. And we have to have a party.'

'A what?' Reece thinks he has heard wrong.

'A party. I'd rather celebrate my life while I'm still alive.'

'Where? In the hospital?'

'No. I'm coming home. The kids. I have to do so much. Leave them rules to live by. Tell them about me, and about them as babies.'

'We can do all of that,' Reece says. 'I can bring a tape recorder. We can start tomorrow.'

'How do we tell the children?' Callie's eyes grow watery again. 'How do I tell our children that I am going to die, that the longest I'm going to be around for is a year?'

Nobody says anything to the children that night.

Reece, Lila and Honor go back to Steffi's to collect them, and Reece stays behind, after the children have gone home, to tell Steffi.

'What?' she keeps repeating, a loud buzzing in her ears. 'What?'

She cannot understand, refuses to understand until after Reece has gone. She sinks down on the floor in the living room, staring numbly at the fireplace, when suddenly a huge sob lifts her up, and she lies, crying, for hours, Fingal curled up by her side.

In the early hours of the morning she pulls herself up to go to bed. Her limbs are so heavy, she can hardly move. This, she realizes, is what they mean when they talk about weighed down with grief.

*

A psychologist comes in the next morning to talk to Callie and Reece. She is warm, understanding and wise. She gives them the words to tell the children, explains that the children have neither the life experience nor the intellectual or emotional development that allows them to understand what is going on in the way adults do.

She sits quietly as Callie and Reece both cry, and works through examples of what to say; but there is no rush, she says. Be honest with them about her illness, and that she is taking medicine for it, but introduce the possibility of it not working. Studies have shown that the more prepared the children are, the better they will handle it.

Mark comes in afterwards, and explains the course of treatment.

'I want to go home. Can I do it from home?'

He is reluctant, concerned about the pain medication, but willing to let her go home if they can get the pain under control in the next couple of days.

'I just want to be in my own bed,' Callie says. With the children. A year,' she keeps repeating to herself, the words seeming to reassure her. 'There's a lot I can get done in a year.'

*

A weight has settled on Steffi's chest during the night. She wakes up with tears already flowing down her cheeks, before she has even consciously remembered the news. She has no more sobs left, but a steady stream of tears trickle down throughout her early morning routine: making coffee, letting Fingal out, feeding the animals.

She is supposed to be cooking ginger almond chicken for Amy this morning, but Amy will understand. She pulls on some leggings, a scarf, slips her feet into thick socks and boots, and climbs in the car to go and see Callie.

Steffi would not say this to anyone, does not even dare think it properly, but she heard a year, and she heard four to six weeks and, while she has never considered herself to have a psychic bone in her body, she knows that she will not have Callie for long, that Callie will not be here by summer. Possibly not even by spring.

And the little time they have left must be wonderful. She will make sure of it.

She stops at the flower market on the way and buys a huge and horrendously expensive bunch of peonies – God only knows where they got them from: who has peonies in winter? – but Callie will love them.

At Mary's she runs in and picks up her own banana and chocolate cake, and a nightgown.

'Are you okay, my dear?' Mary peers closely at Steffi's red, puffy eyes and blotchy cheeks.

'Yes . . . I'm fi –' A sob comes up, and Mary gathers her in her arms as Steffi continues to cry.

'You go and show your sister how much you love her,' she says. 'Go and look after her. Don't worry about cooking for me, and I'll let Amy know you won't be cooking at the moment. You have more important things to do.'

Callie is asleep when Steffi gets there. She puts the bags down softly, slips off her boots and lowers herself, very gently, on the bed next to Callie. Callie opens her eyes and smiles when she sees Steffi, and Steffi scooches down and lays her head on Callie's shoulder as the tears start to drip again.

'Oh God,' she says after a few minutes, while Callie rubs

her back. 'As always, you're the one looking after me. I'm supposed to be here to look after you.'

'Well, you're not doing a very good job,' Callie says.

'I know.' Steffi smiles. 'Cal —' Steffi's voice suddenly breaks. Damn. This isn't what she had intended. 'Oh God. I'm sorry.' She wipes her face. 'I didn't mean to do that.'

'It's okay, baby,' Callie says softly. 'Of course you can cry. I can't stop.'

'Oh Jesus.' Steffi sniffs. 'You can't go anywhere. What am I going to do without my big sister?'

'What am *I* going to do without my little sister?' Callie frowns. 'Oh . . . wait. *You're* not going anywhere. Oh God. I never expected this.'

They sit, both girls in silence, and Steffi's tears continue to fall.

'Will you leave white feathers for me?' she whispers. They both smile as they remember Honor telling them that whenever they found a white feather it was a message from their guardian angels telling them they were looking after them.

'I'll leave you enough for a million pillows.' They lapse into silence again, until Callie eventually asks, 'Do you think there is a heaven?'

Steffi rolls onto her side to look Callie in the eye. 'Well, I don't think death is the end, you know? I once did an Ouija board and I got Uncle Edgar.'

'How did you know it was him?'

'Well, that was the weird thing. I asked him what was his wife's name, just to test, and he said Lavinia.'

'So I guess it wasn't him.'

'I just shrugged it off, but when I spoke to Dad I asked

297

him, just out of curiosity, about Aunt Celia, and whether she'd ever been called anything else. He said she'd always been called Celia, but her actual christened name was Lavinia.'

'Noooo!' Callie's eyes widen.

'I know! Isn't that weird? And I never ever knew that, so now I totally believe in it. Will you talk to me through the Ouija board?'

'I'm not dead yet, baby.' Callie makes a face.

'I *know*. I'm just saying. White feathers, Ouija board, and if you could flick a light on or off or something, just to let me know you're okay.'

'I'll try, but the light thing is hard. Remember we asked Grandma Tollemache if she would do that?'

'Yes, but she never liked us,' Steffi says.

'Only because you were an "exuberant and somewhat rambunctious child".' Callie laughs.

'She was an old bat.'

'Have you spoken to Dad?'

'No. I left him a message last night. I just said to give me a call, but he hasn't rung back. I'll try him again when I get home.'

'Thanks, Steff.'

'Oh Callie,' Steffi says. 'Why is this happening to you? It's not fair.'

'It only happens to five per cent of cancer sufferers,' Callie says. 'Look on the bright side. We always knew I was special. Honestly? I think I'm too good for this earth.' As always, she is using humour to deflect the pain.

'You know what, though?' she says, more seriously. 'It's a year, and that's not counting whatever new treatments they're coming up with. If I can make it to a year, hopefully they'll have come up with something to treat this. I'm not ready to go. I'm telling you. Even though, really, I am too good for this earth.' She grins as Steffi pokes her, then they both look up as the door opens.

'*Dad!* What are *you* doing here?'

Ginger Almond Chicken

4 chicken breasts, boneless and skinless
2 teaspoons ground coriander
1 teaspoon grated fresh ginger
2 teaspoons white wine vinegar
½ teaspoon salt
¼ teaspoon freshly ground pepper
4 teaspoons grapeseed, groundnut or corn oil
½ cup mango chutney
¼ cup chicken stock
1 teaspoon minced garlic
4 large spring onions, thinly sliced, white and green parts separated
¼ cup fresh ginger, julienned
¼ cup sliced almonds, toasted
small bunch chopped coriander

Slice the chicken crosswise into pieces half an inch thick. Toss in a bowl with the coriander, grated ginger, vinegar, salt, pepper and 2 teaspoons of the oil. Marinate at room temperature for 15 minutes minimum.

In a small bowl stir together the chutney, stock and garlic.

Heat the remaining oil in a frying pan or wok over a medium heat. Add the spring onion whites and julienned ginger; stir-fry for 30 seconds. Add the chicken and stir-fry until thoroughly cooked, which should take 4–6 minutes. Add the spring onion greens and chutney mix and cook, stirring, for 2 minutes.

Garnish with almonds and chopped coriander.

Chapter Twenty-Five

Walter knew, as soon as he got home and heard Steffi's voice telling him to call, that it wasn't good. He knew, of course, that Callie had been in hospital, knew they were all waiting for results, which is why, as soon as he heard Steffi's message, he jumped in his car and drove down from Maine.

He stopped halfway, at a little motel. Ordered himself a steak and a beer in the restaurant across the road, and fell asleep to the sound of laughter from the David Letterman show.

From the minute Callie had been taken to hospital he had thought about whether he should come down, but Honor was there, and he couldn't imagine what it would be like, both of them being there at the same time. Reece had assured him it wasn't necessary, there was nothing he could do, but something told him last night that he had to put his hurt feelings aside, and be there for his daughter.

He woke up in the morning, had a shower, folded his pyjamas neatly and put them at the top of his suitcase, paid the bill and climbed back into his old Mercedes wagon, then drove down to Bedford, stopping at the odd coffee shop to fuel his journey.

He doesn't like hospitals. He particularly doesn't like this hospital, for it reminds him of Callie being ill before – the hours spent sitting around in the cancer centre, waiting for the Neupogen shots to raise her white blood cell count, waiting for a chair to come free so she could have her chemo.

Hospitals make Walter aware of his own mortality. God knows he isn't a young man any more, and since his marriage to Hiromi he has felt older than ever. A fool. An old fool. That was how he felt, and how he often still feels, all these years on.

He approaches the thirteenth floor with trepidation, for what if Honor is there? What if Callie doesn't want to see him? What if . . . oh God . . . what if Steffi called because she has died? But a kind nurse points to a door along the corridor and the relief at being directed to Callie's room, at knowing she is still, quite clearly, alive, is immense.

'My little girl!' he croons, softening in a way he was never able to do when he was younger, but willing himself not to show his shock at seeing Callie look so . . . frail. There is nothing to her, and she looks up at him like a frightened little girl.

'Do you *know*?' Steffi asks quietly, after she has given him a huge hug.

'Know what?' His voice catches. 'I came because I felt I was needed. What's the story?'

Callie and Steffi catch each other's eye and smile. This was their father's catchphrase: *What's the story, morning glory?*

'It's not morning glory, that's for sure,' Callie says. 'Basically I have a disease that is called . . . lepto something. Steff? Do you remember?'

'Nope. Leptocarcin something?'

'No. Something to do with meningitis or something. Oh God. I don't know. I feel like my brain's turned to mush.'

'So what is it, whatever this disease is? How do they treat it?'

'I need radiotherapy and then chemotherapy.'

There is a pause. 'So . . . it's cancer? Again.'

'Yes. Same cancer. Different place.'

'Where?' But he already knows it's not good. Meningitis means brain, he thinks, fear settling in a clutch around his heart.

'It's in the CFS.' Callie winces, trying to remember.

'The what?'

'The FCS? The SCF? I don't know. It's in the spinal fluid that goes around my brain and central nervous system. The CSF! That's it.'

'So that's why you've been having these terrible headaches?'

She nods.

'But they can treat it! That's great news, isn't it?'

Callie and Steffi exchange another glance. 'It's not . . . great. It's a very rare disease. Mark has said that if the treatment is successful I have a year.'

'*What?* A year until what?' He cannot comprehend what she is saying.

'Well, a year before I, you know, go to the great big photography studio in the sky,' Callie says, attempting to joke.

'A year?' he repeats. Numb.

'Or six weeks.' She shrugs nonchalantly, and she and Steffi, for some bizarre reason, start to giggle. Hearing those words out loud seems so surreal, so utterly unfeasible that they cannot cry any more, they just have to laugh.

Walter sits down in the armchair and wills himself to hold it together. I am her father, he tells himself. I will not let her see me cry. I will be strong for her. I will not weaken.

He doesn't even hear the girls laughing, but he hears when Steffi's laughter turns to sobs. He stands up and hugs both his little girls, and all the time he imagines himself as having nerves of steel.

I will be strong for them, he thinks. I can do this.

*

Reece looks at the clock, counting down the hours until bedtime. How come weekends have never been this hard before? He supposes it is because he has had Callie with him, and because he has always tended to take the children out to do the fun stuff – the fairs, the festivals, the libraries, the parties – bringing them home for Callie to bathe, and feed, and take up to bed.

Now it is just him, and good *Lord*, this is hard work. When he came back from the hospital this morning he took them to a farmers' market a couple of towns over, and they whined constantly that they were bored. At one point Jack sat down, cross-legged, in the middle of the car park and refused to walk any more. When Reece went to pick him up, he started to scream.

But how can Reece lose patience with him, poor child? When Callie isn't around, when this is exactly what the psychologist told them to expect? They will act out, she warned them, particularly the six-year-old, because he won't understand why his mother isn't there, and his fears, and anger, will come out in unexpected ways.

They have an appointment to take the children to see the psychologist on Tuesday, but until then what is he supposed to do? Eliza is defiant, and Jack is having tantrums.

Neither of them behaves like this usually. They may be out of their comfort zone, but boy, is Reece ever out of his. Where's the handbook that tells you how to do this?

He hears loud screaming from upstairs, and walks up wearily to find Eliza screaming at Jack.

'Get out my room! Get out! I hate you!'

'Eliza!' he says firmly. 'Do not speak to your brother like that.'

'But he touched my American Girl doll,' she says, her voice bordering on hysteria. 'He came in my room and touched my American Girl doll,' her voice is rising, 'and it's private! I hate him. I hate you, Jack!'

'Eliza, stop! We do not use the word hate in our family.'

'I don't care. Aaaaargh!' She throws herself onto the bed, screaming into the pillow, while Jack smirks in the doorway.

'And that's enough smiling from you, Jack,' Reece says. 'Let's go downstairs.'

'What about me?' Eliza raises a tear-stained face. 'I'm coming downstairs too. That's not fair.'

'No!' Jack's face falls. 'It's boy time. Me and Daddy.'

'No!' Eliza shouts. 'That's not fair. Mommy's not here so I don't get to have any girl time. Daddy! Tell him! He can't have boy time when Mommy's not here.'

'Oh Jesus,' Reece mutters under his breath. 'We'll figure it out,' he says, doing his damnedest to keep his voice calm.

In the end, he bribes them. It may be freezing outside, but a trip to the ice-cream store has always worked wonders. They bring the dog with them, and pass Honor, on her way home from a grocery shop, as they leave.

'Who wants to see a movie?' he says, when they have

finished their ice cream. 'How about we drop Elizabeth home and go and see what's on at the Playhouse?'

'Yay!' the kids shout happily in unison, an ice-cream high having long replaced their mutual animosity.

*

Honor is upstairs in the bath when she hears noises in the hallway. Probably Reece is home, she thinks, leaning her head back and wondering when, or if ever, this numbness will disappear. She has spent today just putting one foot in front of the other, trying to get through the long hours.

She has been through this before. This fear. This heaviness. With George. But she never expected to be going through it with her daughter. A year. A death sentence. Climbing wearily out of the bath she wraps a towelling robe around her and goes downstairs to make some tea. She has never been a woman who naps during the day, but it is almost impossible for her to keep her eyes open, and a cup of tea, followed by a nap, suddenly seems like the best idea in the world.

The kettle is on when she hears a man clear his throat, and she almost jumps out of her skin. She turns slowly, standing stock-still when she sees her ex-husband standing awkwardly in the doorway of the kitchen.

'Walter?' she says, confused.

'Hello, Honor.' Oh yes. It's definitely Walter.

'Oh . . . goodness. I wasn't expecting . . . I . . .' She looks down at herself, in a robe, barefooted, and she clutches the robe tightly. 'Clearly, I wasn't expecting anyone.'

'Hey, Mom!' Steffi comes barrelling into the room, trying to suppress her excitement that her parents are in the same room for only the second or third time in almost twenty years. 'Dad drove hours to get here. Callie said he should take the other spare room.'

'Of course,' Honor says, taking a deep breath and regrouping. She walks over to Walter and looks at him closely. 'It's good that you're here.'

Walter breathes in, and finds himself overwhelmed by the fact that Honor still smells exactly the same. He would know her smell anywhere. And it is only now that he feels himself start to crack.

I will be strong. I will not weaken.

He nods, and backs away ever so slightly. Honor puts her arms down. She was going to give him a hug, to thank him for coming, for being the type of father who comes when their daughters need help, and to show him her support. Poor Walter, he still looks as stiff as ever.

'Come on, Dad. I'll help you with your stuff. Mom? Will you make us some tea?'

No matter how old the children, Honor thinks, they still want their parents to get back together. For years after the divorce, when she asked what they wished for Christmas, they always said that they wanted her and Dad to marry each other again. Even when they were both married to other people, and even though they adored George beyond anything imaginable. There will never come a day, she realizes, when they will not want the two people who created them to come together again.

Look at Steffi now, with her parents finally – finally – back in the same room. She is practically skipping up the stairs, looking from her father to her mother with delight in her eyes.

Honor gathers the cups and the teabags, and smiles to

herself. Walter looks very good. She is surprised, but perhaps she should not be. As is so often the case, Walter has got even better-looking with age. His hair is now white, and it suits him. He looks very like his father – an elegant, good-looking patrician man, who has somehow, despite his awkwardness in the doorway, grown into his skin.

But he is still uncomfortable. Poor Walter. She feels now, as she always did, a wave of sympathy. He is a good man. She knew it then, and knows it now, but he is a man always crippled by his background. So stiff. So intent on reserve. Never able to relax and just *be*.

She pours the tea, sets out a plate of cookies. For a moment she is tempted to take her cup and go upstairs, as she had planned, and take a nap. Leave Walter and Steffi to drink their tea by themselves. She is not tired any more. Adrenalin is now pumping through her system, and she suspects a nap is out of the question. Sitting at the table, she pours some milk into her tea, and opens a magazine.

Walter unpacks his suitcase, stacking his clothes neatly in the chest of drawers: underwear on the left, socks on the right, undershirts below and sweaters below that. It is the way he has always organized his chests of drawers, and the way he always will.

He hangs his trousers, making sure all the creases are in the right place, and his shirts next to them, lining up his shoes at the bottom.

His razor and shaving brush go in the bathroom, with the small pot of shaving soap. He has always refused, on principle, to succumb to shaving foam in a can. He still loves the daily ritual of swirling a wet brush in the small pot and working up a lather.

Finally, he can't delay it any more. He has to go back downstairs. Although . . . it wasn't so bad. He has been dreading seeing Honor for all these years, yet seeing her down there was oddly . . . comforting. She looked exactly the same. Obviously older, greyer, more tired, but smelling her for those few seconds, seeing that look in her eyes, swept him back, and instead of feeling the resentment and anger he has felt for so many years, he felt . . . on familiar ground. Perhaps that was the best way to put it.

'So what do you think?' Walter says, sitting at the table.

'I think it's pretty shitty,' Steffi says, and her father gives her a look.

'Language,' he says.

'Sorry. But as Callie was saying earlier, who knows what they'll develop in the next year? They're coming up with new cancer treatments all the time. Mark said a year, but Callie pointed out that they may have come up with a cure by then.'

'She's a fighter, our daughter,' Walter says, looking Honor straight in the eye for the first time.

'She is.' Honor smiles. 'I just don't know whether this is a fight she can win.'

'Mom!' Steffi says. 'We can't think like that. We have to be positive; we have to presume she can get through this.'

'You're right,' Honor says. 'I'm sorry. Did she say anything else to you?'

'Yes. I told her I was going to be with her every day, and she told me absolutely not.'

'She doesn't want you there?'

'That's what I asked, but she said she doesn't want everyone showing up with depressed faces. She understands that this is a huge shock, and we're all going to feel like shit.' She looks at her father. 'Sorry, Dad. She knows we'll all feel horrible for a while, but she doesn't want us to. She said if she can't go out and live her life, we have to live it for her.'

'What does *that* mean?' Walter asks gruffly.

'That means she doesn't want us to mope around her and burst into tears, although, God knows, I'm a disaster. You know Callie – she's never been able to stand being around depressed people, and she says if we all carry on the way we are now she may have to kill herself in way less than a year.'

Honor and Walter both smile. That's their daughter, all over.

'She said it's not that she doesn't want us all around, but she wants us all around in a happy way. Apparently the radiation is going to be rough. She'll be exhausted and sleeping a lot, so when she's awake she wants to hear good things.'

'Any other directives?' Honor asks.

'Yes. Guacamole. She wants me to make her guacamole. She says she has a craving.'

'Well that's good!' Honor is excited. 'If she's showing an appetite that must be a good thing, no?'

'I would think that must be a good thing,' Walter agrees. 'Is there anyone doing any research on this disease of hers?'

Steffi nods. 'Lila's boyfriend, Ed, is a journalist. He's apparently spent all night on the computer doing research. They're going to come over later. I'm going to run down to the store and get some avocado and coriander. Anyone want to come?'

'I'll come,' both Walter and Honor chime at the same time.

'Great!' Steffi cannot hide a big grin. 'I'll drive.'

*

Reece has just paid the pizza-delivery man, and is wondering where in the hell everyone is. He wants to get back to the hospital to see Callie, but there's no one at home. They've done ice cream, done a movie, done the playground on the way home. He was hoping to dump the children on Honor then run off to Callie, but there's no one here, no note, nothing.

As he places the pizza on the table, the back door opens and – thank you, God, for listening! – Steffi and Honor troop in, followed by Walter.

'Walter!' Reece walks over and gives him a man hug just as the children come running into the room.

'*Grandpa!*' they both yell at the same time, climbing up his legs. Walter scoops them up and covers them with kisses.

'Eliza! Look how big you are! And so pretty! When did you get to be so beautiful?'

'I think it was last year,' Eliza says very seriously, laying her head on his shoulder and stroking his cheek.

'And Jack! Show me your muscles!' Jack flexes his little arm proudly and Walter throws his head back and laughs, then squeezes the children tightly, burying his face in their hair and inhaling their smell.

There he is, thinks Honor, watching them in amazement. *There*'s the real Walter. She has never imagined him as a grandfather, has had no idea what he would be like, would never have dreamed that his grandchildren would be able to unlock his stiffness, his awkwardness.

But look at him now! Warm, and easy, and loving.

There he is, at last. She smiles to herself. *Who knew?*

Guacamole

2 ripe avocados
½ red onion, minced (about ½ cup)
2 tablespoons coriander leaves, finely chopped
1 tablespoon fresh lime or lemon juice
½ teaspoon coarse salt
dash of freshly grated black pepper
dried red pepper flakes
½ ripe tomato, seeds and pulp removed, chopped

Much of this is done to taste so start with this recipe and adjust to your liking.

Halve the avocados and remove the stones. Scoop out the flesh, put it in a mixing bowl and mash it with a fork.

Add the onion, coriander, lime or lemon, salt and pepper, and mash some more. Add red pepper flakes according to taste.

Cover with cling film, placing it directly on the surface of the guacamole to prevent oxidation. Refrigerate until ready. Just before serving add the chopped tomato to the guacamole and mix.

Garnish with red radishes or jicama. Serve with tortilla chips.

Chapter Twenty-Six

'What do you need me to do?' Lila has dragged the arm-chair up to the bed, and is holding Callie's hand.

'I need you to look after the children.'

'I will.'

'No, I mean even now, when I'm in the hospital, or when I'm home but can't be around for them. I know you're their godmother, but I want you to really look after them. What I need is for you to do something with them a few times a week, while I'm having radiation. I know they're at school, but if you could take them to a class, or the play-ground, or something.'

'Of course,' Lila says, trying not to show a glimmer of panic, for mothering has never been her strong point. Children, she has always said, are fine in small measure, and as long as they belong to other people.

'I *know* parenting's not your strong point.' Callie squints at her and Lila smiles. 'But they've known you their entire lives, and they love you. My mom's in her late sixties and she's tired, and I'm worried about giving Steffi this kind of responsibility. It won't be for ever, but just while I'm going through the radiotherapy.'

'I would do anything for you,' Lila says. 'Ed too. He's been up all night reading up on your disease.'

'He's a great guy, your boyfriend. Did you know that?'

'I do. I'm lucky.'

'Not lucky. You deserve it. I'm glad you found each other. Did he uncover anything?'

'Well. As you know, it's not great. Apparently, though, there are cases of people living up to two thousand days.'

'Lila, I have no brain cells at the moment. What is two thousand days?'

'Five and a half years.'

'Really?' For the first time in days a light switches on in Callie's eyes.

Lila grins. 'Really.'

'In five and a half years,' she muses, 'Eliza will be thirteen and Jack will be eleven. That would be . . . okay. I could leave them then. Screw the statistics, I'm going to be the one who outlives them all.'

'That's my girl.' Lila squeezes her hand. 'I know you can do it.'

'You know, I have an ulterior motive in having you look after my kids, too, right?'

Lila sighs. 'Go on, then. You're trying to turn me into a mother. Have you been talking to Ed?'

'Not since I've been in here,' Callie says, 'but I did talk to him once and he said he'd love to have more children.'

'Why don't you come right out and say what's on your mind?'

'I have to say these things. I don't have time to mess around. I have to tell the people I love what I really think. I think you should have children with him.'

'No way!' Lila holds up a hand. 'We already had this discussion and I said no.'

'I know. And I'm going to change your mind.'

'By having me take your kids out? That's not going to

change my mind. The only reason I love your kids so much is because I can hand them back at the end of the day. Trust me, if your kids were with Auntie Lila twenty-four/seven, there'd be no love lost between us.'

'What if I asked you to have kids and then I die?' Callie grins, with an evil glint in her eye.

'Don't you dare, because then I'd have to, and I don't want to. I'm serious, Cal. You can ask me anything but don't force something on me that I don't want to do.'

'Oh but, Lila, you'd have these little chubby toddlers with curly black hair who'd speak in plummy English accents. They'd call you "Mummy"! And I know you'd fall completely in love.'

'Hmmm. I told Ed I'd think about it, so that's what I'll say to you. I'll think about it.'

*

Five and a half years.

Five and a half years.

Steffi feels some of the heaviness lift as she drives back home to Sleepy Hollow. Even if it's just one person who lived for five and a half years, why can't Callie? Hell, why can't she live even longer?

'I am putting Callie on a strict vegan diet,' she announced that afternoon, after they all heard the good news that Callie is coming home as soon as they get the pain under control — and it is looking hopeful that this may be in the next day or so. 'I'll make something else for you guys, but Callie cannot eat animal products. If she has any chance at all of making it through this, she has to do everything she can, and there are amazing stories out there of veganism helping people recover from cancer.'

Everyone shrugged their agreement – whatever might help, they are willing to try.

Steffi stops at the big food market on the way home, inspired now to start cooking. She will cook for Mary this week, and for Amy. And she will cook for Callie. For when she does not know what else to do, what else *can* she do but cook?

And she is fired up. Recipes fly through her mind. Cookies and cakes for Mary, fish and chicken for Amy, vegetables and nuts and grains for Callie.

Two hours later she is whizzing round the kitchen in a happy blur. Her iPod is plugged in and Sarah McLachlan is filling the room at top volume as she chops, and blends, and tastes. She doesn't hear the truck, and only hears the knocking on the door after several minutes.

Stanley is standing on the doorstep, with a bunch of gas-station flowers and a six-pack of Budweiser.

'Hey,' she says, surprised. 'It's you again.'

'Yup. Me again.' He shifts from foot to foot, looking uncomfortable. 'I heard that your sister was sick, and I just wanted to say I'm sorry. I brought you these.' He proffers the flowers.

'Wow. They're beautiful,' Steffi lies, touched beyond measure by the gesture. 'Thank you.'

'And I thought maybe you could do with a drink.'

'You know what? I'd *love* a drink. Come in and let's have a beer.'

Stanley surveys the mess in the kitchen. 'Are you ever *not* cooking?' he asks.

Steffi sits down at the kitchen table and looks around, laughing. 'I guess not. It's what makes me happy. And when I'm sad, or depressed, or lonely, the only thing I know to do to make me feel better is cook.'

'Is this all for you?' he says in amazement.

'NO!' She swats him. 'What do you think I am, some kind of glutton?'

'I didn't want to say anything.'

'The cookies and cakes are for Mary's store, and the rest is split between Amy and my family.'

'Is it true you're a vegan?'

'Kinda, sorta,' she says, raising a beer as he cracks off the top and passes it to her. 'I was. I worked in a vegetarian restaurant, so I still used eggs and dairy, even though I didn't eat them myself, but it's harder out here in the country. In New York it's easy to be anything you want, but you're much more limited outside any major city. Also, you kind of see things differently when you know where your meat is coming from. If I'm going to eat it, I want to know it's from an animal that's been raised on a family farm, grass-fed, led a happy life and killed humanely, and there are enough small farms out here that I do know that.'

'Really?' Stanley shrugs. 'I don't much care how it's raised as long as it tastes good.'

'But you *should* care.' Steffi turns serious. 'Most animals are shoved together in tiny pens, filled with diseases, living horrible lives.'

'I guess I've never thought about it much before.'

'I don't want to lecture you about it, but you should think about it. And it tastes better when it's local. Everything does. Here —' she looks around the kitchen, then jumps up and brings back a pot — 'this is home-made pesto. Try it.' She dips a spoon in and holds it out to him, expecting

317

him to take the spoon, but he covers her hand in his and dips his face forward, eating off the spoon they are both now holding.

It is suddenly shockingly intimate, and there is a silence as he holds her eyes while chewing. Steffi feels her stomach lurch. Oh God. She wasn't expecting *this* quite so soon.

'Wow,' he says eventually. 'That's amazing.'

Steffi recovers quickly, smiling with delight. 'See? That's basil grown outside in the garden, with garlic grown next door. Everything's fresh and you can taste the difference, can't you?'

'I don't know whether it's because it's fresh but that is really good.'

'Do you want more?' She grins. 'I've got tons. I was making a fish recipe. Do you like fish?'

'I love it. And yes, I'd love some.'

Steffi is not hungry in the slightest – cooking has always killed her appetite – so she sits and watches Stanley as he eats. He is aggressive, head down, almost shovelling the food in, and she is happy he is such an enthusiastic customer.

'Do you want some salad?' she says, when he is finished.

'Oh man,' he groans. 'I couldn't fit anything else in. This is so nice of you. I came here to see if you were okay, and you end up feeding me. That's just freaky.'

'It's not. It's nice. I like feeding people.' Steffi shivers, aware that, now she has stopped whirling round the kitchen cooking, the temperature in the house has dropped and it is chilly.

'You want me to build a fire?' Stanley says.

'No, it's fine. Don't worry.'

'I'm not worried. I build great fires. I don't mind.'

'Okay,' she says finally, with a shrug. 'Let me clean up in here and then I'll come in.'

Steffi knows what will happen tonight. She didn't expect it to happen quite so quickly, nor quite like this, but she knew, the second she laid eyes on Stanley, that all things being equal – no wives, girlfriends or stalkers to get in the way – they would end up in bed together.

She drags out the cleaning-up process, not sure whether she actually wants this. Her mind feels so full of Callie; but what did Callie say to her just today? She wants Steffi to *live*. She wants Steffi to have adventures. She wants Steffi to be able to come and tell her stories.

If Callie wants to live vicariously through Steffi, let's be honest here, there isn't anything terribly exciting about grocery shopping and spending the rest of the day cooking.

Steffi wipes a cloth over the counters, and bends to check her hair in the dark window. From this angle, she looks pretty damn good. Oh shit, she thinks. Bad underwear. She had shoved the lacy Victoria's Secret stuff to the back of the wardrobe, happy instead to pull on flesh-coloured T-shirt bras and panties – no sex appeal whatsoever, but God, are they comfortable.

'I'll be back in just a minute,' she calls to Stanley, as she races upstairs and roots around for her 'good' underwear.

She runs into the bathroom and scrapes a razor under her arms, then sniffs to make sure. All good. The old underwear is stuffed into the laundry basket, and the new is put on. Her stomach isn't quite as flat as it was when she was living in New York – all that walking definitely helped keep the pounds at bay – but she will have to do.

Back into the living room. Steffi tries to be casual, to pretend that neither of them knows what is on the menu for the rest of the evening. Stanley is lounging back on the sofa, one arm holding his beer, the other resting along the back. He looks perfectly comfortable. And shockingly sexy.

Where should she sit? Well, she knows where she should sit, but it feels too obvious, so she sits in the chair by the fire.

They talk, softly. He asks about Callie, and she finds herself telling him, welling up when she gets to the prognosis.

'Come here,' he says, holding out his arms, and he puts them around her to comfort her. She leans her head on his chest and remembers just how good this feels, to be held in the arms of a man.

And when he finally kisses her, it comes as no surprise whatsoever.

Steffi wakes up slowly, pulling the covers tightly around her, wondering what time it is. It is dark outside, but that means nothing. The mornings have been dark outside for weeks now. She pulls her watch over from the edge of the nightstand and squints: 6.04 a.m. Time to get up – chickens and goats to feed, dogs to let out, heating to be turned on. There must be a way, she thinks, to time the heating so it is off during the night, then comes on automatically at around 5 a.m., so every morning is not like climbing out of bed and into a fridge.

But she hasn't been able to figure it out. It doesn't seem possible to regulate the house. It is either boiling hot, or freezing cold. She has sent an email to Mason but has yet to hear. She will ask Stanley – she knew there was something she had forgotten last night.

Stanley. She smiles to herself as she burrows down in the sheets, in the warmth, trying to remember every detail.

They sat on the sofa last night, for hours. Kissing, and stroking each other, and murmuring.

Steffi expected to jump into bed with him, but that didn't happen. She still isn't sure why, but she is glad. It was enough to be held, and kissed, and comforted.

He left at two in the morning. He stood up and said he really ought to get going. She knew that was the point at which she could have said, stay. She knew that, had she said it, he would have said yes. But she needed some alone time. Needed to process everything that has happened over the last twenty-four hours, this roller coaster of emotions she has been on.

From the devastation of thinking Callie might live for only a few weeks, to the high of thinking it may be as much as five and a half years.

Stanley's sweetness in showing up with flowers; his holding her all those hours, without pushing her, or trying to go further than either of them might have been comfortable doing.

In the old days there would have been no question of her jumping into bed with him, but she feels that if she has learned nothing else through this journey with Callie, it is what it is to be an adult.

Life is indeed short, and she must seize the moment. And yet, and yet . . . She feels she has aged ten years in the past few weeks. She feels, finally, as if Callie's illness is forcing her to grow up, to be patient instead of impulsive, to be calm, even when her insides are raging.

Grown-ups don't always give in to instant gratification. They don't jump into bed with total strangers just because it feels good.

Perhaps she will sleep with him next time. Perhaps not. But for today it feels good to have sent him home, and to have peeled off her Victoria's Secret underwear, all alone, in her bathroom, to have climbed into her long, white, Victorian nightgown, and collapsed into bed with no one but a large, shaggy, snoring deerhound for company.

Better, is waking up on her own. She bites the bullet and jumps out of bed, running downstairs, her teeth chattering, to the thermostat, which she moves to Heat, then to the back door, which she unlocks, shooing Fingal out, before running back upstairs and jumping under the covers again.

This is now her morning routine. The pipes clank ominously as she reaches over for her computer, settling it on her lap while the house quickly starts to heat up. There may only be two temperatures, but at least, and thank God, it doesn't take long to heat.

There is an email from Mason – finally!

To: Steffi Tollemache
From: Mason Gregory
Re: Freezing toes

Dear Steffi,

The heating system in the house has long been a source of discontent. I suspect I have to replace the whole damned thing, but have been putting it off for years by building fires and putting lots of blankets on the bed. I can look into a new system, although be warned – the house will be turned upside down. Failing that, I am happy to provide one, or thirty, space heaters. (A couple should suffice, though, I would think.)

London is . . . not quite what I expected. Rather more changes than I thought, but I shall save that for another time. It continues to be very grey and drizzly, which I did expect, and rather wonderful in many ways. I am finding myself at the theatre on a far too regular basis, and am discovering that we Americans are entirely incorrect in presuming all English food is dreadful.

It is, as they say in England, brilliant! I have eaten some of the best food I have ever eaten in my life here. But I do miss New York, and the neighbourhood restaurants. And of course, Joni's, although I hear the food's gone downhill terribly since their star chef left . . . ;-)

What's fascinating is how much fresher the produce is. You would love it here. The quantities are much smaller, but everything has so much taste. There are extraordinary farmers' markets here at the weekends, and they are huge – I think one day you will have to come over and I will give you a tour.

Again, I am so happy you are so happy in Sleepy Hollow. It is my little corner of paradise, and I'm not sure I have ever before had a tenant who has fallen in love with it quite as much as I, and now you, have.

Do you have any news about your sister? Your last email of three days ago said you were waiting for results. Did they come? Do they know what's wrong with her? The waiting game is, I know, horrific. I am sending you warm hugs across the Atlantic, and much support.

M

Steffi takes a deep breath, and hits Reply.

Yummy White Fish Pesto Sandwich

For the pesto
2 cups fresh basil leaves, packed
½ cup freshly grated Parmesan or Romano cheese
½ cup extra-virgin olive oil
⅓ cup pine nuts or walnuts
3 medium-sized garlic cloves, minced
salt and freshly ground black pepper to taste

For the fish sandwich
zest of 1 lemon
4 white-fish fillets (relatively thin, e.g. tilapia or cod)
1 pack prosciutto
4–5 bunches of cherry tomatoes on the vine
5 sun-dried tomatoes
2 garlic cloves, finely sliced
½ cup black olives, pitted (not the ones in brine – the wrinkly ones)
1 chilli pepper, finely sliced.

Preheat the oven to 350°F.

Put all the ingredients for the pesto in a blender and whizz until ground.

Stir the lemon zest into the pesto, then sandwich the fish fillets together with the pesto sauce, ending up with two sandwiches.

Wrap the fillets with the prosciutto and set aside.

Put the tomatoes, sun-dried tomatoes, garlic, olives and chilli in a roasting pan and roast for around 25 minutes, until the tomatoes have softened and become juicy.

Add the fish on top of the tomatoes, and put back in the oven for a further 20–25 minutes.

Serve warm.

Chapter Twenty-Seven

Reece checks that everything is in the small suitcase. Blanket, the photo frames that Lila brought, clothes, toiletries, iPod. It is all there.

The nurses come in and help Callie sit up, then transfer her into the wheelchair that will take her to the car. Her legs are now so weak they have organized another wheelchair for home. A physical therapist will be coming to the house, who will, they say, hopefully be able to help with restoring some muscle strength.

'Five and a half years,' Reece said to Mark, half an hour earlier, when he came in to tell them her first radiation therapy session would be the next day. 'There are cases of people living that long. Is that possible?'

'It's always possible,' Mark said. 'The odds are not good, but there are always those who beat the odds. Callie is young, she's strong, and that puts her in a far better position than many.'

'So she could have years?'

Mark paused. 'Where there is life, there is hope.'

'I'm going to make it,' Callie said, with surprising strength in her voice. 'I'm going to beat the odds.'

Mark nodded. 'A positive attitude is a wonderful thing. You'd be astonished at what a difference it can make, and Callie? Reece? We're doing everything we can.'

*

Lila stamps her feet in the cold and pretends that she's having a great time, waiting in line for half an hour to get into Ye Olde Christmas Fayre at the Washington Homestead.

Reece was originally taking the children, but when he discovered Callie was coming home Lila and Ed offered to take them instead. Callie could settle in and rest in peace and quiet, they said, ready for the children later that day.

'Are you *sure* Santa's in there?' Jack asks dubiously. 'I thought he was in the North Pole getting ready for Christmas.'

'He is. Except when he visits places to come and see kids,' Ed jumps in, seeing Lila's panicked face. He laughs, knowing that Lila isn't quite sure what the Christmas story is.

'But *why* does he have to come and see us?' Eliza asks. 'Phebe tells him everything every night.'

'What?' Now even Ed is completely lost.

'Phebe. Our Elf on the Shelf.'

Ed stares at Eliza in silence.

'I'm sorry,' he says eventually. 'I have been celebrating Christmas for approximately forty-six years, and I have no idea what you're talking about.'

'Phebe is our house elf, and he flies back to the North Pole every night and reports on our behaviour, so if we're bad he tells Santa and we don't get good Christmas gifts.'

'And also,' Jack adds seriously, 'we tell Phebe what we want for Christmas, and he tells Santa.'

'You tell him?'

'We write to him and he takes our letters to Santa.'

Wow! Ed flashes a grin at Lila. It's all got so ... sophisticated.

'Santa doesn't need to come and see us because he already knows,' Eliza explains.

'I think he probably just wants to come and see for himself,' Lila says. 'Oh look! The line's moving, and they're giving out candy canes!' She breathes a sigh of relief, and squeezes Ed's hand.

While Lila has never actually celebrated Christmas herself, she is secretly a sucker for this time of year. She diligently lights the candles on the menorah every night, but spotting a lit menorah through a darkened window has never quite given her the thrill of spotting a beautiful, lit Christmas tree.

Perhaps because Christmas was forbidden to her when she was a child, it has held a romantic thrill for her throughout her entire life. Driving down Main Street is always so much more exciting when the trees are wrapped with sparkling white lights.

Her own family would go out for Chinese every Christmas Eve, then sit down for bagels and Nova lox on Christmas Day. At college, she would go home with Callie for the holiday, loving their Christmas meal, a hybrid of lunch and dinner, sitting down at the table at around four, and not getting up until long after nine.

George always made a big deal of carving the turkey, and Lila will always remember how welcome they made her feel. She was never, as she thought she would feel, the token Jew, never made to feel she didn't belong. She was welcomed as part of the family. Callie had her pile of gifts, Steffi had hers, and Lila had hers.

Christmas was always a big deal in the Tollemache

household, but what should happen this year? It is fast approaching, and there is no way that Callie will be able to do it. She and Steffi will just have to take over.

Callie takes Christmas seriously. She doesn't do just one tree; she has three. She has colour themes in every room, giant wooden nutcrackers that are positioned outside the front door, delicate glittering snowflake ornaments that she hangs from the magnolia tree in the front yard.

Her ornaments have been collected over the years, and she has a Christmas Eve party every year, when the egg-nog and spiced rum flow, and the children string popcorn and dried cranberries to loop around the tree.

Not this year. This year it will not be done, unless Lila does it with Steffi and Honor.

Lila closes her eyes, just for a second, and puts out a hand to steady herself.

Most of the time, Lila is fine. She carries the weight of sadness with her every minute of every day, but she manages.

Most of the time she has to be fine, because in between thinking about Callie, and worrying about Callie, and caring for Callie, there is life. There is Ed, and Clay, and her work, and running her house, and speaking to clients, and grocery shopping, and doing all the things that have to be done every day.

And then it will hit her. Like now. A wave of dizziness. And she will bury her face in her hands, or break into wrenching sobs out of nowhere, or suddenly find that she has been pushing her trolley around the grocery store and the reason everyone has been looking at her with worried expressions is because she has a trail of tears trickling quietly down her cheeks that just won't stop.

She swallows away the lump for she is with the children and she does not want them to see her cry. Instead she puts her arms around them and squeezes them tightly, and is surprised, and delighted, that Jack, who is so often unwilling to accept embraces of any kind from anyone other than his parents, leans in to her and squeezes her back.

Ed sits with the children at the kiddie craft table in a room at the fair and makes Christmas tree ornaments with them, eventually persuading Lila to join in. She professes she'd prefer to be sitting downstairs drinking peppermint-flavoured hot chocolate, but as soon as she picks up the glue she is, much to the children's delight, absorbed.

She brushes garlands of white glue onto the felt, sprinkles glitter on top and then sticks little sequins all over her Christmas tree.

'That looks awesome!' Eliza breathes, leaning on Lila. She immediately copies exactly what Lila has done.

From the outside, you would think that the children were absolutely fine. That the fact that their mother has been in hospital for the past few weeks has not made any impact on their lives.

Yet they are both more affectionate, and more receptive to affection, than Lila has ever known. Eliza has always been affectionate with her, but today she is positively clingy. And Jack was always Mr Touch Me Not, but today he is holding her hand, letting her hug him, sitting on her lap.

They walk around the fair, stopping to do various crafts or play games – a Christmas beanbag toss, pin the sack on the Santa – and then they join the line to go in to see Santa.

Both children are breathless with excitement, and Lila is

gratified to see they have a real Santa. No cotton-wool beard on a young boy at this fair; this Santa is in his sixties, with round, ruddy cheeks and his own long white beard. He has twinkly eyes and a big soft belly. Even Lila gasps a little. She may not celebrate Christmas, but she knows Santa when she sees him.

Eliza turns very shy when she reaches the front, and Santa gently coaxes her in front of him. 'What's your name, pretty girl?' he asks.

'Eliza,' she whispers.

'And have you been good this Christmas?'

Eliza nods.

'What would you like for Christmas?'

She shrugs.

'Come now. There must be one wonderful thing you'd like from me this Christmas.'

'Can you make my mommy better?' She looks at him hopefully.

Santa smiles. 'I can certainly try,' he says. 'I can't always promise that it works, but I'll get my elves working on that right away. Is there anything else that's for you?'

'Yes,' Eliza says, suddenly confident. 'I'd like a canopy bed for my American Girl doll, please.'

'Done,' Santa says, and they both pose for the obligatory photograph. 'Tell your mom I'm working on it and I wish her well,' he says.

Next it is Jack's turn. He marches up to Santa and looks him square in the eye.

'I'm Jack,' he says. 'And I have a list.'

Lila watches as Santa laughs and Jack fishes a folded and rather crumpled piece of paper out of his pocket and hands it to him.

'Do you want to tell me as well? Can you read it to me?'
'Yes,' Jack says and he starts to read.

Dear Santa, this has mistacs sorry for Christmas cod I have Think fast and talking globe junior and Mystery rock and kids build their own robot and what a opening and calling all rock hounds and look Boing what I made and what spies want and spy shot and kids command and Robbie robot and crystal clear night vision and star wars lego please love Jack

Santa looks surprised, and Lila cracks up with laughter.
'Jack?' she says. 'What *is* all that stuff?'
'It's in the book at home.' Jack looks up at her seriously.
'What book?'
'The catalogues,' Eliza chimes in. 'He goes through all the mail and steals the catalogues, then draws circles around everything he wants.'
Santa chuckles heartily. 'Well, if there is just one thing on that list that you really couldn't live without, what would it be?'
Jack thinks for a minute. '*Star Wars* Lego,' he says eventually.
'Excellent choice.' Santa nods, then leans forward to whisper in Jack's ear, 'Legos are my favourites too,' and Jack grins delightedly from ear to ear.

*

Reece is cooking dinner when Ed and Lila arrive home with the kids.
'Did you have fun?'

'I had the best time!' Lila says truthfully. 'The kids were amazing, and it was just . . . fun. I think they loved it. I also know what they want for Christmas, just in case you are stuck.'

'Oh God,' Reece groans as he slices mushrooms and measures polenta into a jug. 'I haven't even thought.'

'So don't,' Lila says. 'I'll organize everything, and I'll enlist others to help. I didn't know you could cook.'

'Neither did I.' Reece grins. 'But I'm learning. So far the children are big fans of my chicken teriyaki.'

'You make chicken teriyaki?'

'I smother chicken breasts in soy sauce and stick them on the George Foreman. Does that count?'

'I suppose so. I'm impressed. Anything else in your repertoire?'

'I make a mean macaroni cheese.' He gestures to the boxes of organic mac 'n' cheese on the counter, which are waiting to be put away in the pantry. 'And I'm now, slightly ambitiously, I will admit, attempting a wild mushroom polenta for the rest of us tonight.'

'That's amazing.'

'My wife has taught me well.'

'Can I go up?'

'I think she's sleeping, but of course. Go up.'

'Is she thrilled to be home?'

'She really is. She said she feels better just being in her own bed.'

'I can imagine. Where are Honor and Walter?'

'Honor needed some things in town so Walter's giving her a lift.'

'Really? They're in a car together? Walter actually agreed to share air space with Honor?'

'I know,' Reece says with a laugh. 'It must be a Christmas miracle.'

'Some things will never cease to amaze me.' Lila shakes her head. 'I'll go upstairs and see if there's anything she wants.'

The bedroom door is open. Lila tiptoes in to see that Callie is sleeping. It is a restless sleep, her mouth is open and she turns her head frequently. Lila isn't entirely sure she even is asleep, and as she steps on a creaking floorboard Callie opens her eyes and moves them slowly to focus on Lila.

'Hi, sweetie,' Lila says, coming to sit on the bed next to her, leaning over and kissing her cheek. 'I didn't mean to wake you. I just came up to see if you needed anything.'

'I'm thirsty,' Callie says, gesturing to the table where there is a plastic cup of water with a lid and a straw. Lila reaches for the cup and holds the straw to Callie's lips; she sips gratefully, her head falling back on the pillow when she is done.

'How are the kids?' Callie asks.

'They're amazing. We took them to Ye Olde Christmas Fayre today.' Lila tells Callie about their escapades, ending with Jack's long list of gifts pulled from the catalogues. Callie's face lights up and she starts to laugh.

'Thank you,' she says. 'You are the best.'

'Do you want me to do the Christmas decorations?' Lila asks gently.

'No.' Callie covers Lila's hand with her own. 'I want to do them myself with the kids. If I need you, I'll let you know. This radiation stuff sounds like it's going to be pretty brutal so I don't know how I'll feel, but I want to do Christmas with the kids.'

'Are you worried about the side-effects of the radiation?'

Callie nods. 'A bit.'

'I spoke to Mark about it yesterday. He said a lot of it can be controlled with drugs. The Zofran, for example, should still deal with the nausea.'

'I know. He told me.' Callie starts to sit up, and Lila quickly tucks a large foam triangle behind her, brought back from the hospital and now kept permanently beside the bed, so she can get comfortable. 'I'm not so worried about the sickness. Or the hair loss. It's not like I haven't been through that before. It's dementia and brain deterioration that scare me.'

'But that doesn't happen to everyone, right?'

'No. I just have to hope it doesn't happen to me. He also said it's going to knock me out and I'm going to be doing a lot of sleeping.'

'But that's good. That will give your body a chance to heal.'

'I hope so. Where are the kids now?'

'Reece is feeding them. Do you want them to come up?'

'Yes! Let's have a picnic in here! Will you get them? And bring up some wine and some guacamole.'

'You're allowed to drink wine?' Lila is shocked.

'Not me, silly. For you, Reece, Ed and my parents. Hey, speaking of my parents, is that not totally weird, that my dad is actually staying under the same roof as my mom?'

'It's totally weird, and get this: your dad drove your mother into town this afternoon.'

'No! Oh my God. Can you imagine if they got back

together? Wouldn't that be just … amazing? And strange?'

'It would be amazing and strange. I bet they're both lonely.'

'I know they're both lonely. I'm going to try to do some matchmaking.'

'Right. Because you haven't been trying to get them back together since the day they divorced.'

'So? At least now it looks like I have a chance. Maybe I'll make that a dying wish.'

'Will you *stop*?' Lila looks horrified. 'You're not dying.'

'Not today.' And Callie flashes a Callie-like grin.

Lila skips down the stairs, a smile on her face and the heaviness finally gone. This has been the first time in weeks that Callie has looked, and sounded, like her old self. What if she *can* beat the odds? What if she does make it to five and a half years, and they do find a cure and she's fine?

Suddenly this doesn't feel like such a remote possibility after all.

*

Walter parks the car and gets out quickly, walking over to let Honor out of her side.

'Oh, I'm fine.' She smiles, remembering how Walter always used to insist on opening the door. Funny. She hadn't thought about that for years. George had never done it, and she hadn't expected him to. It always seemed ridiculously old-fashioned and formal, but now she realizes she quite likes Walter opening the door, reaching in to take her shopping bags, holding out a hand to help her out of the car.

For let's face it. She's not as young, or as steady, as she once was, and there is something inherently comforting in the elegance of his good manners.

They have not talked much. Even sitting in the car, driving to and from town, there was no small talk. Instead, they listened to NPR, in companionable silence, occasionally swapping thoughts on the discussion they were listening to.

Honor is surprised that Walter has softened with age. She didn't press him, but deduced from his comments that while he may not have moved over quite so far as to be able to join her on the left, he is deeply disturbed with what has happened to the Republican party, and was humiliated by the choice of vice-presidential running mate in the last election.

There is hope for him yet, she thinks, surprising herself with the affection that seems to come along for the ride.

All the lights are on in the house, but there is no one around.

'Where is everyone?' Honor looks at Walter, who shrugs, then turns his head as they both hear a shriek of laughter coming from upstairs.

They walk up to find a smiling Callie sitting up, directing a game of Clue. Reece, Ed and Lila are sitting on the bed, each with a glass of wine, and the kids are bouncing up and down excitedly, not because of the game, but because they are just so damned happy to have their mother home.

'Well!' Honor says, a glow lifting her heart. '*Well!*' And she and Walter drop their bags, and climb on the bed.

Wild Mushroom Polenta

For the polenta
3 cups chicken stock
½ cup single cream
seasoning
2 cups polenta
¼ cup mascarpone
4 tablespoons butter
½ cup Parmesan cheese, grated

For the mushroom sauce
1 cup assorted gourmet mushrooms (porcini, morels, etc.)
olive oil
1 garlic clove
1 onion, finely chopped
1 sprig of thyme
seasoning
4 tablespoons chicken stock
chopped parsley

Combine the stock, cream and salt and bring to a simmer. Add the polenta in a slow steady stream and bring the mixture back to a simmer. Stir with a wooden spoon and cook on a very low heat for 1 hour, stirring frequently. If the mixture begins to thicken too much, add more simmering stock. Finish with mascarpone and butter, then season and add the Parmesan. It should be like loose mashed potatoes.

To make the sauce: rinse the mushrooms thoroughly if fresh, then slice them and sauté them with the garlic and onion in olive oil for about 10 minutes. Add the thyme, seasoning and stock, and turn the heat to high, to reduce and thicken the sauce.

When ready to serve, spoon the sauce over the polenta and sprinkle with the chopped parsley.

Chapter Twenty-Eight

Steffi is lying on Callie's bed, reading out loud from Kris Carr's *Crazy Sexy Cancer Tips*, as Callie drifts in and out of sleep. Her breathing changes each time she sleeps, and Steffi puts the book down and just gazes at her sister, wishing there were something, *anything*, she could do to make this process easier.

Steffi knew the radiation would be bad. *Everyone* knew the radiation would be bad. She didn't think it would be *this* bad, this . . . *exhausting*. Callie barely has the energy to move. Her legs are now so weak she has to be helped out of bed, helped down to the car, and all she wants to do is sleep.

'It's helping,' Steffi whispered earlier. 'You're sleeping because you're healing.'

All Callie knows is she wants to close her eyes, and sleep for ever. Her routine is to force herself awake for breakfast in bed with the children, who are thrilled they get to have breakfast in Mommy's bed every morning, then go to hospital for the radiotherapy, then back home to sleep all day.

In the afternoon she manages two or three hours of awake time, but she doesn't have the strength to get up any more unless it's to go to the hospital. During the afternoons, when she is awake, the family gathers together on her bed, attempting to fill the room with laughter, and hope.

Callie's hair has gone. When the clumps started coming out in her fingers, Reece carried her into the bathroom and gently shaved her head. She joked throughout, her mom and dad sitting in the bedroom, nervous as anything, trying to smile with her when she first emerged, her head shaved, asking if it suited her.

When Callie was back in bed she sent everyone downstairs, claiming she needed a nap. She sank back on her pillow, clutching a lock of her hair. Feeling empty.

They told her this would happen, and it's not like she doesn't know what it feels like, to have no hair, but she hadn't expected it to go so quickly.

'Good job you don't have the energy to go anywhere,' Steffi said, when she first saw her. 'You look terrible.'

Callie laughed. 'Thank God someone's brave enough to be honest with me,' she said. 'Everyone else keeps saying it actually suits me.'

'Nope. You look like a baby bird.'

And it is true. Callie hasn't been able to eat properly for weeks, and she is tiny. Now that her hair has dropped out from the radiation she does indeed look like a fuzzy baby bird.

Steffi has found herself gently taking control, a unique position for her, the baby sister now having to be the big sister. A catheter was inserted just the other day, and when her mom was resting Steffi was the one to open the tube, so carefully, and empty it for Callie.

'I should be embarrassed,' Callie sighed.

'Why? This doesn't bother me.' Steffi shook her head. 'I

was up to my knees in chicken poop this morning. Trust me. This is nothing.'

And it's true. Steffi, and Lila, neither of whom is a mother, have both found themselves stepping into the mothering role, and it is as easy and natural for them as if Callie were a newborn baby.

Callie wakes up to find Steffi smiling at her.

'Hey,' Steffi whispers, reaching out a hand and stroking Callie's scalp.

'Hey, you. I love waking up and seeing you here,' she says. 'Have I been asleep long?'

'A while. I wanted to wait until you woke up before I left.'

'Where are you going?'

'I have to get cooking. Mary put in a late request for more cakes for tomorrow. And I haven't told you yet, but the big night with Stan is tomorrow.'

'Really? You're going on a date?'

Steffi grins. 'I'm not sure about that. We're going to some bar.'

'He can't take you out for dinner?'

Steffi shrugs. 'You know my type. They've usually got no money, and are much happier in grungy clothes.'

'Oh Steff.' Callie's eyes are serious. 'Aren't you getting too old for that?'

'What?' Steffi jumps on the defensive. 'What do you mean?'

'I just mean you deserve someone to treat you wonderfully. You deserve someone like, I don't know, like Reece.'

Steffi looks worried.

'I don't mean that I expect you to marry Reece in my

place!' She laughs. 'I just mean a grown-up. A real man. Someone who values you and respects you enough to take you out for dinner, not to some grungy bar where he's going to drink beer all night.'

'I know he's not the one, sis. But he's cute for now.'

'But Steff, it's time you stopped having *cute for now*. I want you to be with a good guy. A permanent guy.'

'I do too.'

'I want to meet Stan.'

'What? I thought you didn't want any visitors. You said yesterday you didn't want anyone to see you like this.'

'I don't. But what the hell? I'll do a deal with you. I have to meet him and if I think he's a good guy, you can keep seeing him, and if not, you have to end it.'

Steffi is aghast. 'That's horrible! That's emotional black-mail. I can't agree to that.'

'Yes, you can. Go on. I'm an excellent judge of character.'

'Maybe I'll bring him over, but I won't agree to anything else.'

'Okay.' Callie smiles. 'That's enough.'

'Cal?' Steffi says, after a few minutes, swallowing because these are hard words to say. 'If you don't make it, if this . . . doesn't work, have you thought about Reece?'

'What do you mean?'

'I know you. You've probably been going through lists of single or divorced women you know, figuring out if any of them would fit with Reece.'

Callie grins. 'I have. Is this a sick conversation, or what? But yeah, of course I have. There is one woman but I don't really know her. She's a friend of Vicky's, one of the moms in Eliza's class. She's a redhead, and Reece has always had a bit of a secret thing for redheads, and she's very cool. She's fun, and funny. I could see them fitting together.'

'So, if you don't make it,' Steffi can't actually say the word, 'should I try to find her?'

'Give it about a year. He'll need time to grieve. Oh Steff . . .' Callie looks up as Steffi chokes, suddenly, on a sob.

'I'm sorry, Cal.' She struggles to regain her composure. 'I shouldn't have even said anything.'

'Yes, you should. I love that you did. I love you so much, Steffi. You're the best sister anyone could ever have wanted, and I will always love you. Remember that. Wherever you are, and wherever I am, I am still going to love you. Always.'

'Okay.' Steffi's chest is heaving. She can't say anything else.

'And by the way, I'm not going to ask you to marry Reece because you'd drive each other nuts.'

Steffi smiles through her tears. 'Okay. That's one weight off my chest.'

'I have to go back to sleep now, sweetie. I'm so tired. Bring the guy. I don't even remember his name. God-damned chemo radiation brain,' she mumbles, as she closes her eyes and sinks back into sleep.

*

Reece is downstairs in the kitchen, warming up dinner. He peers out of the kitchen window to watch the snowflakes. It is dark outside, and cold, but the external lights are on and Walter is out there with the kids, trying to teach them how to make snow angels.

Lila walks into the kitchen, her arms filled with laundry.

'Reece, honey,' she says. 'I love you, but you need some serious help.'

'What do you mean?'

'I mean, no human being can cope with this amount of laundry. I've got the clothes of four adults and two children, and I can't manage this. We need to find someone to work here, a housekeeper.'

'Honor can do it, can't she? I'll ask her.'

'No, Reece. Honor's, what, almost seventy? You can't ask her to start ironing. She's here to look after Callie, primarily, and her grandkids. Not be a housekeeper. She's already a full-time nurse. We need to find you someone, pronto.'

'Okay.' Reece shrugs. 'Whatever you think.'

'Good. Callie has trained you well.' She disappears for a second, to put the laundry down, then comes back in. 'Want me to set the table?'

'Sure. Hey, Lila?'

'Yes?' She turns around, halfway to the cutlery drawer.

'I just want to say thank you. For everything you're doing, for being the friend you are. You're amazing.'

'Thank you,' she says. Tears well up in her eyes and Reece walks over to give her a hug.

But in the end, it is Reece who can't let go.

By seven o'clock, there are ten people in the kitchen. Immediate family, including Lila, and four friends of Callie's who have arrived with various casseroles and bunches of flowers.

Now that word has got around that it is serious, people keep dropping in unexpectedly. At first, Reece thought they were coming to see Callie, that they would disappear when he told them, as nicely as he could, that she wasn't up to seeing visitors. Still they keep coming, sitting around the island in the kitchen, drinking tea, or, in the late afternoon, wine.

Finally, he has realized that friends keep coming to be with the family. Friends who are as scared, and sad, as everyone else, and who need to have a connection, if not with Callie, then with the next best thing, for there is a tremendous comfort in all of them being together.

It is usually at five o'clock, when everyone is home, winding down, gathering around the island in the kitchen, that the callers start to arrive. It is not until late in the evening that the house is finally quiet. And when everyone has left and Reece goes upstairs to be with Callie, the only hum is that of the boiler, and a steady stream of sadness.

'Is it working?' Callie asked Mark the other day, halfway through the radiation sessions. 'Can you tell? Because I feel horrible, and I'm starting to forget things. My brain is turning to mush. I'm losing words.'

'That's normal,' Mark assured her. 'It's still too early to tell if the radiation is helping the neurological symptoms. We need to finish the course and then we'll do the scans and see where we are.'

'And if it hasn't worked?' she insisted.

'Let's cross that bridge when we come to it,' he said.

But there are other things happening that do not bode well. She is growing weaker and weaker – she needs help to raise herself to a sitting position in bed, she cannot walk, and two days ago she had 'an accident'.

Now, she is in adult diapers, which her mother lovingly

changes, cleaning her up and washing her gently in the bed.

Everyone is scared.

Eliza and Jack seem to be coping – to them it seems as though there is a big party every night, and everyone is making an enormous fuss of them. But Honor has seen Jack punch his pillow, in the quiet of his room, when he thinks no one is watching, a burst of anger that he doesn't want to express anywhere other than in private.

The psychologist, who is now visiting them at home, has said this is normal, and that it is also normal that he is not showing his sadness – at six, he is really too young to understand.

Eliza, though, becomes clingy and upset as the evening wears on. She creeps into her parents' bedroom at night and crawls quietly onto the bed, tucking herself into her mother. This is a child who has never spent a night in her parents' bed in her life, whose parents believed their bed was sacred; but circumstances are different now, and Callie will wake slightly and snuggle into her daughter, stroking her hair until Eliza falls back to sleep.

Honor is exhausted. She does not look in the mirror any more, unless she absolutely has to. Her entire face looks as if it has been pulled down, and she wakes up each morning honestly not knowing how she is going to get through the day, but knowing that she has to. For the sake of Callie, and the kids, and Reece, she has no other choice.

The first time Callie had an accident, she was mortified. Honor tried to reassure her that she didn't mind in the slightest.

'Darling, I first cleaned you up forty-three years ago. It may have been a while, but I haven't forgotten how to do it.'

Reece has been giving Callie her showers – wheeling her into the bathroom and gently washing her – and Honor was shocked when she stripped off Callie's nightdress and saw how she is truly nothing more than skin and bone. Her hip bones are protruding painfully, her thighs now concave. Honor closed her eyes for a second, willing the tears away as she sponged down her daughter then put her in the wheelchair while she changed the sheets, calmly and quickly, chattering away about the kids, telling Callie funny stories about Jack.

She was cheerful and gracious, and when she left the bedroom she gave her daughter a kiss then walked calmly down the corridor with a bundle of sheets that needed washing in her arms, before sinking down outside the laundry room in tears.

Walter found her there. He stood quietly as Honor sobbed, then crouched down, creakily, for he is not as young as he used to be, to awkwardly pat her back. Honor leaned her head on his arm as her body heaved, and after a few minutes he rested his forehead on top of her head, breathing in the smell of her hair, and closing his eyes as the weight of grief descended.

They stayed there for a very long time.

Now, tonight, Honor sits on the sofa closest to the fire, a bowl of soup, which is all she can manage, her appetite having gone, on the table in front of her. The Christmas tree is up, the lights are sparkling and gifts are underneath, but there is nothing festive this year in the Perry household, although everyone is trying, when the children are around.

The fire is dying down. Walter has taken it upon himself to build a roaring fire every night – it's what Callie always does, all winter, and even though she is no longer able to come downstairs, it is important to Walter to keep this going.

Callie would always light a fire as soon as she got up, so the children came downstairs before school to a cosy room, and could start their day with hot chocolate and muffins in front of the fire. And when they returned the fire would again be blazing.

Now Honor stares blankly into the fire, looking up only when she hears a noise.

Walter is standing in the doorway, a cup of tea in his hand.

'I thought you might like some tea,' he says.

'Oh Walter. Thank you. That's so . . . kind.' He places the tea on the table next to her, and she thinks about how much they have both changed.

They should never have been married; she knew that then, and knows it now. But it was because they were so young, and so different – and those differences were so startling back then – that for her there was no way out of feeling trapped.

And now? Walter is still a kind man, as he always was. She has thought, often, these past couple of weeks, of the good things in their marriage. The way he always took care of her. The way he is taking care of her now.

She has thought, often, of how much she must have hurt him. That his hatred for her wasn't in fact *hatred*, but deep resentment and upset. That he couldn't express his pain any other way than to remove himself entirely from her life.

'Come sit,' she says, patting the sofa next to her. Walter isn't sure, but eventually he sits down as Honor takes the tea and sips it.

'This is perfect. Just the way I like it.'

'A drop of milk and half a sugar?'

'Yes. Exactly. You remember.'

'I do.'

'Do you forgive me, Walter?' she says quietly, after a few seconds.

He looks at her, startled.

'I know how you have hated me all these years, and I want to say, now, that I am sorry. I truly did not know what else to do.'

'I didn't hate you,' Walter says slowly. 'You don't have to apologize. It's all . . . water under the bridge.'

'Don't you think we ought to talk about it?' Honor asks.

Walter shakes his head. 'No,' he says. 'I think we ought not to talk about it. The past is the past, and it doesn't matter. We were both young, and different. We made whatever choices we made based on who we were then. I was . . . cloistered, I think. I didn't really know anything about *any-thing*, and you were so . . . so full of fire. I wanted some of that. I wanted to escape this staid, dull existence, the life I was expected to lead, and you were the most exciting woman I had ever met.'

'I thought we weren't going to talk about it,' Honor says.

'We're not.' Walter holds her gaze. 'All that matters now is Callie, and being here for her.' He blinks and turns

350

towards the fire, and Honor watches him, surprised that his eyes look watery. Walter is not a man who has ever been comfortable showing emotion in front of others.

As she watches, Walter makes a noise, halfway between a grunt and a gasp, and, stunned, she realizes that he is crying. He is finally breaking down, and she reaches over and takes him in her arms.

Curried Parsnip and Apple Soup

1 tablespoon butter
1 lb. parsnips, peeled and cut into chunks
2 apples, peeled, cored and sliced
1 medium onion, chopped
2 teaspoons curry powder
1 teaspoon ground cumin
1 teaspoon ground coriander
1 garlic clove, crushed
4 cups good stock
seasoning

Heat the butter, and when it is foaming add the parsnips, apples and onions. Soften them but do not let them colour.

Add the curry powder, spices and garlic; cook for about 2 minutes, stirring well. Pour in the stock slowly, stirring until well mixed. Cover and simmer gently for about 30 minutes, or until the parsnips are quite soft. Purée with a hand-held blender, and add more water or stock if it is too thick.

You can also add cream for a less healthy version. Garnish with chopped chives.

Chapter Twenty-Nine

Steffi is doing the morning rounds, first to Mary's store, to drop off soups, muffins and cookies, then to Amy's with food for the week.

Yesterday she baked gingerbread men, with holes in the top and red velvet ribbons, for children to hang from a tree. 'If anyone wants,' she said to Mary, as she dropped them off, 'I can ice their children's names on them.'

'Lovely idea!' Mary said enthusiastically. 'Why don't we make a sign? Oh Steffi, I am so happy you moved here. People have started coming in telling me they made the journey especially because they heard we had the best food around.'

Steffi's eyes grow wide with joy. 'Seriously? People said that?'

'Yes. Three people came in yesterday, and the local paper called. They left a message saying they wanted to write an article about the food here!'

'Oh Mary. I couldn't be happier that it's working out.'

'What am I going to do when you leave?'

'Leave?' Steffi laughs. 'I'm completely in love with it here. Why would I leave?'

'But I heard Mason was back. I thought he was moving in again.'

'*What?*' Steffi stops still, in shock. 'What are you talking about?'

'Oh, I don't know,' Mary says, capitulating. 'Probably nothing.'

'No, tell me. He emailed me just the other day and he didn't say anything about this. Are you sure it's him? What do you mean, he's back?'

'Mick said he'd run into him down at the inn, and he said he was here for a while.'

'But why would he come back and not tell me?' Steffi feels a clutch of fear around her heart. Maybe he has come back to ask her to leave. Oh God. She has to find him now.

'Is he staying at the inn?'

Mary nods, worried that she has somehow rocked the boat, said something she shouldn't have said.

'I'm going to go and find him,' Steffi says. 'Sorry, Mary. I've got to go.' And she flies out, climbs into the old station wagon and drives down to the inn.

'Hi,' she says to the man sitting behind the old mahogany desk in the reception area. 'I'm looking for Mason Gregory. Is he staying here?'

'Steffi?' She hears her name called from the library, and Mason, who has been sitting in a wing chair by the fire, stands up.

'Mason? What are you *doing* here?' Nerves prevent her from being pleased to see him.

'Well, that's a fine greeting,' he says, his smile now turning into a frown.

'I'm sorry.' She sighs. 'I just . . . why didn't you say anything? Why didn't you tell me you were coming to Sleepy Hollow?'

'I hadn't planned it,' he says. 'It was a last-minute decision.'

'But . . . why are you here?' she blurts out. 'Do you want me to leave?'

'Leave?' He looks confused before bursting into laughter. 'Oh God, no! I'm not here to kick you out. Is that what you thought?'

Sheepishly, she dips her head.

'Oh Steffi. I am so sorry. Let's start again. Steffi! Lovely to see you!'

'Mason!' she says. 'What a gorgeous surprise!' And he kisses her, European style, on each cheek.

'So really,' she says, taking a step back, 'what *are* you doing here?'

'It's a long story,' he says. 'And not a particularly good one.'

'Uh-oh. Sounds ominous. The job?'

'I'd have to start at the beginning and it would take a while.'

'Why don't you come with me? I'm off to Amy Van Peterson's to drop off food. You can tell me all about it on the way.'

'Deal,' he says, following her out to the car.

'So what happened?' Steffi turns her head as they bounce along a dirt road on the way to Amy's. 'Job didn't work out?'

'No, the job's fine. Marriage, on the other hand? Not so good.'

'What!' Steffi pulls the car to a stop and turns to him. 'Your *marriage*? What are you talking about?'

'We separated.'

'*What?*' she blusters, truly shocked.

'Okay. That's not strictly true. Olivia left me.'

There is a silence as Steffi gapes at him. 'What do you mean, she left you?'

'Well. It turns out that during all those frequent trips to London to get the apartment ready, and meet with the decorator, and choose furniture, she was in fact falling in love with the decorator.'

'He's *straight?*' Steffi asks, after a beat.

'Apparently so. Something of a surprise to me too.'

'So that's it? It's over?'

Mason shrugs.

'Where are the kids?'

'They're with her. In London. In this huge Belgravia apartment that's all white.'

'Mason, I'm so sorry.' Sympathetically, Steffi lays a hand on his arm. 'Are you okay?'

He stares at the dashboard for a while, before looking up at Steffi. 'I never thought I'd admit this to anyone but, more than anything, I'm . . . relieved.'

'You are?'

He nods, sadness in his eyes. 'Our marriage hasn't worked for years. I'm not sure if it ever really worked. I was so flattered that someone like Olivia chose me, and she . . . well, I'm not sure why she did, really. I think she expected greater things from me. She has spent our marriage being disappointed in all the things I haven't achieved.'

'What are you talking about? You're this incredible publisher with a string of bestsellers under your belt.'

'Well, thank you for pointing that out, but Olivia didn't much care about strings of bestsellers. She wanted me to support her, and I guess she never felt I made enough money.'

'But what difference does it make to her? I thought she was worth a fortune.'

'She is, but, as she always used to point out, that was *her* money, to be spent on things she wanted, and it was my job, as the man of the family, to pay for everything else.'

'Did you buy that apartment?' Steffi asks in horror.

'Are you kidding? That's one of the most expensive apartments ever to sell in the history of real estate in New York. I couldn't have bought that apartment in my dreams. Come to think of it, I *wouldn't* have bought that apartment in my dreams. That was all Olivia's doing. *Her* apartment, *her* money, in *her* name. I told her it was ridiculous, but Olivia's all about keeping up with those society girls. If they do good, she'll do better. If they buy big, she'll buy bigger. Let's face it,' he says with a shrug, 'she can afford it.'

'So . . . what about your relationship? Was it bad?'

'You know, I don't want to sit here and say bad things about her. She's the mother of my children. I thought we were, if not happy, at least . . . fine. There are many, many kinds of marriages, and relationships, and few of them are great. Most of them just plod along, and even if you think you've made a mistake, you find a way to make it work.'

'*Did* you think you'd made a mistake?'

'I didn't really give it too much thought. I wasn't happy, but I wouldn't have wanted to leave the kids and, honestly, I never wanted to break up the family.'

'What *about* the kids? Are they okay? What are you going to do about custody?'

'I don't know.' For the first time, Mason looks truly pained. 'It's one of those things we'll have to work out.'

'So how long are you back here?'

'I don't know that either. London is great, but I don't want to stay there by myself – I don't have friends there, I don't know it. We thought I'd be needed there for a year, but in fact the company is running itself. The Publishing Director is solid, and my being there just isn't necessary.' He stops. 'I just don't know how it's going to play out. The hardest thing is the kids. I can't stand not being with them every day.'

'Why did you come here?'

'I needed to be in Sleepy Hollow just to . . . digest everything. To be honest, I thought about calling you, but I didn't want to burden you. I just . . . I love this place. It's the one place I feel truly at home, and I needed to feel comforted. John and Kathy, who run the inn, are old friends and they said I could stay as long as I needed to.'

'But I feel horrible, being in your house. It's crazy that you're here. Why don't you come and stay at the house?'

'I couldn't.' Mason shakes his head. 'That would be far too much of an imposition. I'm just here to get some peace and quiet and gather my thoughts. I didn't even plan on seeing you. I don't want to get in your way or make you uncomfortable in any way. Although I do miss Fingal. How is he?'

'Mason!' Steffi slugs him on the arm. 'Don't be such an ass. Fingal misses you, and you have a home here. You're coming home with me, and I won't take no for an answer.'

'You don't have to do this,' Mason says, as Steffi starts up the engine, but he is smiling.

'I know I don't have to. I *want* to.' She shoots him a sideways glance. 'If you're nice I'll even cook for you.'

'How's Callie?' he asks, as they start bumping along the road again. 'How are *you*?'

'Callie's pretty shitty, and I'm much the same way.'

'What can I do?'

'Nothing. I don't think anyone can do anything. Maybe, if you want, you could come with me? I'm going there later.' Steffi has no idea why she says this. She is supposed to be bringing Stan. Not Mason. But the words are out there now, and it is too late.

'I'd love to,' he says. 'Thank you.'

*

Lila stops at Starbucks on the way to Callie's, for a grande non-fat latte, and a chocolate-glazed doughnut to eat in the car.

She knows she isn't supposed to have the doughnut, but when Lila is stressed, or sad, or anxious, she eats. And right now, she is all of the aforementioned, and it is making her starving.

Last night she invented a new dish – pantry chicken and beans. It was for four people, but after she and Ed had eaten she was still hungry, more than hungry, ravenous, so she went back for seconds and then thirds.

'Are you pregnant?' Ed teased her, wickedly.

'You wish,' she shot back. 'I'm very, very, very PMS-y. Do we have any chocolate in the house?'

'No, darling. You ate it all two days ago. Want me to run to the garage?'

'It's not a garage, you big English Wasp. It's a gas station. And yes, I'd love you to.'

'What's on the menu tonight? Snickers? Or M&Ms?'

'How about both? Then I can make up my mind when you get back.'

For years Lila has worried about her weight, and now she has a man who not only doesn't seem to give a damn, but loves her exactly as she is, whatever she weighs.

Which is extremely lucky, given that she is having a very hard time getting any of her trousers to button. She is now in leggings only, with long sweaters that cover her thighs. Every night she lies in bed determined to start a diet the next morning, but then morning comes and she finds herself starving again.

Lila walks into the house, quiet now with the children at school, Honor and Walter out running errands, and Reece working in the office.

Up the stairs and into Callie's bedroom. Callie opens her eyes as soon as Lila walks in.

'Hi, sweetie,' Lila whispers, sitting on Callie's bed. 'How are you today?'

'Not good,' Callie whispers back. 'I don't feel so good at all.'

'What's the matter?'

'Just . . . tired,' Callie says, and Lila notices the whites of her eyes are looking yellow – she makes a mental note to talk to Mark about it later at the hospital. 'Do I have to go today?'

'Yes, sweetie.' Lila strokes her cheek as Callie closes her eyes. 'You do. It's nearly over. Only four more sessions.'

'But I don't want to go. I don't want any more. I don't care any more.'

The colour drains out of Lila's face as she leans forward. 'Callie, you have to care. You have to keep fighting. You can still make it. You're so close to finishing; you can't give up now.'

'But I'm so tired,' Callie mumbles. 'I don't want to do it any more.'

'You're doing it for your kids,' Lila says. 'Four more. That's all. And this afternoon, it will be three more. You can do this, Cal, I know you can.'

Callie opens her eyes and stares at Lila, before eventually nodding. 'Okay,' she says. 'I can do this?'

'Yes, my darling. You can.'

Lila helps her to the edge of the bed, then puts her legs on the floor and arranges the catheter before pulling sweatpants gently on.

'Hey, Lila?'

'Yes, honey?'

'I love you.'

'I know. I love you too.'

'I just want you to know that wherever you are, and wherever I am, I will always love you. Remember that.'

'Oh Jesus, Callie,' Lila says, with a sharp intake of breath. 'Don't say that. That sounds . . . ominous.'

'It's not. It doesn't mean anything other than I love you. If anything happens, I'm going to be your angel.'

'You'd better be,' Lila says, lifting her into the chair. 'Which hat?'

'No hat. Not today. It doesn't matter.'

'Let's go and get your teeth brushed,' Lila says, wheeling her into the bathroom and getting the toothbrush ready. Usually she hands the brush to Callie, but today Callie shakes her head, her arms hanging limply by her sides.

Today she doesn't have the strength.

'Can you do it?' she asks, and Lila pushes down her fear and carefully brushes Callie's teeth, while Callie peers at her in the mirror.

'Li? Open my bottom drawer. See that white packet? Can you get it?'

Lila takes out a white plastic pack and peers at it. 'What is it?'

Callie manages a weak smile. 'It's a pregnancy test.'

'*What?* You think you're *pregnant*? *What?*' If it is possible to shriek in a whisper, Lila is shrieking in a whisper.

'Not me,' Callie says. 'You. Go pee.'

'Why? Because I'm fat? Jesus, Cal. If I didn't love you so much . . .'

'You're not fat. I think you're pregnant.'

'I'm not pregnant.'

'So go pee. I want to know. Indulge me. I'm a dying woman.'

'Don't fucking say that!' Lila spits in horror. 'You're not a dying woman.'

'We're all dying. Not today. Okay, okay, I'm sorry. It was me trying to be funny. Anyway, just do it.'

'What do I have to do?'

'Go and pee, and then we'll see if there's a blue line.'

'Callie, we don't have time for this. You have to be in radiation in half an hour.'

'They always keep us waiting. We can keep them waiting today.'

Lila closes the door of the toilet and gingerly pees on the stick, then puts the cap on and walks back out to the bathroom.

'Did you do it?' Callie asks.

Lila nods.

'Give it to me.'

Lila hands it over.

Callie holds it on her lap and counts down before taking

off the cap to discover the result. 'I knew it!' she says, grinning widely, but Lila feels as if she's going to faint.

'Show me!' Lila grabs the stick, a wave of nausea hitting as she recognizes the strong blue line in the circle. 'Oh shit,' she mumbles. 'Now what?'

'Lila?' Callie's face is lit up with joy. 'Now you get me to goddamned radiation, and then you accept that you are going to have a baby.'

Lila waits until Ed is sitting at the kitchen table, a glass of Scotch in his hand, a bowl of curried parsnip and apple soup in front of him, before placing the stick on the table between them.

Ed lifts the spoon to his mouth. 'This is delicious, my love. What's that?'

'What?'

'That stick on the table?'

'It's a pregnancy test.'

Ed puts down the spoon as a smile spreads over his face.

'What does it say?'

'What do you think the blue line means?'

'You're pregnant?'

Lila nods, and Ed whoops with joy, then stands up and grabs Lila in a huge hug.

'I can't believe it! I can't bloody believe it!' He squeezes her tightly. 'We're going to have a baby!'

'I don't know, Ed,' Lila says. 'I mean, we have to talk about this.'

'What's to talk about? You're pregnant! Jesus. How did you get pregnant, anyway? I thought you were using something.'

'I was. I guess I fall into the two per cent. But, sweetie, I really don't know how I feel about this.'

'You'll be fine.' Ed can't stop grinning and kissing her, not hearing what Lila is saying.

'I know I'll be fine, but I don't know if I can have this . . . if I can have a baby.'

'What?' His face falls. 'Are you talking about an abortion?'

'I haven't even begun to think it through, but yes, if I am clear about not having this baby, then I would have an abortion.'

'You would abort our child?' Ed says in horror.

'It's not a child,' says Lila. 'It's nothing. It's a foetus. I'm only five weeks. I could do it next week and we could just carry on.'

Ed looks as if he is about to cry. 'You can't just announce that you would do that. This is our child. This isn't a decision you can make alone.'

'I know.' Lila's heart is sinking. This isn't what she had expected. Or perhaps she had; perhaps she just hoped that he might see things from her point of view. 'But, sweetie? It's my body. And that's huge. I just don't know how I feel. Maybe I just need time to get used to it.'

'Of course you need time.' Hope fills Ed's voice. 'It's a huge shock, and you can take all the time you need. You will be an amazing mother. I love you so much and the thought of making a baby with you is just incredible. This is what I've always wanted. A partner, a best friend, a lover, a woman I can see myself spending the rest of my life with, who brings me so much joy and peace that I wake up every morning thinking about how lucky I am. And the only thing that could make it better is having a family with you. A proper family.'

'I love you, Ed, and I echo all the things you've just said. Just give me time. Let me figure out how I feel.'

Ed doesn't say anything. His smile says it all as he leans down and kisses her again.

Pantry Chicken and Beans

3 cans beans (chickpeas, black beans, kidney beans
   or lima beans)
1 can diced tomatoes
dried chilli flakes
5 sun-dried tomatoes chopped
handful of black olives, pitted and cut in half
4–5 anchovies, chopped
3 garlic cloves
cherry tomatoes on the vine (completely inessential, but pretty
   if you have some)
6 chicken breasts

Preheat the oven to 350°F.

Oil a casserole dish and pour in the beans (rinsing first in
a colander). Add the rest of the ingredients, except the
chicken and the tomatoes on the vine. Fold in, being careful not to break the beans.

I would also add some finely sliced bacon or pancetta to
the beans, if you have any handy . . .

Add the tomatoes. Roast in the oven for around 25 minutes, until the tomatoes soften and it all starts to smell delicious.

Add the chicken breasts (if they are chicken breasts with
skin, you can brown the skin side in a frying pan first).
Return to the oven for around 30 minutes more, until the
chicken is done.

Garnish with chopped parsley if you have any.

Chapter Thirty

Steffi watches Stan as he walks back from the bathroom, friends of his slapping his back as he passes.

He sits down next to her, giving her leg a squeeze, and tips his head to take a swig of beer. And Steffi sees it. The telltale white powder in his nose. The white powder that she might think was nothing, if she didn't know better, if she hadn't lived in New York all those years, gone out with all those men who took cocaine the way others drank water.

Enough, she thinks, the light switch of attraction turning off for her just as quickly as it flicked on, that sunny morning at Amy Van Peterson's.

Enough of the drugs. Enough of the drinking. Enough of the men who still act as if they are in college.

Enough of the men she can't envision in the heart of her family, getting on with her parents, with Callie.

She hasn't even been able to bring herself to invite Stan to the house. Yes, Callie said she wanted to meet him, but Steffi doesn't have to be a brain surgeon to know what she would say.

Mason, on the other hand . . .

Stan had come to pick her up an hour earlier, as Mason was making her laugh at the kitchen table. Steffi was cleaning up the kitchen, moving round with cloth and Soft Scrub in hand, while he went to the cellar for a bottle of red he was insisting she share with him.

It was comfortable and companionable and, more than that, fun. Steffi felt a flash of irritation when she remembered Stan was picking her up tonight. He was late, by thirty minutes, and she wondered if she could cancel, or pretend to be out, or come up with another excuse.

'I've heard the Post Inn is great,' Mason said, pouring the wine. 'Do you want to see if we can get in there tonight? Might be fun.'

'I'd love to,' Steffi said sadly, 'but I can't. I have . . . plans.'

'Plans?' He looked over at her with a smile. 'That sounds . . . interesting.'

Steffi blushed, bending down to open a cupboard door and pretending to root around looking for a frying pan so he didn't see. Why was she embarrassed?

'Go on, then, who's the lucky guy?'

'What makes you think it's a guy?' Feeling the blush subside, she straightened up.

'Just a feeling. Are there any single men around here?'

'Not many.' She laughed. 'And I'm not telling you.'

'Oh come on. We're friends. You have to tell me. I believe it even says so in the lease.'

'I haven't signed a lease.'

'You haven't? That's terrible. I'll get one drawn up next week. I'm going to see who it is so you might as well tell me. Is he tall, dark and handsome?'

'Well, yes. Oh God, I can't believe you're pressurizing me like this. Okay. It's Stan.'

'Stan who?'

'Stan, Stanley. The handyman.'

'Oh God!' Mason widened his eyes with a huge smile. 'Stanley the handyman? No. Seriously. Who is it?'

'It is,' Steffi mumbled. 'And now I don't want to go.'

'I'm sorry.' Mason wiped the smile off his face. 'It's none of my business, and he seems like a nice guy. I should have realized . . . He's . . . very attractive, right?'

Steffi shrugged. 'I guess.'

'No, I mean, I've always heard that he's a big hit with the women . . . Oh Jesus. I should just shut up. I'm sure you'll have a great time.'

'I'm sure I will.' Steffi glared at him. 'We're going to the Roadhouse to see a band and we'll have a great time.'

Why did it sound like she was trying to convince herself?

And here she is, at the Roadhouse, and it's smoky, and noisy, and crowded, and her date has obviously just done a line of cocaine; and the only place she really wants to be right now is back home, reading her book in front of the fire, with Fingal curled up over her feet to keep them warm, and Mason sitting in the armchair.

It isn't that she's attracted to Mason – good God, he's hardly her type – but it is nice to have him around. It is a welcome break from the crushing sadness in her life right now, and she feels his quiet support.

'Stan, I'm really sorry, but I have a terrible headache and I'm not feeling great,' she says suddenly, watching a flash of irritation in his eyes change to what seems like false concern. 'I have to go home. Would you mind taking me?'

There is a silence, and Steffi fights her own irritation. He's her date, for Christ's sake. Of course he should take her home. What is there to consider?

But she knows why he's considering. It's because

something's changed. A headache is the oldest excuse in the book, and he can tell, instantly, that it isn't that she's not feeling well, it's that she's changed her mind.

Steffi has always been mercurial, has been able to fall in love, then out of love, in less than a second.

Once upon a time a speck of white powder in a nostril would have meant nothing. Once upon a time she would have shrugged it off, because even though cocaine wasn't her thing, it never bothered her that others did it. But once upon a time her sister hadn't been dangerously ill, and she hadn't been forced to question everything in her life.

Not least, as Callie has pointed out, her choices in men. Six months ago and she would have had a fabulous fling with Stan the handyman. But not today. Not any more.

'I can get a cab,' Steffi says eventually, jolting Stan out of his thought process.

'Nah. It's only a few minutes. Of course I'll take you.'

'You know what? A cab is fine.' She realizes she doesn't want to spend any more time in his company, and certainly not spend the journey home feeling his waves of resentment wash over her. 'Don't worry. These are your friends. You stay and enjoy.'

She asks the bartender for a number, and when she has finished the call she looks over to see Stan already talking to a tall blonde girl she noticed when they walked in.

'That was quick.' Mason looks up from his computer as she passes the doorway of his study. 'Did something happen?'

'Kinda, sorta,' she says.

'Come in.' He gestures her in, and she sinks down on the faded sofa under the window.

'I just realized he's not my type.'

'Oh?' Mason smiles. 'What is your type?'

'That's the problem. I have no idea. It's always been guys like Stan, but it's just not doing it for me any more.' She sighs and looks up, catching Mason's eye, and he holds her glance for just a fraction of a second longer than is altogether necessary.

Whoa, she thinks, looking away quickly. What the hell was *that*?

'Did you eat?' Mason says.

'No, but I was thinking about driving over to Bedford.' She looks up at him again. 'Do you want to come?'

The kitchen is quiet. Low TV can be heard from the family room, and Steffi parks Mason at the kitchen counter while she roots around in the fridge for something to eat.

'Are you sure it's okay to help ourselves?'

'Are you kidding?' Steffi peers around the door. 'This is my family, and I'm the one who cooked it all. There's chickpea curry, Asian steak wraps, or home-made mac 'n' cheese. Damn, I made that for the kids. I knew they wouldn't like it. The only mac 'n' cheese they'll eat is the crap that comes out of a box. Here –' she pulls out a bottle of wine and hands it to Mason – 'you open that while I heat this up. Let me just see who's around.'

Upstairs, Eliza and Jack are fast asleep in their beds, Eliza with a cashmere sweater of Callie's wrapped around her, which she now refuses to sleep without.

Callie's door is closed, and Steffi opens it very quietly to find Reece lying on the bed, holding Callie. He looks over at Steffi and raises his finger to his lips, mouthing that he will be down soon. Callie is fast asleep, her body barely registering under the duvet, so tiny is she now.

There is no sign of her mom or dad. She creeps downstairs so as not to wake the children, then peeks into the family room. The light is dim, just the flicker of the television and the dying embers of a fire.

And there, on the sofa, fast asleep and in each other's arms, are Honor and Walter.

Steffi's mouth drops open in shock. She quickly backs away and retreats to the kitchen.

'Are you okay?' Mason looks up with concern as Steffi walks in, her hand on her chest. 'You look like you've seen a ghost.'

'I think so,' Steffi says, her eyes wide. 'I've just seen the weirdest thing ever. My mom and dad are . . . cuddling, on the sofa.'

'Why is that weird?' Mason frowns.

'Because they've been divorced for about thirty years and my dad hates my mom.'

Mason shrugs. 'Clearly not any more.'

Steffi sits down on the stool and pulls her glass of wine over, taking a big swig. 'That is just too bizarre!'

Reece walks into the kitchen, gives Steffi a hug and introduces himself to Mason.

'Okay, before anything, I've just seen something very strange,' Steffi says. 'Mom and Dad have fallen asleep in each other's arms in the TV room.'

'You're kidding.' Reece grins.

'I swear to God. Go and look.'

Reece tiptoes to the doorway, followed by Steffi, both of them peering in.

'My God!' he mouths to Steffi. 'I never thought that day would come.'

'Can we bring Callie down? She'd never believe it!'

He shakes his head. 'She's really not strong enough, but we can capture the evidence.' He pulls his BlackBerry out of the rear pocket of his jeans and smiles, holding it up and snapping a picture.

'Oh shit,' they both mutter as the flash goes off and Walter grunts. They run down the corridor giggling like a pair of schoolchildren.

'Show me, show me.' Back in the kitchen Steffi tries to grab the BlackBerry, shaking her head and marvelling, again, at the sight. 'How did this happen?'

'You know, I'm not entirely surprised,' Reece says. 'I think they've found enormous comfort in each other. And let's face it, both of them have changed. Your dad is softer, and your mom . . . well. She's still nuts, but in the nicest possible way. I think they've found companionship together, and I think it's great.'

'We totally have to go and show Callie,' she says. 'Shall we wake her?'

Reece looks at his watch. 'It's time for her to take the drugs anyway. Let's go up. Mason, are you okay down here?'

'I can help getting the food ready. Just tell me what to do.'

Steffi hands him a large wooden bowl. 'You can get started on the salad.'

'He seems like a great guy.' Reece winks at Steffi as they head upstairs.

'He is. He's truly one of the good ones.'

'And he's your landlord, right?'

'Yes.'

'But married?'

'Separated, it seems.'

'*Reeeaaalllyyy?*' Reece says, with a slow smile.

'Oh stop.' Steffi nudges him. 'It's not like that. We're friends. Plus, even if there were something between us, which there isn't, he's only been separated for five minutes. And he's not my type.'

'*Reeeaaalllyyy?*' Reece says again, and Steffi is surprised to feel a flush rising.

'Oh shut up,' she says finally, not knowing what else to say.

Callie opens her eyes slowly, focusing first on Reece, then on Steffi.

'Where are the kids?' she whispers, confused, her voice now hoarse and rattly.

'In bed, fast asleep.' Reece leans over and kisses her on the forehead, stroking her cheek. 'It's almost nine.'

'How long have I been asleep?'

'Since three.'

'Hi.' She looks at Steffi, but seems puzzled.

'Hi, honey.' Steffi comes over to the bed and kisses her. 'Are you okay? It's me, Steffi.'

'I know,' Callie says, but Steffi isn't sure she did know. Not immediately.

'It's time for your drugs,' Reece says. 'And you have to have something to eat. Here, let's sit you up.' He and Steffi both move her forward to wedge the sponge pillow behind her. Steffi is shocked at how much weaker she is. There is no strength in Callie's arms, and it seems she is unable to sit up by herself.

'What can I bring you to eat?' Steffi asks gently. 'Do you want guacamole?'

Callie shakes her head slightly. 'Chocolate pudding,' she says.

'What?' Reece and Steffi both start to laugh.

'I know!' She cracks a small smile. 'I think I was dreaming about chocolate pudding.'

'Do you have chocolate pudding?'

'Yes. I keep powder on reserve. Top shelf of pantry.'

'I'll go down and make it,' Steffi says, watching as Reece pours a fresh glass of water from the jug on her bedside table and moves the straw to Callie's mouth.

'We just have to show you something bizarre.'

Callie looks up at Steffi. Reece gently lets her head nestle softly on the pillow, then digs out his BlackBerry and holds up the picture.

'What is that?' Callie is struggling to focus, and Steffi wonders if her eyesight has been affected by the radiation.

'Look closely.' Steffi grins. 'It's Mom and Dad!'

'When did you take that?'

'About five minutes ago,' Reece says.

'That's awesome,' Callie says. 'I knew it.'

'You did?'

'I just hoped. Hey,' she asks, looking up at Steffi, 'how's the guy?'

'Which guy?'

'Because there's more than one, right, Steff?' teases Reece.

'Oh shut up, Reece. If you mean Stan, it's a non-starter. You were right. He's not for me.'

'Why don't you tell Callie about who *is* for you?' Reece smiles.

'Mason isn't for me, okay?'

'So how come he's downstairs making salad at the kitchen counter?' Reece shoots back.

'He's downstairs?' A hint of Callie's fire. 'Bring him up!'

Steffi whisks the milk into the chocolate-pudding mix, spooning it carefully into a small glass ramekin. She adds a bowl of tortilla chips, the ever-present guacamole, a bowl of salsa, and some cookies she made earlier, for she knows how much Callie hates being the only one eating in front of an audience of people, all of them watching her.

'You're sure you're okay with this?' she says to Mason.

'Of course! I can't wait to meet her.'

'It's . . . shocking to see her now, though. She doesn't look like that.' She gestures to the photos on the wall, to the glowing, gorgeous, always-smiling Callie and the kids, the photos that Mason admired, that everyone admires every time they walk into the kitchen.

'It's fine.' He rests a hand on her arm and looks her in the eye. 'My mom died of cancer, remember? I know what this is.'

'Okay.' She takes a breath. 'Let's go on up.'

Mason insists on carrying the tray, but Steffi takes it from him when they walk into the bedroom, placing it carefully on the bed.

'You must be Callie.' Mason walks straight over to Callie, and takes her hand. 'I've heard so much about you.'

'Sit,' Callie whispers, gesturing to the bed, and Mason sits, still holding her hand.

'Cal? I made the pudding. Can I give it to you?' Steffi picks up the bowl, for Callie has to be fed now, her big eyes staring into the eyes of whoever carefully spoons the food into her mouth.

Callie blinks her acquiescence and, like a baby bird, opens her mouth on command as the spoon draws close to her lips.

'I don't normally look like this,' she says to Mason, in between mouthfuls.

'I realize that.' Mason smiles. 'I was admiring the photographs in the kitchen. They're beautiful.'

'Thanks.'

'You couldn't have taken them?'

'I set up the shot,' she whispers. 'Reece took them.'

'But the photographs all over the house are beautiful. You have exquisite taste.'

'She took them,' Steffi interjects proudly. 'Those are all Callie's.'

'You're kidding. They're amazing. God. You should be exhibiting.'

Callie shrugs. 'One day.'

'When you're better,' he says, 'I'd like you to meet a friend of mine. He runs one of the top galleries in the city. He'd love your work. Those landscapes are extraordinary. Can I do that?'

Callie nods, with a smile. 'You really think they're that good?'

'I think they're better than that,' he says. 'I think they're stunning.'

Callie's eyes move to Steff. 'Steff? Can I have a banana?'

'Really?' Steff is delighted. 'You're hungry?'

Callie waits until she leaves the room before turning

back to Mason, her hand still in his, and it is clear the banana was a ruse to get Steffi out of the room.

'You'll look after her, won't you?' she says slowly.

Mason tries to swallow the lump that has just risen, that has brought with it memories that are just as sweetly painful as this moment is now. He cannot trust himself to speak.

Callie looks to check that Reece is still in the bathroom, and she turns back to Mason.

'You *know*, don't you?'

And he looks straight into her eyes, and he nods, for he knows exactly what she is saying.

She is dying.

Nobody has spoken about it, the results of the radiation are not known, and yet she knows.

She is dying.

And Mason knows too.

'I know.' She nods to herself. 'I'm ready.' She looks back up at him. 'She doesn't know she loves you yet, but she will. Okay. It's okay,' she says, seemingly to herself again, before smiling at him. 'You're the guy, aren't you?'

Mason doesn't say anything, just squeezes her hand and leans forward to kiss her on the forehead. 'I will look after her. Don't worry. It's all going to be okay.'

And as he walks out, the memories of his mother flooding back and the pain of seeing someone dying . . . Steffi's pain at having to go through this . . . it is all unexpectedly overwhelming.

He doesn't start crying until he makes it out of the room and into the downstairs bathroom, where he leans his head on the mirror and lets a tear or two run silently down his cheeks.

Merry Meringue Christmas Cookies

2 egg whites
⅛ teaspoon salt
⅛ teaspoon cream of tartar
¾ cup sugar
½ teaspoon vanilla extract
1 cup semisweet chocolate chips
1 cup chopped nuts
3 tablespoons crushed peppermint sweets

Preheat the oven to 250°F.

Beat the egg whites until foamy, add the salt and cream of tartar, and continue beating until soft peaks form. Add the sugar, a tablespoon at a time, beating well after each addition. Continue beating until the meringue is stiff(ish). Fold in the rest of the ingredients.

Drop by teaspoonfuls, half an inch apart, on a greased baking sheet. Bake for 40 minutes. Try not to eat them all before they cool . . .

Chapter Thirty-One

Eliza has held Lila's hand the entire time since they stepped off the train at Grand Central Station, and it looks like she won't let go for the rest of the day.

Jack is sitting on Ed's lap, bouncing with excitement and teasing Clay, who's sitting next to Ed, looking around the circus, waiting for something to happen.

'Here you are!' Honor appears at the end of the row, her arms filled with bags of popcorn, closely followed by Walter who has the drinks and bags of something else.

'Is that candyfloss?' Lila asks incredulously. 'They're not allowed candyfloss. Callie will go nuts.'

Walter shakes his head. 'I'm their grandfather and we're supposed to spoil them.'

'Quite right,' Honor agrees. 'We're supposed to fill them with food they're not allowed to have at home and let them go to bed three hours late.'

'Yay!' Eliza and Jack both cheer simultaneously. 'Can we do that tonight?'

'We're not going to have much of a choice.' Lila laughs. 'It certainly won't be an early night,' she adds. 'Not after we take you to Mars 2112 for dinner, then head back to Bedford.'

The four adults have taken the children into the city, for today is the day of scans, the day they see whether anything has changed, and Callie has asked that today it is just her and Reece who sit down with Mark and find out whether the radiation therapy has worked.

Lila wanted to be there too. Callie squeezed her hand and said she wanted her there for the follow-up, but needed it to be just Reece and herself.

And everyone is scared.

They will not let that be known. Not in front of the children, who feel as if it is their birthday, Christmas and summer vacation all rolled into one. Never have they had quite so much attention paid to them, nor had so many fun things presented to them on a plate.

They are on play dates every day, mothers of their friends lavishing attention and praise on them, going to fairs and festivals, theatres and shows every weekend, and now – how great is this! – into New York City for the Big Apple Circus on a weeknight! A Thursday!

No wonder they are jiggling up and down with excitement.

The lights go down and the children roar with laughter as the clown known as Grandma struts into the ring, her handbag clutched tightly to her chest. Walter reaches over and takes Honor's hand, squeezing it gently; they both smile at their grandchildren's delight, then stare into the middle distance, not seeing the show, thinking only of their daughter, with a dread that neither of them can voice, and neither of them can shake.

Lila checks her iPhone every few seconds, waiting for some news. She fires texts off to Reece, who gives her short updates.

Had PET scan, waiting for results

MRI soon

No news yet

It is becoming a compulsion. Her leg jiggles up and down, her eyes flicking down to her hand every few seconds.

'Stop,' Ed whispers, putting his hand over hers. 'There's nothing we can do. You have to just breathe.'

'I know,' she says, leaning her head on his shoulder and digging into his popcorn bucket, her own having been finished ages ago.

Crisps, popcorn, candyfloss, crisps, popcorn, more candyfloss. The nausea isn't bad, but it is enough to warrant carrying crisps everywhere she goes, popping them into her mouth at regular intervals.

And when she isn't eating crisps, she is mostly crying, her emotions, already fragile, sent into overdrive with the pregnancy.

'If I die,' Callie said the other day, 'you have to call her Callie.'

'Don't say that.' Lila's eyes teared up instantly, and no amount of willing them away stopped the sobs that quickly followed. Lila lay her head down on Callie's shoulder and sobbed, Callie weakly stroking her hair.

'Shh,' Callie whispered. 'It's going to be okay.'

'But it's not. Don't say that.'

'It is,' she said calmly. 'It is. And your baby is a girl, and you're going to call her Callie.'

'How do you know it's a girl?' Lila said.

'A feeling,' Callie said. 'I'm sure.'

Lila, still undecided, cried some more; but she couldn't tell Callie that she was still trying to figure out whether to go through with this pregnancy or not.

That night, she couldn't sleep. Most nights, she couldn't sleep. She lay in bed, eyes wide open, thinking of Callie. She would wake up, every few minutes it sometimes seemed, to pee, then climb back into bed, wide awake.

That night, she stood in the bathroom for a long time, looking at herself in the mirror, and all of a sudden she felt a peace wash over her.

She would have this baby, she knew. And it would be a girl.

Going back into the bedroom, she tucked in tight behind Ed, who grunted and moved slightly, reaching back to pull her arm over him.

'Ed?' she whispered in his ear.

'Hmmm?'

'We're going to have a baby,' she said, and when he turned over to take her in his arms she felt, again, wet tears on her cheeks, but now, finally, they were tears of relief. And joy.

The circus finishes and Lila sends a text. Then another. Then another.

She looks at Ed and shrugs. 'Nothing.'

'They're probably having more scans,' Ed says. 'I'm sure you have to turn your BlackBerry off in there.'

'Okay.' She attempts to calm down. 'We'll try later.'

*

Mason is going to the city today, meeting with a divorce lawyer who is said to be the best of the best, trying to map out his future, although right now it seems there are no decisions that can be made.

Would a judge allow Olivia to stay in London? On what grounds? That she has an English boyfriend? It seems . . . risible. Unlikely. But he is terrified that may be the case.

While he loved some of what London has to offer, the thought of leaving home again fills him with horror.

Home. Not London, certainly. Not even New York — that huge, over-decorated, over-grand apartment that has never felt like his. But Sleepy Hollow. With Fingal, and the animals, and now . . . Steffi.

Is he in love with her? There is no doubt. It crept up on him entirely unawares. He didn't even consider it until Callie spoke to him, and with such certainty he almost wondered if his late mother were talking through her.

He didn't realize he had fallen in love with Steffi, because he wasn't looking for it, and because, up until now, he hasn't known what love is. Infatuation, he thought it was, when younger: mad passion, a feeling that you would rather die than be without the person.

Or, as with Olivia, a disbelief that someone like her would fall in love with someone like him. How could he reject that? Wouldn't he be mad not to marry her? He'd never find anyone like her again. She told him so herself. On countless occasions.

In London, when his wife started disappearing, even before she announced she was leaving him, he found the bright spots in the loneliness were when he checked his computer to see an email from Steffi in his inbox.

He would find himself reading them with a smile on his face.

He didn't come back to Sleepy Hollow to see her, but when he heard her voice at the inn that day he realized that, on some level, he had.

And now, sharing a house together, he is getting to know her more; and the more he knows, the more he likes.

Not consciously. Not until he met her sister.

A feeling of . . . safety around her. A feeling of peace.

She feels like – dare he even think it? – a *partner*. Already. And in the truest sense of the word.

Already, and without anything physical happening between them, they have fallen into something of a routine. Mason up first, making tea for her, feeding the animals together.

He cloisters himself in his study during the day, attempting to run the publishing house as best he can from home, happy every time he hears her footsteps on the stairs, or murmuring to Fingal as she lets him out of the back door.

She is often out. Shopping, dropping food off or, of course, at her sister's, and his heart lifts when he hears her car coming back down the driveway.

His favourite times are the afternoons when she is cooking. He will come in for cups of coffee, and she'll insist on his tasting everything, asking his opinion, then they sit and talk about everything under the sun.

And that is what he has missed most, he is beginning to realize. Someone to talk to. Olivia only talked about people, shopping: Bergdorfs was out of those Manolos in her size; her committee meeting that morning was held at Whitney Timsdale's, and God, was the decorating déclassé; how much should they give, this year, to the New York City Ballet?

I was lonelier in my marriage than I have ever been in my life, he thinks, with sudden clarity. And shock.

And I never expected to fall in love. Now. With Steffi. So soon. But there is no rush. It is enough, he knows, that they are friends. It is enough that they are there for each other.

The last thing he needs is a rebound relationship. He will look after Steffi, as he promised, as he would even without a promise. She will need looking after, for she still talks in terms of when Callie gets better, even when the doctors refer to these treatments as palliative, explain that they are merely alleviating her pain, making her comfortable until the end.

No one can let Callie go. He saw that the other night. Callie may be ready, but no one else is, and he understands. He wasn't ready to let his mother go. The doctors kept talking of another treatment, more chemotherapy, something else they could do, and when his mother said she had done enough he was furious with her for giving up.

He gets out of the cab at Grand Central and sends a quick text to Steffi, asking if there is news.

> Not yet. Can't stand it. No one's at house so
> I'm going 2 Bedford 2 wait. Xox

He wonders if he ought to turn around and go back, be with her, but it isn't quite his place.

He will be there for her when she comes home.

*

They have just stepped out of the spaceship to enter Mars 2112, when Lila's mobile phone rings.

'Okay.' She nods, her face ashen. 'Okay.'

'What is it?' The other adults clamour round her.

'It's Reece. They're home. They've seen the medical team and he wants us to come back.'

Chapter Thirty-Two

Callie's family and friends may have thought they were prepared for her death, knowing, as they did, that it was an inevitability, but it is impossible to prepare for the tragedy of losing someone so vibrant, so full of life, so young.

On 21 December 2010, while Reece and Honor sat at Callie's bedside, in her bedroom at home, the children at school, Walter out at the grocery store, there was the tiniest change in Callie's breathing, a rasp, and then . . . nothing.

It wasn't dramatic. No opening of her eyes and final words. There didn't need to be. Callie had lived her life showing the people she loved how much she loved them; there was no unfinished business when the end finally came. She was simply there, and then she was gone.

*

Steffi looks at herself in the mirror as she runs a brush through her hair, and checks that she has no lipstick on her teeth.

Her tears are fewer, now. At first there was nothing but the weight of grief, the tremendous emptiness. Then, some weeks later, the shock wore off and Steffi found she had no idea how to deal with the enormity of the loss, a loss she felt every second of every minute of every day.

But you bear it because you have to. What other choice do you have?

Life, Steffi has learned, carries on around the pain, making room for it, absorbing it until it becomes part of the daily fabric, wrapping itself around you and lodging itself in your heart.

Steffi has come a long way in a year. She plays with Eliza and Jack, makes dinner, creates recipes, goes out with friends, reads books.

Then she cries.

She takes showers, plants seeds, picks vegetables, kisses Mason, goes on vacations, eats too much dessert, surfs the web.

Then she cries.

She plans dinner parties, makes love, makes friends, snorts with laughter, builds fires, reads the papers, brushes her hair.

Then she cries.

And mostly, she just misses her sister.

Apple and Almond Pudding

1 lb. cooking apples, cored and diced
¼ cup brown sugar
½ cup butter at room temperature
½ cup sugar
2 large eggs, beaten
½ cup ground almonds

Preheat the oven to 350°F.

Toss the apples in the brown sugar.

Cream the butter and sugar until pale and fluffy. Slowly add the eggs and continue beating until fully mixed.

Fold in the almonds, then add the apple and sugar mixture.

Place in a greased pie dish, and cook for 45 minutes.

Epilogue

24 December 2011

Walter and Honor are first to arrive, carefully manoeuvring down the driveway that can't be ploughed because it's gravel, and is already dangerously slippery.

There was fresh snow last night, and the farmhouse sits shimmering in the light, a fairy tale come to life, with a wreath on the door and lit candles in each of the windows.

'Do you remember the last time they had a white Christmas here?' Honor turns to Walter, who is unloading the children's Christmas gifts from the back of the car.

'I wouldn't know,' he says, 'but they say we'll have one this year.'

'What a year.' She looks at him, and he puts the boxes and bags down and holds his arms out to her, enveloping her and kissing the top of her head. She closes her eyes and rests for a few seconds against his chest.

'A terrible year,' he says, pulling back to look her in the eyes. 'But, for all the grief and tragedy, in some ways a wonderful one.'

Honor looks at him quizzically.

'Of course I miss Callie every minute of every day,' he says. 'But I have the unexpected joy of you. And Steffi, our wayward daughter, has settled down.' He shrugs, his eyes clouded with sadness. 'It was hard to see that anything good could come out of it, and yet . . . Reece is an amazing father, is raising those children in a way I never would have thought possible.'

He holds her close again, and they turn as a Volvo wagon noses its way down the driveway.

Waving from the front seat is Lila, who jumps out before the car has even stopped, and runs over to Walter and Honor, flinging her arms around both of them.

'Happy Christmukah!' she says. Walter looks puzzled. 'Christmas and Chanukah combined! I've missed you! Was the drive down from Maine hellish?'

'No, it was rather wonderful. A romantic road trip,' Honor confides. 'Now where is that little one? Let me see him.'

They turn to see Ed unstrapping the car seat and proudly bringing their baby boy over to see everyone.

'Oh my word!' Honor gasps, bending down and extending a finger for the baby to grab. 'Isn't he precious! Look at all that curly hair! Hello, sweetie!'

'This is Carl,' Lila says, swallowing the lump in her throat, for this is the first time Callie's parents have met the baby. It was not a girl, as Callie, and consequently Lila, had thought, but a strong, chubby boy.

'May I hold him?' Honor asks.

Lila unclips him, lifting him up gently and handing him over. Honor bounces him up and down, delight in her eyes.

The front door opens and Fingal lopes outside to say hello, sniffing curiously at the baby, wondering what that new, unfamiliar smell is. He is closely followed by Steffi, then Mason, in striped apron, with a bottle of champagne in hand.

'You made it!' He is clearly thrilled to have them all here, and he leans down to kiss Honor and welcomes Walter with a hearty hug.

There are hugs all round for everyone.

'Come inside, quickly.' Steffi picks up stray bags and ushers everyone up the steps. 'It's freezing. Come and sit by the fire. When's Reece getting here? Anyone know?'

'He should be here any minute,' Honor says. 'We spoke to the kids this morning and they were going out to do some last-minute something or other. Oh my, Steffi,' she walks into the hall, still clutching the baby. 'This is beautiful.'

This is Steffi's first Christmas. In previous years they have always gone to Callie's. Steffi has never had to buy a tree, or choose decorations, or, for that matter, do anything other than the cooking.

This year, when Steffi and Mason were out walking, they found a blue spruce on the edge of the property that was perfect. 'Thank you, Callie,' Steffi whispered, looking up at the sky.

She does that a lot. She talks to Callie all the time, convinced that whenever serendipity intervenes it is in fact Callie, her guardian angel, watching over her.

'I am doing Christmas with Callie,' she told Mason, 'and you. The three of us together.' She loved that he didn't question it, that he seemed to understand exactly what she meant.

She has bought wooden nutcrackers from Mary's store, and looped garlands of popcorn and cranberries on the tree, decorating it with home-made gingerbread men and Christmas cookies on red velvet ribbon, side by side with delicate ornaments that had belonged to her grandmother, which Reece gave her after Callie died.

Garlands of mountain laurel are wound around the ban-
isters and candles of differing shapes and sizes sparkle on
every surface.

Mason brought home a box of crystal icicles that he'd
found in a liquidation sale in the city, and Steffi has hung
them from the Victorian chandelier in the hallway. The
entire house is filled with the smells of nutmeg, cinnamon
and cloves.

'Oh honey –' Honor turns to her, with the baby still in
her arms – 'you know she would have loved this.'

'I know.' Steffi smiles. 'I felt her with me every step of
the way.'

It wasn't ever thus. Those first few weeks after Callie died
had indeed been a blur. Steffi kept waiting, expecting to
dream of her, hoping for a sign, but nothing came.

When she finally did dream of Callie, it wasn't Callie
coming to tell her she was fine and happy, and not to worry,
as had happened to other people she had known, although
not with Callie; it was a dream in which Steffi was shocked,
and thrilled, to find Callie was alive, that it had all been a
terrible mistake.

She awoke, the dream as vivid as life, and burst into
tears; for the entire week she bore again the weight of the
loss, suddenly as sharp and searing as it had ever been.

The first few weeks were, in many ways, the easiest.
There were funeral arrangements that had to be made, a
memorial service to organize. Busy, busy, busy, and in deep
shock. It took much longer for the reality to hit her.

When it did, Mason looked after her. She slept. A lot.
Wanted to sleep all day, and sometimes she did. Mason
was the one who brought her tea, sat on her bed and talked

to her, and eventually persuaded her to see a doctor, who diagnosed depression and prescribed Lexapro to bring her back to her self.

He wrapped her in blankets and sat her in front of the fire, or found silly videos on YouTube that started to make her laugh.

He warmed her up again, and she found herself looking at him one night, when he was going into the city to see the children, and thinking: I love this man.

It was unexpected, and yet completely right. For the first time, she knew that this was love.

It was everything about him. From the way he lived his life, his beliefs, his kindness and gentleness, to the way he smiled, and even, she realized, his smell.

His soon-to-be-ex, Olivia, was back in New York. The fling with the decorator had turned out to be just that, a fling, and she had come running back to New York City. Steffi felt a flash of fear that Olivia might attempt to win Mason back, but this was not the case. Steffi quickly shared Mason's delight that his children were home in New York, back at the same schools they had always attended, seeing their father one night a week and every other weekend.

Steffi has come to love the children, and they love her. Olivia refers to Steffi now as the Tenant, which is no improvement from the Chef, but Steffi doesn't much care. Olivia was not, and never will be, a friend. The most she can hope for is a good working relationship, and she tries to stay in the background much of the time if Olivia is involved.

That night, as Mason was leaving, Steffi laid a hand on his arm. He turned to look at her, and she looked him directly in the eye. She hadn't planned to say it, hadn't even thought it before this instant, but the words were out before she could think about them.

'I love you,' she said, and the words hung in the air for a second as Mason registered what she had said.

Mason stood still for a moment, shocked. He was in love with her, but he never dared allow himself to dream she might feel the same way. He drew her close and squeezed her tightly, rocking her back and forth.

'I love you,' he whispered into her hair. 'I love you I love you I love you.'

Later that night, he knocked on her door. She sat up and welcomed him to her. He kissed her with such sweetness, such gentleness, and she felt a swell of emotion that was entirely unfamiliar.

Steffi had always shuddered at the phrase 'making love'. She thought it was cheesy, sentimental, a ridiculous description for such an unbridled animalistic act. That was before Mason.

If he wasn't softly kissing the length of her body, teasing her with his tongue, he was gazing into her eyes and whispering words of love. He moved slowly, and surely, surprising her with the way he seemed to know exactly what she would like.

Afterwards, when he was sleeping, Steffi shifted onto her side and watched him, shocked at how gorgeous she suddenly found him, astonished she had never quite noticed it before.

As Mason pours the champagne and he and Ed hand out the glasses to everyone, the kitchen door opens and Eliza and Jack run into the room.

'Jack! Eliza!' The grandparents crouch down to welcome the children, who fling themselves into their open arms.

Reece follows them into the kitchen, his arms filled with gifts, his cheeks red with cold.

'Reece! We didn't hear your car!'

'You must have been making too much noise.' He smiles, leaning in to kiss Steffi on the cheek. 'The Tollemache family has never exactly been known to be quiet.'

They exchange smiles, for Callie was always the loudest of them all. She was the one always teasing, roaring with laughter at nothing other than the sheer joy she took in living.

'Where've you been?' Lila throws her arms around Reece then steps back to berate him. 'We've barely seen you since Carl was born.'

'Me?' Reece starts laughing. 'You're the one who keeps complaining she's swimming in sterilizers and breast pads every time I phone, and oops, I have to go, the baby just woke up.'

'Okay, okay,' she grumbles. 'Fair enough.'

'Can I hold the baby?' Eliza appears in front of Lila, looking up hopefully.

'Of course. But you have to sit down. I'll bring him to you.' Then she takes Carl from Ed, and places him gently in Eliza's arms. Eliza's face lights up as she gazes at him.

'He's so tiny!' she says.

'He's actually pretty huge.' Lila laughs. 'Off the charts in terms of percentile. Height and weight, I mean. Hey, baby,' she says, leaning down and looking him in the eye, 'what do you think of your Auntie Eliza?'

'Am I really his auntie?'

'Not officially, but I consider you my family, so I'd have to say yes.'

Reece leans back against the kitchen counter and smiles, watching his kids. He loved them from the minute they emerged from Callie's body, but he didn't know them in the way he knows them now, didn't appreciate them the way he does now.

They are amazing. He finds himself hugging them tightly every day, marvelling at how they squirm to get away, how resilient they are, how well they are doing, given everything that has happened.

Callie is still very much present. They talk about her, and talk to her. There are no subjects off-limits, nothing that cannot be said. It is hardest at night, the nights they can't sleep, appearing next to his bed with tear-stained faces. He will take their hands and walk them back to their bedrooms, tuck them into bed and stroke their backs as he whispers stories of when they were babies, of Mommy.

It has been a while since that has happened.

It has been a while since Reece felt the pain and shock and grief overwhelm him to the point when he didn't know how he was going to function.

Those first few weeks, he seemed like a facsimile of himself, there in person, but not all there. Drinking late at night, when everyone was asleep, and railing at a God who wasn't fair.

Exploding at work with such regularity and force that eventually it was agreed it would be better if he took a sabbatical.

A year on, a year of therapists and psychiatrists and treatment for Post-Traumatic Stress, the anger has given way to sad acceptance. Reece has accepted that Callie has gone, that there is a hole in his heart that can never be filled.

A year on, he works from home. Still travelling, but home most of the time, primary caregiver to Eliza and Jack, with the help of Patricia, their own Mrs Doubtfire.

A year on, Reece is starting to believe that it is possible for him to be happy again. He spends time with old friends, and has, unexpectedly, made new ones – a couple on the next street whose kids go to school with his, who Callie would have loved. It felt like an important step – making new friends by himself – and he is grateful they have taken him under their wing, that he and the kids see them most weekends.

There have been a few people who have asked tentatively if he might be interested in meeting someone, and a couple of times he has found himself at dinner parties sitting next to attractive divorcees. But not yet.

He is not ready to tell his stories again, not ready to entertain the thought of a date. Not yet.

For a long time he felt guilty at going out by himself. If he wasn't at work, he felt he had to be with the children, even when he wasn't in a position to look after them. It was Honor who gently sat him down and said he had to stop feeling guilty. It wasn't his fault. Callie may have died, but he had to go on living.

One foot in front of the other, that was all he had to do. He had to act *as if*. As if he were happy, as if life were normal, as if he didn't feel a huge gaping hole inside him. Then, one day, he suddenly realized he *was* happy. It didn't last very long, an hour perhaps, but it was an hour when life seemed . . . normal.

And after that an hour stretched out to two, and life, he has indeed found, is still worth living.

He grabs Jack as he skips past him to find Fingal, and picks him up, swinging him over his shoulder and squeezing his small body tightly, planting a giant kiss on his cheek.

'Geddoff,' Jack squeals, giggling and kicking his legs to get free. 'Put me down.'

'Reece?' Steffi commands. 'Put that giggling monster down and set these crackers out on the table. We're ready to sit down.'

Steffi sits at the head of the table, smiling as Mason blows her a kiss from the other end. Eliza and Jack are ducking underneath to retrieve napkins and party hats that somehow – can't imagine how – keep ending up under the table. Honor and Walter are smiling, both of them more at peace than Steffi would ever have believed. Lila is bouncing her baby, and Ed is deep in conversation with Reece. And Mason. This beautiful man who has brought her to a place she never thought she would reach.

Looking around the table, Steffi sees pain, and grief, sadness and loss. And yet . . . and yet . . . there is love, and laughter, and life.

Love, Steffi suddenly thinks, looking around the table, is actually a *verb*. She didn't realize this before Callie became ill, was too self-absorbed to think about what it meant, *to love someone.*

Now she knows.

Love was all the times she was too tired to drive over to Callie's house, but went anyway. It was thinking of what she could do to make Callie more comfortable and doing it, instead of merely telling Callie that she would be there for her. It was tucking in behind her sister on her giant king-sized bed, and crying with her when Callie said she was done, she'd had enough, she was ready to go.

Steffi looks around the table as she thinks about the journey she has been on the past year. How far she has come, how much she has learned about seizing the moment and appreciating everything she has, showing her love by actions as well as words.

Love was, is and will continue to be Callie. For the way she lived her life, for her spirit, her beauty, her grace, and her unique ability to bring a touch of magic into every room she entered.

Look! Even now, her light remains. It sparkles in the eyes of every single person sitting in this room.

Steffi rests her chin on one palm and smiles, and as she does so a tiny white feather drifts down and lands, as softly as a breath, on her other hand.

Photo by Bruce Green

Heidi's Story

To borrow the words of Erich Segal:

What can you say about a forty-three-year-old girl who died?

That she was beautiful. And brilliant.
And brave.

That she loved, in no particular order, and among other things: her children, her husband and soulmate of twenty-four years, break-up pieces of Munson's chocolate, clothes from Lucy's, her family, haggling to get a bargain (although she never did manage to get the lamp at Bungalow down to the right price), her cottage on the lake in Canada, her camp girls, the Fab Five, Beef Negimaki Bento Boxes at Matsu, skiing, Heidi's Angels, Art Smarts, coaching her son's soccer team.

That she had a smile that lit up the world. That her glass was always half full. That she only ever saw the good in people, in life, in any situation that came her way, and that she had more *joie de vivre* than anyone I have ever met.

Heidi didn't just live life. She sparkled.

She was an extraordinary friend. Through thick and thin, she was always there, offering tremendous wisdom, common sense, support and love.

I called her the Eskimo on my blog because when it snowed here in winter she would take her children outside and build *quinzhees* (snow houses) with them – something she learned to do as a child in Toronto.

She knew everything about survival: you could dump her in a rainforest with a pocketknife and backpack, and I guarantee that a year later she would be thriving, probably having built a small village.

But she couldn't survive the cancer that swept through her body like wildfire over seven months.

I was with her almost every day throughout her illness. One day, as we left the hospital, she turned to me and said, with a twinkle in her eye, 'I hope you're going to write about this.'

And so I did.

Callie is not Heidi, nor is this Heidi's story, although there are some details that are the same. Primarily, that

Heidi fell into the tiny percentage of cancer sufferers who contract Leptomeningeal Carcinomatosis.

As for Steffi and Lila, it was a privilege and an honour for me to accompany my friend on this most heart-breaking of journeys. Her courage, her laughter and her grace taught me extraordinary lessons about life. And love.

Despite dedicating *Girl Friday* to Heidi, this is the book that is really for her, the book that was written with an angel at my shoulder.

She leaves an indelible handprint on all our hearts, and I shall miss her for the rest of my life.

Useful Resources:
www.breastcancer.org
www.carepages.com
www.lotsahelpinghands.com
www.komen.org

Acknowledgements

Dr Richard Zelkowitz and the entire, wonderful staff of the Whittingham Cancer Center at Norwalk Hospital.

Adam Green, Carole Lipson, Bob Armitage Sr, Bobby and Natalie Armitage, Judith Loose, Rachel Horne, Stacy Greenberg, Wendy Gardiner.

Louise Moore, Anthony Goff, the brilliant Clare Parkinson, and the two most unexpected and delightful gifts of the past year: Jennifer Rudolph Walsh and Pamela Dorman.

For her unparalleled wisdom, guidance and friendship these past ten years, my gratitude and thanks go to Deborah Schneider.

Sharon Gitelle and Dani Shapiro, for pointing me, as ever, in the right direction, and in doing so changing the course of my life.

I cannot forget the extraordinary cooks and cookbook writers who inspired some of the recipes in here, and particularly Diana Henry, Hugh Fearnley-Whittingstall, Claudia Roden, Delia Smith and Nigella Lawson. Some of the recipes were culled from other sources, some are my own invention; however, the vast majority are not from cookbooks but from my family. To that end, my endless thanks and love go to my mother and grandmother.

And finally Ian Warburg. My husband, my beloved. Who carries me through.

I love you.